# Sid's Place

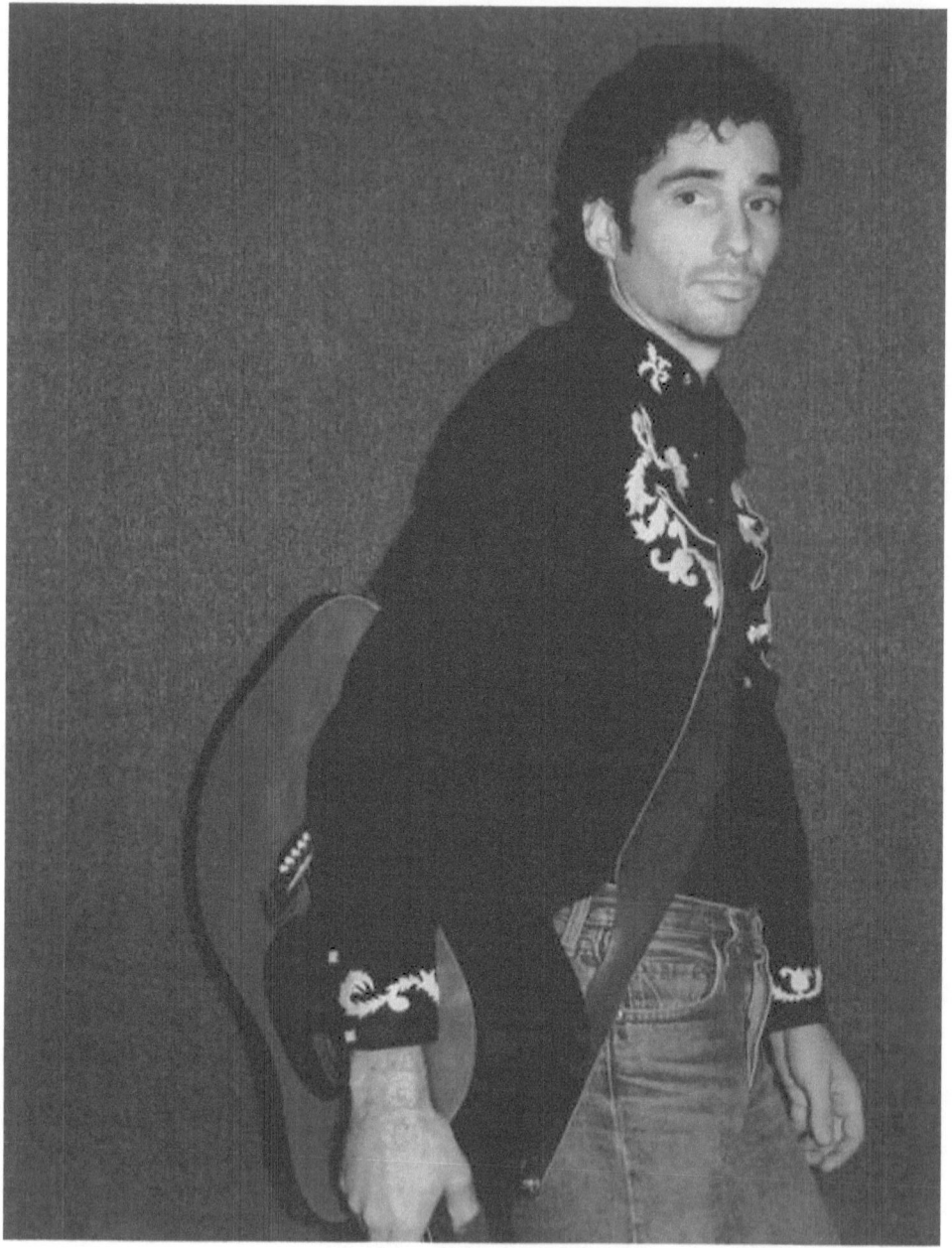

The Coyote 1984

# Sid's Place

*Tom Calder's Life Underground
in the Psychedelic Sixties of California*

*by The Hippy Coyote*

**by Richard Del Connor, "The Hippy Coyote"**
*(American Philosopher Poet, Singer-Songwriter, Novelist, Zen Master)*
Founder of **The Rich** and **American Zen** rock bands.
Founder of Shaolin Chi Mantis Traditional Shaolin Kung Fu.

*produced by*
***Richard Del Connor***
*for*
**SHAOLIN RECORDS**

*A Shaolin Communications company*

# also by RICHARD DEL CONNOR
# "The Hippy Coyote"

**4 DECADES OF LOVE**
Written and composed by Richard Del Connor "The Hippy Coyote."

**SEASON OF FOURS**
Four Seasons of The Hippy Coyote's Life. (1974 - 1980)

**CONNOR BLACK HOLE BUBBLE THEORY**
Origins of Big Bang and Where Black Holes Lead To.

**COYOTE IN A GRAVEYARD**
The 1984 Rock Opera Screenplay.

**HISTORY OF ZEN FROM A TO Z**
Including the Meaning of Life, Creation of Humans . . .

**MASONIC KUNG FU**
Chinese teens rescue British Freemason from Japanese invaders 1937.

**THE POTATOE VALENTINE & OTHER LOVE POEMS**
Love stories and lyrics written 2004.

**RAINBOW IN THE SHADE**
An antiwar poetic memoir of the happy hippie, The Hippy Coyote.

**UTAH - PHASE 1**
Adventures of a California Buddhist Hippy in Mormon Utah.

# Copyright Page

## Sid's Place
## Tom Calder's Life Underground in the Psychedelic Sixties of California

by Richard Del Connor "The Hippy Coyote"

Published by Shaolin Communications.
Publisher contact: *publisher@shaolinCOMMUNICATIONS.com*

Edited and typeset by Richard Del Connor.
    *www.RichardDelConnor.com*
Photography and digital art by Richard Del Connor.
    *www.ShaolinFilm.com*
Cover "Marble Art" by Richard Del Connor.
    *www.ShaolinDigital.com*
"Peace Pendent" by The Hippy Coyote.
    *www.HippyCoyote.com*

**Other Versions:**

| | |
|---|---|
| Audiobook | ISBN: 978-1-57551-302-7 |
| Ebook | ISBN: 978-1-57551-308-9 |
| Hardcover | ISBN: 978-1-57551-301-0 |
| Paperback | ISBN: 978-1-57551-300-3 |
| Paperback | ISBN: 978-1-57551-309-6 |
| shaolinCOM.com PDF download | ISBN: 978-1-57551-305-8 |

10  9  8  7  6  5  4

Author: Richard Del Connor  *www.RichardDelConnor.com*
Richard Del Connor is a "Buddhist Scientist," American philosopher, record producer, singer-songwriter, musician, Shaolin Zen master and founder of Shaolin Records.

**Categories include:**
Fiction > Coming of Age
Fiction > Action & Adventure
Teen & Young Adult > Literature & Fiction>Survival Stories
Teen & Young Adult > Literature & Fiction>Action & Adventure>Travel
Romance > Action & Adventure

For information about Richard Del Connor
Shaolin Communications book releases visit
*www.ShaolinCOM.com/booklist-S.html*

This book contains URL "LINKS" that can be accessed in the PDF version of this book. Even if you own a paperback or hardcover version I recommend you purchase an ebook or PDF version of **Sid's Place** to access all the websites and webpages I've created for you.

Download the PDF version of **Sid's Place** for "CLICKABLE LINKS":
*Sid's Place PDF at Shaolin Records record store*

**Sid's Place NFT Collection** of Shaolin Communications
*https://opensea.io/collection/sids-place*

Published by Shaolin Communications

There are another couple dozen books by me:

*www.ShaolinCOM.com/booklist-S.html*

# DEDICATION

To my hippy friends.  I'm trippin' with you.
I'm singing songs with you sitting on the couch next to me, and across
from me in that tan naugahyde easy chair that leans back with the foot rest.
*"Don't Bogart that joint."*

# RICHARD DEL CONNOR
## *"THE HIPPY COYOTE"*

Richard Del Connor is the author of **Autumn Flavours** in 1974, that hypothesized that life is in seasons of "fours." These four seasons then repeat again, starting with Autumn, Winter, Spring, and then a period of Summer. Each one of these seasons can last one year or several years, depending upon the age, attitude and environment of the individual. The combination of these four seasons is a **Season Of Fours**.

Richard D. Connor became "The Coyote" in 1984 while performing his rock opera, *Coyote In A Graveyard*, in Los Angeles. His fiancee, Jennifer Olds, pressured him to complete this novel. During 1984, Richard wrote this novel sitting in his van, with his cat, Celise, at the LAX airport eating burritos during his lunch breaks, while working as a Journeyman carpenter.

This book, **Sid's Place**, was typeset and released August 8, 2007, from Tujunga, California, before moving to Montrose. The first "preproduction" release, contained a couple dozen typos. If you got one of these PDFs, downloaded, or purchased on CDs, they should be considered a "collector's item."

This 2nd Edition is the first publication in ebook. I'm just about to proofread it again, February 23, 2012.

*RichardDelConnor.com*

I got my "Coyote" nickname in 1984 during a brief friendship with Michael J. Fox. He joined me onstage during a performance of my rock opera, **"Coyote In A Graveyard,"** that I was performing in Santa Monica and Hollywood nightclubs. Thanks to him I got a lot of press and they started writing and talking about my rock opera. Accordingly, the reporters called me, "Coyote," since I was the central character in the show. Michael also called me, "Coyote." I would visit Michael J. while he was onstage recording his **Family Ties** television show. A friend of mine from UCLA film school worked on an adjacent Universal Studios stage, so I became known as "Coyote" by many famous actors as I dined with them regularly in the Universal Studios "Commissary." Then my girlfriend Jennifer started calling me, "Coyote." Okay. I'm Coyote.

I was a photographer specializing in rock concerts. My byline was "Rocktography by The Coyote." Capitol Records called me up and said, "Hey Coyote, we need a first name for our accountant." Sometimes I'd shoot promo shots and do interviews for local newspapers or the record labels.

I replied, "The." I thought that was funny and giggled. But it became my full name, The Coyote.

This worked fine until 1999 when an internet search of, "Coyote," or, "The Coyote," would result in long haired furry faced images that did not resemble me.

So in 2007 I officially became, "The Hippy Coyote." That worked better when people looked for me on the internet. I even got a website:

*www.HippyCoyote.com*

When I released a solo album of me as a singer-songwriter performing my songs live with an acoustic guitar, I created a website for the album.

*www.CoyoteRadioTujunga.com*

Then I started a podcast for my American Zen band at:

*www.CoyoteRadio.NET*

Now I'm building a website of music, music videos as stuff at:

*www.CoyoteRadio.TV*

There I go again… too many websites.

I had a website for my imaginary folk rock band, AMERICAN ZEN at: *www.AmericanZen.org*

After I reached Nirvana and finished that American Zen spiritual journey of 8-LEVELS and 8 ALBUMS I created the *www.AmericanZenPeaceFoundation.org* when I discovered I had cancer. I wanted to create a foundation to keep my websites alive—perhaps even better than I have done while I was alive.

To satisfy my HIPPIE BELIEFS of the 1960s, the trademark slogan of the American Zen Peace Foundation is: *"End All Wars™"*

Despite trashing dozens of websites I still have 55 WEBSITES with Kung Fu, Tai Chi, Buddhism, music, books and my many identities.

The American Zen folk rock band, *"America's First Buddhist Rock Band™,"* is composed of six identities. All these are me:

**Richard O'Connor / Richard Del Connor**   record producer

**Don DelaVega**          recording engineer

**The Hippy Coyote**     songwriter, singer, flute, acoustic guitar

**Rory G**               lead guitar, slide guitar, synthesizer

**Tom Calder**           Rickenbacker bass (with flatwounds)

**Steve Hixon**          drums

My independent record company I founded in 1984 is Shaolin Records. I thought my kids would be running it… but here I am, alone.

I consider Shaolin Communications to be the PARENT COMPANY of all my companies. But they all have separate products and functions.

*NOTE: I'm proofreading my book. I replaced the **"broken links."***

Check out my stuff. I've enjoyed my life that inspired these stories. I enjoy these stories that inspire me to be me some more. I didn't want to be blamed for being a "bad influence" on my kids so I didn't let them read this book. I figured I would wait until they 18 or older. Raising them in Mormon Utah made me paranoid. Unfortunately, both of my kids ostracized me before they turned 18 so neither of them has read and discussed this book with me. I have not had an adult conversation with either of my children. Weird. Although I've never done anything to apologize for and raised my kids the way that I wanted to be raised, we have less of a relationship than I have with both of my crappy parents. Weird. I raised my kids to be good kids. I never got to train them to be good adults. They live with and emulate their mother.

Perhaps my books, stories and websites will inspire you to be you, if you have an artistic or creative nature.

# TABLE OF CONTENTS

*Book Cover*

*Inside Cover*

*Also by Richard Del Connor "The Hippy Coyote"*

*Dedication*

*RDC = THC*

*Copyrights*

*Table of Contents*

*Coyote Trademark Logo*

*About the Author*

*Foreword*

*Song Credits (explanation)*

*Warning*

*Ch1 San Diego*

*Ch 2 Malibu*

*Ch 3 Oceanside*

*Ch 4 Manila*

*Ch 5 San Francisco*

*Ch 6 Redwoods Commune*

*Ch 7 Underground Railroad*

*Ch 8 Soledad Prison*

*Ch 9 Sid's Place*

*Song Credits (lyrics)*

*Discography*

*Audiobook: Sid's Place*

*Sid's Place BOOK NFTs*

*Rear Cover*

*"Table of Contents" links work in Ebook and PDF book versions.*

*All the WEBSITE LINKS work also!*

My *"Coyote"* Trademark since 1986.

Created in "The Bat Cave" rehearsal room, NoHo, California.

# ABOUT THE AUTHOR:

In 1970 Richard was exiled from the United States for LSD-25 and marijuana trafficking.
San Diego, California, USA

*www.HippyCoyote.com/*


In 1971 Richard graduated the Prince of Wales Collegiate High School.
St. John's, Newfoundland, Canada

*www.RichardDelConnor.com*


In 1971 Richard was a DJ for MUNR Radio, Memorial University of Newfoundland.
St. John's, Newfoundland, Canada

*www.CoyotePodcast.com*


In 1972 Richard took the oath of the Apprentice Carpenter in United Brotherhood.
San Diego, California

*wwwCoyoteRadio.TV*


In 1973 Richard attended San Diego State University.
Allied Gardens, California

*www.CoyoteRadio.TV "about"*

In 1974 Richard graduated the RIAA Recording Engineer Programs.
La Mesa, California

*www.shaolinRECORDS.com*

In 1975 Richard is staff recording engineer-producer at Bonita Recording
Studio.  His first record album is recorded and titled, **Bonita**.
Bonita, California

*Bonita album by Lotus 1974*

In 1976 Richard performs for keg parties, backyards, and garages as
Lotus, playing bass and lead vocals.
El Cajon, California

*www.CoyoteRadio.NET*

In 1977 Richard graduated the United Brotherhood of Carpenters
Apprenticeship as a Journeyman Carpenter.
Spring Valley, California

*Autumn Flavours  poetry book*

In 1978 Richard moved from San Diego to Venice Beach, California
with The Rich while remodeling the Beach Boys recording studio.
Venice Beach, California

*"The Pauper" rock opera*

In 1979 Richard remodels LA recording studios, performs with The Rich and hired as a staff carpenter of The Village Recorder and Frank Zappa.
Santa Monica, California

### *Richard Del Connor RESUMES*

In 1980 Richard records **Live In Venice** album with The Rich power pop trio featuring Richard on Rickenbacker bass and lead vocals singing his romantic songs.
Venice Beach, California

### *The Rich - Live in Venice*

In 1981 Richard designs, draws blueprints, builds Future Disk Systems mastering lab after working for RCA, MCA, and Capitol Records.
Hollywood, California

### *Richard Del Connor RECORD PRODUCER*

In 1982 Richard's band, The Rich, transforms to Richard Connor or Rich Connor, with horn section and future members of The Eagles, Chicago, and Red Hot Chili Peppers.
Santa Monica, California

### *History of Shaolin Records*

In 1983 Richard records album, **Temptation**, by Richard O'Connor to become the first release of Shaolin Records.
Hollywood, California

### *Temptation EP 1984*

In 1984 Richard founded Shaolin Communications and Shaolin Film & Records Records to release his books, movies and albums.
Santa Monica, California

### *www.ShaolinCommunications.com*

In 1985 Richard enrolled in the UCLA Motion Picture Program to be a Director-Producer. Richard worked in music videos, commercials and with Special EFX studio Apogee who made first Star Wars movie.
St. John's, Newfoundland, Canada

### *Shaolin Pictures VIDEO CATALOG*

In 1986 Richard meets Raquel King-Hayata at UCLA. They are married the day after Christmas in San Diego, California.
North Hollywood, California

### *Richard Del Connor MARRIAGE 1986*

In 1988 Richard works commercials as Cinematographer-Lighting Director for MTV and as concert photojournalist for magazines and newspapers.
Los Angeles, California

### *Cool Commercials by Coyote*

In 1988 Richard completes year as Union carpenter building Maximum Security Prison, then divorced Raquel on the day he was laid off.
North Hollywood, California

### *www.CoyoteSolo.com*

In 1988 Richard graduates with Certificate from the UCLA Motion Picture Program writing Coyote in a Graveyard screenplay for New World Pictures.
Los Angeles, California

### *www.ShaolinPictures.com*

In 1989 Richard publishes **Love, Always & Forever!** printed by Michelle McCarty.
North Hollywood, California

### *ShaolinCOM.com BOOK: Love, Always & Forever!*

In 1990 Richard and Shaolin Records intern, Michelle McCarty, decide to have a baby. She has been the booking agent of Richard's band, Coyote Graveyard, and concert photography assistant.
North Hollywood, California

*www.shaolinMUSIC.com*

In 1991 Richard moves to Utah with Michelle McCarty because she promises to make Richard Del Connor more successful than he can be by performing in Hollywood, California. Richard launches American Zen.
Salt Lake City, Utah.

*NFTs of American Zen LEVEL 1*

In 1992 The Coyote composes 2nd album of American Zen as musical journal while performing concerts in the only 3 venues in Salt Lake City.
Salt Lake City, Utah

*NFTs of American Zen LEVEL 2*

In 1993 Master Zhen composes and records **Tai Chi Magic** album used for Shaolin Chi Mantis tournament and State Fair performances.
Salt Lake City, Utah

*www.TaiChiMagic.com*

In 1994 Richard records American Zen **LEVEL 5** album during Lakota Sioux pipe ceremonies performing his flute for sweat lodges.
Salt Lake City, Utah

*American Zen LEVEL 5 = Pipe Carrier*

In 1995 Richard's Hanblechia at Pine Ridge Reservation, Bear Butte, and Medicine Wheel becoming a disciple of Fools Crow and Lakota elder.
Rosebud, Pine Ridge Reservation, North Dakota

*American Zen LEVEL 6 = Vision Quest*

In 1996 Richard incorporates Tai Chi Youth as a 501(c)(3) nonprofit organization for troubled youth in prisons, rehabs and public schools.
    Salt Lake City, Utah

*www.TaiChiYouth.org*


In 1997 Richard writes grants for NEA National Endowment for the Arts.
    Salt Lake City, Utah

*www.TaiChiYouth.org/donate*


In 1998 Rory O'Connor is born amidst sewer geysers and windy tempest rains. Richard lectures and performs Zen Buddhism workshops.
    Salt Lake City, Utah

*www.RoryDibdenOConnor.com*


In 1999 Richard moves back to Los Angeles with family to relaunch Shaolin Records and make music videos like he did in the 1980s.
    Canoga Park, California

*Webmaster Richard Del Connor*


In 2000 Richard moves to cabin in Angeles Forest north of Los Angeles.
    Angeles Forest, California

*www.ShaolinKungFuBeginner.com*


In 2001 Richard moves to Tujunga producing live cable shows with kids.
    Tujunga, California

*www.CoyoteRadioTujunga.com*


In 2002 Richard recuperates from black widow spider bite for two years.
    Tujunga, California

*Live Recordings of Singer-Songwriter RDC*

In 2003 Richard publishes first digital poetry book, **Autumn Flavours**, after homeschooling his daughter for several years.
Tujunga, California

*www.coyotePOETRY.com*

In 2004 Richard launches **Zen Buddhist Podcast of Shaolin Zen** to teach the world and his children what Chinese Zen Buddhism really is.
Tujunga, California

*www.ZenBuddhistPodcast.com*

In 2005 Richard launches **American Zen Buddhist Rock Podcast**. The roles of all 6 American Zen band members are being acted by Richard.
Tujunga, California

*www.CoyoteRadio.NET*

In 2005 Richard releases American Zen's first album, **Peace Of Mind** on CD and distributed to internet radio stations.
Tujunga, California

*LEVEL 1 = Peace Of Mind*

In 2006 Richard launches **The Coyote Poetry Podcast** to perform is poetry books, **Rainbow in the Shade**, and **Potatoe Valentine & Other Love Poems** published by Shaolin Communications.
Tujunga, California

*www.coyotePODCAST.com*

In 2007 Richard releases **Christ Killer** album by American Zen. Richard hopes for scandal and publicity but the world promotes Christ killing as a pathway to Heaven. So no one is upset about this album.
Tujunga, California

*American Zen LEVEL 2 = Christ Killer*

In 2008 Richard publishes his first novel, **Sid's Place**, as PDF download. Millennials do not appreciate the counterculture revolution of the 1960s because "Women's Rights," "Equal Opportunity," "Black Rights," and the antiwar and "Ban The Bomb" movements have been attained or are not of interest any more. All the food colorings and preservatives removed from products are back in modern foods—and no one cares.
     Tujunga, California

*Hey!  This is the webpage for THIS BOOK!*


In 2008 Richard releases **I Want You To Love Me** album by American Zen. Although these "commercial" songs are mostly romantic love songs, Millennials want "Free Music" on iPods.
     Montrose, California

*American Zen LEVEL 3 = I Want You To Love Me*


In 2009 Richard becomes 3rd Degree Master Mason in Burbank Lodge 406 while being transferred from Hollywood lodges to Burbank amidst Freemason legal scandals and Masonic Court trials.

*www.HippieBuddha.com*


In 2009 Richard releases first music album by Buddha Zhen on Shaolin Records, **Tai Chi Magic 1**. Songs can also be downloaded from special album website: *www.TaiChiMagic.com*
     Montrose, California

*www.TaiChiBuddha.com*


In 2009 Richard discovers, ***"Masonic Kung Fu"*** coded within ***"Ling Po / Lian Bu"*** form he learned from Grandmaster Wong Jack Man in San Francisco who is famous for fighting Bruce Lee in 1964. His other Shaolin Kung Fu master, Kam Yuen, said, "If I only learned one Kung Fu Form I'd want to learn this one."
     Los Angeles, California

*www.RichardDelConnor.com  "Project 14"*

In 2009 Richard is "Organist" of Panamericana 513 Masonic Lodge performing guitar and flute. *"Flintridge Fire"* was written in the lodge while performing for Initiations, ceremonies and Masonic meetings.
Los Angeles, California

*"Flintridge Fire" by American Zen*


In 2010 Richard releases **LEVEL 4 = Kung Fu Cowboy Part 1: King Solomon's Temple** to be last CD manufactured by Shaolin Records.
Montrose, California

*American Zen LEVEL 4 = Kung Fu Cowboy*


In 2010 Richard is Assistant Secretary of Panamericana 513, resigns with loss of computer, and acoustic guitar. He writes novel, **Masonic Kung Fu**.
Los Angeles, California

*Masonic Kung Fu*


In 2010 Richard authors book **Human Values for Success in Family and Business**.
Montrose, California

*Human Values for Success BOOK 1 of 4*


In 2011 Richard authored the following poetry books:
*Rainbow In The Shade*

*The Potatoe Valentine & Other Love Poems*

*The AntiChrist*


In 2011 Richard authored the following poetry novels:
*Masonic Kung Fu*
*History of Zen from A to Z.*

*www.shaolinCOM.com*

In 2011 Richard as TCY Patriarch becomes grant writer to create TCY Online School.

Montrose, California

### *www.TaiChiYouth.com*

## Times Interview

### Richard Del Connor
### Philosopher Poet

*Here's a book I just released a couple days ago in October, 2022.*

### *Times Interview of Richard Del Connor Philosopher Poet*

A Shaolin Communications Publication

## NFTs for this Sid's Place BOOK and PODCASTS:

### *https://opensea.io/collection/sids-place*

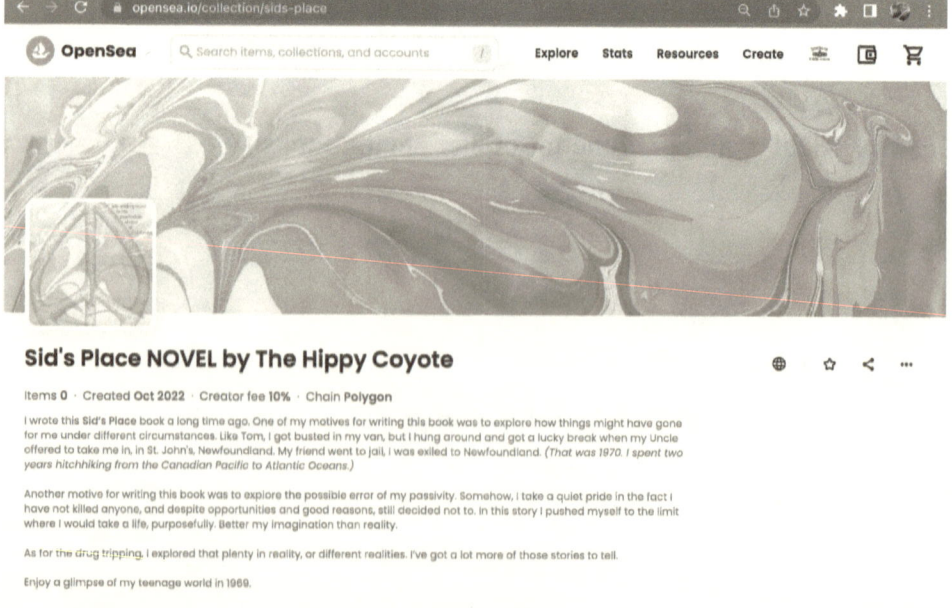

### Sid's Place NOVEL by The Hippy Coyote

Items 0 · Created Oct 2022 · Creator fee 10% · Chain Polygon

I wrote this Sid's Place book a long time ago. One of my motives for writing this book was to explore how things might have gone for me under different circumstances. Like Tom, I got busted in my van, but I hung around and got a lucky break when my Uncle offered to take me in, in St. John's, Newfoundland. My friend went to jail, I was exiled to Newfoundland. *(That was 1970. I spent two years hitchhiking from the Canadian Pacific to Atlantic Oceans.)*

Another motive for writing this book was to explore the eventual error of my passivity. Somehow, I take a quiet pride in the fact I have not killed anyone, and despite opportunities and good reasons, still decided not to. In this story I pushed myself to the limit where I would take a life, purposefully. Better my imagination than reality.

As for the drug tripping, I explored that plenty in reality, or different realities. I've got a lot more of those stories to tell.

Enjoy a glimpse of my teenage world in 1969.

# Foreword (2008)

I wrote this **Sid's Place** book a long time ago. One of my motives for writing this book was to explore how things might have gone for me under different circumstances. Like Tom, I got busted in my van, but I hung around and got a lucky break when my Uncle offered to take me in, in St. John's, Newfoundland. My friend went to jail, I was exiled to Newfoundland. *(That was 1970. I spent two years hitchhiking from the Canadian Pacific to Atlantic Oceans.)*

Another motive for writing this book was to explore the possible error of my passivity. Somehow, I take a quiet pride in the fact I have not killed anyone, and despite opportunities and good reasons, still decided not to. In this story I pushed myself to the limit where I would take a life, purposefully. Better my imagination than reality.

As for the drug tripping, I explored that plenty in reality, or different realities. I've got a lot more of those stories to tell.

So enjoy a glimpse of my teenage world. Sadly, as civilization seems to be heading toward less love and more war, you can see a generation that fought this trend of violence.


Love,
 Coyote


# Foreword (2022)

Special thanks to the Bantam Books editor who helped me edit this book in the 1980s. Unfortunately for me, the chief editor of Bantam Books told my editor that we were not allowed to publish this book while Ronald Reagan was controlling the government. His genocide of drug dealers meant that no publisher was allowed to publish a book with a "drug dealer hero."

So my editor said he would help me finish editing the book "outside of Bantam" and then see who we could sell it to.  He evidently was also doing a similar deal with the writer of the Jeffrey Dahlmer cannibal book that Bantam wouldn't publish.  He finished that book first, got a huge book deal and told me he had to quit my deal to work full-time on this cannibal book.

So my book was edited by an anonymous editor who dropped my acid-popping book for a finger licking good story.

I've never known how to put that stroke of bad luck in perspective.

My book sat in its notebook for twenty years until a girlfriend of mine who worked at the Endeavor Talent Agency got my book to one of their literary agents.

He wrote up a positive review that they call, *"Coverage,"* in the entertainment industry.  But before he could get me signed to the agency as an author he took off for Australia with one of his clients to work for him.

Sheesh.  Abandoned again.

So I self-published it as an ebook in 2007.

Times were hard.  Unknowingly, I'd be homeless in a few years.

Due to bad advice from what friends I had, who knew nothing about book publishing, they told me to reduce my inventory of websites since they were costing me hosting fees, not generating income, and not of interest to them.

So I trashed a dozen websites to save expenses and upkeep.

This was a very bad idea because this **Sid's Place** book had links to some of these websites I trashed.

I'm just sorting out today, all my files and editions and edits and graphics… so I can REPUBLISH **Sid's Place** in the beginning of 2023. Maybe I would have made money if this book would have been for sale since 1985 when I finished the first draft.  Maybe I could have got a movie deal for this story.  At any rate, here I go.  Today is October 29, 2022.  Let's see how quickly I can turn this book into a paperback, hardcover and Kindle ebook without *"broken links."*

# SONG CREDITS

When you see a number in parenthesis. e.g. *(9)*. This represents the song credit at the rear of the book. This would be song credit #9, ***"Run Run Run"*** by The Hippy Coyote.

**9. *"Run, Run, Run"***
Lyrics by The Hippy Coyote
Written for the book, **Sid's Place**
Used by permission of *Shaolin Records*
Copyright 2008 *www.shaolinMUSIC.com*
All rights reserved. ASCAP

# WARNING: FOR MATURE AUDIENCES ONLY

This book contains:

**cuss words**: lots of them

**sex**: graphic, lesbian, and romantic

**violence**: people are shot, stabbed, and blown up

**drugs**: marijuana, LSD, heroin, amphetamines, hashish

**terrorism**: as told by the terrorists

Sorry, but these things offend me. I don't like cuss words. However, because I've strived to capture the language and beliefs of these characters, even when I disagreed with them—I have captured their thoughts and words as they spoke them. Oh yeah, this is fiction.

There, you've been warned.

*NOTE: I wrote that "WARNING" back in 1987. Cuss words are common in most YouTube comedy shows. In 2022 YouTube millennial newscasters seem to be motivated to throw in "shit," "fuck," and whatever other words align them with today's young audience. Ironically, all the racist and slander words of my youth are BANNED by these foul-mouthed "influencers." The word, "nigger," is also banned, although when I was homeless this last decade or living in the homeless shelter I would hear that word in the lunchroom every day a dozen times. Movies have more nudity, sex, and vulgarity than when I first wrote this book. I considered removing the "WARNING" but decided to leave it in because I still don't cuss or talk vulgar. Especially after being a Mr. Mom for 20 years and teaching Tai Chi Youth classes in churches, YMCAs and public schools. I'm 68 years old now, and I still can't see why people need cuss swords to express their thoughts. I guess millennials and modern adults have more crap and filth in their minds than I've ever allowed into my brain. I have cleaner thoughts and ambitions than the "normal" or "common" man.*

*https://www.AmericanZenPeaceFoundation.org*

# Chapter One
## *San Diego*

"Hey, c'mon man, it's not my stash. Ninety-five each no matter how many you buy. That's the price and all I want is a few kilos for pulling it off."

Tom listened to the payphone receiver for a positive response. "But hey," Tom continued, "I'd really rather not get involved."

Tom's sleeveless arms informed him of the bright sun as he stood on the sidewalk outside the supermarket. He looked around to make sure no one could hear their payphone conversation. Although Tom had moved out of his parents' home a year ago, he was still wearing some of the same clothes he wore in high school. Tom was realizing he needed to replace his dark blue ivy-league shirt with purple pin stripes—

"Just a minute," finally came the reply, "and your cut?"

"Hey I'm just doing you a favor. The guys a friend of mind. Say, six kilos'll do me. I'm tellin' ya this stuff is great. From Guerrero. You know, that's where they grow Acapulco Gold."

"Yeah, thanks Tom. Gimme 75--hold on . . .that's . . .7,125. Then you keep six of 'em."

"That sounds about right."

"Stop by later tonight and pick up my van."

"Okay, see you 'bout eight."

"Later."

Tom hung up the payphone receiver and smiled to himself. Why should he let this guy know that he was getting the kilos for a lot less?

Why should he let him know that he wasn't just a friend of the dealer. He was actually a runner. Not across the border though. Tom was only 19 and he disliked the border towns anyway. But it was romantic to think of actually running the kilos from their source in Mexico. The jungles, Sierra Madres, the deserts, planes, horseback, banditos, the campesinos, and the women . . .

Tom enjoyed the thrill of being a rebel, a Robin Hood, but not really a criminal. Nixon had been cracking down hard on San Diego, pot capitol of the US. It was getting riskier all the time. Maybe by next year in 1970 they'd realize you can't put one-tenth of America in prison for getting high. Tom didn't believe anyone had a right to prohibit smoking any kind of leaf, root or berry he wanted to puff in his pipe. He was selling modern moonshine in 1969. A Robin Hood of the new prohibition.

This supermarket was half-way between the house he grew up in and his apartment in El Cajon. The Food King looked the same as the one in his childhood neighborhood. The similarity bothered him. The uniformity. The corporateness. Too big for one person or one family to own. Maybe every store is a box with food inside. This was just a bigger box. More cash registers. Futuristic? The future was square.

Tom's van was like an oven. Quickly he rolled his windows down. Sweat beaded on his forehead. The California beach sun, unimpeded by clouds, had turned his van into a four-wheeled oven. He took off his collared shirt. The swimsuit he'd brought was sitting on the engine cover, dry. He tossed it back onto the bed, disgusted at not having had time to go swimming that afternoon.

He slipped the van into neutral at the top of the hill and let it coast down Fletcher Parkway. Tom knew it was illegal, a fact that his girlfriend, Barbara, had pointed out to him just about a week ago. When he had asked her what was so dangerous about it, she was unable to think of a reason. So, he figured it was one way to save a little gas, especially since gas prices were now up to 35 cents a gallon. As he drove deeper into El Cajon, the streets narrowed and the sidewalks disappeared. With the windows rolled down and his hair tossed by the wind, he turned up the volume on his 8-track player. It was one of those late sixties songs that echoed of reality as it wore a heavy cloak of surrealism. The trumpets from the preceding song descended like birds landing, and the single guitar hammered out the rhythm like an introductional fanfare for an oracle stepping into the castle courtyard. Tom had turned up the song as loud as his speakers could handle without getting distorted.

He knew the words: he'd been singing them along with his record player for the last two years.

> *Soldiers yell, "Out of my way!"*
> *Battles rage through every day*
> *What was yours--now is mine*
> *Heaven in smoke*
> *"More women. More wine"*
> *The strongest God rules again today (1)*

There were many memories attached to the song. As he sat in the van with his engine off and eyes half-open, he remembered an old girlfriend who he met in Driver's Ed. class . . . seventeen years old and shopping for an engagement ring . The one they had chosen was a pearl in a gold baroque setting. Not just any pearl, but a black pearl. This made it seem different. It made the vow, promise, commitment... whatever it was, seem different. A unique promise required a unique ring. Tom didn't want to duplicate the marriage of his parents. That didn't end well. They were divorced. The image of the ring brought a slight smile to his face. Never did manage to afford it back then. Maybe it was—

> *In the streets of broken dreams*
> *The tears of angels glitter and gleam (1)*

"Hey Tom!"

Tom jumped in his seat, jolted out of his daydream and hit the eject button on his 8-track player. He hadn't noticed Bob walk up from behind the van.

"Wow. Hey I'm really sorry. I didn't mean to scare you." Bob sounded sincere, although his tightened lips were twitching with the effort of stifling a smile.

"Shit," Tom sighed, turning towards Bob as he draped himself over his steering wheel. "I didn't hear you walk up man."

"How could you with the music up so loud? What are you playing, The Stones?"

"Yeah. One of my favorite songs off **'Their Satanic Majesty's Request,'**" Tom replied.

"Right. Isn't that the album with *"2,000 Light Years From Home"* on it, and the 3-D picture on the front?"

"Yep. Now they're just sticking a picture on 'em. The original issues with the 3-D pictures are already collector items." Tom sat up. "I've got one at home," he remarked proudly.

"Cool. Aren't there pictures of the Beatles hidden in the flowers or something like that?"

"Yeah, and I've found them all, including a couple of other guys I've never recognized." Tom paused. "Hey, is Jimmy home?"

"Sure is. He's inside trying out some black hash."

"Oh no. I've got a kilo deal set up for him. He'll want to try it out too."

* * *

White robed sheep blocked the downtown sidewalk next to the bus stop, dancing and chanting in an eastern holy trance. A crowd of people who were waiting for the next bus reluctantly gathered near them. The rhythm of the dance was simple, the lyrics monotonous and repetitious. Their white robes and shaved heads were a striking contrast to the suit-and-tie American middle class audience. However, the most amusing aspect of their appearance were the tennis shoes they wore; out of place with the otherwise religious Eastern identification. These were probably all young Americans who didn't even understand the language they were chanting. Just the same, none of them actually spoke to each other in any language. They all seemed oblivious to everything. Many of the staring audience poked fun at them.

While the majority of the sect danced, several others mingled with the crowd and held out tambourines or cups like downbeat beggars do. The ten story buildings on both sides of the street dramatized the trespassing of these religious renovators in San Diego's mechanized downtown.

Unable to pass through the glutted sidewalk, Tom waited patiently as the bus finally arrived. Most of the observers clambered aboard still glancing amusedly back over their shoulders at the tambourine splashing spectacle. Tom pushed his way through the crowd and the disciples, muttering, "Excuse me," a couple of times, but careful not to look anyone directly in the face. For a moment he contemplated the picture on the sidewalk that the dancers had drowned in flowers. He couldn't visualize completely the face in that picture, but the bright colors stuck in his mind as possible color schemes for his van.

Tom hadn't walked downtown for quite some time. There was always too much traffic, and the parking meters reminded him of little taxmen with no arms, but endless appetites. He was also reminded, by the increased numbers of hovering police cars and sheriffs, how near he was to the courthouse and jail. Like a beehive, the nearer you got to the honeycomb, more bees would buzz threateningly around you. As he turned the corner, he couldn't help looking up at the huge grey hive across the street. Tom couldn't see in the jailhouse windows, but he knew that the inside was packed with people who had been sealed into their paraffin cells.

Tom wondered what time it was. Oh yeah, he was wearing a watch. He looked at it. Still an hour before the pick-up. Tom looked at his watch again. Hard to get used to wearing it. The only time Tom wore a watch was when he was running a deal like now; or when he used to be in high school. It felt strange to wear a watch. As strange as those kids in white bed sheets. With an hour to kill, Tom decided to pop into a record store.

* * *

As planned, Tom's van, was waiting in the parking lot. He pulled the stub out from under the wiper blade and took two quarters out of his pocket for the parking lot attendant. He had left the van in another lot four blocks away. Another runner, had driven it here after loading the side walls with 69 kilos of killer pot. Tom had left $4,750 in a prearranged spot behind the paneling. He knew the money had been removed when he drew the curtain back to see the piñata sitting atop a half-dozen plastic wrapped kilos in a cardboard grocery box.

Jerry had a strange sense of humor. The kilos in the box were for Tom, a small part of his commission. Last time Tom got a sombrero. Jerry was always bringing gifts back from Mexico, besides the plastic wrapped ones he smuggled in his station wagon side panels and tires.

It was a forty-five minute drive to where he would deliver the kilos, so he lit a cigarette and tried to relax. His eyes spent almost as much time on the speedometer as they did on the road. He was taking special care not to exceed the speed limit. As he neared the freeway on-ramp he saw the light change to yellow. He did not have much time to stop but didn't want to chance running a red light. As he put on the brakes, he felt them begin to lock up and knew he couldn't stop before the line. His teeth clenched and the radio seemed to be blasting too loud to think. A fast talking DJ came on the air as Tom down-shifted into second gear and quickly accelerated into the intersection.

His front wheels were just over the white line when he saw the light overhead turn red.

He wanted to see if there were any police cars near the intersection, but was too busy maneuvering up the narrow on-ramp. He squeezed in front of a silver Mercedes which seemed to have no intention of slowing down to let him on the freeway. He slid over a couple of more lanes into the fast lane and reduced his speed to the 65 mile per hour limit.

The disc jockey with the bubblegum amphetamine hard-sell voice hadn't stopped jabbering commercials since he was back at the red light. Tom hadn't listened to a word he'd said, but now that he was starting to relax with the affirmation that no police had pursued him, he turned off the radio. He pushed in the 8-track cartridge and lit another cigarette.

*Changing lanes they drive too fast*
*Not knowing who they pass*
*Where they've been, who they know*
*Dented bumpers do not glow*
*Horses drink the poison stench*
*People died to build a fence*
*Time was here, time has passed*
*Trying to be first and last (1)*

The freeway was crowded. He glanced at his diver's watch; it was 4:05. The freeway was slowing down minute by minute. Tom thought of the rush hour traffic in L.A.

San Diego wasn't as bad yet, but seemed to be getting worse all the time.

Once off the freeway, he had only a few miles to go until he reached the house where they would unload the keys into the buyer's van. As he waited for the red light to change on Mollison Avenue, he thought for the umpteenth time of how he wished he could find a steady occupation. A legal one, of course.

School hadn't exactly enlightened him in any career direction. In electronics, he felt he was being prepared for a life of television repairing in the back of a dusty shop. In English, he saw himself only as another bored instructor confronting a mob of screaming children. Mathematics? No thanks; calculus had burned out his appreciation of that subject. School wasn't his direction anymore. He felt like he was on a boat, but couldn't jump off. He was stranded, almost in the mainstream of society, earning a living no less scrupulously than the majority of other Americans. One buys something for a particular price and resells it at a profit to cover expenses. This particular sales market was very risky and Tom only wanted to get far enough ahead to put himself through another three years of college and graduate. Maybe with a bachelor's degree some opportunities would open up. That's what they keep telling him.

\* \* \*

Mrs. MacGregor was already running late for supper. The roast still had at least half-an-hour to cook in the oven. The table was set for four. She stood over the sink, peeling the carrots with the water running. Turning, she opened the refrigerator and reached inside for the lettuce. There wasn't enough for a salad.

The front screen door slammed shut as the spring pulled it closed.

"Is dinner ready yet?"

"No. Now go back outside and play. I'll call you when dinner is ready. Leave me alone. Go on."

The boy turned around and walked to the door. He stopped as he was holding the screen door open and looked at the back of his father's head. Mr. MacGregor was watching a game show on television. The boy didn't understand how they played it. He blinked his eyes and ran outside to join his buddies down the street.

"Fred, would you go the store for some lettuce?"

"Aw, hon. I'm in the middle of a show."

Disappointed, she looked in the refrigerator to make sure she hadn't overlooked any lettuce. As she began to resign herself to a supper without salad, she noticed that she was also out of milk. She shook the last gallon container to discover only about a glass left.

"Fred, I'm going to run to the store. Would you keep an eye on the roast in the oven for me?"

"Sure, sure," he mumbled, not turning away from the television set.

She stepped out into the San Diego sunshine suburb through the screen door which automatically slammed shut after leaving the wooden front door open.

It was an affordable neighborhood. Built in the fifties, the blocks and blocks of 3-bedroom homes were all of just two designs. The homes with an attached garage would be mirror images of each other. On this street, sometimes the attached 2-car garage would face west, and their neighbor's home would face east. The only other design was to detach the garage from the house and put at the back edge of the back yard. This created a longer straight driveway and made the backyard smaller. But even this design could still fit a swimming pool in the back yard next to the garage.

By changing the trees in the front yard, between the sidewalk and curbed asphalt, all the homes appeared completely different. None of them would be painted the same color except on the opposite side of the street or towards the end of the block.

To make these homes even more affordable, none of them had backyard fences. The fencing business was very lucrative in the fifties and sixties.

Some houses would be differentiated with a flower pot shelf under the kitchen window facing the street and some would have a small brick curb for a flower garden.

Any WWII veteran with a job could get a bank loan for one of these homes with starting prices of $13,000. And every home had a grass seeded front yard and back yard which was cherished like their Christian souls. There was never a single home with a dead lawn. These lawns were the souls of middle class life. Maintained by the parents until the kids were old enough to earn a weekly allowance by mowing and watering them. Perhaps this also established the middle class work ethic in the children.

Her lime green Chrysler was parked in the driveway. It barely fit into the garage, and like many people who parked their cars in front of their homes in the street, the automobile was also an ornament of success or perhaps another way to differentiate one home from the other in this single story conformity.

Mrs. MacGregor didn't bother to warm up the car engine or put on her seatbelt. She merely revved the engine several times, shifted from park to forward, backed up in the driveway, and jetted down the street in her husband's Chrysler. The store was less than a mile away. As she neared Mollison, she swerved into the left turn lane as the green light changed to yellow. The car in the adjacent lane hit his brakes to stop making a slight screech.  She passed him and entered the intersection as the light turned red.

Tom was tired of waiting for his green light.  He turned his head to the left to watch the signal for the other street turn to yellow, he shifted into first, let out the clutch slowly and edged forward into the intersection with music causing his head to bob slightly in harmony with the music.

Mrs. MacGregor swung into the intersection, her tires hissing from the ton of steel making an aggressive left turn.

Tom watched the light ahead of him turn green at last, although he was already moving into the intersection.

Mrs. MacGregor barely had time to slam on the brakes before her car ripped into the passenger door of Tom's van.  Her chest struck the steering wheel with a cracking sound, then her head snapped up into the windshield in a whiplash she never heard.

Tom lifted his head off his van's steering wheel and opened the door.  Slumped forward, he put his hands to his head to stop the dizziness.  As he reached down to unfasten the waist seatbelt, he saw the wet blood on his hands and patted the top of his head to find where he'd hit his head on his steering wheel.  He didn't notice that his .357 had slid from under his seat to beneath the brake pedal as he stepped out of his van and staggered to the woman's car.  With one hand tightly holding the front of his skull, he looked through the passenger window of her car as someone opened the driver's door for her.  Mrs. MacGregor's head drooped over the steering wheel, dead.  As Tom stood back up, he watched the woman who had come to the dead driver's aid.  She was vomiting quietly into her hands.

Tom, even dizzier than before turned around to see two policemen.  One was running over to them and the other cop was picking up the pistol from inside his van.

\* \* \*

"C'mon Jimmy, you've got to give me the money. Jesus, do you know what I'm going through? I'm a fugitive man. I'm like a duck sittin' alone on a lake with a hundred shotguns pointed at me."

"I know, I know," sighed Jimmy as he turned to look for his pack of cigarettes. "But you know we all lost a lot of money on that deal. And well, the money's just not available. Hell, Tom, I'd give you the money myself but I just don't have it. I lost my ass in that deal. You know--"

"Yeah, yeah, yeah. Sure. So now here I am without a car, the twenty five dollars I happened to have in my pocket, a warrant for my arrest, and no home. And now you, my friend and buddy, whose stash I was carrying, won't get me the money to split town. Fuck, what about my commission on that run?"

Jimmy lit up a cigarette.

"Don't you realize that if I'm busted you could be too? We're in this together," Tom shouted, his face flushed, eyes burning. "Remember?"

The fear, frustration and paranoia were becoming too much for Tom to handle.

Jimmy felt badly for his friend, but "The Director" had told him to handle it just the way he was doing. Jimmy pulled out the piece of paper he'd written the address on.

The paper rustled against the inside of his nylon windbreaker. Jimmy maintained his poker face, except for the nervous twitch of his upper lip which his walrus mustache couldn't conceal. He held the paper out.

Tom looked at the paper, then into Jimmy's eyes as if discerning by telepathy what it said. Tom pulled off his navy blue ski cap as he stepped towards the outstretched arm. He slowly reached out and slid the paper from between Jim's fingers and held the note before his eyes. He stuffed the small piece of paper into the watch pocket of his only slightly faded 501 button-crotch Levi's. Tom shoved his hands into his front pockets and, looking down at nothing in particular, sighed loudly and kicked gently at an invisible stone on the carpet.

"You've gotta understand, Tom. I had no voice in it. They said that if you needed more money you'd have to do another deal. They'll pay you $500 to pull this off."

"What do I do?"

"Go to that address and pick up five parcels. They'll tell you what to do next. No purchasing. You just deliver it."

"When do I get the money?"

"Tonight I'm sure."

"Is it smack or coke?"

"Really important coke I heard. Peruvian flake. Pure, just the way it left South America."

"Damn it, Jimmy. You promised me I'd never have to run anything but grass and hash. You—"

"I know, but fucking don't whine at me about it. It's not my fault you're in this jam. You couldn't have made a finer finale. You made the headlines: DOPE SMUGGLER KILLS WOMAN IN CAR CRASH. Shit, you ought to feel lucky they're gonna give you this chance."

"Lucky?" Tom bellowed as he slammed his cap on the motel couch. "I'm fucking out of luck and I'm scared shitless! I don't even want to do this, but I obviously have no choice." Tom sat down.

"Good. I'll have a car here in the next couple of hours for you." Jimmy walked towards the door of the motel room. He grasped the doorknob and turned around without opening it. "They said this is your last chance."

It took a moment for Tom to respond. "They, they, they!" he almost yelled, startling Jimmy. "You mean him, 'The Director,'" Tom drawled with a Texas accent.

Jimmy looked sadly at Tom and shook his head as if Tom had said a nasty word.

"Don't blow it," he said softly.

"Yeah? Well buddy, go fuck yourself."


\* \* \*

"Are you sure that you were supposed to come along?" Tom asked.

"Well, actually no. But I figure it's better that I do," Daniel laughed to himself. "Especially with your driving record. Don't worry, I don't want any of the money. I just want to make sure you get out of the country. Consider this my own personal favor for you. I'll do all the driving, and together, we'll pull off this deal."

Tom was smiling for the first time since the crash. He wished he had more friends like Daniel. They had gone to junior high and high school together. Tom remembered when his parent's house was broken into and someone told him Daniel had done it. Maybe Dan was trying to make up for when he messed around with Michelle behind his back. It didn't matter. Tom was in deep trouble and Daniel was here.

"Okay Dan, you drive."

Daniel's straight blonde hair hung almost to his shoulders, just a little bit longer than Tom's brown hair. Tom could see his nose silhouetted as they drove down the freeway in Dan's white Impala. 'Ski jump,' Tom thought to himself. He wanted to make a joke about Daniel's nose, but humor seemed strangely out of place. Tom ached deep inside for peace, but until he was safe, he knew that the uneasiness would persist.

"Acid, that's what this is, it's a bad acid trip," Tom exclaimed as if discovering the meaning of life. "I've just gotta ride this whole thing out until it wears off."

They laughed together. It was a relief to laugh.

Daniel pulled the white Chevy into the driveway and parked.

"This is it. Keep the car running and I'll go to the door," said Tom.

Tom left his car door partially open and moved briskly up the porch steps. He knocked on the aluminum screen, which rattled in that familiar annoying way. no one answered. He waited patiently, listening for any noises inside. The lights were all on. It seemed as if someone were there. He opened the screen and knocked on the wooden door. Still no one answered. He pressed the buzzer, but it was apparently out of order.

Tom walked back to the car and sat down in the front seat, leaving the car door propped open against his knee. He continued to stare at the house as he spoke. "I don't understand." Confused, he reached into his watch pocket again and pulled out the scrap of paper. He "uh-huhed," as he looked at the address on the paper and compared it to the numbers on the house.

"Should we check the backyard?" asked Daniel.

"No. There's probably a dog back there. We don't need the neighbors on us as burglars."

Tom looked at his diver's watch; 9:40.

"We'll wait until ten o'clock. There aren't any cars here. Let's just hang tight for a few minutes."

"But if they don't show by then, then what?" asked Daniel, worried.

"Then I'll call Jimmy and see what he says."

It was only five minutes before a Lincoln Continental pulled into the driveway behind them, but left them enough room to still pull out beside it. It was a deep scarlet red with white vinyl top and nearly glowed in the dark. A small fat man stepped out and walked to the driver's side.

Daniel rolled down the window.

His fat face glanced around in the car. "I thought there was only one of you coming over."

Daniel started to make an excuse when Tom butted in. "Change in plans, but that's not your concern."

The fat man accepted the additional presence with shrugged shoulders. "Okay," the fat man groaned. "Follow me," as he walked towards the house.

"Wait here, Dan."

"Hey," Daniel argued, "he said it was all right."

"But I didn't," retorted Tom firmly.

Tom stepped into the living room just as the fat man carried the fifth parcel out from one of the bedrooms. Each one had been wrapped with white butcher paper and taped with black electrician's tape.

14

The fat man looked Tom over and then handed him the keys to the Continental. "Go get the attache out of the back seat."

Tom walked out to the driveway and opened the red driver's door with the key, then reached in to pull up the rear door lock on the driver's side. The attache lay on the floor of the car. He reached for the briefcase but then hesitated. He got down on his knees and reached under the seat for the revolver that, as expected, was there.

Tom dropped the attache down on the table next to the pounds of cocaine.

"Well," the fat man scolded. "Put them in the case."

Jimmy had told Tom that there would be no exchange of money and sure enough, none was mentioned. Tom felt especially uneasy about this cargo, although perhaps it was just a composite of all the other things on his mind. Not to mention the fact that he hadn't yet spoken to Barbara. He could imagine the thoughts that she was having by this time. She knew that he was dealing and had tried to talk him out of it many times, even though she never hesitated to enjoy its financial benefits whenever possible.

Tom tried to think negative thoughts about her to ease his mind, but it didn't work. He missed her terribly.

*  *  *

It was going to be a long drive from San Diego to Malibu, so Tom closed his eyes and tried to relax.

The tires hummed in the highway breeze. The smog filtered California night stars moved quietly overhead as the white Impala proceeded northbound on Highway 5.

At 65 miles per hour, it was a two-hour drive and there wasn't much to talk about. The radio filled in for the lack of conversation, and the traffic camouflaged the car that was following them.

It was about one o'clock in the morning when they drove slowly past the small beach house whose address was given to Tom by the fat man. The house stood fifteen steps above the street. They parked a couple of houses away and Tom got out.

"Don't forget the cargo, Tom," Daniel reminded.

"Stay with it here, and kill the radio."

Tom disappeared up the steps to the unlit porch. The screen door had a wooden frame and two of the four screen panels were torn. There was no name on the mailbox.

Tom knocked gently. He heard footsteps inside the house. A voice in another room spoke too softly for him to hear. Tom heard the receiver of a telephone drop in its cradle and then the footsteps again.

The door opened. "Come on in."

Daniel just happened to glance into his rear view mirror as the car that had followed them from San Diego pulled around the corner with its lights out. Daniel's immediate reaction was to think it was the police. The car parked about five houses behind him.

Tom opened the passenger door, and Daniel, thinking they'd been busted, nearly screamed.

"Calm down," said Tom soothingly. "What's wrong?"

Daniel was still trying to catch his breath. "A car just parked about six houses back there. It came around the corner with its lights out."

They both craned their necks backward over the front seat to stare out the back window. No movement.

"Did anyone get out of the car?" asked Tom.

"No."

"Do you have a gun?" he asked hopefully.

"No."

"Okay then, just wait right here. I'll get this over with right now."

Tom grabbed the attache out of the back seat and proceeded swiftly towards the house again. The night seemed to swallow him alive as he zipped up the stairs.

Daniel was jittery. He was starting to wonder what he'd gotten into this time. He had run a few errands for these Texans before, but this one reeked of trouble. He heard a car door shut softly behind him and turned around to watch as a man walked from the car that had parked somewhere behind him. He walked towards him, and then turned and walked up the steps into the same house that Tom had gone into. Daniel didn't like the way things were going at all.

Tom heard the front door open behind him. He flinched and prepared to dash out the back door.

Russ welcomed the tall slim faced man into the house. "Hey, are you their escort?"

"Yeah. Who is the other guy out there?"

Tom looked scared. 'How did he know there was someone else out there?' "Uh--That's my friend Daniel. He's worked for us before."

"Bring him in," the man demanded.

"No. Just give me my $500 and I'll split."

"Sure, sure," the stranger murmured angrily. "I want him inside . . .now!"

"Leave him out of this," Tom pleaded. "Look, just give me the money and we'll go."

The escort pulled a gun and pointed it at Tom.

Russ remained silent . . .dead silent.

"Russ," the stranger commanded, "put these on him." He pulled a pair of handcuffs from his dark blue coat pocket. Russ stepped over to him and took the cuffs. Tom was petrified. Russ grasped each of his arms, which hung limp at his sides, and pulled them behind Tom's back as he cuffed them. Tom remained hypnotized by the small .38 police special that was still trained on his chest.

"Russ, do you have a gun?" the stranger asked.

In a daze, he stammered, "Uh, yeah. In the bedroom."

"Get it."

Russ returned carrying a .357 with a Wyatt Earp barrel about seven inches long.

"If he moves, shoot him in the head," he told Russ calmly. He turned and walked out the front door.

It was only about a minute before Daniel walked in with his hands up and the .38 pushed into his back. "What's going on?" he asked nervously.

"I don't know yet," was all Tom could say.

"No more talking," the stranger yelled. "Get a couple of handkerchiefs and some rope."

Russ disappeared into his bedroom.

"All right, now sit on the couch, slowly" he said to Tom and Dan. "And you Daniel, keep your hands up."

Russ returned with the handkerchiefs and a couple of brightly colored ties. "I couldn't find any rope," he whined.

"That'll do," said the stranger as he sat down in front of them. "First tie Daniel's hands behind his back and then gag them."

Daniel and Tom looked at each other in desperation. Russ stepped behind the couch and tied Daniel's hands together with a tie. Daniel sat up again. "How do I gag them?" Russ asked.

"Stuff a handkerchief down their throats and then tie up their mouths with one of your lovely ties," replied the escort sarcastically.

Russ retreated into the bedroom for more ties. With one hand pointing the gun, the unsmiling escort reached into his coat pocket and removed a pack of cigarettes. He then reached in front of him to the coffee table and grabbed a book of matches. He had to lay the gun in his lap to light his cigarette. Daniel and Tom stared frozen at the gun. Tom struggled without success to slip out of the handcuffs.

Russ emerged from his bedroom with more ties.

"Well dummy, tie them up!"

Russ walked nervously around the couch. Daniel tried to keep his teeth clenched as Russ pulled the tie tight against his mouth.

"No, asshole." The stranger stood up and pointed the gun at Russ. "First you cram a handkerchief in his mouth like this." After changing the pistol from his right hand to this left hand, he round-housed Daniel in the jaw, almost knocking him off the couch with his right fist that reminded Tom of John Wayne. Daniel struggled to say something, but the stranger dealt another fist to his face. Then one blow followed another… keeping the pistol held tightly in his left hand.

Daniel's body hung limp over the end of the couch, unconscious. This amused the stranger. "How about you, kid?" he leered at Tom. "You planning to give me any trouble?"

Tom slowly shook his head back and forth.

The stranger was perspiring heavily from his brief workout. He took off his dark blue blazer and tossed it over Daniel's head. "Fine coat rack we got here," he mocked.

Russ tried to smile but couldn't. Although he had never met Tom before, he was beginning to feel a great deal of sympathy for his predicament. He didn't know who the escort was either, but as long as he wasn't the target of his abuse, he didn't care to ask questions.

The stranger's face was covered with a thin sheen of sweat. He started to walk towards the bathroom, panting in an abnormal fashion. "Russ, shoot them if they move." He left the door ajar after stepping in. Tom could see the stranger roll up one of his shirt sleeves and place a small metal cigarette box on the sink. The bathroom door slammed shut.

With the stranger out of the room, Tom tried to influence Russ. "Please let us go. That guy's crazy, I mean, I think he's going to kill us all. Please man, I'll owe ya. You've gotta let us go."

Russ looked as frightened as Tom felt. He paced nervously, waving his cowboy gun as he spoke. "Tom, if I can get you out of this, I will. But I'm not gonna risk getting myself killed. I'm sorry, but there's not much I can do."

"Yes there is," Tom pleaded, "you--"

"I told you to gag him," interrupted the escort. He no longer looked sweaty and uncomfortable. On the contrary, he appeared refreshed, invigorated.

Russ quickly grabbed the ties and handkerchiefs and completed his task. After cramming a handkerchief into Daniel's lolling mouth, he gagged him securely with the tie. Tom received the same treatment.

"Come here, Russ," the stranger motioned. They stepped into the kitchen.

Tom rocked and squirmed on the couch, slipping his cuffed hands beneath his legs and under his feet until the chain cleared his shoes. His hands were now in front of him instead of behind his back. Tom frantically shook Daniel, but he was still unconscious.

He untied the gag and pulled the handkerchief down from his mouth to look more like a necktie. He glanced furtively around the room. They'd see him if he ran for the front door, but he could hide behind the kitchen door. Yeah, and then possibly jump the stranger when he came through. Tom tiptoed over and pressed his back against the wall behind the kitchen door. Hold it. What was he going to do when they came through the door? Give them the 'Spock'? No. Yes, over by the table was an empty Coca-Cola bottle. Tom moved quickly back towards the couch. Just as his hand grasped the neck of the bottle--

"Freeze!" shouted the stranger from behind him. "Turn around slowly or I'll put a bullet in your back. I'm not particular about a clean kill."

Tom turned mechanically around without the bottle in his hand. The stranger cold-cocked him in the face with his gun, spinning Tom across the room like a Duncan top. Tom fell into the lamp on the wooden end table, pulling it down with him. The tall ceramic lamp smashed as it hit the floor.

The kitchen light was now the only light on in the house.

Tom sprang up into the darkness. Still cuffed together, he clasped his hands as if to pray and swung his clenched fists like a bludgeon, knocking the gun out of the stranger's hand. They wrestled desperately in the darkness to retrieve the pistol. Tom was first to grab the revolver, but the stranger quickly grasped Tom's hands. The seconds seemed like hours as they thrashed on the floor, each struggling to point the gun in the other's direction. Kicking and hitting with elbows and knees, Tom bit the stranger's arm as hard as he could. A shot rang out. Blood soaked the white shirt of the stranger. He coiled up like a snake, clutching his hands to his abdomen in a futile effort to stop the pain. Tom jumped up and pointed the revolver at the stranger's head.

"Where are the keys?" he demanded, the handcuff chain dangling below the gun. The escort writhed in agony, but refused to answer. "I'll kill you, you son of a bitch!" Tom screamed. "Now give me the keys!"

There was no reply.

Tom stepped carefully around the stranger's body and reached into his pants pocket. Before he could withdraw his hand, the stranger rolled into him, pulling him down. The gun slipped from Tom's hand as he tried to break his fall. The hitman pounced on the gun as Tom scuttled behind the sofa.

"Shoot him!" the stranger yelled at Russ. "Shoot him now!"

Confused, Russ stood in the kitchen doorway. The light behind him barely illuminating the far corner of the room where the stranger lay bleeding with the .38 in his hands. Tom, still crouched behind the sofa, gestured for Russ to throw him the gun. A violent whirlwind swirled through Russ's ears. He could no longer hear the stranger's repeated commands to kill Tom. Dizzy, he began to spin and step back into the kitchen.

"God damn it, I told you to get him!  RUSS! DO YOU HEAR ME?" The stranger tried to stand, but the pain seared through him like a raging fire. He clenched his teeth, nearly hyperventilating as he screamed at Russ. When he saw that Russ was abandoning him, he raised his gun. "RUSS!" he bellowed, as he pulled the trigger.

The bullet entered at the base of Russ's skull and exited out of his mouth. Russ fell like a tree to the linoleum floor, dead. Tom's mouth hung open in petrified amazement.

Suddenly, he heard the sound of someone crawling in the darkness toward the couch, towards him. Tom thought fleetingly of Daniel laying on the couch, unconscious, helpless. Of Russ; dead. Of himself; handcuffed. 'Oh God,' his mind roared, 'he's gonna fuckin' kill me!'

The stranger slithered towards Tom. The carpet soaking up the blood trail.

Like a frightened rabbit, Tom jumped from behind the couch and dashed towards the kitchen. He heard the gun fire behind him and felt the splinters of wood splatter in his face as the bullet shattered the door jamb. Tom leaped over Russ's body, his shoes landing in a puddle of blood which was draining from the dead young man's mouth.

His feet flew out from under him and he landed flat on his ass, skidding painfully into the closed oven door.  Without hesitating long enough to feel the aches from the collision, he clambered on all fours past the water heater and, reaching up, turned the knob and shoved the back door open.  A bullet shattered the single pane of the kitchen door as Tom rolled down the two concrete steps into the back yard.

*  *  *

Barbara Selma had a lot of money, at least her parents did, and they made sure she showed it.  Not too many other girls wore real silk, and her pink 911 Porsche stuck out like a flare in the high school parking lot.  But Barbara was nervous, very nervous.  She had told her parents that she was sick, but they had insisted that she attend school anyways.

"Where's Killer-Boy?" Nancy sneered.

Barbara's thin blonde hair ruffled as she spun to face her heckler.  The lockers were crowded with students digging into them between classes.  The flow of body traffic pushed the two girls closer together as they stood glaring.

"Just fine, I hope," replied Barbara, shrugging as if she didn't care.

Nancy laughed maliciously.    "Aren't you aiding and abetting a fugitive?"

"No," Barbara snapped back.  "I haven't seen him since before the accident.  I don't know anything about it." Her long Hawaiian muumuu fluttered about her legs as she disappeared into the crowd of high school students.  Barbara scratched nervously at her notebook cover.  She knew that sooner or later she and Nancy were going to have it out.  Nancy had been antagonizing her all year.  Barbara had never really been in a fight before and the more she thought about it, the harder she scratched at the canvas book cover.

Nancy had always despised Barbara.  Barbara's angelic blonde hair and fine clothes had always attracted the attention of the best looking boys in school. Nancy's brown hair was too common and ordinary to strengthen her confidence, and there weren't too many girls who could compete with the way Barbara dressed. Nancy wasn't allowed to wear much makeup by her parents. But once she was at school she wore a little bit of everything on her face as if to compensate for her average features. She plucked her eyebrows and painted them on again at a new and, she thought, more stunning angle. She surrounded her eyes, which could have been her best aspect, with thick black liner and several coats of black mascara because her eyelashes seemed too short.

Of course she had to take it all off before returning home. Her Bible belting father would whip her as a prostitute if he saw her in so much makeup. Nancy wanted to go braless like some of the other girls but still wasn't sure if that was a sin.

Nancy slammed her hallway locker shut and pushed through the idle traffic that always congregated around the corner from the restrooms, joining the mainstream of students that flowed through the corridors. She shook her long brown hair, fluffing it with her left hand. Her experiment in hair streaking had almost grown out; good riddance.

Nancy's thin lips tightened with determined hatred. She felt a newly gained confidence as she realized that Barbara actually feared her.

* * *

Mrs. Selma had liked Tom from the beginning. He was very respectful, had good manners, and always brought Barbara expensive gifts. She had suspected that Tom probably experimented with drugs, but to read in the paper that Tom was now wanted by the police for second-degree murder, marijuana trafficking, and possible mafia connections, well; the death penalty seemed reasonable to her. Barbara, of course, claimed to know nothing about it.

Mrs. Selma was reclining in her white upholstered chair reading the **San Diego Union** when Barbara walked into the house through the front door.  Mrs. Selma lowered her newspaper and folded it across her lap. "Barb," she asked kindly, "would you step into the living room for a moment?"

Barbara plopped her books on a dresser in the hall and stepped onto the deep white shag carpet of the living room.  Her mother crossed her arms and briefly closed her eyes.  "Barb," she said with her eyes still closed, "It seems that Tommy," she paused, opened her eyes, and looked up into Barbara's anxious face, "has committed another murder."

"What?" Barbara exclaimed.

"Tommy's fingerprints were found in a home in Malibu where a drug dealer was shot in the head.  Here," she said, handing the newspaper to Barbara, "read it yourself."


## YOUTH KILLED IN MALIBU SHOOTOUT

*Malibu, California.    A young UCLA college student, Russ A. Shekowitz, was killed during an early morning gun battle at 3381 Weston Blvd.    The coroner's office estimated death at 2 a.m. from a bullet through the back of the head.  A nineteen year old youth from San Diego was held captive at the home.   No motive for the murder has been officially disclosed.*

*Russ Shekowitz had been arrested for drug trafficking previously this year.    Police Chief Robert Waltman hinted of possible 'drug rip-offs' being responsible for the death.   Fingerprints of Tom Calder, a San Diego teenager, wanted for a drug related murder in San Diego, were found at the scene and a search for the murder weapon continues.  A large amount of blood was found in the home not belonging to the deceased . . .*


Barbara dropped the newspaper to the floor and drifted towards her bedroom with a look of blank fright in her eyes.  Mrs. Selma decided not to question her.

The walls of Barbara's room were decorated with posters of the Rolling Stones, Moby Grape, The Monkees, Jimi Hendrix, Jim Morrison, and Paul Revere and the Raiders.  She threw herself down on the satin comforter and began to sob violently.

Eventually, she sat up in her bed and noticed how quiet it was in her room. Every sniffle seemed amplified. She decided not to cry anymore about it. 'I'll never see him again,' she thought to herself.

On top of her dresser was a picture in a gold frame. The picture was taken on a camping trip at the Colorado River. Tom's chest was burnt red from the desert sun, as were both their faces. Their hair was windblown into curls and frizz so that, with their heads leaned together, they seemed to be of one body.

Tom was unshaven in the picture, the dark bristles dramatized his partial Latin heritage, shading the sideburns, goatee, mustache, and upper cheeks. To his dismay, no hair ever seemed to grow in that one neutral zone where goatee should join sideburns. Sometimes his hair appeared to be almost black, at others is was a smooth brown. And sometimes, as in the picture, the summer sun bleached his hair with red streaks. The picture depressed Barbara . . . it was from another time, a happiness she thought she would never feel again.

She dropped her dress onto the floor and scooped it up with her foot, flicking it up onto the bed. It was Friday night, and there was a dance at school. She and Tom had made plans for it, and, well, Barbara somehow felt she must follow through. Better than staying home to be interrogated again by her parents.

She gently smoothed on fresh makeup, lacking the usual sense of anticipation that she felt before her dates with Tom. There would be no more dates with him, she knew, and her actions took on a hypnotized form. No matter how much rouge she applied, her cheeks still felt cold and pale. She thought of how she'd never touch him again . . . never hold him . . . never kiss him. Never see him again. Her thoughts were all the loneliness of her loss. He'd been a part of her life . . . now he was gone. She wondered what her life would be like if she'd never known him. Somehow, she was glad he'd loved her. Somehow, she still loved him.

\* \* \*

The morning air wasn't really chilly along the Coast Highway that morning, but Tom was cold and hungry as he crawled up the gravel shoulder to the road. A thin fog blew in wisps from the ocean across the silent highway. It was only an hour or two after sunrise and Tom was heading north. He didn't know where he was going, but that didn't bother him. What did bother him was the feeling of being pursued by an unseen enemy. He was being hounded by more than just policemen. He sensed a larger monster behind him; one that was not content to merely capture him, preferring to shred him with its teeth. Tom felt as though he were a very small rabbit being chased by a Tyrannosaurus Rex. It had his scent and would chase him to death.

His thoughts popped back to the highway as a solitary car approached from the South. Tom gathered his composure, running his fingers through his sleep tousled hair and straightening his shoulders . . . he stuck out his thumb.

The car whirred past.

Pulling his arm in he massaged first his right wrist and then his left wrist. He could still feel the handcuffs. His wrists were still red bruised. He chuckled as he remembered breaking into that garage last night for a hacksaw. Chained. Like a wild animal. Humans chaining humans.

Tom relaxed and began to take in his surroundings. The California weather seemed more like winter than summer. It had been hot and cloudless for weeks. In a couple of hours the fog would hopefully burn off and the waves would be full of surfers.

The swells hissed and crashed, one over another. The noise level was like that of a distant battle, yet it was somehow comforting in its consistency. The waves sounded louder than ever before. The waves were more than water. The waves were breaths of the world. Breaths of the earth.

The surf made Tom feel alive. The waves, the water, the movement was life itself.

Tom didn't have a swimsuit but decided to walk up the highway until he found a good place to bodysurf. There were too many rocks in the surrounding area.

By the time Tom had walked a mile or two, and had not been picked up by any of the several cars that passed, he was near Zuma Beach. He still needed a bathing suit, so he continued walking northward until he reached a small shopping center. Very small. One of the shops sold swimsuits but it was still too early for it to be open. Tom went next door to the grocery store for a quart of chocolate milk and a box of glazed donuts and waited for the shops to open.

Although he didn't have much money, a swimsuit seemed to be a necessity. Eventually he selected a pair of black jams with a Hawaiian print of purple orchids and bright green leaves. He walked out of the store wearing them, carrying his 'smileys' tennis shoes and Levi's wrapped in his brand new beach towel with bright colored horizontal stripes. Not psychedelic, kind of Indian. Not Indian of the east. American Indian. The horizontal stripes were like rows of bright collared mountains. The flat bumpy ocean plus the jagged mountain outlines gave him comfort. Alone between frosted moving waves or standing amidst forest trees…

Tom didn't have any dreams of success… but he did have dreams of freedom now. Peace. A space. Air, waves, pine trees and sky.

He walked back towards the ocean and felt content viewing the ocean horizon.

Since school wasn't out for summer vacation, he knew that the beach wouldn't get too crowded before three o'clock. By four o'clock it would be teen-city. Tom just wanted to get in the water.

# CHAPTER TWO
## *Malibu*

He decided to take one more dip. He strolled leisurely into the water until it was waist high then dived under an oncoming wave. Tom shook his head and wiped the saltwater from his eyes before opening them. When he did, he was looking at a blonde haired girl who, from behind, resembled Barbara. Tom knew it couldn't be her, but he had to be sure. He swam outside a little more until he was beside her. Either she was very tall or was standing on her fins. Tom could barely touch the bottom and keep his head above water as she bobbed comfortably over the swells, staring out to sea.

"I hope the best waves aren't all gone," Tom said to make conversation.

She turned toward him impatiently. "There aren't any good waves today!"

Well, she wasn't Barbara, that was certain. He was curious what she meant by saying there weren't any good waves. In fact, the waves had been excellent. Even without fins, Tom had ridden quite a few in fine form. "I've had some pretty good rides today," he remarked.

She turned to him, about to crack another rude remark. Then she stopped. Her expression changed from hostility to interest as she really looked at Tom. She chuckled.

Tom smiled hesitantly.

"I'm sorry," she confessed. "I was thinking of things."

"Oh," said Tom. "That's all right. I've got a lot on my mind too. My name is Tom...uh . . .Tom Brady," he stuttered, quickly changing his name.

"Hi. I'm Carey Finely. You from this area?"

"No. I'm from Del Mar." Tom realized he'd have to get his story straight. "I'm just hitching up the coast for a while."

"How long you gonna be in this neighborhood?"

"I don't know."

"Why don't you come over for a barbecue?" she asked politely.

"Sounds great!"

"My parents are out--"

"Hey Carey!" a girl shouted from shore. "Let's go!"

"Okay!" Carey yelled back. "C'mon, let's go," she smiled.


* * *


'Now this is a nice place,' Tom thought to himself. He could see the ocean from his lofty perch on the brick patio, almost at the top of the chaparral mountain. The patio took up most of the backyard; a red brick carpet that was sculpted into circular planters. The green fiberglass awning covered only a small portion of the bricked area.

Just as everyone would water their lawn, add some bushes and maybe a tree to their front yard, the next step in owning a middle class home was to create a back yard. Each homeowner could find self-expression in the paving, curbing, patio building, bush planting and tree shading of their back yard. But this back yard didn't really say anything to Tom. It didn't really express anything personal.

Tom shook his head in realization. Carey's parents probably picked out this design from a catalog. Like choosing a hairstyle from a magazine, a backyard was usually a default goal. Nothing a homeowner ever dreamed of or planned. Tom thought about he'd design a back yard. A swimming pool? Too much hassle. Better to know someone with a swimming pool. A tennis court. No, you'd need two backyards for that.

Tom remembered helping his mother and father build their back yard fence. It turned out to be more than they could handle, with concrete post holes and lining up all the posts. Tom remembered one of their neighbors using a string line to line them up.

But his parents wanted privacy. The fence was about seven feet high so you couldn't see over it, and no one could see into their back yard.

Tom smiled at how the wooden backyard fence he'd grown up with would be a mistake here on this ocean hilltop.

Tom leaned on the waist high chain link fence as he stared out to sea. This was a backyard with a view. It was awesome. There wasn't a swimming pool, but they did have a redwood jacuzzi and sauna.

Tom hadn't been thinking in terms of which day of the week it was. The past three days seemed like one long nightmare. He needed to get things back into perspective. It was Friday, almost the end of the school year. He was in Zuma at Carey's house. Her parents were on a two week vacation and tonight there was going to be a keg party with a live band.

As Tom watched the band setting up he thought how drugs had totally messed up his life. The past was gone. His future was gone. He couldn't go back to his family, his relatives, to his friends, to Barbara, to the neighborhood he had grown up in. Although he was only a hundred miles from San Diego, it could just as well have been a thousand, because it was all so far out of reach.

The band would begin after dinner. Teenagers were scattered in little clusters over the entire backyard. Some sat inside the house, listening to the stereo as they ate. It was loud enough to hear clearly outside. The orchestrations to pop music were a compromise between background music and melodic words. Tom thought of Barbara as The Moody Blues played softly.

*And when my time to join you*
*Comes to save me at long last*

31

*I'll climb aboard that final ride*
*I'll be there soon by your side*
*I'm blind to your reflection*
*I'm deaf to your sweet words*
*Our lips again will taste*
*The nectar of our love (2)*

Romantic memories agitated Tom's comfort here, the music reminded
. . .

*Be there for me*
*I'll be there for you*
*Until our time is through (3)*

As the last song on the album wound to a close and a poem was recited, the band members stepped towards their instruments in Carey's living room.

*Another kiss will quench my fire*
*Whisper to the wind your true desire*
*even though life has its own conclusion (4)*

The drummer tapped a tattoo on his snare. The guitarist tuned to the organ one more time. The bass player let his Gibson EB-3 dangle from his neck like an ornament as he drank beer from a paper cup. He held a joint in his other hand. The keyboard player's face, lowered to his keys, was obscured in his own shadow.

*Somehow I know we've lived before*
*Seen the sunset from this earthen shore*
*What I seek is something more*
*Hidden behind a hidden door*
*Where windows reveal the real illusion (4)*

The sun was starting to set. The few puffs of clouds that occupied the sky dramatized the violent orange above the dark sea. As the sun dropped behind the water, it yellowed to the point where it was possible to look directly at it without discomfort.

Tom sat in his lounge chair, finishing his second hamburger, and stared at the sun through the chain link fence. He began to fully relax, realizing that his problems were small when compared with the larger scheme of things. He thought of the brilliantly colored sunset as a movie screen and began to project mental images up on it. He saw the fat man; Russ being blown away; Daniel driving; the gun on the floor. He envisioned the hitman grimacing at him from the sky. Tom pictured Barbara in a white gauze dress, her body silhouetted by the half-sun so that her hips, waist, and breasts were visible beneath her transparent dress. All of these scenes, and many more, flashed upon the fiery background like scenes from a movie. Tom felt detached, and watched the sun drown away like the smoldering ember of a candle whose flame had been snuffed out.

With the last tip of sun in view, the band began playing their first song. The guitarist started off first, droning an open string against the melody of an adjacent string. The organist gently joined the melody.

*Clouds gather in grey matter crevices*
*Conspiring softly*
*Eyeless notions and confusing colors*
*Sift through the shapeless mind (5)*

The band's first song had been dramatically arranged. The teenagers listened to what no one had expected, and they appreciated the complexity of the song, although its meanings soared rhythmically over their heads. The theme within the song intrigued Tom, something he felt he already knew. But he didn't know what it was either.

Tom's philosophical intrigue was cut off with a chainsaw as the band ground full volume into an uptempo song, invigorating the entire crowd. People began to bob and bounce and, as the rhythm became constant, girls began pulling boys up to dance. By the end of the song, the area in front of the band in the living room was packed with gyrating bodies. The rest of the people crowded around to watch the band. Even Tom was on a chair, standing, watching the band over the pulsating sea of heads from the backyard patio.

At the beginning of the third song Tom felt a tap on his right shoulder blade. He turned around to see a smiling Carey looking up at him on his pedestal. She tossed her head and said, "C'mon, let's dance." She reached for his hand, he popped to the ground. She led him into the ocean of bodies.

After several songs, Tom asked Carey to take a break outside. He led her back to the backyard. The night air was still warm, but much cooler than inside. They sat side by side on a redwood picnic bench.

"Whew," Tom panted. "That was fun."

Carey smiled a little, yet sadly.

"What's wrong?" Tom inquired.

"Ah, nothing."

"Something's bothering you. Is it me?"

"No," she assured him. "It's not you. It's, well, it's my boyfriend--or ex-boyfriend as the case may be."

Tom considered. He hadn't been chasing her, nor had he taken a sexual interest in her. But now something stirred in him. He was intensely curious about the other man. "What about him?" he asked, trying to sound as if he didn't care.

Carey snorted bitterly. "One of my girlfriends stole him from me."

"Stole him?"

"I hope they're happy in Hell together!" she exploded.

"Hold on," Tom laughed. "Is she holding him for ransom?"

The remark drew first a shocked expression, then a soft smile. "No, you idiot," she laughed reluctantly. "His birthday was a week ago and she gave him a special present. I haven't seen the son-of-a-bitch since. And I threw the party!" She looked down between her legs. "I lined up the whole thing, bought a cake--"

"Okay, okay. So he dumped you," Tom said bluntly.

Surprised again, Carey drew back from him.

"Do you still want him back?"

"I don't know," she mumbled.

"How long were you going with him?"

"Since last Christmas."

"That's a long time," Tom commented.

"Yeah. But we broke up twice."

"Then I guess this makes strike three for him."

"Yeah, Carey laughed, "he's struck out!"

"Alright," Tom cheered. "C'mon, let's have some fun. No sense crying over spilt milk."

Carey grasped Tom's upraised arm and they strolled back into the party. The next song was a slow one. Carey melted into Tom's arms as they swayed. Her body relaxed into his so that he felt her press into him from his knees to his chest, where she nestled her head. When Tom altered his grip around her, or hugged her tighter, she would respond by snuggling into him. Thoughts of Barbara were fleeting. For the first time in what seemed like months, Tom found comfort. He felt strong and responsible as he sheltered her from the other dancers. It didn't seem as if they had only met that day. All that seemed important was to enjoy the evening and relax inside what comfort he could find.

When the band took their first break, the guitarist approached Tom and Carey.

"Hey, cool turn out. And thanks for the eats."

Carey smiled at him as she sipped her beer.

"My name's Jim," he told Tom, holding out his hand.

Tom shook it and replied, "My name's Tom."

"I've got some really good Purple Barrel," the guitarist told Carey. "Did you still want a hit?"

"Yes," she replied, "two hits."

The guitarist smiled, glancing at Tom. "Follow me. They're in my guitar case."

The band members were sprawled out in Carey's bedroom. Guitar cases and accessories were strewn over her furniture, floor and bed.

Several girls were smoking joints with the organist and drummer. The bass player was absent. Tom slid a guitar case out of his way and perched on the edge of the dresser. The guitarist pulled out a baggy that contained a couple dozen small purple pellets. Carey stood anxiously behind him, holding out her hand as he dropped them one at a time into her palm. She pulled a five dollar bill from her back pocket and said, "Thanks."

The guitarist laughed, "Don't do anything I wouldn't do."

Carey motioned for Tom to follow her as she stepped out of her bedroom and led him through a door that opened into the garage. "Shut the door," she whispered as he clunked down the wooden steps. Carey walked straight to a refrigerator on the other side of the garage and pulled out an imported beer from Germany that Tom didn't recognize.

"I've been saving this for a special occasion; and I guess it's now," she announced, handing him the bottle to open. He ended up opening it by placing the cap against the edge of her dad's workbench and slapping down with his palm until it popped off on the third try.

They sat inside her father's milky-yellow Jaguar XKE and listened to the radio. Carey handed Tom one of the two tabs of Purple Barrel and unceremoniously popped the other into her mouth, following it with a swig of beer. Tom held his tab on the tips of his fingers and, as he put it into his mouth, tried to bite off half of it without her noticing. He ended up with a very small portion in his fingertips. Less than half. A few crumbles. Maybe a quarter. He reached for the beer and took several burning swallows. He rubbed the rest of the acid debris into his shirt pocket when Carey wasn't looking.

"I wish we had a joint," Carey sighed.

"Yeah, that would be nice."

"Wait here," she commanded, getting out of the car and leaving the garage.

Tom sat in the car and listened to the radio. He was a little nervous about the trip that he was heading into. Tom had dropped acid at least a dozen times before, but every trip was different. The fear was always the same, like stage fright.

Carey accidentally startled Tom as she opened the car door and popped back inside.

"What a score!" she exclaimed. "Jim gave me some Red. Have you ever had any?"

"Yes," Tom replied. "It's great stuff." He wondered if it was the same Panama Red he'd been moving about a month ago.

Carey pushed in the car's cigarette lighter and held the joint near her mouth.

The Chambers Brothers began to play *"Time."* The electric guitar and cowbell clinked away the moments.

> *Life may fade away*
> *Time will never tell*
> *The past is here to stay (6)*

Carey puffed at the joint and, holding her hit, passed it to Tom with her cheeks puffed up like a chipmunk's.

Tom snatched the joint and took a hit. It singed his throat and expanded instantly in his lungs like an explosion. He tried as hard as he could to hold it, but the dry itchy cough burst out of him on its own volition. Carey smiled and exhaled as Tom hunched forward, coughing incessantly. She took another hit, patting Tom briskly on the back. Tom eventually regained his composure and with teary eyes, took back the joint.

The pot was definitely powerful stuff. Tom felt drowsy and weighed down. The lower half of his body seemed as heavy as concrete, the upper half filled with helium. He was floating away. Tom's head was getting dizzy from the changed altitude. Carey passed the joint, now much smaller, but he refused it.

The song softened to the cowbell beating away the seconds in a tick-tock, tick-tock, tick-tock. The bass guitar plodded double-time beneath the cowbell. The cowbell began to echo and repeat, as do images on acid that strobe into sequences.

Tom checked to see if he was coming-on to the acid by waving his open hand back and forth in front of his face like a metronome. The strobe light effect wasn't happening yet. Tom knew that sometimes it took a while to come-on to the acid.  He was in no hurry.

The 'paranoia' Red had really stoned him.

"Man!" Tom exclaimed.  "I'm Moto-ed."

"So am I," Carey monotoned, staring directly forward at the bare garage wall.

"You coming-on to the acid yet?"

"No," Tom forced out.  "Not yet."

Finally, the song returned to its verses and choruses.

*Colorful skies*
*Kaleidoscope clouds*
*Flowers in your eyes*
*Butterflies talk too loud*
*My psychedelic soul -- sings and flies (6)*

Tom began to fear the LSD that was now somewhere within his digestive system sneaking up on his consciousness.  Tom knew better than to take a whole hit of anybody's acid the first time.  Sometimes a whole hit was just too hard to handle.  He'd only wanted to take half the tab, but in his attempt at being inconspicuous he'd eaten at least 3/4.  This made him even more nervous.  Being stoned on acid wasn't too bad, but if the acid was fresh, the hallucinations might be uncontrollably 4th-dimensional.

"Let's finish the beer and go back inside."

Tom's marijuana thoughts were rattled away . . .

"Yeah . . .sure," Tom replied hesitantly, not knowing where he wanted to go.

The house was completely packed now with teenagers.  Tom lost Carey in the crowd as he waded through.  Although Tom was a little taller than average at 6' 1", he felt too crowded and squished.  So he zig-zagged his way outside for elbow room and fresh air.  Tom found the same lounge chair he'd had earlier and laid back comfortably to stare at the night sky as the band played their second set.

It was sometime during the second break that Tom noticed a lot of activity in the sky. Jets were streaking across overhead and colored lights blinked in erratic patterns. There seemed to be a lot of falling stars also. Maybe even meteors.

People were dispersing from the house to the backyard for fresh air while the band took an intermission. Tom's eyes were riveted to the heavens.

After a short while Tom was able to pick out which stars were going to break loose and burn a path towards the black horizon. It seemed that a star would first begin to vibrate then shake back and forth as if shedding extra weight until it would become so tense that like a slingshot releasing its stone; the star would suddenly bolt off and burn up in the distance. This utterly fascinated Tom for the longest time.

Someone in the house put on Jimi Hendrix's first album, **Are You Experienced?**

> *Acid burns the innocent mind*
> *Searching for what I cannot find*
> *My body moves by some control*
> *Am I free or doing what I'm told (7)*

Shit. Now Tom remembered. He was hallucinating. How stupid he felt as he realized the source of his visions. His body was numb and heavy like a wet mattress.

Acid was like a horror movie you'd get engulfed in; you'd forget it was only a movie. Maybe it was real. Then he remembered Carey. She must be coming-on also. But where is she? Tom looked to his left. Like a robot he could hear his neck creak and groan as it slowly panned. Tom thought he'd better find her and stood up. Whoops.

The world spun. He was standing on water. Tom was barely able to sit back down without landing on the bricks.

People were scattered all over the backyard talking but none were familiar to him. In fact the longer he stared at the faces the more unfamiliar they became as their features twisted and their hair changed colors.

Tom knew that he was in for one Hell of a ride as he slowly stood up again.

Staggering like a drunk, he made his way to the sliding glass doors and like a blind man imitating a mime, he moved along the glass door feeling it open-handed like a gecko. When he reached the half-opening he stumbled inside the house onto a girl's shoulders who almost fell with Tom's weight upon her.

"HEY! WHAT ARE YOU DOING?" the girl exclaimed turning to scold the molester.

"I'm sorry," Tom mumbled softly as his head wavered side to side. "I'm really wasted."

Realizing the truth of his confession the girl gently commanded, "Well, maintain man, maintain."

"Yeah. Maintain. Maintain," Tom repeated like a mantra.

"Are you a friend of Carey's?" the girl asked.

"Yes I am," Tom said now more briskly. "Where is she?"

"I don't know," she replied watching Tom's head sway.

"Would you help me find her? We both dropped acid and I want to make sure she's all right," Tom explained in wavering pitches.

The girl appeared a little more concerned now. "Okay, let's check the bedrooms first," she suggested.

The girl led Tom by the hand from room to room often balancing him or leaning him against a wall like a big broom, while she looked around.

The rooms were blurs of heads and shoulders that would flash brightly and jump away from his. The ceiling was much lower now and Tom had to duck under all the doorways. Sometimes when someone bumped into him it was as if he'd been hit by a large beach ball as he bounced away into furniture or potted plants.

When the band started playing again they seemed much, much louder and certain notes or rhythms set up flashes of colors that lit up the rooms in oranges and yellows. The carpet was a lot thicker now like high brown grass. Tom couldn't lift his feet high enough to clear the tall grass or keep from tripping on the indoor weeds.

Standing in the hallway as the girl called out Carey's name for an answer behind the locked bathroom door, Tom rubbed his face. It felt good as he rubbed it but his hand began to stick within the soft Play-do texture of his skin. Then Tom realized he'd pushed his nose over onto his right cheek and his eyes were out of arrangement with the left one too high on his forehead. Frantically Tom tried to rearrange his face like a sculptor using melting ice cream. His face was now dripping and nothing was in place.

Tom looked at his hands with sheer terror to see them covered with a red-violet goopey substance that shimmered and flowed around upon his palms.

"I think she's in the bathroom," the girl spoke.

Tom could only stare open-mouthed at his hands.

The girl went back into one of the bedrooms and found a hairpin which she used to pick the bathroom door lock through the hole in the knob. The door swung open to reveal Carey huddled next to the toilet on the linoleum floor crying. Tom snapped out of his trance when he heard Carey crying and stumbled quickly into the bathroom behind the girl. Together, Tom and the girl helped Carey stand up. Carey embraced Tom like a long lost friend as they stumbled out.

Somehow the girl led Tom and Carey back outside through the crowd with Carey clutching desperately to Tom, and Tom holding desperately onto the girl leading them with a hand on her shoulder.

After seating them down the girl said she'd go find something to calm her down and to wait there for her to return.

Seated on the lawn huddled together, Tom and Carey would have waited forever (or at least until the acid wore off).

The band had quit playing for their third break when the police arrived. The police had responded to complaints from the neighbors and were now at the front door.

Seeing so many minors and smelling so much pot inspired them to call in a couple back-up units. Within ten minutes they barged into the house causing a wide scale panic. Girls screamed and guys were shouting. People stormed out of the house at full race and ran around the seated pair of hallucinating vegetables.

Scared for the both of them Tom couldn't stay seated any longer and drug Carey back to the low chain link fence. Many of the kids were jumping this low fence and dashing into the sagebrush beach cliff canyon. Tom decided to follow their lead. He helped Carey over to the glistening, shiny checkerboard boundary and with adrenaline pumping and fear commanding, picked her up and set her over the top of the waist high barricade.

The next step they both took was into a black vacuum as they tumbled down the ice plant for what seemed forever. The jagged green back hairs of the high steep hill poked and jabbed their rubberized bodies. By the time they tumbled and rolled almost twenty feet onto an unlandscaped plateau, they were half wet from the ice plant juice that had exploded into their glowing fluorescent clothing in the moon light.

Tom dragged Carey into a large bush and as before he huddled up with her as the lights flashed all around and screams and shouts echoed in the night.

*  *  *

The Senator drove up the narrow windy road like a mouse in a memorized maze. Night blooming jasmine would occasionally breathe through the convertible wind that tasseled his graying hair. A quick left here, up a little past the ivy covered embankment, then left on Oriole, up to Blue Jay Way, then left. The white house overlooked the Hollywood side of the hills. Across the street were the deluxe custom homes which overlooked "The Valley."

The driveway was vacant so the Senator had no reason to expect guests. He unlocked the front door deadbolt. Then he reached up above the intercom and turned off the alarm. Next, he unlocked the brass door handle shaped like a giant thumb, and walked inside. The house was dark except for the kitchen lights which came on automatically at night. Since it was past midnight the timer had already turned the bedroom light off.

The Senator put his coat on a chair and walked straight for the bar. He didn't hear the footsteps behind him as he clinked the ice into his glass. When he started to pour the Scotch the voice behind him injected enough fright to send the bottle of Scotch flying halfway across the room.

"Pour me one also Senator," the voice repeated sarcastically.

The Senator's eyes were dilated with fear as he panted heavily with his back arched backward against the bar.

"How'd you get in here?" the panicked Senator puffed.

"Same way I get into any house; whatever way suits me best," the intruder replied calmly. He wore a dark grey woolen suit jacket over polyester black pants. The shoes were black also but didn't have leather soles or heels. The shoes were as quiet as tennies as he walked past the Senator into the kitchen. He pulled out a steak and turned to the Senator, "Did you want a steak also?"

The Senator didn't say a word but shook his head back and forth watching the intruder's every move.

As the intruder prepared his dinner, the Senator mopped up the Scotch in his carpet with paper towels and picked the broken glass bottle pieces from his ivory white shag carpet.

The intruder grimaced in pain as he bent to insert the steak into the broiler.

"You probably heard about that fuck-up in Malibu, didn't you?" He cut up a potato.

"Yes, I did. What happened?"

"This fuckin' kid from San Diego got away from me."

"What happened to Russ?"

"I shot him," the intruder said coldly.

The Senator was astonished. "Why?"

"Cuz he froze up on me when the kid shot me."

"You got shot?"

"Yeah, that fuckin' little asshole. Look!" he barked, unbuttoning his shirt to show the chest wrapped in bandages. "I'm gonna waste that fuckin' kid," he continued through clenched teeth.

Without letting on that he'd heard the kid's name before, the Senator asked, "What's his name?"

"Tom Calder."

\* \* \*

The house was quiet above Tom and Carey where they still crouched inside the large scrub oak bush. Above them stretched the tall ice plant hill they had rolled down.

Below and around them stretched sagebrush canyons and small ravines. Beyond that were train tracks that bordered the white California beach sand. Tom couldn't hear the surf because of its distance, but he could smell the ocean and taste it in the air.

"My body still feels numb," Carey whined.

"It's okay. Hey relax. Try to maintain and think about fun things-- like Disneyland," Tom said cheerfully.

Much of the consuming stone effect that seemed to make the body feel full of gravel had subsided. The hallucinations were now more like mescaline. A flash of color here, a puff of smoke there. Occasionally a shadow would walk by or fly overhead.

"We're gonna just hang out here until your trip wears off; then we'll go back to your house," Tom consoled her. "Just relax, relax."

Tom put his arm around her again and she responded by putting her head on his chest and hugging him tightly. Then she started crying.

"Oh shit," Tom said jokingly. "C'mon don't cry. Why heck, just look at that view!" Tom exclaimed pointing upward through the bush branches.

Carey looked to the sky and then laid her head in Tom's lap looking upward. "I used to dream about being captured by aliens from another planet," Carey began. "The ones who caught me were always small and ugly but when I was aboard their ship, they'd turn me over to the Captain who was very tall and handsome . . . even though he was green."

"Sounds sexy," Tom interrupted jokingly.

"And then they'd take me to their planet where I was treated like a queen. Because I was from Earth I was really special and given a high rank in their government. But I couldn't have any children. For some reason there was too much of a genetic difference and I was like a cat who couldn't get pregnant from a dog. So--after so many years they let me return to Earth where I came back almost as young as when I left. Of course I could never tell anybody the truth because nobody'd believe me."

"Hmmm," Tom said, as if the story were true.

When the trip had passed enough for them to make the steep climb back up the ice plant, Tom asked Carey, "Was your boyfriend at the party tonight?"

"Yes," she replied.

"Well, who was he?"

"In the band."

"The guitarist who gave us the acid?" Tom asked startled.

"No," she laughed. "The bass player. That was my ex-friend Debby who helped me out of the bathroom."

"Oh yeah?"

"C'mon," Carey said. "I've got to go to the bathroom again."

"Only this time you won't need any help," Tom snickered. "Right?"

The house was depressing despite the Rolling Stones record which played at a conservatively low volume. The band was tearing down their equipment.

"Where were you guys?" asked the guitarist as Tom and Carey entered the house through the sliding glass windows.

"We split," Carey answered. "What happened?"

"Well," the guitarist started, as if repeating a school lesson, "Jack and John Backle were arrested for under the influence and Barry got arrested cause he gave them a bunch of lip."

"Barry got arrested?" she asked in amazement.

"Debby went to get money from her parents to bail him out."

"Oh," Carey said as if disappointed.

"How was the acid?" Jim asked as he latched the lid on his Echoplex.

"A dandy," Tom interjected.

Jim looked at Tom to figure if he meant to compliment or insult.

"It was powerful enough," Tom continued, "but the environment wasn't right."

Jim smiled. "Yeah--the pigs got heavy tonight. Too bad. At least they didn't take our equipment."

"Take your equipment?" Tom questioned.

"They always say they will," Jim laughed.

"But maybe someday they will," the drummer added pessimistically. "I'm done loadin' up. I'll see you tomorrow at rehearsal."

"Okay," said the guitarist.

"Where do you rehearse?" asked Tom.

"Just down the street a few blocks. Stop on by. Carey'll tell you where it's at."

"Did you get Barry's equipment out already?" asked Carey.

"No. None of us had room. We'll come back for it tomorrow. It's all in the garage," answered Jim.

"Okay."

Carey and Tom were still pretty loaded and the house cleaning would obviously wait until tomorrow.

"Let's jump in the jacuzzi," suggested Carey.

"Okay."

* * *

The knocking at the front door was combined with the doorbell ringing simultaneously.

Tom reached over and shook Carey. "Someone's at the door," Tom whispered.

"Yeah-yeah," Carey groaned.

So Tom got up, put on a pair of boxers and walked to the front door. Opening the door he found himself face-to-face with Carey's ex-boyfriend, bass player Barry.

Barry slowly eyed Tom up and down with disgust and proclaimed, "I came for my equipment."

"Sure," Tom said, stepping aside.

Tom returned to the bedroom to tell Carey who was here.

"He is?" she exploded. Then she calmed down and seemed to smile like a cat who ate the canary. She realized Barry had seen Tom dressed in his underwear and was probably jealous. "Good."

Carey stepped into the bathroom and closed the door. Tom sat on the edge of the bed and for the first time looked around to see where he was. He was in Carey's bedroom again. Only this time Tom noticed that all of the original paintings were signed, C. Finely. He got up for closer examination of the various works. Tom's favorite was the charcoal rendering of an Indian Chief. The watercolor print of the white swan was pretty. The oil painting still life was excellent but boringly common. Tom figured it was probably an art class assignment.

The sculpture on the bookcase was the last thing Tom noticed. It was a sea monster, menacing and vicious, yet at the same time it wasn't frightening. It was as if this man eating beast was tamed like a watchdog.

The shower was running and Tom decided to make breakfast. It was too late for modesty so Tom didn't put his jeans on.

Tom sensed that he could get Barry to stay for breakfast and made enough scrambled eggs and pancakes for three persons. As he was setting the table, Barry approached him.

"Who are you?" he asked rudely.

"I met your girlfriend, Debby, last night," Tom said avoiding Barry's question. "She helped us out before the police broke up the party."

"Oh yeah. She said something--"

"The last I heard she'd gone to bail you out of jail."

"They wouldn't release me until this morning, fuckheads," Barry said lowering his head with resentment towards the police and perhaps Tom also.

"You had breakfast?" Tom asked as if totally unaware of Barry's hostility.

"They tried to feed me some jail slop this morning but I wasn't gonna touch it."

"Have a seat, I'll tell Carey breakfast's ready," Tom informed as he bopped across the living room in his boxer shorts.

The breakfast went smoothly with a little jail talk and band talk before Carey finally referred to Tom by his name, providing Barry with the answer he'd originally sought.

Barry looked at Tom and said, "Where you from, Tom?"

"Del Mar."

"Oh. You visiting family up here?" Barry went on.

"Well--"

"Hey!" Carey interrupted. "Enough of the second-degree."

"Are you rehearsing today?" asked Tom as he now gained the floor.

"Yes."

"I'd like to come watch," Tom said innocently.

"Uh--"

"Sure," Carey answered for Barry. "I'll show you where it is. What time are you guys starting?"

"Three o'clock," Barry grudgingly replied.

*  *  *

The rehearsal room was the garage of Barry's house about three blocks down the hill. The walls were covered with egg cartons, foam, carpet, and even a mattress on the garage door. A few posters decorated the uneven surfaces. A Jethro Tull poster, a Led Zeppelin poster, and a poster of Moby Grape; the one where the guy in the middle is 'flipping the bird'! (Some of the later posters had been censored and the middle fuck-finger on the washboard artistically removed.)

The bass player and organist were drinking orange juice while the drummer and guitarist drank beers. By the first break the drummer and Jim were getting tipsy.

"What's the name of your band anyway," asked Tom.

"The Razors, man. We're The Razors," Jim replied with a smile. "By the way, I forgot your name."

"Tom," he replied as they shook again. "My name is Tom."

"Yeah, that's it. I'm bad with names. If my name weren't on my guitar case I'd probably forget it too."

Tom looked to the guitar case next to his amp and saw the stenciled name, Jim Foster.

"Hey, you want a line of crank?" Jim asked Tom quietly.

Tom had never done crank before, but he'd heard it was a kind of speed. Tom liked speed. "Sure."

Jim grabbed another beer from the ice chest in the corner and led Tom into the house. Barry's mother was preparing something in the kitchen as they walked through.

She eyed Tom so he decided to introduce himself.

"Hello. I'm Tom," he said with outstretched hand.

Mrs. Smith put down her soft white lump of dough and wiped her hands off on a towel.

"Hello," she said enthusiastically. "I'm Barry's mom, but the kids all call me 'Sis,'" she smiled. As she put down the towel she shook Tom's hand and asked, "Where you two going?"

"The bathroom," Jim answered. "You wanna come?"

Mrs. Smith smiled again. "Give me a minute to finish here. I'll be along shortly."

Once inside the bathroom Jim locked the door and pulled a vial out of his green velvet vest with silver embroidery. A small mirror leaning in the corner had obviously been used for this purpose before because the glass was rimmed with white dust.

Jim poured out a small amount of beige crystal powder onto the mirror and spread them out into six lines about inch-and-a-half long each. Then a knock on the door announced Mrs. Smith's arrival.

Jim said, "Let her in."

As she stepped into the larger than average bathroom she hungrily eyed the mirror. But Jim took his lines first, then passed the brass tube to Tom.

Tom looked at Mrs. Smith and holding out the tube to her said, "Ladies first."

She smiled, took the tube, and agilely sniffed up her two lines of crank. When she looked at Tom to hand him the snorter her eyes were red and teary. She pinched her nose shut with her free hand in an effort to stop the pain.

Tom took the tube and reluctantly did his two lines of Hell fire. The pain was immediate, like Drano. A thousand onions would have been more pleasurable than the pain to his nostrils. His eyes watered and his nose began to run a little. He sniffed to keep from losing any of his nasal contents. Ouch again! The pain subsided after about sixty-seconds.

By the time all three of them stepped out of the bathroom, Tom felt his teeth clenching and gums vibrating. He felt very, very awake and wanted to jump out of his skin and run a lap.

"You a musician Tom?" Sis asked.

"No. But I play the harp a little bit."

"Really?" Jim asked with interest. "Maybe you could sit in with us on a tune later."

Tom smiled into the hungry anxious leopard eyes of Sis. She may have been over 30, but she was cool. Her straight dark brown hair hung almost to her shoulders. Her dark brown eyes seemed to glow black as the speed amped her brain like a Daytona race car.

Tom wasn't sure what to say to her intense stare. He wasn't sure how to stop staring himself.

Finally his eyes broke the laser connection with Sis as his head mechanically snapped to look at Jim—who had a strange Cheshire Cat smile.

The Razors picked up their instruments, wandered a few steps into their molecular positions within the musical universe and began to play a Doors song called, *"Moonlight Drive."* The guitarist whipped out a really slick slide guitar solo.

> *Sitting together by the sea*
> *The world exists for you and me*
> *Shake the moon, let's jump and dive*
> *On our warm moonlit drive (8)*

Tom turned around to see that Mrs. Smith was sitting next to Carey on the couch. As Carey watched Jim singing, Mrs. Smith was staring at Tom, tapping her feet wildly to the song. Tom felt a little uncomfortable as she obviously turned thoughts of him over in her mind. Maybe she knew who he was. Tom had been checking the newspapers, but as of yet, the articles had shown no pictures of him. So probably she was . . .

"Play *'Light My Fire,'*" Mrs. Smith blurted out as the song ended.

Jim mumbled how they were tired of that song. "But there is another Doors song we haven't played in a while." Turning to the band, "Let's play *'Let's Run'*!"

Barry started the song with a steady bass heartbeat. The big wooden organ whistled spookily. The guitar added a few bended notes setting up an eerie presence.

> *Feet upon the ground*
> *Burning from the sun*
> *It hurts less*
> *To run, run, run*
> *Take me to your house*

*Take me to your home*
*Shadows of the past*
*Catching up at last (9)*

Somehow the band was capturing Tom's life with this song.  He was grasped by the music and lyrics like a soundtrack to his life.

*Your cavern is warm*
*From the fire inside*
*Soft pillowed bed*
*Empties out my head (9)*

The music began to break up as the instruments separated melodically.  Tension grew.

*Policemen die*
*Protecting the bigger lie*
*It all seems so insane*
*To play this deadly game (9)*

Although Tom had found a place to be right now, he wondered with an empty feeling in his stomach where he'd be tomorrow.  No food.  No car.  No money.  Hunted by the law.  That hitman.  He was a castaway.  Lost.  Where was he going to go?

*Run to somewhere far*
*Run to somewhere near*
*Run, run, run (9)*

The air was amazingly silent.  No one played.  The song had somehow abruptly stopped.  Shot--

Then Jim groaned and screamed as the drummer smashed his cymbals violently and the beat continued only much faster.  Jim used the metal finger slide for some unguitar-like effects. The musical key was changed again.  Higher.

*Outlaws hide behind their guns*
*Keeping peace where freedom runs*
*Take a girl, get married today*
*This could be your very last day (9)*

The organ groaned and roared. The guitarist raced up and down his guitar neck. The drummer thundered. The singer chanted.

*Run, run, run*
*Fast, fast, fast*
*Go, go, go*
*Too slow, too slow, too slow (9)*

Tom felt the shadow of death over him. Like an animal in a trap. The hunter was about to pluck him.

*Eyes in the night*
*Seeking (9)*

Tom squirmed uncomfortably.

*Hunting (9)*

His heart pounded wildly in his chest.

*Attacking (9)*

Then as if the musicians were all simultaneously stabbing a beast they stomped down the chaotic ending into a full hysteria which quieted down slowly like an animal dying, gasping for its last breaths. Jim spoke softly in a low voice:

*Death has no fear*
*She is always here (9)*

The organ screamed its last breath and the apparition vanished. Tom was back in the rehearsal room as if awakened suddenly.  He clapped automatically, especially glad to be back in reality.  Carey and Mrs. Smith joined in the applause.

*  *  *

That evening, as Tom and Carey ate dinner back at her house, Tom asked about Mrs. Smith.

"Oh, she's a character," Carey laughed.  "She waters Barry's pot plants and then helps smoke them too."

"What about Mr. Smith?"

"Divorced," Carey replied between mouthfuls. "He's an attorney for ABS Records and says he can get them a break when they're ready."

"They're ready!" Tom said abruptly.  "They're ready now."

"Yeah. I know," Carey sighed.  "They've had a few people check them out, but nothing yet.  Barry says they've still got to tighten their arrangements but--"

"Man," Tom interrupted, "I think that they're one of the best bands I've ever seen. They should be playing concerts, not parties."

Carey laughed as if she'd heard that before.  "Well, they're playing a gig next week if you want to see them perform."

"Yeah. Let's go," Tom rooted.

"But it's all the way down in Oceanside at the Marine Base at Camp Pendleton."

"I don't care. I wanna go."

"Actually, because it's the Marine Base they might not let you in unless you were part of the band or the road crew."

"No problem. I'll be a roadie. That'd be great."

Carrie nodded in agreement.

* * *

Tom was tired tonight. The acid and police, the rehearsal and crank, cleaning up the house. Tom was ready to crash. He wandered about Carey's room looking at her artwork some more.

"You're very talented," he awarded.

"Thanks," she smiled while straightening up her room. "You wanna see some more?"

"Definitely."

From the white bookcase she pulled an oversized black hardbound book. No printing on it. She sat on the edge of her bed and opened the book on her lap. Tom sat beside her.

Charcoal sketches, pen and ink, pencil . . . what an imagination! Strange animals and warrior men graced the pages drawn by Carey. She skipped a few pages and continued.

"Hey. What were those drawings you skipped?"

Carey acted embarrassed. "Oh, some drawings of Barry."

"Well, let's see 'em."

"You probably don't want to see them. He's nude."

Tom thought for a moment. "If he's nude, you're probably right." Barry nude didn't sound so interesting.

"If you want I could draw you?"

"Uh--" 'That would definitely be a mistake,' Tom thought. 'No pictures. I'm a fugitive.' "I'm not too photogenic."

"Sure you are," she giggled. "You're very good looking. I could--"

"No. Really. No. I don't like to have my picture taken."

"But I could--"

The phone rang. Carey got up and answered it.

"Yeah, this is Carey. Uh-huh . . . No, I don't think so . . . Yeah . . .

55

Well, he's helping me over here now . . . Sure . . . Okay . . . I'll tell him . . . Bye." Carey put the phone down in a very mechanical manner as if part of her wanted to slam the phone and the other part was restraining herself.

"Who was that?"

Carey walked to her bedroom door and shut it firmly. "Barry's mom."

"Sis? Did she ask for me?"

Carey boiled hostile, "Why, you wanna go fuck her?"

"Hey, easy does it. I just--"

"You wanna go play with her . . . Go ahead."

"Carey!" Tom tried to calm her. He stood up and approached her, leaving the art book on the bed. "Kinda jealous aren't you?"

Carey walked away from him to the other side of the bed.

Tom talked softly. "I want to be with you."

"Well, she wants to be with you. Maybe the two of you have something in common."

"Maybe," Tom said casually, trying not to chuckle at her behavior. "But that doesn't matter."

Carey turned half circle to face Tom as if cornered now and ready to attack.

"And what does matter? Huh?"

Tom reached for her hand but she slapped his arm. Hard. He retracted. "What matters is that you are very special to me. Even though we only met yesterday in the ocean, I know that we are special together. We have a lot in common."

"You hardly know me," she rebuked.

"I know you intimately," he teased.

Carey pushed Tom aside to walk away. Tom grabbed her waist. She pushed at him. He held onto her. She turned away from him. Tom held her gently, his arms wrapped around her from behind. He nestled her into his chest. She made weak prying efforts with her fingers to loosen his grasp.

"Now come on Carey. You've got no reason to be upset."

"I've got plenty of reasons!"

"Well I'm not one of them." Tom spun her around, their eyes locked. "Let's--"

She interrupted him with a kiss. They stood in a long embrace changing head positions but all the while keeping lip-locked. When they finally broke the kiss she was a different person. Like a happy-go-lucky little girl she smiled, stepped back, giggled, and started peeling off her clothes, keeping her eyes locked with his. When she was fully undressed she climbed on her bed like a cat on all fours. She put the art book on the end table and then laid face down atop her bed, cuddling a pillow, with her bare ass invitingly upraised.

\* \* \*

Ah . . . springtime in California. One of those things best not described but felt. In fact the less known and written about, the better. It's already too crowded. The bloated midwestern beachballs and East Coast litterbugs would be better advised of the riptides and stingrays than the bikinis and suntans.

Zuma Beach has course dark sand, but feels like an island as it juts out into the Pacific. The fact that Tom was on the run was easy to forget with Carey. In the comfort of her parents' home, or on the beach, fear was a world away. Anyway, when his nerves did get subconsciously bristled, there was the solace of good pot, great music, and Carey's passion. She was an only child. Raised with everything. She owned what she wanted and what she shared was her exclusivity. That was shared in abundance.

They were together all day long. Barbara was well-to-do also, but her sophistication and upbringing had been too rigid and unemotional. Carey was much more hedonistic. She enjoyed pleasure. It was a luxury her family could afford, and now Tom was an adopted child. Sex was sport. Sex was relaxing. Sex was for love. Sex was for loneliness. Sex was for comfort, and best of all her sex was for Tom. It wasn't really love. It wasn't really lust. It was pleasure and passion. Tom was her toy and she was his paradise.

They fucked in every room of the house. They screwed all day long, or at least whenever either of them felt like it. No one ever had a headache, and they were naked almost all the time. Some people resented their always touching, cuddling and kissing. So what. They were together and neither time nor location were of any consequence.

After several days of seducing each other and going through the normal courtship or foreplay rituals, the body language simplified. A certain stroking of the thighs or even a look in the eyes was all that was necessary. Carey had beautiful breasts that she tried not to flaunt. She downplayed them a lot. It was mostly her beautifully firm ocean toned buttocks that she would pose or adjust, that alerted Tom's adolescent radar to a mission at hand. They licked, kissed, probed, loved, tickled and stroked each other's entire bodies until they seemed to develop a telepathic linkage. She knew where to rub him and he knew where to scratch her. There was never a lonely itch as they practiced preventative medicine.

No real worries, no hassles, and no conflicts. Well, a few very minor ones. Mrs. Smith kept trying to get Tom fucked up, in more ways that one. And Tom's lack of identity (and identification), meant he was unable to provide a masculine umbrella for Carey's maternal nature which was developing. He couldn't even drive a car, no license. The lies and half-lies to conceal his identity must have affected Carey to some extent, despite her willingness to accept Tom as a trusted partner.

Tom worked hard to invent a new background for himself, but it was after all, full of holes and deceptions. He didn't enjoy lying. Trust is an intuitive child. You can trick the mind but you can't fool the heart.

*Happiness is a place*
*Have you ever been there?*
*Dreams are memories*
*That you've never had*
*Love's a holy word*
*With someone else you share*
*Sins are just a judgement*
*When judgement has gone bad*
*I've got my life to life (10)*

# Chapter Three
## *Oceanside*

Camp Pendleton occupies a large expanse of beachfront property all around Oceanside. In fact, Oceanside exists only because Camp Pendleton is there.

Entering the marine base checkpoint the band was scrutinized and approved for entry. An MP jeep escorted the three-vehicle caravan to the Officer's Club.

The band equipment was loaded through a side door. Tom helped load in the Hammond organ which was no easy chore. Although Russell, the organist, had a dolly that strapped right onto the piano case, it was still so heavy that it took four guys to lower it out of the van like a lead-filled casket. The drums, as always, comprised the most pieces per member, but they're all pretty light; except the trap case which holds all the metal hardware and cymbal stands.

Tom enjoyed his new job with vigor and hustled about as busy as a worker ant. He didn't know how to assemble the equipment yet but got a lot of instructions from each member.

"Usually we bring a light show also," Russell explained. "But here at Pendleton we don't bother."

The band did a sound check playing an original and a Beatles song. Then they took an hour break until show time.

Barry had a jet black Ford van with a new-smelling interior. For tonight the secluded partying took place here within the carpeted walls and paneled van ceiling. The front seats swiveled around to face the rear where Tom, Jim, and Gordon sat on the sofa bed. Russell sat shotgun.

Barry always had smoke, usually of a new variety, and tonight he had Lebanese hash. Jim offered the use of his small porcelain hash pipe but Barry insisted on using his hookah. It was homemade, using some kind of fancy bathwater bottle to hold the water. A black rubber chemistry class stopper with two holes in it supported two brass tubes. One tube reached down into the bottom of the water to produce a stream of bubbles with each hit. The other tube sucked out the smoke that gathered in stormy clouds below the stopper and above the water with floating ashes. Into the black brass lined bowl, which looked like a crow's nest on a fishing boat, Barry crumbled up a half gram of the yellow hashish and put the clear plastic tubing in his mouth. Quickly the top half of the bottle's interior, above the water, filled with smoke and jetted through the clear tunnel into Barry's mouth.

Jim told Tom that smoking hash was better here because they could cover up the smell easier with their cigarettes.

Barry passed it clockwise to Russell and then Tom took a hit. Jim lit a match as Tom took his hit and the crumbled hash which was half-ignited lit to a bright red glow as its smoke discharged into the hookah water. The density of smoke in the pipe thickened to opaque white. Tom got more than he bargained for and couldn't even finish inhaling as he exploded with coughing spasms that sandblasted his lungs. Everyone laughed and Tom was embarrassed. Shit! He was no novice toker but the water cooled smoke had tricked him into taking more than he could handle. Tom remained bent-over and motioned them to continue. Gordon also fell victim to the expanding smoke. His coughing was of consolation to Tom.

When the pipe returned he more cautiously took a smaller hit. Tom held his next toke down with all his might, he felt it grinding and pushing against his lung interior and finally exhaled smoothly without coughing. Bruce and Jim had a couple beers and by the time they were to begin the first set everyone was totally wasted.

Before going on stage the band hurriedly worked at consuming as much as possible in five minutes. Gordon, the drummer, drank from a bottle of Jack Daniels--helped his timing no doubt. Russell nursed a beer, but not to get high. Russell was a hype. He indiscriminately went about his ritual in the back of the van as if no one was really watching. Tom realized what the distilled water was for when Russ popped the plastic lid off. With the needle pulled off of the syringe, Russell sucked up some water. He gently squirted some water into the spoon. The remainder of water in the syringe was shot like a squirt gun at Jim.

"Hey!" Jim barked. "Knock it off!"

Russell ignored him without expression and reached over for the fat red candle that sat in an aluminum pie pan on the floor in the middle of the van. The bottom of the tablespoon was already black sooted from previous usage. Russell moved the spoon in a circular motion over the candle flame. The light-brown Mexican poppy powder quickly dissolved and in a rapid succession of movements Russell set the spoon down next to him, put the needle back on the syringe, sucked up the contents of the spoon, pointed the needle to the paneled ceiling and pushed up the plunger until a drop appeared.

"Tie off my arm Jim will you?" Russell asked in a tone he'd delivered many times before.

"Where's the surgical tube?" Jim asked, sounding perturbed.

"I forgot it. You got a hanky or something? A bandanna?"

"No," Jim said flatly.

"No," Barry offered before he was asked.

"Sorry Russ," they chorused sarcastically.

Russell looked about the interior for something, in a slightly frantic bug-eyed tilt. He held his syringe pointed at his skinny arm; so near yet so far.

"Grip my arm tight," Russell appealed to Jim.

"Aw c'mon man," Jim moaned.

"Damn it Jim," Russell demanded.

Jim scooted on his knees over to Russell and choked his left bicep. Russell opened and closed his fist in a pumping action. He chose a vein in his forearm for injection. He poked in twice before backing up the plunger a little bit with his thumb. All this being done with only his right hand as Tom watched. Russell clasped the syringe tightly between his index and middle finger, and operated the plunger with his thumb. When a little blood was sucked into the bottom of the hypodermic he knew he was on track. The blood didn't even have a chance to mix with the heroin solution. Russell shoved the blood back into his vein and followed it with a heroin chaser.

Jim let go of Russell's bicep. Russell pulled the emptied syringe out of his arm in a flowing wrist motion and then he leaned back against the carpeted van wall.

Jim had crawled back to the other side of the van and began to roll a joint.

Tom reached for a beer. "Uh--shouldn't we be getting ready to play?"

"We are," Jim commented as he lit the joint.

None of the band really looked forward to this gig. It was money. The "Jugheads," as Jim called them, were like another breed of animal compared to the band members. Their marine stubble heads differed only in shape; they all had the same haircuts.

Tom was excited to see The Razors perform. It didn't matter that they were in a Marine Officer's Club. He was also nervously excited, he had been entrusted with operating the house lights. Tom sat in front of the mixer and light board amidst the audience about forty-five degrees off stage right.

"After most songs it's cool to black out the stage," Jim explained to Tom. "Just pull all the sliders down like this or hit the master switch. This switch is for the strobe light. We're not going to use it until the third or fourth set. I'll tell you about that later. Careful how you mix some of the colors like green and red, but feel free to play around."

Black to yellow with a pink spot light. Red-toned Hammond organ. The songs were current and recognized by all. Despite this being the Officer's Club on a marine base there were almost as many women as men. These girls were chasing uniforms with stripes in their eyes. The dance floor was waves of undulating, bobbing heads of prickles and locks. Even the slow songs kept the dance floor full.

*Loving you*
*The best that I can*
*When a woman*
*Holds a man (11)*

The first set finished with no complications . Tom was "getting the hang" of his new job.  The set was smooth and the songs were paced well.  The band could have played those songs in their sleep.

The Razors and Tom regrouped in the van.

"The place is packed tonight!" exclaimed Barry.

"Yeah.  Good turnout," agreed Russell.

"They're really whooping it up.  Seems like they're celebrating or something," Barry added.

"Yeah," Jim chuckled.  "It's probably National Jughead Day."

The band laughed loudly through the smoke that poured up from the hookah bowl.  Like smoke signal warnings, the hash clouds filled the van interior again.

"Anybody need an Opetrol?" Barry offered.

"Yeah.  Give me one," Jim quickly replied.

"I'm fine," Russell groaned.

"You want one Tom," Jim asked.  He knew there was still a little tension between Barry and Tom.

"Sure," Tom replied.  "What the heck."

"Give me two of them," demanded the drummer with outstretched hand.

"Hey--these are the orange ones.  You know, the OP-20's.  You eat two of these and you won't be able to sit on your drum stool for more than five-seconds at a time."

"I know, I know.  I'll save the other one for later."  Gordon took one OP immediately with a swig of Jack and put the other in his black cowboy shirt. The white on black embroidered pockets and shoulders were bright and flashy. He was an aggressive drummer who when playing hard appeared to be riding a brahma bull as he bucked, bounced and cringed.

"Who's got a joint?" asked Russell impatiently.

Better to smoke hash here," Barry reminded.

The second set went smoothly until the last couple numbers. Jim was so animated as he spun around that he knocked over his mike stand into the dancing crowd. It hit a marine on the head with the microphone. The marine cussed at him but there was no big scene of it. Jim's mood seemed dampened by the commie killers.

The van was again full of hash and cigarette smoke. Everyone was talking a mile-a-minute simultaneously. Tom bounced from conversation to conversation as certain key words caught his attention. Everyone was talking to everyone. Barry and Tom drank a couple of beers as Jim and Gordon worked on their Jack Daniel's. Russell performed his candle act. No one saw Gordon pop his second OP-20 into his mouth, as he washed it down with a gulp of whiskey.

The band was warmed up now.

The third set was The Razor's favorite set. This was when they played most of their originals and a few Doors songs. This was also usually the high point in getting high. No matter how dead an audience might be, The Razors were gonna have fun.

Despite being very wasted, modern science was 'O-patrolling' their blood veins and keeping The Razors wide awake.

Gordon started right into some extended drum riffs the minute he sat down on stage. He soloed hard. Without the accompaniment of his fellow musicians he seemed even louder yet.

Russell double-checked his Leslie cabinet and sat down at his Hammond C-3, adjusting the draw bars.

Barry fiddled with his amp settings as his black Gibson bass hung suspended from his shoulders.

Jim walked to the bar. He was the only one old enough to buy liquor. He bought a beer and picked up a few cokes for the boys.

Tom experimented with some light combinations on stage; totally involved and engrossed in his new creative function: red and yellow, fader up, switch off, pair on . . .

The Razors started the third set with the same song they'd started the party at Carey's, *"Headin' To Heaven."* Within its poetic descriptions of altered realities Tom found ample space to experiment and try bold color changes and combinations. The song finished with the dance floor only half-occupied. *"Headin' To Heaven"* was an ethereal, changing series of moods. But these marines had come here tonight to have a good time, not transcend their consciousness! Other than getting drunk, a couple of them shouted requests like "Creedence Clearwater," *"Wipe Out,"* and *"Gloria."*

Jim was a little peeved that the song had not been received better. "Was that song a bit too thought provoking?" Jim taunted the audience through his microphone. "Well here's a song that shouldn't go too far over your--"

Barry gave Jim a dirty look hoping he wouldn't say . . .

"--heads. You asked for it and now you've got it!" Jim turned to the band as the crowd murmured restlessly. "Let's do *"Gloria."*"

"Aw c'mon," whined Russ. "I don't want to do that song."

"Let's do a Stones song," interrupted Barry.

Jim wasn't listening to anyone else and was intent on doing *"Gloria."* "Gordon, count if off," he demanded.

The drum sticks clicked together four times and continued clicking another four as the drummer counted aloud, "One, two, three, four."

Jim's guitar was cut down in volume to give a cleaner, jangly sound with a bit of a rough edge on it. The words were easily audible over the simple arrangement. The song was sung and played the same as countless other bands had; until Jim got to the intimate verse:

> *Then I walked up those steps*
> *To her apartment door*
> *I knocked in that same pattern*
> *Like so many times before*

*And she knew it was me*
*She didn't want to hide*
*She opened up the door*
*And I slipped inside*
*Inside her little room*
*She's getting all undressed*
*She's looking good*
*I also get undressed*
*I put my arms around her*
*We kiss: I throw her to the floor*
*I don't give her any choice*
*I'm gonna FUCK HER 'TIL SHE'S SORE! (12)*

Gordon picked up on the new lyric flow and started embellishing with snare drum flourishes and sexy high hat accents.

*I made her groan and purr*
*It felt so good to be — deep inside of her (12)*

Jim was consumed as his body acted out the song with eyes closed.

*And I moved fast*
*And I moved slow*
*I used every loving trick*
*Some she didn't know*
*She started to shiver*
*She began to shake*

Russell looked nervously to Barry who shrugged his shoulders. Neither of them could stop Jim. Just hold up the song…

Jim began to sing louder and build up his intensity.

*And she felt so good*
*I felt the same*
*We both shouted!*
*We both came*

*And I shouted out*
*Yeah! I yelled her name!*
*And I said, M*

The crowd was aghast.

Gordon was loving it as he pounded harder on his simple rhythm.

*A*

Even the dancers stared at Jim.

*R*

Several marines ran for the manager.

*I*

Fingers were pointing at the singer.

*I - I - I - I - I - I - A*

Some angry soldiers were pushing to the front lines.

*M - A - R - I - N - A*
*Marina*

One of the marines reached for the mike stand.

*M - A - R - I - N - A*
*Mar--*

The mike stand was pulled down.  Jim in reflexive anger kicked at one of the marines then ran to Barry's microphone.  He sang as loud as he could, almost shouting.

*--I - N - A*
*Marina! - You shout it every day*
*Marina! - You fuckers can kiss my ass!*
*"Marina!"*

One of the other angry marines jumped on stage. Barry backed up to his amp but Jim attacked the stage trespasser. Still strumming his guitar he shouldered the marine off the stage into the dancers with the power of a football linebacker. He sang the song's new name, letter by letter.

*M - A - R - I - N - A (12)*

The drummer and keyboardist continued singing, using the new lyrics, "Ma-ri-na." Another marine jumped up the side of the stage by Barry. Gordon saw him and with the deadly accuracy of an ancient hunter, threw a drum stick which hit point first in his chest. The marine buckled over and Barry, in a frightened attempt to just get him away, pushed him off the stage with a boot heel.

The crowd was crazy; yelling and shouting cuss words and cheers. A fist fight broke out on the dance floor. The band kept playing as the dancers cleared a circular arena for the two male bulldogs to roll on the ground and punch each other to military oblivion, or at least the war planet of Mars.

Jim went into a guitar solo and was looking down at his guitar neck when the beer bottle struck him in the shoulder. Gordon jumped over his kit to rescue Jim as three marines stormed the stage. Gordon grabbed a mike stand and in one sweep took two of them down with the weighted bottom. The third uniform tackled him. Gordon wrestled like a wild animal and pummeled the marine's face, but the soldier was much bigger and had gotten on top of Gordon as Tom took a last glance over the mix board. Tom pulled all the light faders down and as he stood up flicked on the strobe light.

The club was a manic swirl of violence; girls and guys screaming and yelling. The absence of music was replaced by the percussion of fists striking bones, bodies and skulls. The strobe light dramatized this brawling rumble into a nightmarish panic that no one could focus upon.

Tom made it only halfway across the dance floor before he got caught in a whirlpool of arms and shouting faces. He never even saw the fist coming which hit him in the side of the head and knocked him down. He wasn't quite unconscious until a few boot kicks curled him up into a ball.

When Tom awoke it was still night and his face was in dirt. Ooh . . . ooh, really dizzy with excruciating pain he rolled over onto his back and realized he was under a bush. Tom wasn't sure but he figured he'd crawled to his present hiding place while in shock and half-unconscious. His head throbbed and his ribs were afire with pain every time he tried to take a breath.

As Tom lay beneath the bush he listened to an argument about fifteen feet away in the parking lot. They were trying to talk so no one could hear, but the man's anger prevented his volume control.

"I don't have to put up with this," said the man. "What the Hell's gotten into you?" the man said even louder. "You've been bitching at me all night."

"Yes, it's been a wonderful evening," the woman replied coolly. "I love to see marines banging their jarheads together."

"There you go again. Now listen here. This is ridiculous and I've heard enough. Let's spend the night at the Oceanside Motel and put all this behind us." The man was being much more diplomatic now.

"No thanks. I think I'd be safer alone. Aren't you missing the Officer Club victory celebration?"

Tom listened as he heard the man stomp back into the club. Tom could hear the lady fumbling through her purse for her car keys. He realized she could be his ticket out of Camp Pendleton. He tried to get up but the pain made him 'yelp' and tighten up.

She must have heard him because the jingling in her purse stopped. Tom rolled onto his side and used his arms to push his torso up a little bit.

"Oh shit," he moaned. His ribs really hurt bad.

"Who's in there?" the lady asked. "Are you all right?"

"I don't know, I'm hurt in a few places," Tom groaned as he crawled out of the bush. He couldn't keep a calm expression on his face due to the constant throbbing pain; especially when he inhaled.

As Tom crawled on the sidewalk he got his first look at Jane, kind of; white knee high boots, pink nylons, and a miniskirt of some shade of purple. Unable to arch his back or neck up, Tom was prevented from seeing any further up than her waist.

Jane kneeled down in front of Tom and asked softly, "Were you with the band?"

Tom was panting in short breaths. Leaning sideways on his elbow he waited for the pain to subside . . . it didn't.

With Jane now kneeling he tried to look up enough to talk face to face. But his neck was stiff, and the bottom of her chin was the best he could do. Of course that wasn't too bad considering Jane was a shapely woman. Gravity distended her blouse and ballooned her features with her low cut top. Rhinestones gave the shoulders and low neckline a wester flair a-la-Britain. Tom's attention was appropriately diverted from the pain. As she leaned forward a little more . . . her breasts seemed larger yet . . . and Tom could see some of her white lace bra . . ."

"Your friends are all gone I think. They were escorted or arrested at least an hour ago."

"Great," he moaned sarcastically.

"Did you drive?" Jane asked, concerned.

"No. They drove me down from LA. I've got to get out of here. Will you drive me out of the gates?" Tom asked as he winced and clenched.

"--sure," she said after a reluctant pause. "Let me help you into my car."


* * *


Jane's townhouse in Oceanside was a two-story home only a couple of years old. Her ex-husband, (almost--they were legally separated and the divorce would soon be final), had given her the house as part of the settlement. It was flanked on both sides by adjoining townhouses all the same stucco brown with white wood moulding and trim. The shrubbery was well tended but all the trees were still skinny and scrawny.

Jane had to assist Tom up the several steps. The small front porch and overhang were just a bit wider than the white double doors. Jane leaned him against one of the two posts and hastily opened one of the two doors. Putting her shoulder once again beneath Tom's armpit, she walked him inside. The thick sky blue shag carpet was like walking on a marshmallow. Tom stumbled forward with Jane's assistance.

Tom's shirt had to be removed with scissors. Unable to raise his arms much, she pulled off his T-shirt in sections.

The large bruises on Tom's sides were from marine boots that had accidentally drop-kicked his ribs after mistaking him for a soccer ball (accidentally of course).

There were no open wounds, other than scrapes and scratches, so Jane placed her hands upon Tom's chest and sides as she felt for any broken bones. Grimacing and grunting, Tom tried as best he could not to cry or scream. Eventually though she found all the tender spots and Tom's body rebelled; he flinched back into a prone position away from her on the couch.

"I'm sorry. But I've got to check for any breaks."

"Let's assume it's broke and wait for it to heal," suggested Tom sarcastically.

"That's fine if it's set properly," Jane informed. "However, any splinters or improperly aligned bones will cause you big problems. Now just be brave and grit your teeth for a minute more."

Without further explanation she went back to the most painful area again on Tom's right side and traced the bone with her fingers.

"Ouch!" Tom yelled in pain.

Jane continued without even looking up. Finally she sat up and looked Tom in the eye. "It's probably a cracked rib. I can't feel anything irregular so you'll probably heal up okay, if you take it easy for a few weeks.

"A few weeks?" Tom gasped.

"Yes, and I still recommend you get X-rays," she concluded firmly.

"I told you already in the car. I'm not going to any hospital. No way!"

"I'll tell you what," Jane bargained. "I'll even pay for the hospital visit myself. It's no big deal--"

"No. No. No," Tom repeated stubbornly wrinkling his face. "No doctors and no hospitals. You said yourself that it's probably okay."

"I'm not a doctor though," Jane said despairingly.

"Close enough for me," Tom quipped.

"How's the headache of yours?" Jane quickly asked without letting Tom's aversion for doctors finalize the discussion.

"I'm getting used to it," Tom tried to joke.

"Lemme see--"

"It's all right," Tom snapped as he whipped his head back, away from Jane.

Jane relaxed and retracted her half-outstretched arms and said, "It probably is all right. I just want to see where you were hit. You've got too much hair covering it up."

"I'm sorry," he said in a lower volume voice. "I guess I'm punchy from all the punching."

Jane smiled and asked, "Can I have a look?"

Tom reconsidered. "Okay," he groaned.

Jane slid up a little closer to Tom's horizontal torso on the couch and sat beside his chest. She leaned over him. Tom felt warm and focused on Jane's lavender blouse material as it shifted with her arm movements.

"You've got a nasty bump back here, and one on this side here. Ooh . . . and you've bled a little. We should treat it as a minor concussion."

"Aren't you getting a little carried away with this nurse routine?" Tom asked mockingly.

Jane stood up quickly; offended and angry. "Perhaps you'd rather be back in that bush where I found you? I don't need to be insulted."

Tom realized he'd hurt her feelings.

"It's just a bump on the head," he pleaded.

"And your ribs are probably just bruised," Jane snapped back.

"Yeah," said Tom hopefully.

"Well, you have three choices Mr. Tom. Number one, you can go to a doctor--I'll take you of course. Number two, you can stay here under my care and authority." She emphasized the word, "authority." "And number three, you can walk out the door right now and take care of yourself."

Jane was pretty mad . . . and pretty . . . her expression burned impatiently down at him.

"Your care," he replied softly.

"And authority," she repeated sternly.

Tom took a deep breath-- "Uh!" he grimaced with pain. "Okay."

Jane probably predicted this outcome and relaxed a little. "Then first we'll wrap your ribs and then we're going to have to stay up for awhile."

"Why?"

"Because any head injury could be a concussion and the person might not wake up if they fall asleep." Jane smiled as if she'd just won a bet and continued, "I'll make some coffee."

Tom probably didn't need the coffee, he could still feel the opetrol speed buzz a little. No need to mention it to her though. She seemed pretty straight.

Tom and Jane talked all night about nothing and everything. Tom's fugitive status was not a topic of conversation. As of yet he'd revealed himself to no one. She was still adapting to her newly divorced life and seemed a little lonely still. As the sun rose into a cloudless California sky . . . Jane ended their conversation. "I'll get you some blankets. You need some sleep now, and maybe some aspirins too."

Tom lay comfortably in pain beneath the two soft blankets and watched from the couch as she stepped away from him. He trusted her, and she didn't fear him. Tom wondered if he'd die in his sleep. He figured if he did, it would be from the chest bandages.

She made him exhale before wrapping up his chest. Now every time he tied to inhale the bandages confined him. Strangled by a band-aid.

Jane closed her bedroom door.

Tom couldn't fall asleep right away. Between the coffee and new changes of habitat; life felt so unsteady, so unpredictable, so helpless, so painful . . . oh well . . . life on the run.

Tom heard a sliding glass door open and shut. He raised his head enough to see Jane in loose white pajamas run across the backyard. She disappeared behind a row of potted bamboo. He lay awake about ten minutes longer before he heard the sliding glass door of Jane's bedroom open and shut again.


* * *


Jane kept Tom bandaged up for a few days before officially inviting him to stay until fully recuperated. He did have a broken rib it seemed, and a month's rest was safely appealing. Tom wore some of Jane's husband's clothes--all of them too big.

Sometimes Jane poked fun at him and said he looked like a "little boy."

It was towards the end of his first week's stay at Jane's, as he pulled himself out of bed (he got the master bedroom, she said there were too many memories there for her), that he heard the sliding glass doors to her bedroom downstairs open and close.

He decided to finally investigate. Tom imagined a lover sneaking in or out. He had to see. Sneaking downstairs he peered through the kitchen windows. Her curtains were closed but as he looked out into the backyard he noticed movement on the other side of the bamboo hedge.

Tom tip-toed out the kitchen door and closed it silently without hardly a click of the latch. He snuck across the lawn and peered through the thin green bamboo leaves.

It was Jane, by herself, dancing in slow motion. Some form of martial

74

art, a new kind of combat dance with invisible enemies.

"Come on around this side," Jane spoke calmly without ever noticeably glancing at Tom. "You'll be able to see better." She kept moving in her memorized dance.

Tom was a little surprised at being noticed so easily. When he'd stepped around the bamboo, Jane began to explain what she was doing, continuing her movements without looking at Tom. Her concentration remained fixed on invisible targets and her hands changed from open to flat to fists . . .

"It's called Tai Chi Chuan. Kind of a moving meditation. You do Karate?"

"No."

"Anyway, it promotes better health, energy control, balance, coordination, and concentration. And of course, it can be used for self-defense."

She explained a few of the movements as she did them and pointed out a few fighting techniques.

"Could I learn that?"

"Of course you could," she laughed. "Perhaps when you heal enough to move and breathe easier, I'll teach it to you."

After another week of TV, Tom was getting antsy. No drinking, no drugs, no girls, no money, no car, no friends, and no pot. He didn't even call Carey. Her parents were probably back now and where would he go now? Just television commercials, and a gorgeous voluptuous pseudo-stepmother.

Jane bounced into the room looking more girlish than usual.

"Well--you look a lot better. You must be healing up all right. And--" she skipped a dance step sideways and then poised herself with her arm and index finger pointed at Tom, "--I've got a few surprises for you."

Hmmm. Tom was alert with curiosity. Jane seemed a lot more animated than usual. He felt like he was on a TV game show.

"Your first surprise is at the far left end of the hall closet. The second surprise is at the far right end."

Not sure what to expect, he shoved all the clothes from the left side and squished them together into the middle of the closet. Cool. No one that Tom knew had a suit like this. Kind of like a gangster movie. It was a heavy reddish-brown woolen fabric with matching pants. Dotted ivory dashes formed vertical lines in the material.

Those couple of shirts are for you too. And a pair of Levi's."

"These are great but--"

"That's only surprise number one," Jane smiled. "Check out the right end of the closet."

Tom had never seen an outfit quite like this. It was a heavy black cotton fabric. Matching pants. The shirt was all black except for the large white, roll-up cuffs and short double layer collar. The shirt was kind of priest-like with the inside collar being white and the outside black.

Tom unwound his chest bandages.

"It's a Chinese Tai Chi outfit," Jane explained. "We were planning to give it to one of Rex's nephews."

"What the heck are these buttons?" He twisted the knots in his fingers.

"Frog buttons."

"Frog?"

"Yes, frog. They are frog buttons," she teased elongating the word "frog" in a mocking way.


\* \* \*


"There," Jane said with a smile. "That's the whole Tai Chi form. You've learned it quickly--and well."

"Thanks," Tom said as he went over a few of the moves.

In the last three weeks Tom had taken responsibility for the


76

housework and some yard maintenance. They were like a family. He didn't really mind doing the dishes all the time. Sometimes he cooked.

Jane was planning to take a job in the fall working for her old boss. She said she had too much time on her hands. She explained how she had been a "buyer" for a clothing company. She used to travel in Asia picking up fabrics. That was where she'd met Rex, her husband. He was on leave in India when they met. She also told Tom why they were separated. She found out that Rex had been keeping a mistress in Manila during their marriage. She told Tom, "What's a relationship without trust? And now I don't trust him."

* * *

During the sixth week of Tom's stay Jane received a telephone call from a friend of Rex whom she knew also. It was the middle of August and Tom was recuperated.

The officer explained to Jane that Rex had been killed in a restaurant in Saigon. Some little kid had brought a bomb in. Even the little kid had been blown to bits when the bomb went off before he could get out himself. Rex's remains were being shipped back to the States the next day and he'd have a full honor burial ceremony.

* * *

The stands were filled with civilians. Two dozen caskets were lined up with American flags draped over them. Camp Pendleton felt strange to Tom. Not just the ceremony and mood, but this whole strange war concept; he pictured this cartoonish war-meat-grinder with Uncle Sam twisting the handle, spewing out mortal debris into these civilian laps. He also hoped none of these marines recognized him from the brawl at the Officer's Club. Jane and Tom were front row in front of the caskets.

Several officers moved down the line offering condolences to the families of the war victims. A lot of crying. Senator McLean first shook Jane's hand, then after a few impartial words told her that there would be an informal banquet at the Oceanside Hilton Hotel tonight.

Jane thanked him for the invitation and introduced Tom as her nephew. "I'm not sure how I'll feel later. Perhaps."

Senator McLean shook Tom's hand a little longer than necessary. Tom felt uncomfortable as the Senator inspected him, very intensely.

As Tom and Jane were retreating back to her car, Senator McLean approached them again and offered his sympathies. He kept staring at Tom. "I really hope that I'll see you tonight at the dinner," said the Senator. "Whatever time suits your convenience is fine." He was trying too hard. "And please, bring your nephew along. There's plenty of food."

Jane just smiled and waved through the car window as she drove off. Tom got a funny feeling from this Senator McLean. This whole military facility gave him the creeps, like a prison or something, but something about him . . .

The Hilton had a view of the ocean like a boat at sea. There are no islands or even mountains at the waterside to give you the perspective of being on land. From Senator McLean's suite the ocean seemed to surround the hotel.

"You've got to keep as low a profile as possible," the Senator instructed. "If anyone asks, or whatever, you are a . . . a . . . an insurance salesman. Yes, I think that will work fine. You've come to Oceanside here to sell me an insurance policy that we spoke of over the phone."

The Senator thought for a moment and turned back to the closed bathroom door for a response.

"You got that Sid?" the Senator asked louder.

"Yeah . . . I'm an insurance underwriter for Mutual of Deathville," came the reply.

"Seriously Sid," the Senator said sternly. "Don't let your picture be taken."

"Got it!" Sid snapped back.

The toilet flushed and the door immediately opened.

"You really think this is the kid?" Sid asked.

"Looks just like him," Senator McLean said with a shrug of his shoulders.

"Do you think he'll come tonight?"

The Honorable Senator McLean replied matter of factly, "If he doesn't come tonight I know how to find him. The late Captain's wife introduced him as her nephew."

Sid smiled and squinted his eyes.

* * *

Jane and Tom didn't go to the Senator's hotel that night. Instead they took a drive to Los Angeles. They ate dinner at a fancy restaurant, whose name Tom wasn't sure how to pronounce, and saw a movie at the Cinerama Dome in Hollywood. Jane was tired but not interested in going home. So she rented them adjoining rooms at the Sunset Hilton.

Hollywood sparkled at night from their hillside perch. The different colors and sizes of moving lights flickered like neon fireflies. Somehow the city seemed clean at night when darkness could shadow the filthy corners of the supposedly glorious history.

Tom and Jane had an almost mother-son relationship. Tonight Jane was very melancholy. No sooner had they sat down in the hotel lounge than a waiter approached and asked if she cared for a drink. It was uncustomary for Jane to drink liquor. Tom had not ever seen her drink at all.

"Yes. I'll have a--" Jane thought for a moment with a wrinkled look on her face. Finally she replied, "A white Russian, thank you."

"Very good mam," the waiter replied like a butler. He didn't even give Tom a second glance. Tom would have liked a beer but he knew that they'd ask his age. Being only nineteen years old he couldn't easily pass for drinking age, no 'ID' anyway.

Very quickly another waiter brought Jane her creamy intoxicant. Although Jane had been calm and composed all day long, she seemed especially shaken now. She drank the White Russian quickly. No communication passed between them until after she ordered her second drink. Tom sipped at his Hires root beer.

"I really appreciate you coming to the funeral Tom," she said with a slight lilt in her voice.

"No problem," Tom quipped. He thought for a moment. "I'm sorry that your husband was killed."

Jane exhaled a chuckle of air through her nostrils then shook her head side to side. "He was always cursing the anti-war protesters. He was always proclaiming the United States' responsibility to protect these countries from communism. He was so proud to be "the vanguard of freedom," as he would say. He said war was a necessary part of our peace." Jane paused a moment and took a couple gulps. She flagged down a waiter and ordered another drink while hurrying to finish her second.

She was leaning on Tom in a new way, emotionally. It made them closer. Only later as Tom lay on his bed thinking did it seem unusual when she kissed him, "Good night." Of course he found her very attractive. For a woman in her thirties she was incredibly youthful. Her skin tone and fitness were par with a high school girl. She didn't wear a lot of makeup, but spent a bit of time painting her blue crystal eyes. Sometimes she'd even wear false eyelashes. Most of the time she just framed them in hues that emphasized how big, round, and intent her gaze was; in a dreamy sort of way. Jane had a unique contrast of sexy confidence and shy demure.

The morning sun rose to illuminate the LA smog like a purple sunset. The blue background made a sharp contrast to the scattered small clouds that were lit in shades of crimson. The benefit of smog is the dramatic sunsets and sunrises it provides. As Tom and Jane strolled in the back garden of the hotel, the clouds seemed more like smoke, and the colors they glowed were like a reflection of fires burning on Earth.

Jane mentioned to Tom, "I feel tense this morning. Perhaps I didn't sleep well in the hotel bed."

"I feel rather tense also."

"Oh well," Jane shrugged. "Let's work out over there," pointing at a grassy area beneath a cluster of palms.

Jane was tall and graceful without high heels. When she performed her Tai Chi she was like a swan stretching its wings.

"When you're doing your Tai Chi," Jane instructed, "sometimes you want to try different attitudes and different speeds. Not always is it just for relaxing or breathing. Although you want to be fluid and relaxed, you should still imagine your energies behind your movements, being externalized. For instance, imagine flames shooting from your palms or fingers."

"Be like a whip in slow motion, flexible, circular, and then snap at full extension. Effortless power like a mythological God throwing lightning bolts."

They mirrored each other as they moved in unison.

"When you are confronted with a dangerous situation the memorized movements should instinctively occur without having to plan or think what to do. Yes . . . good . . . now vary your pace."

As they practiced their Tai Chi a desperate fear urged both of them to quicker and harder movements. The invisible enemies seemed to materialize easier today.

\* \* \*

Jane's house seemed different somehow. It wasn't the sanctuary it had provided all summer. Somehow transformed, it seemed like a living nightmarish shark with windows for eyes as they pulled up into the driveway.

Tom uneasily followed Jane inside the front door (shark jaws), after she unlocked the dead bolt. Jane was nervous but didn't say anything about it. Instead she went straight for her jewelry chest in her bedroom.

Tom stepped like a man on a high wire. He edged into the kitchen and opened all the closets. He looked in every cupboard big enough for a person to fit in, in the study and even in the shower.

Jane reappeared in the living room and announced, "Someone's been here while we were gone."

"I know," Tom acknowledged. "I feel really spooky. Did they steal anything?"

"That's the strangest part, I can't find anything missing. My desk has been rummaged through and the files have been searched. I think that even Rex's guns were checked out."

That night was especially nervous in Jane's house. Neither of them had much appetite and they kept the TV on despite no one watching it. Of course they kept the volume low so they could hear any strange sounds.

Jane interrupted Tom as he practiced his Tai Chi in the living room. "Tom, I'm going to teach you some more fighting techniques now. You'd best learn some direct applications. Tai Chi is more a foundation. When you learn to move fluidly you can move faster. Now grab my wrist," she instructed as she held her arm out.

Tom grabbed her wrist and Jane used her other hand to lock his hand in place then made a small circular motion from her wrist while twisting her waist that pulled Tom to the ground effortlessly.

"Body mechanics," Jane said proudly. "Once you've learned the body's inabilities you can use these techniques like leverage to control someone. Try it on me."

Occasionally Jane went out with a girlfriend Sandy. A few evenings she went out alone. Most of the time she was content to stay at home or go to the beach with Tom.

They practiced Tai Chi and Kung Fu moves. Although they watched television a lot, they mostly read. Tom enjoyed reading more than ever before. Often he wouldn't even finish the book. Just glance through, find a good chapter, or just read an ending. And of course Tom found Rex's **Playboy** collection in the garage. Tom secretly checked out issues from the garage library for private bathroom perusal when she was out.

In late August, as summer burns the sand into a white hot griddle, Tom met Melanie. He'd gone to the beach with Jane and met Melanie while body surfing. Tom memorized her phone number and called her that same evening. She invited him over.

"Could I borrow the station wagon tonight? I'd like to visit a new friend I met today at the beach."

Jane was a little surprised. Tom borrowed the car to do shopping and run errands for her. He never bothered to tell her he had no driver's license. He'd thrown away all his identification a couple months ago after the accident. He said he'd lost it on the beach.

"What's his name?"

Tom stumbled with his reply. "Mel," he answered. "He doesn't live too far from here."

"Yeah. Go ahead. But I'd prefer you didn't keep the car out late."

Melanie was waiting outside her parent's house when Tom arrived.

"C'mon. Let's get out of here," Melanie said angrily as she sat down and closed the car door.

"What's wrong?"

"Oh my fucking parents. They're so fucking lame. They found some grass in my coat pocket and think they can suspend me from going out the rest of the summer. That house is a prison. Every time I go home it's like entering the Pentagon. I've had it. Next year I graduate high school and then it's 'Bye-bye family. Later mom,' and, 'So long poppa.'"

Melanie paused briefly as she jumbled through her purse for her pack of cigarettes. "Those stupid fucking assholes stole my smokes! Can you believe that? They even took my smokes! Shit! Turn left at the next light. There's a seven-eleven down a couple blocks. You smoke pot don't you?"

"Yeah," Tom answered thinking how long it'd been.

"Well I know where we can get some. You got any money?"

"Five bucks I think."

"Hmmm, okay. That's cool, I've got ten. We can get a lid of some good stash for fifteen dollars."

The dirt road went all the way down to the sand. Tom was a little concerned about Jane's car as he bounced it through pot holes and small gulleys.

"Park over there," Melanie pointed. "By those bushes."

*Come on, little woman*
*Let's drive*
*I'm hot tonight*
*I really feel alive*
*I know where we'll go*
*It's not too far*
*Where we can play*
*In the backseat of my car (13)*

She pulled a pack of zig-zags out of her purse. "At least they didn't get my papers."

Tom especially enjoyed the taste of the pot. It'd been a long time since he'd smoked anything. Tom turned up the radio as they finished their first joint. Melanie had already rolled another one, but before she lit it she leaned over and kissed Tom on the lips. Pulling her face back a few inches, she opened her eyes, sparkled, and smiled as she turned up the radio even more.

*So back into the backseat*
*Where*
*We will make love*
*With the radio loud*
*The windows cloud*
*With you*

*My backseat love (13)*

There wasn't even a blanket in the back of the station wagon. Fortunately it was a warm summer night, temperature in the upper seventies. Tom was sweating. Melanie was steaming. Her skin dark, like an Indian. Her long straight dark brown hair was everywhere. It stuck to her forehead and got in their mouths. It was great.

Tom raised his torso up as he lay naked atop Melanie. He found her as beautiful as she had looked at the beach. He lowered his lips to hers and kissed her. She wasn't as responsive as he'd like. Not much magic. After all they were still strangers. It felt good though, kissing her even when she seemed so unfamiliar. The sensation of her lips against his was a soft ethereal sensation that relaxed and warmed his entire body. She kissed him back and swayed her head as she commanded his mouth with her tongue.

Even in its newness, making love was like being with an old young friend.

She was very different from Barbara. Somehow, when he thought of Barbara while making love to Melanie, he felt no sense of guilt. He loved Barbara still. He could even close his eyes and while remembering Barbara almost pretend to be with her. It was nice to be intimate with Melanie.

They walked naked in the warm sand. The night clothed them in darkness. A thin moon lit their footsteps and hid them from view. The light breeze, the bombing of the waves, and Melanie's dark brown straight hair twirling in his face made all his senses whirlpool. The pot accelerated his visual and slowed the physical. She spirited off down the beach.

Tom chased her. She ran into the water. Tom stampeded behind her in a flurry of flying white foam. He tackled her and with a loud flop they crashed into the black ocean water. The water was warm, even at night. They played, and splashed at each other like human otters.

Back in the car Melanie passed Tom the joint.  She was dry enough now to get dressed.  She put on her light-brown see-through bra as Tom took a hit.

"I don't want to go home," Melanie stated.

Tom watched her continue to dress.

"Can I stay with you?"

Tom didn't know.

"Where do you live?"

"Uh, just a couple blocks away from you.  Remember?  On Fenton."

"Oh yeah?"

"But I don't know if it'd be cool.  I mean like . . . well . . . I'm stayin' with . . . staying with my aunt.  She just lost her husband.  He was killed in Vietnam."

"Your uncle was killed?"

"Uh . . . yeah.  He was.. .my uncle Rex."  Wow did it feel strange to tell that lie.

"I don't want to go home."

"Well--"

"Let's just stay here.  It's midnight now and plenty warm."

"No.  I really can't.  I told my aunt that I'd have her car back tonight."

"Then leave me here."

"Now come on.  Don't get weird."

Her eyes exclaimed, "I'm not weird.  My dad calls me weird."  She started sobbing.

"I'm sorry.  I'm sorry.  Come on really.  Don't cry."  He pleaded with her, "Hey.  Come on . . . maintain.  It's not that bad."

"Yes it is."  She snatched up her woven purse bag.  Melanie got out of the car and ran towards the beach.

"Shit," Tom said to himself as he got out of the car and watched her run off into the dark of a knife thin moon.  He felt responsible.  He ran after her.

It had been probably a half an hour since Melanie had dashed. Tom had looked everywhere. He'd yelled her name a hundred times. He felt hurt, lonely and somehow guilty. He was leaving her on the beach in the dead of night. He felt confused and depressed as he started the engine.

Jane was still up with the TV on.

"Have fun?"

"Yeah. We went to the beach."

"Looks like you went in the water."

"Yeah, we did."

Jane was instinctively inquisitive. Tom was instinctively defensive.

"I'm going to bed." Tom slipped away to escape conversation.

"Goodnight."

"Goodnight."

Tom closed his bedroom door and tried to figure out a hiding place for the partially burned joint that he'd started to share with Melanie. No, not the chest of drawers. Not under the mattress. Not anywhere in the room. Jane owned everything, except the clothes on his back. So he decided to just keep it in his shirt pocket.

Jane woke up Tom with a knock on the bedroom door. "Breakfast in five minutes," she said through the closed door.

Tom put the same clothes he'd worn last night back on and joined Jane at the table. Jane was drinking coffee. Unusual for her. Without looking at him, she got up for the biscuits in the oven and turned over the bacon on the stove.

"You already done your Tai Chi?" Tom asked.

"Yes," Jane said with her back to Tom.

"Why didn't you wake me?"

"I thought you'd want to sleep."

Strange. Why would she think that. Many times they'd stayed up late watching TV and still got up early.

"Move your napkin."

Tom put it on his thigh as Jane quickly dumped a pile of hash browns.

Something was amiss. She was mad at him it seemed. For what?

Unceremoniously she plopped several strips of bacon down.

"What's wrong?"

Jane turned around as she walked back into the kitchen with an empty skillet. She wore a tense expression. She wanted to say something. "Nothing."

Tom didn't know what to say. He looked down to his plate and began eating.

It was almost time for dinner. Tom spent the day sunning in the backyard. Jane worked all day cleaning the house.

"Tom?" Jane shouted from the sliding glass windows.

Tom sat up in his lounge chair. "Yeah?"

"Would you go to the store for me? I need some things for dinner."

"Okay."

He left his shorts on, put the same shirt back on and left barefoot.

\* \* \*

Jane was in the kitchen when Sid entered the house through the sliding glass doors. She ducked her head into the refrigerator for a jar of mayonnaise. When she pulled her torso out of the refrigerator's jaw she looked up to see Sid pointing a pistol at her face.

"Move slow and put the jar on the counter."

Jane obeyed.

"Where's your nephew?"

Jane was shocked. How did he know of "her nephew?"

"Where is he?"

"I don't know."

Sid shoved the gun into her mouth and chipped a tooth.

Jane's body automatically kicked up, shifted sideways, blocked Sid's arms and the gun out of her mouth. She kicked him in the legs and as he fell he grabbed a foot and pulled Jane down but away from him.

Jane scrambled around the counter into the living room.

Sid jumped atop the counter and pointed the gun straight down at her.

"Make a move sister and I'll kill you. Lay face down. Arms above your head. Stretch 'em out! You move again and it'll be your last move, I swear."

Sid handcuffed her hands together.

"Now get up and slowly walk into the bedroom."

Sid followed her with his gun pressed into her back, pushing her along.

"Lay down on the bed face up. Now reach for the headboard."

Sid unfastened one of her handcuffs and looped it around one of its wooden rails. He refastened it to her temporarily free arm.

"Now, if you behave--you'll live."

Sid ripped her blouse in half with his left hand while holding the pistol still in Jane's mouth. He fondled her breasts roughly through the bra cups that encased them.

He pumped the barrel in and out of her mouth.

Tom laid the bag of groceries on the kitchen table. The sink in the bathroom could be heard through the closed door. Tom decided to sneak out back and finish the joint he'd saved from last night while Jane was in the bathroom.

Tom sat down in the shade of the tool shed. He lit up the joint.

Like a bullet up his spine he heard Jane scream from the house. He stood up. She cried again.

Tom ran to the windows outside her room. The bamboo blinds were down but Tom could see through when he pressed his face to the glass. He saw Jane stark naked on the bed and Sid was wiping off his gun.

Tom's heart stopped.

The sliding glass doors were still open. Tom snuck back into the living room. He grabbed a samurai sword from its black stand atop the fireplace mantel. He poised himself beside the entrance into the living room from the hallway. He waited.

Sid stepped out into the hallway from Jane's room. He walked past the entrance to the living room and entered the study. From the study's windows he saw Jane's car parked in the driveway.

If Sid came through the other end of the living room Tom would be a sitting duck. Tom's heart beat so loud it was difficult to think over its drumming.

Tom barefootedly stepped into the hallway. He decided to wait for Sid to return and poised himself in the bathroom door, frozen in position, sword raised, like an executioner.

Tom listened for footsteps but heard only his heart pounding.

Sid's gun slid into Tom's view at waist level. Tom snapped his arms out and down. The sword struck the gun with all of Tom's might, metal flying as the blade shattered. The gun fired as it rocketed to the floor. Blood shot in several directions.

Sid never even screamed. His right thumb lay beside the gun on the carpet. Tom remained in the bath opening without looking around the corner into the hall.

"Tom?" Jane screamed. "Tom!"

No reply. Tom remained silent. Scared and listening for Sid. Tom took one step into the hall, kicked the gun down the hall towards Jane's room, following in a gallop behind the pistol and never looking back. Like a soccer player he kicked the gun again scooting it under Jane's bed as he dashed into her room.

Tom was stunned. He'd never seen Jane naked, but here she was before him unable to cover herself. She stared at Tom and paused her crying.

They stared at each other until Jane let out a bug-eyed scream.

Sid jumped Tom from behind. The half sword was knocked loose of Tom's grip.

They wrestled. Tom was blocking punches more than giving them. A few punches hit Tom's face very hard. Tom could taste blood in his mouth and his nose smelled only the dry bitterness of violence.

Tom broke away and rolled for his broken sword. Like a whirlwind Tom swung his half-saber above his crouched body slicing up the air between them. Sid hopped out and above its reach like a girl with a jump rope.

Tom broke the pattern, as Sid jumped, Tom stabbed outward with his whole body following the sword like a striking snake. The jagged edge tore through Sid's thigh and stabbed entirely through his leg as Sid descended down upon the sword. He fell atop Tom with the sword pushed through nearly up to the hilt.

Tom rolled out from underneath as Sid scuffled out using both hands, one leg and dragging the skewered limb.

Tom jumped up to Jane's side.

"We need the key for these handcuffs," she said quickly.

Tom turned to see the path of blood Sid had left as he had crawled out. Tom slipped under the bed and got the gun of Sid's.

As Tom followed the blood trail down the hallway he felt as if in another world.

The hallway was a cave. The doors were traps and monsters hungered in every opening.

Tom turned into the living room stepping on the wet blood trail.

Sid lunged out from where Tom had stood before. Tom couldn't turn in time as Sid grappled him to the floor. The sword still in Sid's leg cut Tom's knees. Sid was weakened now and Tom was able to maneuver out of his hold and strike Sid's head with the gun butt. Sid rolled over to face down. Motionless.

Tom held the gun pushed against Sid's head, just in case, ready to pull the trigger.

Tom grabbed the keys from Sid's pocket and went back for Jane.

Tom quickly returned to the living room after freeing Jane.

"Forget about calling the police." Tom could see the blood on the fence in the backyard where Sid had escaped over.

"WHAT?" yelled Jane from the bedroom.

"He's gone!"

*White laced tongues — "lick your black veins"*
*Waiting for me — "blind cat and dog"*
*Satin fences glitter — "electric barbed wire"*
*Green lakes surround — "an island"*
*We won't be found — "don't go"*
*In my world — "in my land"*
*In my time — "in my hand"*
*Come visit my castle — "made of sand" (14)*

# Chapter Four
## *Manila*

"No way!" Tom snarled.

"But you've got to," Jane pleaded.

"No way. Why do I want to go to jail for a murder I didn't even commit."

"What about the lady in the Cadillac?"

"I told you. She ran a red light."

"Then prove it in court."

"There's nothing to prove. I had a seventy-five kilos of grass in my van. When we hit and she went through the windshield I lost all my rights because I was holding a lot of weed. Even if I beat the murder rap they'd put me away for twenty years on drug trafficking. I don't have a chance in court."

"So what're you going to do? Run away?"

"Yeah." Tom shrugged.

"And I suppose they're never gonna find you?"

"That's the plan."

"Oh yeah. Sure thing." Jane stomped across the motel carpet. "And you're a fugitive for the rest of your life."

"Yeah," Tom hummed as a lightbulb glowed overhead. "Just like the TV show... Ben Gazarra."

"Very funny. But wrong show. That's **Run For Your Life.**"

"You know the one I mean--"

"Just shut up!" Jane yelled covering her ears. She marched furiously with her ears muffed, back and forth, back and forth . . .

Tom silently waited and watched her pacing like a lion in a cage.

"Okay," she said lowering her hands. "You don't take this very seriously I feel." She paused with her back to Tom. "Just yesterday," she paused, "you saw me raped with a gun muzzle by a maniacal killer. I can't report it to the police," she paused again, "just to protect you, a wanted fugitive also. My own home is unsafe to return to because of you. Because of you . . . him . . . because he tracked you . . . because of YOU! Because of you, I don't have a home. You've brought YOUR tragedy into MY life."

"I'm really--"

"Shut up! And now after all this . . . after what I've suffered . . . you have the callousness to say it's all like a TV show?"

"I didn't say--"

"Shut up! God damn it just keep your mouth shut!" she hissed through tight clenched teeth.

Tom was shocked. She was angrier than any woman he'd ever seen. It scared him a little.

"I don't think you understand . . . Thomas . . . how it feels to a woman to be raped." She looked straight at him. "It's not just violent sex. It's a . . . a . . . it strips off part of your heart, tears out something inside of you," she motioned as if ripping off her breast. "It's a violent murder!" she almost yelled. Jane looked up at nothing and repeated softly, "a murder . . . a murder . . ."

\* \* \*

After bouncing from airport to airport like a truck on a milk run, Tom and Jane finally arrived in Manila. All flights were being booked up by the military. A lot more men were going to East Asia than coming home. The streets of Manila were constantly flooded with people. Ants, body to body. Some cars, many small motorbikes, lots of bicycles, and thousands of people. Tom felt like a corpuscle in a blood vein as he bumped through the crowds making a path for Jane. A lot of the side streets were dirt or gravel. Houses were crowded together like a monopoly board. No one had a yard and everything was dirty despite the frequent rain. It was late summer and very hot and humid. Always eighty degrees or better. The rain was warm and when you weren't wet you were sticky.

"Sorry. No vacancy."

They tromped on to the next hotel.

"Sorry. No vacancy."

After a few more rejections Jane began to look very tired and cranky. She'd remained a bit 'snappy' since the . . . incident. But today was a new high--or new low, depending on how you rate it. She even yelled at one hotel manager and used a swear word. Whew.

Tom decided to try a different angle. Whenever Tom saw a teenager dressed clean and usually walking a bicycle through the crowd, he'd ask if, "You rent room? We pay room and board."

Many of them didn't speak English. Some spoke Spanish, or something that sounded kinda like Spanish, but Tom wasn't good enough to complete the conversations.

Jane was ragged and hungry following silently behind him.

"You got money?" the dark skinned teen replied.

"Sure. Ten dollars a day," Tom excitedly spoke.

"Fifteen."

"Three meals a day?"

"Well . . . maybe two."

"Then twelve dollars a day."

"Okay," the youth smiled. "You want to go home now?"

"Yes. Let's go there right now. How far is it?"

"Back that way about half a mile," he said, pointing in the direction they had come from.

"Fine."

The kid held out his hand and said, "Twelve."

Tom started to turn to Jane for the money, but reversed his motion back to the kid. "Let's see the place."

The kid laughed. "This way. Follow me."

The houses were joined together with rarely a space between them. Most houses had some vegetation like some uncut grass or shrubbery, but not really gardens or lawns. Most houses were unpainted and the grey wood made the street look like a black and white picture. Roofs were irregular and often patched with a sheet of plywood or metal awning scraps, which contrasted with their preexisting shingles. Small picket fences were flimsy and only a couple feet high. Their purpose was just to keep pedestrians off the porches.

Gary Lang led them up the several steps, onto the porch, and in through the front screen door.

"My mother and sister appear to be gone. Follow me and I'll show you your room."

Up a flight of stairs and down a very narrow hallway that two people going opposite directions would have difficulty passing, to the end of the hall. A single door was on the left side and another door on the right side. It appeared to Tom that the upstairs was two entire bedrooms. The floor was bouncy in spots and creaky everywhere.

Tom figured if it hadn't fallen through yet, it wouldn't now.

"I'll go get you a door key and as you can see there is even a private bathroom."

Tom dropped the suitcase he'd been carrying. There was a window at each end, one in the bathroom and one over the bed.

"Tom, there's only one bed."

"Yeah. I noticed. Go ahead . . . lay down. We'll figure it out later. At least we've got a roof over our head and two meals a day."

Jane plopped down upon the bed like a falling tree.

Tom investigated the bathroom. Not bad. The toilet seat was cracked. At least it looked pretty clean. An old fashioned bathtub with four legs was especially inviting to Tom. He closed the door and ran the water. No hot water, but cold would suffice in this climate.

When he finished bathing he threw his clothes in to soak. Tom peeked out of the bathroom, dripping wet, and naked. Jane appeared to be asleep on top of the bed, in the same spot she'd originally fallen. Tom had forgotten a towel. The suitcase was next to Jane. Either he'd have to wake her up to bring him a towel or sneak over and get one. He decided to sneak.

Walking on tiptoes he approached her. He opened the suitcase and began to pull a towel out when a knock upon the door woke Jane and thoroughly startled Tom. The suitcase rolled backward away from him like an open clam doing a half roll and Jane sat up to see Tom kneeling over it butt-naked. She laughed as Tom fumbled for the towel. He wrapped it around himself before he stood up, blushed and embarrassed.

"Come in," Jane announced, still giggling.

Tom started for the bathroom but realized he would look even sillier trying to escape.

Gary's sister entered. Now Tom was really shocked. He expected it to be Gary.

He fidgeted and adjusted the towel tighter.

The girl was short. Or regular height for this area of the world, about five-foot-two. Her hair was long black and very straight all the way to her hips. Her brown skin and almond shaped eyes gave her the appearance of an island girl. She was dressed in a green silk dress, oriental styled that had Nehru-type collar.

"I brought you the keys," she explained, holding them out to Tom.

Tom didn't even move so Jane got up from the bed and took them.

"I am Ko," she said in a friendly voice with an accent.

"I'm Jane and he is Tom."

The girls both smiled as if they now knew a funny secret.

"How long will you be staying?"

"I'm not sure.  I've come to square up some business.  Maybe a week," Jane replied.

"That will be fine.  We will be serving dinner in another hour.  Come down whenever you want or we'll call you when it's ready."

"Thanks."

Ko left, shutting the door.

Jane turned to the silent boy in a towel.  "You dressing for a luau?"

The round dining table was big enough for another five people.  Gary, Ko, and Mrs. Lang all sat with their faces buried in the fried rice.  An assortment of cooked vegetables completed the meal.

"Had I known we would be feeding guests I would have brought home a chicken," Mrs. Lang apologized.

"That's all right," Tom reassured as the rice fell off his chopsticks.

"Incidentally," Jane began, "Tom is my nephew and we'd like to rent the other upstairs room."

"Well, perhaps," Mrs. Lang thought.

Ko looked sternly at her mother and chastisingly reminded, "Mr. Quon will return in a few days.  We must save it for him."

Mrs. Lang was not thoroughly impressed as she still pondered how to make some more rent money.

"We could separate the two mattresses on the bed and put one of them on the floor," Gary suggested.

Mrs. Lang was disappointed at this suggestion.

"That would be cool," Tom spoke up.

Jane thought about it.  Mrs. Lang thought about it.

"Of course we'd have to charge another two dollars for the extra sheets," Gary grinned.

"Okay," Jane replied.

Mrs. Lang smiled ear to ear. "Good. We pay a few days advance?" Mrs. Lang asked happily in her accent that Tom was getting used to.

"Sure."

"We have big dinner tomorrow," Mrs. Lang announced.

Pouring, drenching, wind swept rain kept Jane and Tom indoors for the next few days. The small radio gave a thin hollow metallic sound to all the songs and voices like a mouse-size megaphone. Still, the music was enjoyable and prevented mental boredom.

Due to the influx of American personnel the music of Manila was programmed similar to back in the U.S. Tom didn't feel so far removed from his homeland listening to The Beatles, Zeppelin, Hendrix and others. At the same time he could realize how far from home he was.

*She lives in luxury*
*Sipping her tea with milk and honey*
*She has at least one hundred men*
*Somehow I must replace all of them . . . (15)*

The rain didn't keep Ko in though. At least once a day, and sometimes twice, a peddle rickshaw arrived out in front of the house. The driver, wearing a large basket-like woven cone, would jingle his bike bell. Ko would be dressed well and smelling of perfume as she ran to the rickshaw with umbrella in hand.

Tom stood up in the bathtub when he heard the familiar bike bell. Ko ran through the whipping rain to the rickshaw. She looked like a little girl off to school. Hardly a woman going to work. Ko said she was a waitress at a club frequented mostly by GI's. She wouldn't return until three in the morning.

Tom felt somehow concerned for her, like a little sister. He also felt attracted to her. She was very pretty. Tom guessed her to be about sixteen years old. His hand automatically fell on his groin as he stood in the tub watching her leave. Instinctively he massaged himself.

Thursday was finally a clear day. Hot and humid but sunny. Jane had gone into town to find out some info on some property or business her husband had owned. She wasn't talking too much to Tom since they'd left California a few days after Sid's visit.

Tom went downstairs for a snack. He found some corn left from last night's dinner. He ate it cold.

"Are you going into town also?" Ko's voice asked from behind a beaded blind that separated the back patio area.

"I dunno. Maybe."

"I'll show you around a little before I go to work."

Tom smiled as she stepped through the blind. "All right."

The town seemed a little cleaner after a few days of rain. Most of the trash was washed from the streets. But many of the streets were yet unpaved. They walked around mud puddles as Ko explained about her country and its volatile politics.

"Our newest President is General Marcos. Manila needs the stability of a steady government. Perhaps he will be an improvement, but I fear he is another greedy pig who has plans to destroy local governments and kill any opposition . . ."

Tom could sense her emotional involvement growing. Ko's words became even more vicious. " . . .and they may help out as henchmen besides his military support."

"Who?" Tom interrupted, realizing he'd missed some important words of hers.

Ko looked at Tom puzzled. "Your government. The American army. The CIA. They put him in power. We don't have any say in our government. With your support Marcos is a stone puppet."

"You don't elect your President?"

"Ha!" she laughed cynically. "You Americans are all either blind or dumb."

"Hey!"

She lowered her head. "I'm sorry. You don't understand." With a fresh composure she finalized, "Our politics is still determined by bullets, not votes."

The club was green with white trim. New looking and small. Next to this was a red and white one next to a brown and black next to . . .

The clubs at each end of the block flashed the biggest signs of them all. So big that Ko's little green and white club looked teeny with its neon name tag the size of a mailbox, in comparison with the corner huge rectangular flashy signs bigger than a standing human.

One corner sign was a picture of a long red fox on a twisted corkscrew snake body, headed downward. Neon letters stuck on the outside of the sign spelled, "RED FOX." You couldn't miss it.

The other corner sign really got your attention. A white inner sign light made a silhouette of a girl in a bikini, standing with knees bent, and her hands on her own buttocks. With her arms behind and her body turned to the side, her large breasts jutted out round and firm, in profile. This club didn't really have a name. It just said, "NITELY," in capitals and under the painted girl said, "LADIES."

These formidable signs made Tom feel humbled and young. At only nineteen, Tom was not unfamiliar with bars. He'd been in a few strip joints with a borrowed driver's license of an older friend. But that was safe. The club was in a beach area next to the San Diego Stadium. Not even a neighborhood. Just parking lots and freeways all around. The sin store of San Diego was a block oasis in a controlled environment.

But this street in Manila was an environment that obviously spawned and interbred with itself. The clubs were all different yet all the same. The three-story buildings all crammed together side by side made the street look like Tom was walking into the belly of an evil dinosaur.

Lights on the roof--Christmas lights?    And neon in the windows advertised everything from beer and cigarettes to dancing girls.

"I'll come back later tonight and walk you home."

"No. That's alright." She searched for an explanation. "I don't really know what time I get off."

"That's cool. I'll wait around for you."

She flustered a bit trying to think up another excuse. "I may have to attend a party tonight."

Tom looked excitedly at her for the opportunity to accompany her to a party.

"I'll be escorted."

"Oh." Tom looked down.

"Maybe another time," she reassured him.

"Yeah. Sure." Tom scuffed his shoe on the sidewalk.

"I've got to get inside and go to work. I'll see you tomorrow. Okay?"

"Okay."

Ko turned and stepped inside the bar.   She closed the wooden door behind her.

"Hey Yank!"

Tom turned to see a bicycle rickshaw approach him.

"Hey Yank!"

"Yeah?" Tom snarled.

"Oooh," the brown skinned kid cooed. He wore an American baseball cap. It read, NY Yankees. "Unhappy in Manila?" he joked. "You need 'Boy Johnson.'"

"Who's Boy Johnson?" Tom half-heartedly asked as he turned away to continue walking down the half-crowded street.

The kid followed close behind and beside Tom. "Me."

"So what."

"Boy Johnson put smile back on Yankee face."

Tom half-smiled.

"Yes. Boy Johnson get you girl. Boy Johnson get you grass."

Tom looked at the rickshaw kid. The way things were going Tom really felt like smoking some weed.

"What kind?"

Boy Johnson continued his ear to ear smile and knew the fish had bit. "Good stuff, Thai sticks and even some 'killah' weed."

"What's the 'killah' weed," Tom mimicked.

"Good, good stuff. It change tears to cheers," he laughed as if to congratulate his rhyme.

"How much?"

"Five dollah bags."

"Got any on you?"

"We go now. Not fah."

Tom finally stopped walking and Boy Johnson ran into him with the rickshaw before he could stop.

"Get in. We go. Not fah."

Tom waited outside the shop, seated in the rickshaw. Boy Johnson had run into one of the small stores but Tom wasn't sure which one. The sidewalk was bustling with people at this part of town. After only a couple minutes he reappeared with his constant Cheshire Cat grin. He climbed promptly onto his bike seat and began peddling before talking.

"Wait 'til around next cohnah."

Boy Johnson parked on the next street between a couple of small foreign cars that Tom didn't recognize. He dismounted and handed Tom a cigarette pack half-full of nonfilter cigarettes.

"Hey. What the Hell is this?"

"Killer weed," B.J. replied, with a better sounding "er" than before.

Tom pulled a machine rolled joint out. He sniffed it. Sure enough. Smelled great.

"Got a light?" Tom asked softly.

B.J. pulled out a gold flip top lighter.  Tom puffed on the cig while B.J. held out the flame.

"Where to?" B.J. asked as he peddled out of their parking space.

"I don't know.  Show me around."

\* \* \*

Jane had found some cancelled checks of large amounts of money and references in Rex's journals to "investments of ours."  It appeared that Rex was a partner in a couple clubs and an import-export business.  Rex had never told her anything about them.  When they returned his remains from Vietnam they of course sent her all of his personal effects.  An account at the Manila Bank contained over $200,000.  Jane changed it into cashier's checks and mailed them to herself care of her sister in Florida.  The safety box at another bank was her plan for tomorrow.  Jane felt more nervous than excited as she returned to their rented room.  She was disappointed not to find Tom.

\* \* \*

It was an effort for Tom to stay awake.  This was definitely killer weed and with the heat and humidity, Tom was melting into the rickshaw.  There present course was up a small hill where B.J. had mentioned a park.

From the park Tom could see the town of Manila below him.  B.J. pointed out a few places as Tom asked questions.

"What've you got for a tired Yankee?"

B.J. thought.    "We go back and I see.    We find something," he assured.

It was cooler now as the sun set over the harbor.    Tom sat on the concrete bench.    Sections of these poured in place benches circled the Spanish fountain.    Tom didn't feel good.    Tom worried about spending all the money he had in one day.    The weed, rickshaw taxi, and food were all chewing at his low holdings.    Tom gnashed his teeth and continued to gaze at the mosaic fountain.

It looked very Spanish.    Tom imagined he were in Spain.    Boy Johnson was right.    These "Pick me Up" pills Boy Johnson got him were powerful.    His heart pounded and his eyes were straining to explode. Were it not for the "killer weed," Tom would probably be doing a hat dance, uncontrollably.

*Winds of the gypsies - fill my sails*
*Take me along on your midnight trails*
*Forests and valleys fill with stars*
*Guiding my caravan with horse pulled carts*
*Don't leave behind*
*Dreams of your mind (16)*

The brown skinned Asians became Spanish matadors and senoritas in Tom's eyes.    A bull fight in the distance echoed in choruses of cheers. Tom could imagine the bull being harpooned by bright colored spears.

*Blizzards and rain block what I see*
*Searching for treasure to set me free*
*Rubies and gold*
*The mountains may hide*
*Tracks in the snow*
*On our caravan ride (16)*

Tom felt oddly heavy. His head was numb, but inflated with warm liquid. He hadn't eaten for hours but he wanted to throw up. He held it down. Nothing appealed to his mind's appetite. He knew he hadn't eaten dinner and it was nighttime now.

Tom wandered back into town. Not as much traffic as the daytime. Yet a lot of people were walking and traveling. Smells were more annoying, enough to barf-

"Hey Yankee!"

Tom turned to see beside him Boy Johnson on his rickshaw.

"Oh you." He continued walking.

"Hey, Yankee, you don't look well. What happened?"

"You happened. That's what! I think that weed is dragging me down."

"Oh . . . maybe you've never done opium."

"Opium? I thought that was pot?"

"It is pot. But they spice it."

Tom stopped walking beside the rickshaw and grabbed B.J.s arm.

"You mean this stuff is laced with opium?"

B.J. meekly nodded his head.

Tom dug out the cigarette pack from his coat pocket and shoved it at B.J. "Go get my money back!"

B.J's eyes dilated. "I can't do that. I told you it was "killah weed.""

"Yeah . . . well you can kill someone else with it!"

"Bu' these people ah not too nice abou' retuhns," he said shaking his head and using his Chinese accent again.

"Tough! I don't want any of this shit. I'm no junkie and don't plan to be by learning to like this fucking shit!"

B.J. hesitated trying to think of an argument.

Tom didn't feel good. He was nauseous and even getting emotional made the discomfort swell up.

"Goddamnit. I'll kick your ass motherfucker if you don't take this shit back."

Now his head was pounding.

Boy Johnson realized Tom was beyond conversation. "I'll be back. Wait here."

As Tom waited for B.J.'s possible return, he realized he wasn't far from the club that Ko worked at. He decided to stop in on her as soon as B.J. returned--hopefully returned.

It didn't take long before B.J. returned and very disgruntled, explained how he exchanged the pot for this Thai stick and even had to shell out another buck.

Tom looked at the small brown-green frond. He felt better. "You want to smoke some with me?"

"No. No drugs for Boy Johnson."

Ironic. This kid seemed like the devil's courier. Then again he did seem to have a good heart. Still, this downtown area was Hell's playground and purity was definitely misplaced here.

"How 'bout a ride to a club down the street."

"Two bucks."

"It's not that far."

"Then walk."

"Hey!"

"I've got to make my money back."

"You said it was only a buck."

"Gotta make a profit," he smiled.

"Two bucks if you take me home too. And, I'll buy you a drink."

"Two-fifty and I don't drink."

"Okay you Manilan money monger . . . let's go."

There were several other pedal cars outside the club, like taxis at an airport.

Tom handed B.J. a buck and walked into the club.

The club was dimly lit. Red glassed candles lit the tables and cigarette smoke was thick enough to swim in. Tom sat near the wall and tried to locate Ko through the haze.

After a few minutes and no service Tom was about to get up and search the joint. Then he saw her. Ko was dressed as he'd last seen her. She looked figuresque even from this distance in the artificial fog. Her red silk dress clung tightly to her showing off her narrow waist. Tom didn't like the way men grabbed her arms for her attention or tried to kiss her. A slovenly, mostly American crowd.

The couple now entering had obviously been here before. One gentleman of this establishment immediately greeted them and ushered them to a booth. Tom watched this same gentleman quickly scoop up Ko and escort her out back somewhere. Meanwhile, the couple were being treated like royalty. They were immediately given a plate of appetizers. Tom looked around and saw no one else eating anything. Finally a girl approached Tom and asked what he wanted to drink.

"A beer. Whatever's on tap."

This special couple were fairly young. Late twenties. Early thirties. The man seemed like a college boy. He wore a nice grey tweed suit, white shirt and a black tie. The girl was very attractive and perhaps pretty, were it not for an obvious air of snobbishness about her. Tom figured they must be blue eyes because her hair appeared naturally yellow-blonde. A small upturned petite nose and curt lips; not turned down at the corners, but a frown just the same. She wore a silver dress that displayed her thinness and lack of chest. She was sexy in a mean manner.

"Fifty cents."

Tom gave her three quarters.

"Who's the couple over there."

"He's some military officer and she's his wife."

"They appear to be treated very well here."

"They spend a lot of money."

"Oh."

When Ko reappeared her hair was seductively pinned up. She looked more cheerful than before. A quick transition like a costume change. Tom wondered if she was going to perform.

Ko walked straight to the table where the couple sat. They greeted her warmly. They greeted her very warmly. The woman stroked Ko's arm as they talked.

After a few minutes of talking and giggling the blonde pointed at the front door while explaining something. Ko nodded agreement and headed out of the club. Was she leaving or retrieving something?

Tom gulped his beer faster.

The couple got up and walked out the front door.

Tom guzzled the last . . . oooh . . . stomach still queezy . . .

When he reached the sidewalk a large black car pulled out from the curb and drove away slowly with its red tail lights burning a strange suspicion into Tom's mind.

He wanted to follow her to see where they were going. Ko must've waited for them in the car.

Several rickshaw drivers conversed behind Tom. He scanned them until he picked out Boy Johnson, gabbing away with his peddle buddies.

"Boy Johnson!" Tom yelled.


\* \* \*


Jane was getting worried about Tom. It was 1:30 in the morning. Tom hadn't been out this late before, and this was the Philippines with a war around the corner.

Manila was a tough town at night. And here she was with so much to tell him. Over $200,000 and still more leads to follow tomorrow morning. Tomorrow morning? This morning! Jane looked at her watch again. Where was he? Investigating these strange businesses that Rex owned was a little disconcerting, she wanted to talk to Tom. And now Tom was out on the town carousing. She realized she'd been cold and unfriendly to Tom since Sid . . .

Maybe it wasn't really Tom's fault, yet, it still was connected with his deception and falsehoods. The same type of selfish distrust that Rex had been involved in also. For all she hated Rex, it was hard not to channel some of it also at Tom. But tonight she felt willing to put all of that behind them if he'd only come home so she could share her newfound success. Her excitement also made her lonely. After all, what is success if there's no one to share it with.

* * *

This was a nice neighborhood. Obviously the wealthy people lived on this hill. Stone walls and black iron gates blocked Tom's view of what he knew were large houses and mansions.

The small round tail lights turned up a driveway ahead.

"Park here. Wait for me. I won't be long."

Tom walked the rest of the way up the street and tiptoed up the cobblestone driveway. At the top of the driveway he turned right and stepped quickly across the lawn, hunched over, to the side of the house. He had to go almost into the backyard to find a window that offered a view of the living room.

There were several tall palms indoors and ferns in hanging baskets. A large overstuffed looking floral couch was where the blonde sat. Across the room at a chrome rolling bar the officer was mixing drinks. Ko stood in the middle of the living room at a kind of attention. As if she was waiting for further orders. When the man sat down, the blonde girl waved her cigarette wielding hand at Ko as if to say, "Get on with it."

Ko got on with it! Tom could not hear any music at all. She didn't need it. She rotated her hips like a belly dancer and moved her flowing arms and fingers in sensuous circles. Then she began unbuttoning her red silk dress. Tom was aghast. A strip tease! Ko was performing a strip tease. And she was performing a very sexy strip tease.

Now Tom finally got nervous. His headache was coming back. He could feel his stomach tighten again, his heart was pounding . . . He realized he was trespassing. He remembered leaving B.J. waiting. What if there were dogs here? He dropped lower below the window sill crouching. What if Ko saw him watching her? His heart was pounding.

He was scared. He was mad. He was hurt. He was aroused.

Tom felt betrayed. Ko in a few days time was a casual friend, but housemate, none the less. Kind of a sister. A sister. A friend. Being prostituted! Tom couldn't believe it. He would leave and sort this out later. He raised his head up and peered through the window. 'Oh my God!' he thought to himself. Ko was kneeling, naked before the couch, offering Tom a clear side view. She was giving the man head! And even more, the blonde was forcing her head up and down on his cock!

Tom ran for the street.

* * *

In a couple hours the sun would rise over Manila. The streets still had a few sailors stumbling about. Tom was almost back at the house. Boy Johnson wasn't waiting back on the hill so Tom had to walk across town. As he walked, he thought. The world was a huge blender of two-sided faces. Someone would appear like someone . . . then they'd turn around to reveal someone else. Honesty and truth seemed to exist until the back was turned and a new face appeared with new rules. Tom didn't know if he could trust anyone. Anyone! Could anyone trust him? After all he had two faces also. He tried to appear as a college hitchhiker . . . Heaven help him if he was found out to be a murderer wanted by the police back in California. So what is the truth?

Though Tom was a fugitive, he thought of himself as a safe, honest, trustworthy person. "Shit, do I really even know myself?" Tom said out loud into the darkness of an unlit street. "My name is Tom-- My name is Tom--My name is Tom--," he kept pausing because he no longer had a last name. He didn't like the name, Tom Brady.

"My name is Tom. My name is Tom . . ." he spoke methodically as he walked.

When Tom got home he realized Ko was already back also. He didn't want to talk to her, he just wanted to go to bed. He slipped upstairs into the dark room.

"Tom?" Jane asked in the black filled room.

"Yeah. It's me," he replied, stripping in the darkness.

"Where've you been all night?"

"I wandered around downtown . . . and around." He clunked onto his bed.

"I was in town also."

"Oh yeah? How was it?" Tom rolled over on his side with his back to the end of the room Jane occupied.

"I found a bank account of Rex's. He had a lot of money in it."

"Huh," he moaned sleepily.

"Over two hundred grand."

"Tom didn't feel so sleepy now. He rolled over. "Where'd that come from?"

"I don't know, but he's got other accounts I think."

"Far out!" Tom wondered if Rex was selling drugs. No. He didn't look the type. Of course, how could he? All marines look the same. Buzzhead robots. Sure a lot of them must get high . . . Wow! A military connection . . . the blackmarket? . . . An American Viking . . . Rape and plunder . . . the spoils of war . . . Oh well, all part of the job.

"I'm kind of nervous about all that money."

"What did you do with it?"

"I sent it by checks back to my sister in Florida."

"Sarah?"

"Yeah. I addressed them to me."

"Tomorrow you're gonna check out some other banks?"

"Uh-huh. Would you mind coming along with me?"

Jane's voice sounded very demure and helpless.

"Sure. Of course."

"Thanks. I'll see you in the morning."

"Okay."

"Good night Tom," she said softly.

"Good night."

\* \* \*

"I'm sorry Mrs. Thompson. You must have a key to open the box." The bank's squatty, oriental manager was obviously a stickler for rules. Courteous and mechanical.

"I've shown you the papers," Jane frustratedly explained again. "See. This is the death certificate. Here is our marriage certificate. This is my military ID card. Here is a copy of the will and insurance statements. So you have to open it for me."

"I'm sorry Mrs Thompson. You must--"

"I'll pay you a couple years rent on the box," Jane interrupted, "and I'll pay you $100 for your inconvenience."

"Well . . . I'll have a locksmith over here this afternoon. I'm sure we can get it open somehow." His tune changed when the money sang.

"Thanks. I'll be back about 2:00."

Tom smiled as they walked out of the bank. "That was pretty slick," he congratulated.

Jane smiled.

It wasn't too far to the Manila harbor. They picked up some hot dogs and walked to a spot near the water to eat.

"What do you want to do with your life Tom?"

Tom stopped in mid-chew. "I dunno."

"What do you mean, "You don't know?" You've got to want something."

"Well . . . When I was a kid I wanted to be an ice cream man."

Jane laughed a little.

"Yeah. I know. But I wanted to be wanted, and appreciated, I guess. I mean, I loved the ice cream man. When I heard his song I'd run to my mother and ask for a quarter. I tried 'em all. I liked the sidewalk sundaes. I loved pushups, half-n-halfs, and eskimo pies. In fact, I really dug those cones with the nuts and chocolate on top."

"Drum sticks."

"Yeah . . . drum sticks! They were really a treat. And I loved those sugar cones--"

"Okay, I get the picture. You wanted to be an ice cream man."

"Right. But as I got older I realized that anybody could be an ice cream man and that it wasn't a very good job. At least it didn't pay much, and being an ice cream man is not very prestigious."

"They do make people happy," she reassured.

"Yeah. And that's what I guess I really liked about it: making people happy. And I'd like to see them smile the way I did. Yeah. Making people happy. That's what I'd like to somehow do with my life."

"Like selling drugs."

"No. Well . . . heck, I never thought of it that way. But yeah. Maybe. I mean . . . well . . . Wow! I don't believe it. I guess I did achieve that goal in my own way." Tom thought for a moment. "Funny how things turn out, isn't it?"

"Yes it is," Jane reflected.

"But I do like to help people somehow. Be an Ambassador of goodwill, somehow."

"I don't think that with your background you're all too eligible for civil service or government work."

Tom chuckled. "I guess not. But there must be something I can do. I don't want to just run around all my life. I'd like to settle down somewhere. Preferably by the beach. Heck. Maybe even have a family. I know I'm not cut out to be a nine-to-fiver like my dad. I don't want to just work and work and work. I want to enjoy life. Be with my family.

Still travel. And I do want to help people. Maybe runaways and fugitives, like me. Maybe even change some laws. Did you know that two million people in America supposedly smoke pot? That means that one-tenth of our population are all criminals for just smoking pot. What's the sense of having a law that makes that many people fugitives and criminals. It's like: US against THEM. It's not a generation gap. It's a justice gap. You have to afford justice. If you can't buy justice you're just hamburger in the big meat grinder . . ."

Jane listened.

"I'd like to have a place," he continued, "where people could go to be free. To find justice. A home . . . or a country . . . heck, I'd like to have a hashish bar. I hear that in Amsterdam they have hashish dens and you can go there and openly smoke your brains out. I'd like a place that. Free like that. People could just go there and enjoy themselves. Now that would be a great place. That would be my kind of place. What do you think?"

"Pretty interesting."

\* \* \*

When they returned to the bank they were informed that the locksmith had already begun working on the safety deposit box.

"I will need your signature on these forms," the manager explained.

Tom eyed the clerks with their dark blue suits and ties. All had white shirts and polished black shoes, a standard uniform. The manager's only deviation from the norm was his black mustache. Tom thought, 'the sinister rise to the top of sour milk . . .'

"And here's the $100," Jane offered.

"Thank you," he replied, not offering a receipt. "There, he appears about done."

The manager pulled a large chunk of keys out of a drawer and led them into the safety box vault. The locksmith handed the manager one key. He opened the box door with the new key and one on the chain, pulled out the metal rectangle halfway, larger than a shoe box, then stepped back for Jane to remove it from its mausoleum-like wall space.

Jane took it to a booth as Tom waited with the manager. Jane stuffed all of the paperwork into her large brown burlap handbag and returned with the empty tin.

"Thank you," she said, hardly glancing at the bank manager. Then they left.

* * *

Back at home they reviewed the paperwork. There were stocks, and there were deeds and contracts. Rex was a part-owner of some business in Vietnam, and one here in Manila, a real estate company. There were also a few letters. Letters that Rex had received from a Miss Mon Set Hong. Some of these real estate transactions were detailed in the letters. And, Mon Set appeared to be Rex's mistress.

There business was more than pleasure. A lot of families were uprooted during Vietnam's constant upheaval. It was evidently very easy to buy out businesses and make a substantial profit from the occupying forces . . . Night clubs boomed and farms were evacuated. The letters even referred to abandoned homes bought for nothing.

Rex was quite enterprising. Mon Set sounded shrewd also. A monopoly game using the spoils of war.

The addresses on the envelopes were the same as the real estate office contract for which Rex was a ten percent owner.

"I want to go to this real estate office tomorrow," Jane announced.

Tom nodded agreement as he read through the documents. He was overtaken by a strange foreboding feeling though. This was an evil enterprise. He could sense that there was power and danger within this paperwork.

* * *

The real estate company was also near the Manila harbor, not too far from the bank they'd visited yesterday. As Tom and Jane stood outside and read the storefront sign, Jane spoke, "Somehow it all seems like a mistaken identity. I can't believe Rex was involved in all of this. He kept it a secret from me."

They entered the old grey doors and approached the counter that separated those who entered from those who worked there. A Mexican or Spanish or Portuguese looking woman got up from a desk and asked if she could help.

"I'm looking for Mon Set Hong."

"Your name?"

"Mrs. Rex Thompson."

The heavyset woman's eyes widened and she nervously replied, "Just a minute."

She exited into an office.

Tom and Jane waited several minutes. It felt uncomfortable in this old house converted into an office. Mon Set Hong appeared followed by the first woman who watched intently.

"May I help you?" she asked coldly.

"I would like to speak to Mon Set Hong."

"I am Mon Set Hong."

"I am Rex Thompson's wife."

"Oh?" she acknowledged with little interest.

"Rex was killed in Vietnam."

"I know," she replied flatly.

"He evidently was in business with you."

"Did he tell you this?" Mon Set wore an unemotional straight-face.

"No. I found out after his death."

"So what can I do for you?"

"I am his surviving wife and now own his business interests."

"You were divorced."

"No. We were separated. The divorce was not final."

Mon Set looked slightly distressed now. Jane was beginning to boil.

"So what can I do for you?" Mon Set repeated, but not as calmly.

"I want to liquidate his business interests."

"What business interests?"

"Don't toy with me. I now possess the deeds and paperwork to several business interests of yours!"

"What paperwork?"

Jane reached into her large handbag and produced the documents. Tom watched with stern squinted eyes as Mon Set glanced at each one individually.

"I must talk with my partners."

Mon Set Hong talked secretively to the first woman before reentering her office and closing the door. She left the other woman to watch Tom and Jane like a big fat guard dog.

After a few more minutes of waiting, Tom was getting very restless, and nervous.

"Let's get out of here. Something's fishy here."

Jane stood as still as a mountain. For her this was a showdown.

Before they could have even turned around, the doors behind them opened and two heavyweight Polynesians walked in. One stayed to block the front door and the other brushed rudely past them to lift up a section of counter top and walk under it like a draw bridge. He went straight to the office of Mon Set and knocked on its door.

"Finally, you're here." Then Mon Set began to talk in Chinese or Vietnamese or something, so as not to be understood by Tom and Jane.

Mon Set approached them with a confident look upon her face. "I will buy all of these for $1,000."

"One-thousand dollars?" Jane exclaimed. "Are you kidding? One of these is ten percent of your real estate operation."

"$1,000. Take it or leave it," she grinned.

The two thugs converged, one from behind and one from in front. Jane was doing business with the very same woman who had broken her marriage and seduced her husband into this greedy, cancerous empire. She despised this woman. She hated this woman. She hated this business. She hated these documents. She had been deceived, and cheated, and now she was being pushed around?!

Jane swiftly back-kicked the guy behind them and as he bent forward in intestinal pain she grabbed his ears and smashed his head forward into the counter top. She was breathing hard and ready to jump over the counter. Tom jumped to the side as the other bighead plodded to the draw bridge. Mon Set Hong held out her hand and spoke in oriental again. He halted.

"$10,000 for everything," Mon Set offered.

Jane shook her head 'no' as she kept an eye on the kneeling thug cupping his bleeding nose.

But Tom wasn't interested in risking their lives for bidding purposes. He stepped over the grumbling thug to Jane's side. "Take it. Let's get out of here!"

"Forty-thousand dollars," Jane demanded. "Take it or leave it!"

The other thug beside Mon Set looked at his mistress for an order to kill. Mon Set stared forward into Jane's spiteful eyes. This was a showdown and these looks could kill.

"Come back at 3:00," Mon Set calmly stated.

Jane shook her head as she spoke, "Deliver it to the Manila Star Restaurant at three o'clock."

Mon set stared Jane in the eyes without blinking, then nodded in agreement.

Jane began to shuffle the papers together. Mon Set stepped forward to stop her but Jane pulled them quickly out of reach.

"When you bring the money, you get these."

Tom and Jane kept an eye behind them as they walked out the doors. Before the doors closed Jane yelled back, "US dollars!"

* * *

A skinny oriental with glasses and a standard issue suit arrived at the Manila Star right on time. He knew what papers to expect as he checked them each individually. Then he summoned another accomplice who had been waiting inside across the restaurant. This man set down on the table a large reddish-brown lacquered wood box almost a foot square.

Tom and Jane counted the raggedy bundles of bills. There were bundles of fives, tens, and twenties, but no fifties or hundreds. The box was stuffed full.

"I wish they would have used bigger bills," Tom mumbled as he counted bundles of fives and tens.

"It seems to all be here," Jane stated coldly.

The oriental skeleton man picked up the papers and walked away with the second man following behind.

Tom held up his glass of coca-cola and offered a toast.

When they exited the restaurant there was a taxi waiting.

"Need a ride?" the Polynesian asked through the taxi's passenger window.

"Yes," Jane replied.

Tom was carrying the box.

As Jane got into the back seat Tom remembered the doggey bag of Peking duck that they had left on their table. "Oh. I just remembered. I'm gonna go get the doggey bag."

"Leave it," Jane said.

"Naw. I want it. I'll eat it later."

"You can leave the box in the car," the cab driver suggested to Tom as he was walking away from the taxi.

"That's okay," Tom replied as he went back into the club and hurried up the stairs to the restaurant.

Tom got the doggey bag and as he walked back down the steps he became suspicious of the cab driver's helpfulness. Maybe he was set up by Mon Set. After all he was conveniently available.

Tom approached the cab and holding the box under his left arm motioned for Jane to get out of the taxi. The driver seemed to panic.

"What's wrong?" the driver asked nervously.

"Nothing. We just want to walk."

"Tom. What's the matter?"

"I don't know. I just got suspicious of that driver," he whispered.

"Now Tom . . . don't get paranoid," she laughed as they walked away.

"Maybe. But I don't trust that lady."

They got about two blocks down the street before it became easily apparent that they were being followed by a small black squarish car.

At Tom's command he and Jane ran down a narrow alley filled with trash cans to another narrow street. Pushing aside some sidewalkers and dodging bicycles, they crossed the street, then ran a little further before Tom ushered Jane quickly into a sleazy hotel.

Still out of breath they approached the deskman.

"We'd like a room," Tom panted.

The deskman eyed them suspiciously. Tom put the box on the floor so the deskman couldn't see its contents. He pulled out three twenty dollar bills and asked for a nice quiet room.

It was probably the best this dive had to offer. The room's furnishings were a mixture of plastic and wood grain formica. A couple of oriental knickknacks, like the imitation jade ashtray, were the only signs of this part of the world. They could easily have been in any cheap hotel in America.

Tom closed the blinds and curtains. There was a king-size bed which Jane sat upon as Tom peeked out the curtains.

"I don't think they saw us enter here," he said.  "Let's wait 'til dark and then we'll find a way back to the house."

Tom sat next to Jane on the bed.  She was frozen stiff.  She hadn't panicked; she'd been amazingly forceful and brave all day long.  Now however, she was succumbing to the scared after affects and was worn out from the adrenaline rushes.

"Don't worry, we'll make it.  Those fuckers don't know where we're from or where we're going."

"It's just all so strange," she began,  "This running, and money, Rex and--"

"Yeah. I know what you mean.  Maybe I'm getting used to it."

Jane looked Tom in the face.  "What's next?  My home's for sale and that Sid is still on the loose, and now this?"

"What about your sister?  You could go stay with her in Florida."

"What about you?"

"I don't know.  I was thinking about going to San Francisco."

"But what will you do there?"

"I don't know."  Tom looked down, looked to the left, looked to right . . . he shrugged his shoulders, "I'll figure something out."

"Will I see you again?" she asked shyly.

"I hope so," Tom stated politely.

"Do you?" she asked doe eyed.

"What do you mean?  "Do you?"" he teased.  "Of course I do.  You've been a tremendous help to me.  You've been kind and generous.  You taught me Tai Chi.  You've been like a mother to me."

Jane turned away.  Oops.  Maybe "mother" was not the best word to use.

"Some mother I've been.  I didn't want kids.  I was too selfish to want . . ." She paused with her face lowered away from Tom, "I've been too much like a parent, not enough like a friend.  I wish we were closer now."

"We are close.  You're my best friend."

Quietly she confessed, "Closer than that."

Tom suddenly realized what Jane was saying. Somehow the age barrier was always there. He was 19, she was 29. Now it all seemed like a stupid illusion that both of them had conceded to. Like two children suddenly without their parents they were stranded, afraid, and lonely. Rules began to dissolve . . . they hugged in sad desperation, sitting on the edge of the bed. They clung emotionally to each other as they slowly rocked back and forth.

They parted briefly as Jane sniffled, her eyes were watery. He gently placed his hand on hers. She moved her hand out from underneath and instantly grasped his hand firmly. As she raised her head up Tom bent forward and kissed her on the cheek.

She looked him in the eyes with a helpless expression and kissed him on the lips.

They embraced again, passionately this time. She allowed herself to fall back onto the bed as they continued kissing. They were passionate but reserved; very sensitive and gentle. Her breathing quickened. She was panting. He nuzzled her neck and she squirmed and twisted like a warm snake. She breathed harder, seeming wilder now. Tom was overcome by a tingly feeling over his entire body. All of the ignored lust was surfacing between them. He stroked her sides and back as she began to scratch and rub him frantically.

They struggled out of their clothes; never totally parting, still kissing and undressing awkwardly.

In a sweaty slick, they entwined atop the bed. Constantly kissing and licking each other from head to . . . like feeding cats they devoured each other's bodies shamelessly.

They didn't want it to stop so they kept it at a high sensual plateau for at least a half-hour before Tom accidentally came inside of her. He wanted to hold back longer.

No problem though. She was so jazzed and electric she didn't notice his orgasm as she wriggled and danced beneath him. Tom never lost his erection and they continued for almost another hour. Exhausted, they slept clung together, her head resting on his chest.

It was dark when they woke. They kissed, cuddled and beamed their smiles to each other with loving eyes that wanted to say much more. Even their legs brushing each other was intercourse. Tom was filled with her love and she felt nourished and comforted by him. They tried to ignore the time.

"This box is a giveaway," Tom said as he pulled on his pants. "I'll bet they gave it to us intentionally."

So they stuffed their pockets and her purse. There were still some wads of bills left. Tom stuffed his socks. She put a couple in her panties.

Smiling and holding hands they walked out of the hotel anointed with the sweat of each other like newborn spirits.

*Sometimes the hardest words to share*
*Are the easiest emotions to feel*
*And to express my feelings for you*
*I find myself stumbling head over heel*
*So I will sing a simple song*
*To you*
*Together and free*
*And the love I will bring*
*We will share*
*Together and free (17)*

# Chapter Five
## *San Francisco*

"Hey! Watch where you're stepping!"

"Oh. Sorry," Tom replied to the shapeless form somehow sleeping on the stairs. He continued up to the second floor. A door was partly ajar. Blue light glowed around the door's perimeter giving it the appearance of a portal to Heaven. Tom looked around. There were a couple of other doors, closed. The guy on the phone said he'd be waiting. Tom didn't carry a watch but he knew it was about two in the morning.

Tom peeked through the door's narrow opening. He saw the far wall with an Indian paisley print hung on it, a few lit candles, and low stacked book shelves. Jasmine incense burned in the room.

Tom knocked gently. He could hear someone walk to the door and then open it.

A tall fellow, Tom's height with shoulder length light-brown hair and a long brown beard, asked if he was Tom.

"Yes, that's me."

"Come on in."

A girl sat on a cushion facing the stereo turntable with headphones on.

125

She bopped to the music and with her eyes closed was obviously in another world.

"I'm Jack and that's Muffin."

Tom made a waving gesture at Muffin, but she didn't see it.

"You said you were new in town when we spoke on the phone."

"Yes," replied Tom.    "I've just got in from a short stay in the Philippines, and before that Los Angeles."

"How do you like San Francisco?"

"I've only been here a couple weeks, but I really like it a lot.    The people here are very friendly.    It's almost like coming home, even though I'm a total stranger."

"We're all strangers.    We're all family.    After all we've all got the same grandparents, Adam and Eve.    Are you religious?"

"I'm raised Catholic.    I figure I'm religious by nature."

"Christian."

"Well, I guess so.    I'm not sure though.    I figure Christ was a prophet, but I don't buy all that Virgin Mary stuff."

"We're all Christ.    We're all God."

"What religion are you?" Tom asked the apparent sage.

"Faith."

"Faith?"

"Faith."

"What do you mean?"

"My religion is faith.    Faith in religion.    Faith in self."

"Oh."

"You ever read the Bible?" he asked Tom with calm yet somehow piercing eyes.

"I've read bits of it.    I appreciate its ideals and messages.    I believe in many of its teachings.    Like the *Golden Rule*."

"Rules are made.    What's made is eventually broken."

"Sure, but you've got to have rules."    Tom felt like the Devil's advocate taking sides with society. "This is society, and for people to coexist you need rules. You need speed limits."

"You ever take the written driver's test Tom?"

"Of course."

"What is the **Basic Speed Law**?"

"Don't drive faster than is safe."

"Correct. And that is the **Golden Rule**."

Tom interrupted, "I thought the **Golden Rule** is: 'Do unto others as you'd have them do unto you.'"

Jack hardly varied from his calm hypnotic tone, "Many people endanger their lives or even destroy themselves knowingly. If they're willing to do that to themselves, would you want them to do that to you?"

"No."

Silence. The discussion was completed. Tom was amazed. This Jack was very intelligent and very spiritual, and rather weird. Tom respected him already and realized he had much to learn from him.

Tom broke the silence. "What about the job you advertised?"

"You ever do sound before?"

"Yeah. I told you on the phone. I did a short stint with this band called The Razors. I even worked the lights."

Tom was exaggerating. He hardly knew what he was doing at all. It was, however, the only job Tom ever had besides selling dope and having a paper route as a kid.

"Why do you want this job?"

"I really enjoyed doing sound and augmenting the performance. I felt like I was playing an instrument in the band. I felt I was part of the performance."

Jack grinned at Tom.

"You know where The Cuckoo's Nest is?"

"I'll find it."

"Show up tomorrow at six o'clock and we'll put you to work."

"Great!" Tom beamed.

"You got a place to stay?"

"Yeah.  A couple girls I met are putting me up over by the Golden Gate."

They shook hands and as Tom got up to leave he remembered how late it was.

"You don't mean six in the morning I hope?"

"No," Jack laughed.

Tom paused for Jack to specify that he meant six in the evening but Jack had answered his question and accordingly offered no further explanation.

"Okay. See you tomorrow."


                                *  *  *


When Tom opened the front door with the spare key that the girls had given him, he knew immediately they were awake.  A solitary red light in the dining room gave a warm dark feeling to the apartment.  Many of the concert posters on the wall lost their color because of the red light, and even looked like black and white faded pictures now.  Anything colored red was invisible.  The light, unmistakable smell of hash scented the air unobtrusively.  The record player was spinning *"A Beautiful Day."* Flute and acoustic guitar lent an angelic air to this airborne environment. Tom heard a voice, a moan, then became aware of heavy breathing around the corner of the living room near the kitchen.  Whoever was here had not heard him enter.  He'd already closed and locked the front door. He sensed that he was intruding.  He stepped forward anyway in the dark red glow.

A huge black simulated fur bean bag chair rustled and shifted with its foam BBs inside.  Tom watched Tawny and Tammy embraced like an M. C. Escher drawing of two lizards swallowing each other's tails.  Lapping and sucking they clutched each other's buttocks and swayed like boats on a rough sea.

Tom was awed. He'd never seen two girls make love. Tammy was on top. She raised her head up with eyes shut and mouth agape panting. Tawny continued to chew Tammy's buried treasure. Tammy gave several short howls and began to tremble. She shivered, then trembled, then vibrated then spasmed uncontrollably for several seconds before rolling off and away from Tawny's tongue to escape her pleasure.

With Tammy off of her face, Tawny was staring coldly at Tom. Her look was not surprise or even embarrassment. She was protective and harsh. Tawny glanced at Tammy who lay panting on her back with eyes closed beside her, then back at Tom.

Tawny flicked her head to the side as a cue for Tom to step out of the room.

He did.

Tom knew they slept together and figured 'so what.' Seeing them in action was awakening though. He wasn't offended or shocked. He was just a little dazed by it, and excited. He pulled a Hawaiian Punch out of the refrigerator. Tawny entered the kitchen with a robe on.

"How was your job interview?"

"Fine. I think I got the job."

"Good." She sat down across from him at the kitchen table. "What club is it?"

"A place called The Cuckoo's Nest."

"You're kidding," she exclaimed, now showing some warmth.

"Yeah. Is it a cool place?"

"Cool? Are you kidding. That's a happening place. The Airplane, Santana, Dead and touring groups play there."

"Really?"

"And they do have a great light show. Wild stuff!"

"Great. And the guy is really cool. I mean he's something else. He was blowing my mind with some heavy trips."

Just then Tammy walked into the kitchen. Her shoulder length blonde hair was tussled and teased from her bean bag sports. She was a contrast to Tawny's darker stronger look. Tammy was thin, frail, and small breasted. Tawny was big boned, big breasted, brown chest length thick hair and even her face was strong and confident.

Tammy was cute and Tawny was attractive but so stout as to appear a little masculine.

"Tom's gonna do sound for The Cuckoo's Nest!"

"Wow, what a gas. That's cool." Tammy looked at Tom, "It's a far out place; great groups and hip people all week long." She turned back to Tawny, "Remember when we saw Moby Grape there?"

Tawny laughed, "And Lee Michaels."

"Yeah. I really love him. He's so cute."

"So I guess I've got a good job?"

"A good job? Maybe you'll be able to get us backstage. This is worth celebrating. Where'd you put the hash T?"

"On the book case."

Tammy left the room. Tom watched her walk out and could better visualize her small pert ass beneath her thin cotton robe.

Tawny interrupted him and spoke bluntly, "I love her."

Tom looked to face her and saw the same cold expression he'd seen when she'd caught him spying.


*  *  *


California, as Tom had known it in San Diego, was summer from May to October; then sometime before Halloween it switched to Fall until March. A short Spring was hot like Summer but the ocean was still chilly until June. Winter? Not in San Diego. Fall was a masquerade.

San Francisco however had a real autumn. The offshore fog was darker, greyer, colder; like the Crawling Eye movie. Here, now, October in San Francisco was darker than Tom had ever felt before. Being a homeless fugitive was not quite a plus for anyone's situation, but the gloom was really external here. San Francisco was grey and cold like an old Chicago gangster movie. Autumn: wet streets, low clouds, cold nights and steep hills.

This impending muscle flex of Nature was not so strange to Nancy. She'd been raised as a child in the midwest. She took the damp twilight air in stride as she walked briskly up the sidewalk with her hood-covered brown hair. She'd been in San Francisco all summer. After she graduated from Patrick Henry High in San Diego, she left home. Hardly a runaway at eighteen, but definitely a young girl, with a tough attitude. Family life was all a jumble of anger-filled memories. Her father had slapped her enough times, her mother had only two volumes: one was so soft you'd have to ask her to repeat what she said, and the other equalled the exhaust of a jet plane.

Tonight as Nancy made her familiar path to her favorite club, The Cuckoo's Nest, she was remembering Barbara. Tonight was Monday, Nancy's day off. She'd had a great weekend waitressing in Fishermen's Wharf. In the last four days she'd made enough money in tips to pay her rent for the month and buy a new blouse. Nancy felt proud and strong. Barbara had always had it so easy. Well, Nancy could have anything that Barbara could have and be stronger for it, because Nancy would work for her earnings. Working made her independent. Barbara was weak, too much too easy.

Nancy felt as if she was having the last laugh. She walked faster uphill.

* * *

"You think you've got it?"

"Yes, I think so . . . except, these foot switches, I can't see them when I'm working the console switches."

131

"No, 'fraid not.  You'll just have to feel where they are like an organist playing bass pedals."

"Aren't any of the floor fills on the board?"

"Just the two on each side of the stage, a yellow and a blue.  Just flip this toggle up and both blues come on.  Flip it down and the yellows are on.  The middle position is off.  The same with the three overhead switches to the left of it; up is blue, down is yellow.  You understand the others, right?"

"Yes, but I'm not too familiar with the overhead projector."

"Don't worry about that.  Moonchild handles that."

"Who's Moonchild?" Tom asked loudly as the band soundchecked another song.

Jack laughed, "You'll see.  Now go get something to eat and be back in an hour."

* * *

It was only Monday night so the club wasn't too full.  The first band had almost finished their show.  Tom wasn't doing bad, but he felt retarded.  The Razors, or Marine Officer's Club, didn't have near the light show this club had.  Frustration and determination fueled Tom with the ambition to get a handle on this.  He knew he could be good at it.  He was concentrating on it so hard that he'd been unaware of the soundman, Jack, and special effects person, Moonchild.

Moonchild stood off to Tom's left and a little in front of him.  His super-long knotty curly hair was like an unopened mushroom cone on his head.  It totally enshrouded his head with a slot in the front for his face to view through.  From where Tom sat he was a phallic silhouette of a gushing volcano.  The blobs, flashes, designs and liquid colors he painted on the stage backdrop and also onto the performers transformed them into lava puppets within a kaleidoscope.

Jack had instructed Tom to give Moonchild enough darkness to paint his moving images. Tom was glad to. Occasionally Tom would become mesmerized and fascinated by the color combinations of Moonchild and watch them like a member of the audience.

The first band left the stage to a warm applause. Tom hit the stage with yellow, red, blue floors and a couple white spots. Moonchild withdrew his visions entirely.

"Not bad novice," Moonchild commented.

Tom looked at Moonchild as he pulled a pyrex tray of colored oils off the overhead projector.

"You follow the music, that's good. Feeling is important in lights. Becoming part of the song is as necessary for us as the players themselves."

"I enjoy playing along with the band," Tom added.

"What's your name?"

"Tom. My name is Tom."

He turned to face Tom and held out his hand. "I am Moonchild."

His face was shadowed and his eyes were even darker removed from the light, yet, somehow Tom could see his reflection in their blackness.

"You been here long?" Tom asked.

"Six months. I've been working different gigs here for several years though. And you?"

"I'm new in town."

"San Francisco will be good for you. Your spirit is a thirsty bird. There are many fountains here to drink from. Remember," Moonchild said pointing upwards.

Tom looked up.

"Remember when you drink, like a bird, you must look up to swallow."

Tom was getting hit with some more of this heavy head trip stuff.

He continued, "Or you may choke."

Tom was still being jolted by these impromptu sermons but he wasn't uncomfortable with them like church sermons. Tom remembered how sitting through a Catholic service was like being chained to sit on top of an anthill. After so long, his boy brain would shut itself off. Heck it was like anything that was too monotonous, the body would turn off sensory perception, like smelling a rose. A sniff or two was fine, but after a dozen sniffs it becomes odorless. These sermons were different though. Jack was like his conscience speaking. Now this Moonchild character was talking as if he was Tom's soul.

"All of us who come here," Moonchild continued, "are searching for something. For all of us it's different. For all of us it's the same. Your search is benevolent Tom. I like that. Many come with violence in their hearts. All of us must meet here, together. Only when we can look at each other and understand what-we-are-not, will we understand what-we-are."

Moonchild paused to assess Tom's attentiveness. Moonchild was not rambling. He was talking to Tom. "When we understand: we are."

"Okay Moon. It's time for Tom to get to his next class, phys' ed.," Jack interrupted. "Go on down and check out the club. Have a drink on the house. Tell 'em Jack said to. I've done this next band before. They're nothing flashy so Moon and I can handle it. Find a girl and work your legs on the dance floor."

Tom started down the ladder to the main floor.

Jack yelled down the hole behind Tom, "And tell 'em to send up a couple drinks for the crew!"

"What kind?" Tom yelled back up.

"They know."

Tom headed to the bar first and placed the orders. With beer in hand he strolled the perimeter of the club. People here didn't dress funny or weird, they dressed bizarre. Tie-dyes and velvets, feathers, brass, leather fringe, and more beaded necklaces in this club than the Sioux Nation. Hats too. Tom was really taken by the Daniel Boone cap. Looked like a real raccoon all right.

Tom found a chair to sit in on one of the side platforms. From there he could see all the club and gawk at the attendees.

A real solid band, they drove into a hard rocker as Tom finished his beer. He felt a tap on his shoulder and leisurely turned around to see a smiling girl's face.

"Wanna dance?" she asked.

"Sure."

After a few dances Tom began to notice a strangely familiar face bobbing amidst the heads of the other dancers. He tried to get a good look but she was dwarfed by the dancers between them. He felt compelled to find her. When the song finished Tom thanked his dance partner and pushed through the idle bodies to where he had seen her. He couldn't find her.

Tom walked back to the bar and ordered another beer to cool him off. When he turned around he saw her only a couple tables away. It was Nancy. He was sure of it. Sitting there. In real life talking to a couple of other girls at her table and drinking. It was Nancy. God, how he wanted to run to her and embrace her like a soldier coming home from war. They had been good friends. Her and Barbara were bitter enemies. Still, he and Nancy had some wild times together, partying and hanging out.

Tom grabbed his brain with a bear hug. What if she now disowned him? The press referred to him as a murderer. And she may not be his friend anymore. She could turn him in and destroy his chance at a new life. It hurt deep inside Tom's heart to not trust her. He wanted to trust her. What if she told a friend? . . .

Tom pivoted around and leaned on the bar with his back to her. What was she doing here? Could she know he was here? No way! 'Maintain!' Tom told himself mentally. 'Now I'm really getting paranoid.'

Tom took his beer for a walk back to the sound booth. There he was safe between Moses and Mohammed. Tom felt hurt by the dishonor he presumed and a bit stronger in his independence from the past. Yet now he realized that his past would be closer than he could ever travel. Somehow, Tom felt he'd have to become unrecognizable. He decided to grow a beard.

* * *


The job was going fine and Tom had finally found a studio apartment near the club. Jane had been very generous to Tom. He had enough money for a car but didn't have a license. His old license was a death card so he'd thrown it out with all identification bearing his correct name of Tom Calder. His new name was now Tom Hastings.

After a couple weeks, Tom's beard was hardly a beard at all. A goatee maybe and mustache, but between his sideburns and chin was a barren wasteland of adolescent skin. Tom decided to keep the mustache and keep shaving.

Nancy had been back several times to The Cuckoo's Nest. Tom kept his distance. Sometimes he felt invisible, as if he could jump before her face and go unnoticed. He knew better than to push his luck.

Tom felt very differently about his past and future. Many evenings after work he went home with Moonchild or Jack. They rapped, got wasted and dropped acid and mescaline. Jack said that the past can be a punishment of possible futures. Moonchild said the future was a reward of past learning. Tom said both are frightening and exciting perspectives. Now the fears were almost gone. Caution and care should be exercised by everyone. Tom understood the limitations of his world. He was guardian of many secrets. Kindness and compassion would guide him. Tom pictured himself a puppy in the dog pound.


* * *


Christmas was approaching and yet somehow it wasn't. Without family and loved ones it seemed obsolete. Of course he had some friends, but they had family . . .

Tom's hair remained uncut since arriving in San Francisco. Light brown waves now touched his shoulders for the first time. As a 'runner' in San Diego he always kept his hair 'old fashioned' so as to attract less attention. It was unbelievable what some hippie-longhairs would have to endure, even here in California. They wouldn't allow you into Disneyland with long hair. They would run you off the road if you were hitchhiking. They would hassle you about getting a job or being a deserter. They were everywhere. 'They' wore the masks of normality. 'They' would lay dormant amidst the drowning fish of mediocrity and surfaced like angry sharks for a solo swimmer whenever 'their?' territory was penetrated. It was dangerous to be yourself in 1969.

San Francisco was different in that there were more of 'us' and fewer of 'them.'

Old men wore long grey hair with bald crowns. The campuses were breeding grounds of 'us.' The educational institutions were the focal points of discontent and patriotism.

The streets were mellow and fun. Everyday was like a festival. People here seemed to always behave as if they were at a carnival--or in a carnival. A lighthearted spirit predominated everywhere in this oasis from the Vietnam warring world.

Tom had already visited the intersection of Haight and Ashbury. The hippie seed had germinated there. However, having grown up, all that were left behind were the children with too little vision to sow their own seed or bury their addictions to the past.

Addictions to the past, Tom knew that topic by his own heart's unsettled nature. No one had rekindled the fire that Barbara had left untended for a half year now. It seemed like years ago that Tom had been completely in love and enjoyed the infinite security of a real relationship. Not being able to trust or share completely with anyone was disheartening and hardening. The look in Tom's eyes had even toughened slightly. The relaxed contentment still showed, the sexy warmth was still there, even the boyish charm was still with him, but the constant abrasion of difficult living had calloused him accordingly. Independent aloofness was a way of life and 'no roots' was a fact of life.

It was 2:00 a.m. before the stage was clear and Tom's job was done.

"Tom. We're going to a Christmas party in Berkeley. Wanna come?"

Jack asked.

"Sure. Who's place?"

"Some girls.   It's supposed to be a real happening," Jack said strangely with a lilt in his voice and a tip of his head.

"So . . . what's happening?"

Jack moved closer to whisper more discretely.  "I'm bringing a dozen tabs of 'Aviation Blue' and Silky Sam has some great organic mescaline. The girls are making punch and said we're welcome to spend the weekend."

"The weekend?"

"Yeah," Jack laughed like an old pirate.   With his long beard he looked like one too when he smiled like this.   "Seems that this whole apartment building is full of chicks and the party is gonna be everywhere at once."

"Huh!  Well count me in.  Can I ride with you?"

"I'm not driving but we'll squeeze you in."

Squeeze was hardly the word.   Cram more suitable.   Tom had the habit lately of wearing a leather dark brown western type wide brimmed hat with lacing on its crown.

The weather was too often wet and the hat made walking in the drizzles to and from The Cuckoo's Nest more bearable.   There were four or five people in the front seat so that was out of the question.   The backseat had four girls and one was already on Jack's lap.

"C'mon Tom, the more the merrier," he laughed as he playfully bounced the girl on his thighs.

"Well, perhaps if someone will sit on my lap."

"Lay crosswise," someone in the front seat suggested.

"Yeah!" a couple girls in the back confirmed patting their laps.

Tom took off his hat and stood at attention.  Bending his knees with hands clasped together holding his hat, like a high-diver, he prepared to plunge. The girls giggled at his expected leap headfirst into the backseat. Tom was about to try something as radical as jumping in when he noticed that one of the giggling girls was Nancy from San Diego. He stiffened.

"Maybe I could get a ride with another car."

"Aw . . .c'mon," several girls chided at once.

"Everyone else is long gone," Jack informed.

"C'mon, get in, we don't mind," the girl next to Nancy offered.

Tom gently crawled in over their laps. Nancy was next to the opposite side door so Tom's head was on her lap. He kept his head low and didn't look up. When he was stretched out prone he placed his hat over his head and said, "Wake me when we get there."

"Boy, this is a live one," the girl next to Nancy poked.

"He's been working all night as lightman," Jack tried to substantiate.

"Perhaps he'll get his second wind at our house," Nancy giggled.

'Oh my God!' Tom thought to himself. 'I'm going to Nancy's house. Shit!'

The car drove on with Tom lying across everyone's lap, face covered by his leather wide-brimmed hat.

The apartments weren't in Berkeley but actually Oakland. Most of the tenants attended the university in Berkeley. Somehow most of these students were girls. Tom entered the black iron gates into the apex of this two-story horseshoe. All of the apartments had a front door towards the pool. The second story had a black iron rail all the way around with stairs at each end of the front and one in the rear next to the laundry room. Parking for tenants was in the rear of the building. Blue and green flood lights at the bases of some of the palm trees gave an otherworldly spookiness to this otherwise plain stucco complex. Although it was almost three in the morning, a couple were swimming nude in the pool and music blasted from several different apartments at once. It seemed that almost every apartment was engaged in a party with curtains wide open exposing joint smoking, drinking and dancing.

The girls that Tom had come with huddled into the complex together.

Tom watched where they went on the first floor and thus decided to find a happening on the second floor.

"Tom, where been . . . you?" Jack glurbed.

"Right here man. This is Toni. Toni - Jack."

"Well . . .wow . . .man . . .this is there . . .on . . .the party . . .Down in . . .Great punch . . ."

"Yeah, sure," Tom laughed helping Jack sit down. "Keep an eye on him for me. I'm gonna search for this cup of grail," he told Toni.

"Bring me back one too," she said as he left.

"Okay."

Tom wandered in and out of a couple parties looking for punch and finally found it. Something cheap and childlike... sugar powder and water. Yeah, 'what kind of powders?' Tom thought. He remembered Jack telling him about the acid he and his friend had brought. Tom wondered how much to drink. With a pill it was easier. Divide it in half or quarters. But punch? No one really knew the potency until after it was too late.

Tom filled two paper cups.

When Tom returned upstairs Jack was on the floor closely examining the legs of a wooden coffee table and feeling them delicately as if reading braille. Toni and Tom sat on the couch drinking the "cool-aid" and keeping an eye on their pet dog Jack.

Tom was a veteran of a few dozen acid trips now. He took it as recreation and entertainment. It was like a roller coaster for the optical nervous system. Disorientation and often gruesome images and monsters were a definitely scary part. Sometimes the intoxication affect that accompanied the hallucinations made it harder to tell one's self, 'It's only a movie.' Often people identified or attached themselves to their images. Tom attributed this to a weak self-confidence. Sometimes when he'd look in the mirror and see his own face dripping like a melting candle or bubbling like lava in a volcano, an instinctive panic would jet through his veins and embody itself in a state of fear. Every time this happened however, Tom would click into automatic pilot, Captain Calm. Captain Calm would talk Tom down to a detached bewilderment.

It was as if Tom would separate into three separate realities. The first reality was the state of motion; this is where everyone hangs out in 3-D ignorance, moving from one spot to another or just one minute to another (this is where LSD stoned the body). The second reality was the mental identity; the knowledge or belief of who you are (this is where LSD destroyed time and reality -- Captain Calm was stationed here). The third reality was the soul or spirit; a nameless vagabond hitchhiking inside our body (unemotional and inquisitive).

This third reality was where Tom would view the world from as he stared bewildered through acid lenses, searching for the meaning of life, or a good song.

It seemed that anyone who used LSD regularly would eventually click into these three separate realities. It was necessary to survive some trips. Tom had seen several people "wig-out" on acid. Sure they probably had emotional weaknesses to begin with. But perhaps those weaknesses could have been strengthened or eliminated had they been given proper guidance and lessons in acid travel. Tom knew that LSD had strengthened his self-control and forced him to decide who he was in his own mind's eye.

Tom had tripped with a lot of people and had a lot of fun. As he sank deeper into the couch cushions he started to fear that he would suffocate like falling into the center of a giant marshmallow. Thoughts of quicksand and drowning underwater raced through his mind. Tom's heart was audibly pounding away like a choo-choo train.

Oops. Captain Calm to the rescue.

'Tom you're hallucinating again,' the deep masculine voice commented in his mind.

'Oh yeah!' thought Tom back to himself.

From Tom's new vantage point deep within the couch cushions, Tom could look out and see only the ceiling from his dark marshmallow tunnel. Glimpses of the ceiling were like viewing the moon on a cloudy night. Wispy thin smoke-like steam circled and vibrated, zig-zagged and evaporated as more clouds formed indoors.

'Here we go again,' Tom thought.

Like cold water on an unsuspecting cat, Tom was riveted from this tranquil third reality by sobbing and crying. Tom surfaced from his marshmallow pit like a freight elevator until he was raised high enough to turn his head and look to his left. Toni was crying with both hands clenching her hair. Her mouth hung open, her eyes were agape and tears streamed down her face like a diamond crystal waterfall.

Tom's body was unfortunately made of granite tonight. More of Tom's body was off the couch than on it. Somehow Tom had slid down to where his head was next to Toni's lap and his butt was almost touching the floor.

Tom tried to roll over to his left side and scoot back up onto the couch.

Slow . . .motion . . .strobe . . .light . . .arms . . .of . . .granite cracked and crumbled as they slowly arced over Tom's head. He pushed... with...his...legs...but...his...body...of... stone__ was__ too__ heavy__ to__ push...

So . . .here Tom froze in mid-motion; arm extended upward, body stiff and straight from couch to floor forming a triangular void beneath him.

Toni kept crying, eyes transfixed forward. People in the room began shifting away to avoid the 'vibes' and even the wag-tailed Jack crawled off into another room.

Tom was frozen like a brain inside a stone statue, immobile and powerless, arm still extended upward like an outfielder. No one was helping. People were avoiding them as if they were just irregular hallucinations (ignore it and it'll go away).

Then trumpets sounded loudly and echoed through the cavernous wasteland of Tom's brain. The King's Court, no: the orchestral fanfare of--, no; just two french horns proudly sounding the fox hunt, no; it was a solitary bugle, a call to arms, the cavalry, YES!

The US cavalry in blue. A stampede of horses and sabers drawn coming directly at them. But Tom was an Indian . . .and . . .oh no . . .realized this beautiful war cavalcade was after him. No chance fighting them off, he was outnumbered badly. Tom sprang to his feet like a cat landing on a hot frying pan. His feet were automatically in a gallop though he wasn't moving in any direction. He got his bearings and aimed at the apartment door.

Toni's crying . . . a helpless squaw, to be brutally murdered by a bayonet or trampled under Custer's hooves. NO! He grabbed her in his arms and ran through the panicked tribe knocking bodies like bowling pins. He carried her high along the cliff over the blue-lit lake below. Down the stone ladder and then into the protective seclusion of a dark tipi.

Toni clung to Tom desperately as they huddled in the dark void of hiding. The screaming and roaring of the massacre outside was like ghostly haunted spirits crying.

"Try not to listen to them," Tom comforted. "Try just to imagine pleasant music, pleasant music, pleasant places. Remember something fun to make you feel better."

"Like Disneyland?" she asked, no longer crying.

Tom looked to see if somehow he was with Carey again . . . too dark to see . . . "Yeah. Like Disneyland. I like the Matterhorn the best. How about you?"

"The spinning tea cups."

'Yuck!' Tom thought. He didn't like spinning rides and found drugs like downers that produced that sensation most nauseating.

"Okay, tea cups. How about Mr. Toad's Wild Ride?"

She began to laugh hysterically. "Mr. Toad's Wild--" she broke off into laughter again.

Tom began to laugh also, picturing a frog peddling a bicycle. She laughed and he laughed until their sides ached and Tom got the hiccups.

"Oh--hic--shit! I've got--hic--the hic--hic--hiccups."

Toni looked sadly into Tom's face as if Tom had told her his dog died. Then her frown turned to a smile, the smile to a laugh and they were both laughing to their hearts--"hic"--content.

Toni was still hugging Tom, but now the hug was affectionate instead of fearful.

Tom could feel the roundness of her arms like tubular rubber, soft and squishy. Her legs were tangled with his and he became aware of the heat like glowing snakes. Even her hands began to humm with electrons being absorbed by Tom's skin.

Tom reached his arm behind her and shifted his weight a little. They seemed to be on a shag carpet leaning up against a metal bed frame. It was pretty dark and Tom realized his hand was not behind Toni but inside the back of her dress. Her skin was smooth, warm and charging. His hand was heated and his crotch burned with energy.

He moved his hand around a bit more producing a cooing sound from Toni. She snuggled closer. Tom's other hand found an arm to rub. Tom's crotch burned like a mound of energy. His entire groin area was a fire with desire. Tom's hand rubbed down the length of her arm. He massaged her wrist. He felt her hands clutching. He touched her fingers and tried to figure out what she was holding. Her hand moved up and down bumping his hand off and on the short post. She was stroking the wooden object like a cock. She was masturbating it. Tom was aroused beyond belief. His head was exploding. Areas of his skull seemed to be expanding with helium. His groin was still a raging fire. He wanted Toni and he wanted to have sex with her and he wanted to be inside of her.

He could imagine himself with her, moist and suctioning. He reached down for her hand and found her head, face down, bobbing in his lap. What! She was simulating a blow job! No! He could feel now amidst the raging waterfall current of sexual electricity down there, she was giving him head! That hadn't been a wooden post. That was him! But no, he didn't want to come in her mouth. Tom wanted to be inside of her.

With both hands on her head he lifted her 'noggin' and raised her up to a sitting position.

Passionately he kissed her mouth and at the same time unbuttoned her blouse, unhooked her bra, then lifted her body up onto the bed where he unfastened her pants, pulled off the shoes, pulled off her pants, slid down her panties, hopped out of his own clothes and like two pieces of a puzzle he refastened himself to her game board.

* * *

Bright white twinkles danced beneath Tom's eyelids as he lay asleep atop Toni.

"Look at this!  Hey Becky c'mere and get a load of these two sleeping on my bed."

Becky laughed and covered her mouth realizing Tom and Toni were still asleep.

"Who are they?"

"I don't know," replied Nancy.  "But they're gonna have to get up because I don't feel like sleeping on the couch."

Nancy stepped over the scattered clothes on her way to the bed.  "Hey you two!  Party's over.  Out of my bed."

Tom rolled off Toni and was blinded by the ceiling light.  He covered his eyes.

"It's Toni!" Nancy gasped.

"What?" Becky widemouthed.

Toni squinted her eyes open and suddenly realized she was naked and uncovered.  She sprang up knocking Tom entirely off the side of the brass bed and onto the floor with a resounding thump-crash and exclamation from the half-asleep Tom, "<u>What the?!?</u>"

"Toni, what are you doing?" Nancy asked like an angry mother.

Toni pulled the comforter around her with her knees huddled up against her chest.

Becky began to laugh and Tom achingly raised his head up like a periscope to realize that the sun was rising outside, he'd slept with the frightened girl on the bed, and the bed belonged to none other than Nancy!  And he was stark naked!

Toni was humble, "We slept together."

"Obviously."

"I didn't know it was your bed."

"Sure thing."

"I didn't. Really."

"If you--"

"Hey! Hold on a minute!" Tom barked.

Tom stood up in his naked glory with one hand covering his genitals and the other serving as a visor against the light, and his identity. Tom looked down enough so that Nancy couldn't see his face. He could sense the girls' shock. Good.

"I and Toni had a wild time upstairs with the kool-aid. We came down here because she was a little hysterical. We didn't know whose place it was. I'm sorry for any inconvenience. Now close the door, give us a minute to get dressed and we'll be gone."

Tom could feel Nancy's angry eyes beating down on him. Her footsteps retreated and the door closed firmly.

Toni was still sitting in the middle of the bed huddled in the comforter and looking as sad as last night.

"Hey kid." Tom bent over the bed and kissed her brow. "Let's get dressed and go for some breakfast."

"I'd better go home."

"Ok, but let's get something to eat first. I'm starved."

"I'm not hungry."

Tom was already pulling his pants up. "Here's your blouse," as he tossed it on the bed. Tom put his shirt on and sat on the edge of the bed to put on his socks and shoes. "What's wrong?"

"I'm not a virgin."

"So, I've never slept with a virgin."

"Yes you have."

Tom began to tie his shoelaces as he bent forward. "When?"

"Last night."

Tom paused for a moment and finished dressing. "Now listen to me.

We're getting out now. Let's get dressed, I'll see you home."

"No. You go on. I want to stay and talk to Nancy."

This was depressing. He wanted to cheer her up like last night. Get her to think of happy things and snap her out of this doldrum.

"Okay."

Tom leaned over to kiss her goodbye but she turned her head slightly, leaving only a cheek target. He kissed her cheek. He realized he'd left his hat somewhere, it wasn't in the bedroom. Now he was doubly pissed. How was he gonna conceal his face? Nancy would surely recognize him up this close.

Junipers were visible outside the bedroom window and Tom realized he was on the first floor, fortunately. Tom opened the window, popped the screen out and began to climb out.

"What are you doing?" Toni asked.

"Leaving."

*Dear Mom,*
*I'm writing a short letter*
*To tell you that everything's fine*
*I'm going to be gone*
*For a long, long time*
*I know I'll miss you very much*
*Give my love to all the family*
*And good luck explaining to Dad*
*I'm sorry for my mistakes*
*It's not your fault that it turned out so bad*
*And take good care of my cat and dog*
*My dog, she's probably still waiting for me*
*I won't be home for the holidays*
*My face you may never again see*
*But please, remember I love you*
*I appreciate all those years*
*You spent on me*
*With no return*
*I'm sorry, I really tried*
*So please think of me*
*With good memories*
*Just pretend that I died (18)*

# Chapter Six
## *Green Valley Commune*

The Cuckoo's Nest was packed tonight. Of course, Fridays usually were. Tom was running the lights as Moonchild and Jack held their posts from their balcony perch.

"Man these guys are raw," Jack said with frustration.

"Most LA bands are," replied Moonchild.

"These guys give new meaning to 'garage band.'"

"L.A. is an unhappy town," Moon summarized. "Bitterness in their world. Bitterness in their sound."

Tom broke in between fader moves, "I've heard an L.A. band that's got bite without bitterness," sounding like a TV commercial.

"Probably folk music," groaned Jack.

"No," Tom stated, "they're The Razors. I used to do sound and lights for them. They were spacey, hard, melodic, and really good! I really like them. They did a really cool version of "Gloria" that--"

Both Moonchild and Jack broke out laughing.

"What's so funny?" asked Tom.

"Gloria?" Jack spewed and continued laughing.

"Yeah. "Gloria,"" Tom said defiantly. "They did a version of it that would knock your socks off.

Tom remembered how someone knocked his socks off last time he heard it.

"Message for Tom," piped the waitress as she stuck her head into the sound booth, or crow's nest, as they called it. Jack reached down and took the note.

"A round of beers for us crows," Jack pirated to the waitress as she climbed back down the ladder.

Jack handed the note to Tom.


*Dear Tom,*
*I'm a friend of Toni. She should*
*arrive here later when she gets off work.*
*Becky*


Oh no! The sharks were closing in on him. Toni was a friend of Nancy and so was this Becky. What a mess. They were trying to be friends. Shit, then Nancy would recognize him, his cover blown, Tom would have to . . . Unless he could scare them off. Maybe if he came-on to this Becky they'd all be pissed off at him. After all Toni had been a virgin, and now Tom was holding the golden ring. This Toni probably had a crush and unless he could scare her off, or piss her off, she'd hound him like a lost puppy.

The waitress popped her head up through the floor again. "Three beers," she announced.

"Great!" cheered Jack as he scooped them off the tray. "Hey, how come you don't use the ramp like the other girls?"

"This way's quicker, and I can look up your skirt Jack," she replied with a smile and a wink.

Tom interrupted the foreplay, "Where's the girl who gave you this note?"

"The other side, by the cove. She's alone--wearing a black and white dress."

"I'm gonna make a run when this band's off," Tom told the other guys.

"Hi. I'm Tom."

"I remember," Becky smiled sipping her drink.

"Is Toni upset with me?"

"Upset about what?"

"I don't know. She seemed pretty bummed last time I saw her."

"Oh . . . she's just a little . . . moody. Do you like her?"

"I don't know her."

"You slept with her."

"We were on acid. I took her down to that apartment to calm her, you know . . . The noise and all . . ."

"Yeah. She told us. She said she was balling, I mean crying her eyes out," Becky giggled. "She appreciated your taking care of her."

"And I suppose she appreciated my taking her cherry," Tom said bluntly trying to offend Becky.

"Even if she doesn't, she will." Becky was cool and calm. "We all appreciate it."

"All?"

"Me, Nancy, Sue. We're friends of hers. She's so damn shy she could have been a virgin through menopause."

"Uh . . . where are Nancy, Sue and Toni?"

"Nancy and Toni work together at that restaurant on the wharf. I don't know about Sue tonight." Becky sipped and studied Tom.

Tom started to feel panicked. His stomach got butterflies. How was Tom going to cause enough trouble to scare them off? Nancy was a ticket to jail (do not pass Go . . .).

Tom reached under the table and put his hand on Becky's leg. He expected her to flinch but she remained calm.

Tom slid his hand up her thigh under her short dress. He even had to lean forward a little to accomplish this.

Becky was cute. Very curly dishwater brown hair down to her shoulders. Tom couldn't tell what color her eyes were in the low light as she slowly blinked then smiled.

Wow. This girl was relaxed . . . too cool.

"Wanna smoke a joint?" Becky asked with his hand still massaging her thigh.

"Well, yeah," Tom replied with hesitation.

Tom led the way out the back service door. He had a key so they could get back in.

"I'm parked over there in the lot if you'd rather sit in my car?" Becky suggested.

Tom still didn't have a car. "Sure," he shrugged.

He didn't have much of a plan except that he was gonna come on to her sexually. As blatantly as possible. Hopefully she'd get pissed, slap him, and later tell Toni and Nancy who'd all hate his guts and leave him alone.

Tom and Becky sat in the font seat of her small Japanese shoebox car. Tom liked big cars. 'Coffin on wheels,' he thought to himself. The joint was almost gone. Tom in a rush of bravado leaned over and assaulted Becky with a firmly planted French kiss.

Becky moaned. Tom put his right hand to her breasts and kneaded them roughly. She kissed harder. He pinched her nipples.

"Oh!"

'Oh?' This wasn't working right. Nothing was happening. Or, nothing as Tom had planned it. Becky began to retaliate, she moaned louder and now was rubbing the crotch of his Levi's.

Tom was desperate. He went for shock value. He unbuttoned his jeans and pulled his pants down revealing a half-hard weapon.

Becky pushed Tom back into his seat. Great. She was mad. Or was she? Becky leaned forward and began licking him, and flicking him and . . . oh . . .

Damn. Tom came out here to make an enemy . . . got a lover instead. Tom accepted this tragic defeat like a good sport and undressed her. In full view of anyone who should walk by; they copulated doggey style across the front seats. The Jap-junk-ship bobbed on the black shocky sea; side-to-side-to-side-to . . . in the parking lot.

"Tom, you're late! The band went on ten minutes ago," Jack scolded. "What's the big--"

"I got held up in the back lot. Sorry."

"A girl with a gun I suppose," Jack fumed.

Moonchild glanced at Tom getting into the swing of the performance and laughed angelically. "A girl with his gun!"

Tom ignored both of them as he worked the lights. His mind was banging around trying to sort out his situation. Now he was really confused. Tom kept glancing and looking for them, but they never surfaced. None of the girls bothered him that night.

Maybe his plan worked.

The next night Tom got another note:

*Dear Tom,*

*Want to ride in my car?*

*I'm alone.*

*Becky*


Becky and Tom put more bumps in her import than Mario Andretti had during a year of racing. Of course the wheels never rolled, but the shocks got quite a workout in their trophy quest of the "Frisco 500."

After almost a week of blissful encounters, Tom asked, "Whatever happened to Toni?"

"I told her you weren't interested." Becky rolled over dreamily.

Tom smiled at his cunning paramour. "How'd she take it?"

"Fine. I told her you'd fuck anything on two legs." She hid a smile.

"What about you?" Tom asked with surprise. Perhaps insulted.

"I've got two legs." She rubbed them against Tom's bare . . .

Tom was always thrilled to look over the San Francisco Bay. Despite the presence of Alcatraz prison, Tom felt free--well, at least less nervous. San Francisco was an oasis, a concrete gray fogged paradise, a psychedelic sanctuary. With its pastel painted two-story homes packed together like kipper snacks, they bulged at the street like cozy windowed ripples of residence. Anywhere else this compactness would have seemed crammed and uncomfortable. Not here, it accentuated the closeness of the community.

Becky's car was parked in the lot at Coit Tower. They sat on their hilltop eating fried chicken and enjoying the view.

"There's going to be another bash at those apartments on New Year's Eve."

"I'd rather not," he mumbled with food in his mouth.

"Why not? It should be lots of fun." She smiled mischievously, "Probably be more of that cool-aid again."

Tom continued eating, not wanting to look her in the eye, "I got in enough trouble last time."

"What trouble? You did Toni a favor and I got a chance to meet you."

"Well, I'd rather not see them again, right now."

"What's to see? It's a costume party and nobody's gonna see you if you don't take your mask off." She watched him continue to eat. "Well I'm going, and hope you do too."

Tom didn't want to bullshit her anymore. He'd like to just lay his cards on the table and tell her his life story. She was going regardless. It must have been easier in prehistoric days . . . pull her hair . . . tell her what to do… Plus, he wanted to be the guy who kissed her at midnight.

He exhaled, "Okay." He meant to say, "No way."

"Groovy. I'll get some cool costumes together."

Becky was spending the night at Tom's pad frequently. He avoided her place entirely. Her constant presence was never a nuisance because she was so playful, and knew so many ways to initiate sex; after breakfast, before breakfast, in the bathtub, at night in the parking lot, and even in the middle of the night she'd wake Tom up for a "dream fuck," as she called it.

Becky was a tight companion who didn't cling. Occasionally she'd sense Tom's fear of entrapment and say she'd be busy for a day or two.

She'd left town for Christmas. Her parents lived in Tennessee. He'd missed her, but wouldn't dare admit it. It was the loneliest Christmas he'd ever known.

Her wild smile was like a smart cat; sharp teeth, ready to jump, and ready to be jumped. Tom tried not to get serious, but he always looked forward to seeing her, a.s.a.p.

This was a strange holiday season, he wanted to contact his family. Let them know he was all right . . . Say, "Hi" . . .see someone . . .

Tom had finagled his way out of working New Year's Eve. Becky was excited.

She'd been raving about her costume for days. She even planned his outfit, but kept it a secret from him.

"Time to get into costume," Becky sang as Tom finished the Cornish game hen she'd cooked at his place.

Tom turned around to see Becky dressed in a black police uniform. He dropped his fork.

"Not bad huh? I rented this and yours for only 15 bucks."

"Am I a cop too?" he stuttered.

"Nope," she grinned with sexy mischief. "You're my prisoner."

"Your--?"

"It's in the bedroom," she giggled excitedly. "Now get a move-on or I'll put you under arrest."

Her uniform was complete with holster, badge, and a black officer's cap. Becky wore black stockings and a pair of black riding boots. Black gloves too.

Tom was flabbergasted and thrilled. Becky's dark blonde curls puffed out form beneath her cap and seemed golden against the black collar and shoulders. As he walked humbly past he noticed a pair of handcuffs dangling behind her from the wide gun belt.

On the bed was an old fashioned convict's uniform, white with wide black horizontal stripes. It even included a striped convict hat like in the old movies. Keystone blackout.

"Not bad, prisoner," Becky stated with authority as Tom entered the living room.

"And because you didn't want to be seen I got you a mask," she said holding out a Lone Ranger style black mask by its elastic strap. "I got one too," she said proudly.

When Becky put her mask on, Tom felt flushed with a fearful excitement. Now she was less recognizable, and shapely gorgeous. She was a sensuous Gestapo, a sexual warden, a correctional officer who had captured him; physically, sexually, and emotionally.

Becky flexed sadistically as she enjoyed the newfound role. With Tom's mask on he became depersonalized. He realized how his identity, his own face, were limits to his personal freedom. If only--

"Hands in the air!" she demanded. "Let's see if you're carrying any weapons."

Becky began frisking her prisoner… everywhere. She kneeled in front of Tom and padded his legs from ankle to groin, from ankle to groin, from ankle to… "Hmmm."

"What's this?" she asked patting his pistola.

Tom's pants were held up by a draw string. She pulled out the bow and tugged them down. Tom's boxers were unusually distended. Very slowly Becky slid the light blue cotton down until Tom's revolver sprang out from the waistband like a diving board.

Tom's arms automatically dropped--

"<u>Keep those hands in the air!</u>" Becky scolded as she grabbed his lower trigger finger firmly in her fist. His hands reached for the ceiling.

"Well now," she disciplined. "Prisoner appears a little restless. Perhaps you haven't been getting enough exercise." She toyed with Tom's head (both of them).

"Perhaps you need some extracurricular activities." She backed away slightly. "That's enough for now." Her tone changed to professional. "Prisoners aren't allowed special privileges."

Becky stood up straight-faced. "Maybe if you're lucky I'll get you off... for good behavior."

She smiled wickedly.

Tom didn't smile. He was in the agony of ecstasy--withheld.

\* \* \*

Nancy's apartment wasn't occupied by its tenants. A dozen people milled around or sat on the counters and tables. The rest huddled.

"Lets go in the bedroom."

Tom hesitated. This whole thing was becoming a rerun.

"Hey . . . it's cool. I told you. Nancy said I could spend the night if I wanted to. She has to work late to cover for--"

"Well, I don't really want to. Let's go back upstairs--"

"Tom!" she scolded. "Now I'm in charge and I've planned an exciting evening for us." She pulled the handcuffs out and playfully shook them at him. "Don't make me use force."

Tom was shook up.   Even his own logic was shook.   Too many strange variables here; the costumes, her role playing, the party, Nancy, and being here in her . . . Becky closed the bedroom door.

"Here, take a hit.  And relax," she instructed, holding in her first hash hit.  She passed the pipe.

They sat on the bed and smoked hash out of a briar pipe with aluminum foil wrapped around it.   The pipe had been in the room already, as if it were expecting them.

After a few huge hash hits Becky asked, "How's the punch?"

"If it's spiked I don't feel it yet.  But I'm stoned on the hash."

"Give it a chance," Becky assured with a smile.

They smoked some more.  Tom felt groggy.  "That's enough for me," he confided.  "I'm blasted." He was.

"Good," she smiled crookedly.

Becky put down the pipe and then began to sexually assault him.  She kissed him a lot and was rougher than usual.  She wouldn't let him gain control or touch her back.   She held his arms down and ferociously kissed his neck.  He tried to get on top.

"Lay on your back!" she commanded.

She continued kissing and rubbing.

"I'm starting to feel the acid I think."

"Good."  She chewed and licked his ears.

Tom closed his eyes and was lost in a tube of plasma colors.  Green and yellow blobs wriggled past his head.  White jets of static electricity jumped from glowing red balls of light.

Tom could feel his legs burning like hot metal.  He raised his head up and saw that Becky had pulled his pants down and was licking his thighs. He tried to reach down and steer her head elsewhere but once again his arms were locked, immobile.   He pulled but his joints rattled and clanged.

"Oh . . .Oh . . .please," he moaned in a drunken rapture.

"I'm gonna go for a drink.  I'll be back in a minute," she spoke curtly.

"What?" Tom panicked. "No. Don't leave me . . . just--"

She was gone.

Tom reached to pull up his pants but no use. It hurt his wrists to move. Acid froze his movements. He watched the overlapping color grids gently dissolve into each other below the ceiling. Where was Becky? He was stoned. Stoned and alone. He felt the acid hummmm, that vibrating pulsation of his body mechanics amplified by his increased sensitivity. Ouch! His wrists hurt. He looked up from his prone position on the bed. A brass bed. The headboard glistened and had bouncing white spots on it. And his wrists were bandaged. No not bandages. Bracelets. Chains on the headboard.

'Chains? Wrists? Handcuffs! What the fuck? Handcuffs? No. Ouch!' They hurt. They rattled loudly. 'Damn. Fuck. Why--Becky? No, yes, but . . . she must've. Why? Oh please. God. Where is Becky? What the . . . What was she doing?'

Tom snapped his arm up. Crunch, pain, intense noise. His head pounded. His heart pounded. His feet kicked. Tom flashed policemen. Policemen entering the room.

No. He saw Gestapo women stomp into the interrogation room. The bright light blinded his eyes. He turned away. Boots. Black leather boots. Tall black . . . legs. "No. I don't know anything!" Tom pleaded. They shook their heads in disgust.

Tom remembered seeing Jane . . . raped by a . . . He saw Sid. Sid was laughing. Hiss face close. Bending over. <u>'This was a trap by Sid!'</u>

Tom's heart pounded hard like a piston in his head. This was a death bed. A trap. His chest felt like a huge slab of concrete was laying across him. Hard to breathe. Breathing difficult. Tom gasped for air. Tom was strangulating. He shook and rattled at the handcuffs. Metal bit and dug into the tender skin and nerves of his wrists. Hard bones and soft skin jammed up in pinching metal. The ceiling was lowering down on top of him. A trap. No escape. Tom was still gasping for air. Short bursts, little breaths, need more . . .

'Maintain!' he tried to say to himself. Panic. He struggled. 'Maintain. Got to relax.' Choking. 'Got to escape! Maintain! Breathe slow, deep breaths. Maintain. Got to maintain.' Lungs: stiff and dry.

'It's the acid.  Relax.  Gain control.  I'm just tripping heavily.  Ride it out.  In a while--come down.  Come down, in a while.  All will be okay.  Yeah.  Just ride it out.  Relax.'

'Where did Becky go?  Oh Becky.  Please come back.  Rescue me.'

His mind conversed with itself.    He began to calm down.  'Handcuffed.  By Becky?  No, she wouldn't.  Why?'

'It's just a prank.  Becky got carried away.  Only a party.  Ha-ha… some joke.  Now let me out of here!  Shit.  You're handcuffed man.  Fuckin' handcuffed to Nancy's bed.  Yeah.'

'No.  Oh no.  End of the line.  How you gonna get out of this one?  Your pants are even pulled down.  Hah!  Caught with your pants down!  Naked.  Shit.  Try to laugh.  Half naked, stuck on acid.'

Tom looked down at his striped convict pants bundled up over his ankles.  He shifted, twisted, put his legs up in the air.  Finally, Tom worked his pants back up to a level of semi-decency.

The door opened.  Becky walked in.

"How ya doin' babe?"  Becky asked with genuine concern.

"Hey man!  Take these things off now!  I was like freakin' a minute ago on 'em.  Please!  Now!  I don't dig it!"

"Okay, okay, I'm sorry, really sorry," she whimpered as she used the key.

"Why'd you do that?"  Tom asked sitting up on the edge of the bed and massaging his wrists.  'Uh-oh.  Still acid dizzy . . .'

Becky huddled forward next to him pensively.  "I was gonna let Toni fuck you."

"YOU WHAT!?!"  he yelled.  His voice hurt his own ears.

"Well, I like really stole you from her and all."

"Huh?  Are you out of your mind?"

"You know.  I was supposed to get you interested in her--not me," Becky spoke as she dangled the handcuffs by their chain.

Tom grabbed the cuffs and threw them against the wall.  Ouch ouch ouch that banging sound really hurt!  He turned to her angrily; her features distorted like seeing them in a carnival mirror . . . "I wasn't interested in her to begin with," Tom snapped.

"Yeah. Well she felt bad sometimes. Kinda lonely. So I felt bad and made her a deal." Becky hung her head down.

Tom lifted her head up with his left hand. He could feel his arm repeating and vibrating through the movement over and over and over and over . . .

"What kind of fucking deal?" he asked sternly yet calm.

"Just that," she half-smiled, half-laughed and looked him in the eye. "I was gonna get you wasted and then let you fuck her. Once more."

"Shit!" Tom hissed through a staccato exasperated laugh. "How could . . . so--" he took a deep breath, then exhaled. "So what happened... to Toni?" He felt sea sick. Reality is stranger than acid.

"Oh, she couldn't go through with it. She chickened out in the living room and went back upstairs." Becky touched his arm.

Tom leaned too far and fell against her. She sat him back up. "I'm sorry Tom. I guess I really fucked up." She pulled back.

Tom wanted to comfort her. The pain in his red glowing wrists reminded him he was pissed at her. "And why the fucking handcuffs?"

"I don't know. I didn't plan that. I just happened to have them."

"I hate these things. YOU GOT THAT?!" he yelled louder. "I hate handcuffs. Not cool. I DON'T EVER WANT TO SEE A PAIR OF FUCKING HANDCUFFS AGAIN THE REST OF MY LIFE!!! YOU GOT THAT?!" he yelled, making himself super dizzy. "That was the stupidest thing you've ever done!" Tom swayed a little. "Scared the shit outta me--," he said less loudly.

"I'm sorry," she softly interrupted. "But you know I was almost turned on by the thought of you screwing Toni."

Tom looked at her and tilted his head. She still looked distorted.

"But somehow," she continued, "I felt better about you having your arms and hands immobilized." Becky looked down. "I didn't want you to touch her."

Jealousy had never been a part of their relationship. Both Becky and Tom were free spirits. They went out of their way to prove they weren't jealous of anything. Way too far.

Becky's voice was soft and sullen. "I'm glad she didn't do it . . . and I'm sorry."

She looked up.

Tom felt a new swell of emotion. Probably love. But on acid, swells are swells are more swells and Tom felt a little dizzy again . . . 'Ahoy!'

"I love you Tom."

'Wow!' Big swell again.

She hugged and kissed him.

* * *

"What do you mean you're moving to a commune?" Nancy fumed.

"Well, Tom and I visited this great big commune in Mendocino. It's beautiful. There are trees and forest. They've built a big huge dinner house. There's group activities and parties. Everybody lives off the land. Some are craftsmen . . . a silversmith, there are leather workers. Most of the families are into farming and operating a store where they sell stuff they make--"

"Bitchen!" Nancy bitterly broke in. "You're gonna sleep in a tipi?"

"Some people have tipis. But we want to build a house."

"Tipis?! I was only kidding. This is the twentieth century. People don't live in tipis!"

"It's not bad. People have families and kids there," Becky pleaded.

"Great. You're pregnant, and now you want to freeze to death in a tipi. This doesn't make sense. You're not being responsible!"

Nancy slapped her hands against her thighs and stomped around the room. "You've been seeing this Tom for how many months now?"

"Almost a year."

"Six months," Nancy corrected. "And now you're going off into the wilderness to have a baby."

"A commune."

"And I still haven't even met him."

"You did once," Becky laughed. "I know that doesn't count. But you guys have different schedules."

"Don't give me that again," Nancy scolded. "You got a picture of him?"

"No. I told you. Tom doesn't like pictures. Don't worry. You'll meet him . . . soon."

"Sure! Soon you'll be a billy goat in the wilderness with Tommy Boone and a son named Cheetah!"

\* \* \*

The commune existed within the forest like an ant hive in the forest's backyard. Life poured in and out of the human landing spot. A dozen to twenty kids seemed to always be yelling and screaming like wild parrots--day and night.

But it was beautifully vibrant here, like a pregnant woman (preferably your own wife), here in this rich life giving environment. The forest couldn't be dented, only penetrated. The forest remained unchanged around them. They merely plucked a few rodent fruits, and sifted salads from her dirt dandruffed surface. What wasn't edible, was beautiful; lush fern gardens and wild honeysuckle flowers. (Tom enjoyed plucking these long yellow flower tubes and with his tongue, scoop out what small taste of nectar was possible.)

Erika's first birthday party had really been a circus, but this, her second birthday, was like a children's peace convention. Some of these kids definitely had their own languages. They were foreigners, especially to Tom. They were climbing up the walls, climbing up the curtains, pulling out the records, and not responding, in the least, to his stifled, "Noes," and, "Stop that," and, "Don't," and, "Holy Shit!"

The innocent looks these kids would return seemed all the more realistic when they calmly explained, "Glub-glub-ooogey-ah-ah."

Tom bit his lip to redirect his anguish to a simple pain in the lip. 'Soon this birthday would be over . . .'

Make no mistake, Tom loved his daughter to death; literally. His freedom, his life, his dreams and unlimited potentials were bestowed upon Erika. She was the white pigeon who would escape and never know the fear of Tom's past. Erika was his golden child. In a few years her hair would darken to Becky's beautiful light brown. But now, Erika was a Norwegian import. Two years old this twenty-ninth of October, a couple years into the seventies. Tom and Becky were never without her. Alone or together, neither of them could be with her too much. Erika's love was fertilized fully in this wealth of affection.

Christmas is a strange way to summarize the year, but it does reflect it--at its worst. If the year was a struggle, Christmas was a battle. If the year was lonely, Christmas was suicidal. But Tom was as far from melancholy as Heaven is from Hell. Becky was pregnant again, about four months.

Erika was talking to Daddy, and Daddy was "goo-gooing" back. Erika really did understand more than she could say. Tom talked calmly to her like a miniature adult. Often he expressed his philosophies, his concepts on reality, the meaning of happiness... Even religion was already a topic of conversation when she was only two. Erika's eagle-wise eyes seemed to reflect a confident understanding of everything Tom told his daughter. Tom could only guess what she was saying.

Erika's Christmas present was a beautiful rocking horse. Carved by one of the commune's carpenters, it was a work of art. Not a flat piece of shaped and painted wood with foot pegs. No, this was a wooden pony, in every detail. It was carved to the finest detail, with cream-colored hair and grinning teeth. It smiled in mid stride as it appeared to be hurdling an obstacle. A flying horse, unimpeded by the tallest barrier.

Tom kept this Christmas pony in the attic. It was Erika's surprise, almost two months early. He wanted to give it to her for her birthday.

But he knew that come Christmas, he'd be unable to match this magic horse with another present.

Tom decided the big party was her main birthday present. That was a week ago and it left a heavy hangover. Tom snickered to himself as he remembered the one little kid who'd climbed onto the record player at the party. Spinning around on the turntable he'd even tore the arm off... 'Kids are amazing.'

Becky was amazing also. Her love for Erika deepened his love for her. Watching them play together made him feel so . . .

"Beck, I think I'm gonna go with Bobby to our 'shiny pool' this weekend." He felt like cancelling it and being with her and Erika.

Becky continued washing the breakfast dishes in the pair of washing basins as she spoke, "No Tom, why don't you spend a weekend here. I'd like to go away for a change. I haven't seen any of my Bay-friends, Sue or Nancy, for some time."

Tom continued reading the **San Francisco Tribune**. "Heck Beck! This commune life is getting more like a factory that a retreat."

"Now Tom," she paused, trying not to repeat any previous arguments, "You have a family, and that requires a lot of work."

"Yeah. I'll stay home with the kids, you go get a job." He was comical but sincere.

"Tom, I'm pregnant."

"Then we'll demand twice your hourly wage."

"Tom--"

"Becky!" Tom bent over the newspaper on the table. He didn't notice part of it in his bowl of shredded wheat as it soaked up milk. "I don't believe it!" he exclaimed.

"The Razors are playing The Cuckoo's Nest."

From the kitchen Becky asked unconcerned, "Isn't that the band you always rave about?"

"You bet! And I'm gonna go. You wanna come too?"

"Oh Tom, that does sound fun." Becky looked out the kitchen window. "The neighbors'll take care of Erika."

Becky thought of Nancy, "And you'll finally get to meet--"

"Hey Becky, what's today's date?"

"Look at the paper."

"Saturday, November fourth."

"And today's Tuesday--"

"Well, that makes today November seventh."

"Brilliant Tom."

"Hey, today's election day, isn't it?"

She sounded bored. "Yes Tom."

"Becky are you voting?"

"Tom, you're the one who refused to register. I registered--"

"Yeah, I know. But since you're voting I'll help you out. Okay . . . Now if a picture tells a story then this guy… No not this one either . . . Wow! These guys are all geeks!"

Tom studied the newspaper pictures. "This guy's ugly… Another long nose… Forget him . . . Shit! That leaves Pinocchio!" Nixon smiled up at Tom.

Tom reflected on his old buddy Daniel. Dan and Dick had one thing in common, a ski jump. Tom wondered what ever became of Daniel. Nancy probably knew. Sometimes he wanted to talk to her. Nancy was always protector of the underdog. She was like one of the guys. Tom remembered when she drank tequila the first time and got sick--

"He has finally got us out of Vietnam," Becky informed as she walked in from the kitchen.

"Hold it, this ad says they're playing November seventh, that's tonight!" Tom stood up spilling his cereal. "C'mon Beck, let's go!"

"I'll meet you in the parking lot." Becky threw the dish towel across the room at him.

Tom watched her denim derriere dance into the bedroom.

"Go see if the neighbors'll take Erika," she shouted unseen.

* * *

The same doorman.  Tom liked that about The Cuckoo's Nest.  It was a family business.  Nobody was related, but they were a family operation.  Jerry, the manager, was like Humphrey Bogart, great tough guy in the movies, but for a dad he was a little too calloused and hard-nosed to get close to.  But he kept this family together, and they prospered.  Moonchild and Jack were still working there, the doorman said.

"Tom, where's Mother Earth?" Jack asked with outstretched arm.

"She's here."  They shook.  "She's calling her old friends."

Moonchild shook Tom's hand.  A long shake.

Jack interrupted, "Heard you got another one comin'."

"She's four months pregnant."

"Great!  And I heard Erika's birthday party was a real smash."  Jack laughed.  "Got a new turntable yet?"

'Jack was amazingly well-informed,' Tom thought.  Tom turned from Moonchild's brotherly eye-lock.  "Jack, how'd you know--"

Jack laughed his pirate laugh some more.  "I've been seeing Nancy."

Tom's breathing stopped.

"She's always complaining about Becky disappearing and--"

"Shit Jack, we didn't disappear.  We're just . . . just . . . a little--"

"Remote," completed Moonchild.

"Uh . . . yeah.  Hey it's great.  Tucked away and removed from the--"

"Sounds like you've found peace of mind," Moon commented.

'Peace of mind?'  Tom thought of Jack dating Nancy from San Diego.  'So that's how he knows whenever he farts or sneezes.'  Nancy called occasionally.  Fortunately, only one visit.  Tom went fishing.

"Sit down," Jack motioned.  "Help with the lights.  Oh . . . by the way, Tom, this is our new lightman, Fred."

Tom and Fred shook hands.  Tom could see Fred, but he wasn't really

Fred.  Tom could see . . . of course!  Fred was an alias.  Shit bad choice Bub, or whatever your name really is.  Heck.  You don't even look like a Fred . . . Oh well, nice guy though… another underground life . . .

"Hey Fred.  Take a break.  Tom'll handle the next set."

Fred left.  The cycle continues . . .

"Old times," Tom said as he put his hands on the board, before he sat down.

"No such thing," Jack mumbled.  Tom didn't hear him.

"You're still pretty good," Moonchild complimented in his restrained manner.

"This place misses you."

"Tom, maybe you shouldn't be here--" Jack stopped himself.

"What?" Tom asked as he swung faders for the opening act.

"Ah . . . I can't say," Jack finalized.

"Jack, you on drugs?"  Tom smiled but didn't look towards Jack.  Tom danced the stage lights as the band played.

"You really happy Tom?" Jack asked meekly.

"Hell yes!" Tom confirmed.

"Then perhaps not all opportunities are golden opportunities."

Tom laughed, "What are you trying to say Jack?"  Tom laughed some more.  He felt good.  "Jack?  This next band is that band I told you about a long time ago."

"I know," Jack deadpanned.

"Yeah?  Well, these guys are excellent."

"They have a musical force," Jack deadpanned.

That one hit Tom strange.  Not the kind of enthusiasm he'd expect. "Jack?"

"Yeah?"  Jack boosted the guitar player for his solo.

"How were they for soundcheck?"

"I told you."

"What do you mean, they had musical farts?" Tom laughed loudly.

"That's not what I said!" Jack defensively overreacted.

Tom laughed. "Oh-kay. You'll see. Can I run the lights for them?"

Jack thought. No, Jack wasn't thinking. Jack knew. "What about our lightman Fred?"

"Fred Shmed, that guy's--" Tom laughed at himself now. "Hey Jack."

"Yeah?"

"Jack you're like my father sometimes." Still chuckling to himself, "You knew I was coming tonight, didn't you?"

"Yes."

"Then why you being so weird?"

"Your friends."

"What friends?" 'Shit,' Tom thought. 'I don't have many friends except--'

"The Razors. I smoked with them."

Tom was chuckling again. "Well, Jack. I'm gall-derned proud of you!"

"Tom, the boys are good boys, but they're very alone now."

"Alone?" 'Man, this Jack was a character. Hard not to laugh at him sometimes.'

"Tom, they ride a black horse."

"Jack, you priestly pirate you, I can't make hide nor hair of what you're saying."

Tom was happy to be back. He loved this job. He was happy, like on shrooms. He still chuckled, "Jack, you been smoking hair?" Tom burst out laughing some more.

Jack remained frozen, emotionless. "Tom, things are going really good out there on the commune, right?"

"Jack, I think you're getting too old to be smoking--"

"Tom, I'm not toying with you. For all the medicine we shared, you know the nature of the pipe, the friendship of the smoke... You know how to see!"

Tom nodded. Jack was serious. Way serious.

"Tom, those boys are courting big trouble.  Sure, big success too, but they're junkies, cold . . . and alone.  They don't speak for themselves anymore, not as persons, they--"

"Jack, that's ridiculous.  Sure they party hard and do drugs.  So do we. I don't know where you're going with this . . . but I'll see for myself."

Jack adjusted the faders and watched the stage.  "I hope so."

Tom was back in the swing of it again.  Running the lights was fun. Hell, there wasn't much money in it, but you do get to be part of the show.  The first band was tearing down, the second band setting up.  Tom ran backstage to see The Razors.

The dressing room door was closed.  Tom raised his hand to knock . . . He smiled with self-assurance and just walked right in.

"Hello guys!" Tom trumpeted.

Jim looked up from his guitar as he tuned it.  "Holy Moly!  TOM!"

Hearing this, Gordon peered out from the bathroom half dressed. "Tom!  YOU'RE ALIVE!"

Jim stood with guitar in one hand and approached warmly for a handshake.

"Tom, this is great!  What happened to you?"  They shook.  "We thought you were dead.  Carey was really upset-- for a long time."  Jim's voice lowered, "You should've called or something."

"Yeah, I know.  I was pretty banged up."

Barry and Russell walked into the dressing room.

"Look guys!" announced Jim, "It's Tom!"

Barry looked at Tom with that same old microscope glance.  He studied Tom disdainfully.

Russell pushed in for a handshake.  "Tom, Tom.  We really thought you bit the big one.  Where you been?"

Russell was thinner now.  His eyes darkly rimmed.  Tom felt good as Russ smiled and eagerly shook his hand.  Yeah, he was till a hype.  But the rest of the band seemed okay.

Tom spoke quick, "I've got a kid, Erika, she's two now, gorgeous and smart too.  And my woman, Becky, she's pregnant again.  We live on a commune north of here, in the Redwoods."

Barry silently watched Tom as if he were taking notes, mentally.

"I hear you guys are doing real good," Tom complimented.

Gordon walked in from the bathroom, putting on his shirt. He was thin before, now he was skinny. His white skin seemed whiter as he buttoned up his black shirt hurrying over to greet Tom. He jumped a guitar case and landed in front of Tom.

"Wow, now I do believe in ghosts!" They shook hands very dramatically. Gordon tried to complete it with a "soul handshake" but Tom didn't know it. They slapped hands like teammates. "Why the Hell'd you disappear like that?"

Tom just smiled. "Incidentally boys," Tom informed like a mock schoolteacher with outstretched arms quieting the class, "I've worked lights in this club for a long time and I'm looking forward to electrifying you Razors tonight."

Gordon let out a series of cowboy yips and yells.

"Great!" Jim grinned. "Sit down and we'll get you in the mood." He pulled a partially burned joint out of the ashtray and lit it with his cigarette.

Tom was totally wasted as he floated back to the sound booth. The second band was finishing its set and Tom plugged an ear as he walked in front of the P.A. speakers.

He walked around the dance floor, which was packed with dancers, and looked up to the sound booth.

'Shit! Nancy was up there, with Becky. Fuck! Now what?' He felt pinned in. He didn't want to run. The crow's nest was his domain and he felt more imposed than nervous . . . or maybe just too stoned to be scared. Tom leaned forward. Like a drunk stumbling home, he knew this confrontation was inevitable. But not now, he just wanted to have fun and be a Razor. Well, if he was gonna confront her, he didn't want to make a scene in front of everybody . . . Maybe he could still keep it under wraps . . . even from Becky . . .

The grass buzz kept his mind churning . . . He had to get her alone . . .

The waitress popped her head up the ladder trap door into the sound booth. "A note for Becky."


*Dear Becky,*
*Wait for me in the sound booth.*
*Send Nancy down to the bar. I've got a*
*surprise for her.*
*Love you,*
*Tom*


"Oh that Tom, always playing secret agent man," complained Becky with a smirk. "He wants you to meet him at the bar Nancy, alone."

Nancy looked quizzically back at Becky. "What does he even look like?"

"You know . . . He's shaved his mustache, but he's got dark brown hair down to--"

"Oh I'll find him," Nancy cut off impatiently. She tromped down the ramp towards the bar.

Nancy circled the bar. Tom stood back waiting for the right moment. There wasn't one. He just pushed himself forward and approached from behind her.

"Hello Nancy," he said over her shoulder.

She turned, "Well hello Tom. Tom? Tom!" Nancy's cold expression went from icy to electric shock. "You're Tom Calder. Tom from--"

"Shh--" Tom hissed as he reached out and steered her by the arm away from the bar. "Yes, and no one but you knows."

Nancy couldn't take her eyes off him as they pushed through the crowd. "But you're not Tom, Becky's husband?"

He wanted to get this over with. "Yes, I'm Becky's husband, Erika's father--" he stopped and turned her toward him, "--and your friend."

"I don't believe it!" She tried to laugh but she wasn't happy about this at all.

"You're still wanted for—"

"Shit Nance, keep it down!" he hissed. "I've started a new life. A good life. That's all behind me now. Don't blow it for me." Tom paused. "I'm tired of trying to avoid you. I recognized you here before I even spent the night with Toni."

Nancy was still retabulating events and filling in missing pieces as she spoke,

"Then you've been . . . man . . . Tom I don't know what to think—"

"Nancy, nobody knows. Nobody. I want to keep it that way." Tom's eyes penetrated her. He was speaking to an old friend somewhere behind her confused glaze. "Can you keep it from Becky too?"

Nancy thought. With a still-puzzled look she nodded.

The band finished playing and were leaving the stage.

Tom felt more conspicuous about talking without the loud music. "Good. I'll fill you in later. Let's get back to the booth."

Tom kept his hand touching her arm or shoulder as they zig-zagged back to the sound booth. He was trying to reassure her. Nancy was thinking, and thinking . . .

* * *

"Becky, it's only a month. They're already part way done with the tour. It'd be great. I'd love to go. Ah, Becky come on."

Tom sounded Erika's age.

Becky solemnly continued folding the laundry. As she silently contemplated and folded a red towel; Tom flashbacked to Rex's military funeral . . . They gave Jane a folded flag.

"I hope you're back when I give birth.  I would--"

"Becky!"  Tom shouted gallantly.  "I'll be back before Christmas. You're not due until next spring!"

"I wish you'd stay home."

Tom walked up and over to Becky.  She continued silently folding clothes.  Tom embraced her from behind.  She pretended to ignore him. He hugged her, bent over, so his chest pressed against her back. Gently, he rocked and hugged her.  She swayed with him.  He pressed tighter, his groin into her seat.

"I love you Becky.  I love you."

She was hugging her towel, "I love you Tom," she spoke sadly.

"Good," Tom moaned.  And then in a sudden flurry, as if struck by lightning, he began to "bunny-hump" her as he laughed and held her hips.  She laughed and they rolled over into the laundry and unfolded blankets.  Fully dressed, they kissed and rubbed all over each other.

\* \* \*

*Now here, before your eyes*
*I stand outside,*
*A separate life*
*The guttered rivers through your city*
*Always return, to the poisoned lake*
*I am, I am (19)*

The **LA Times** has its highest circulation on Sunday.  The best reason for this Sabbath popularity is its *"Calendar Section."*  Since L.A. is an entertainment community, the *"Calendar"* caters to not only the movie industry but literature and the music scene.

Sid set the spread-eagled *"Calendar"* on the glass table.  Sullen and consumed in thought he walked to his veranda of his twenty-sixth floor condo dressed in a grey robe and terry shorts.

The view was splendid, a harbor full to its brim with white and blue sailed boats of all sizes. Sid didn't have a boat, although on occasion he'd rent one if an assignment or a project required it.

Sid rubbed his leg where the broken samurai sword had left a scarred depression on both the front and back of his leg. He walked to the bookcase and pulled out a book which had a white envelope taped behind the cover flap. Emptying the photos on the table he selected a couple newspaper photos of Tom. Sid placed the pictures side by side with a small space between them over a "Calendar" photo of The Razors, backstage, so that only one face was between Tom's photo clippings. Sid grinned to himself as he confirmed that the face in the Sunday paper was indeed Tom.

The caption beneath the picture read: *Razors Raid The Henhouse in Chicago. Shown backstage with members of the entourage are bluesman Jack Dempsey and local D.J . . .*

\* \* \*

Milwaukee, Detroit, Chicago, Philadonia, St. Roosey . . . the cities blurred together.

Holiday Inn, Ramada Inn, Howard Johnson's . . . Hotel room to taxi cab, to stage, to soundcheck, to dinner, to hotel to stage to taxi... A nightly circus with four electric priests; a sermon, a chant, a celebration, a party, a loudness that echoed through the concrete and metal of gymnasiums, amphitheaters, small clubs and even the hotel rooms where impromptu jams would bring the hotel managers running... Taxis and rent-a-cars, occasionally a limo--whenever the record execs were attending--became part of this American rock 'n' roll whirlwind.

Drink . . . party . . . smoke . . . party . . . eat . . . swim . . . drink . . . then when you were either too stoned to dance, or stripped by a stranger . . . crash . . . ahh sleep . . . then that fucking tour manager would be banging on the door: "WAKE UP."

Tom envisioned himself a minuscule ant feeding the queen bee as he loaded up the tour bus.

* * *

The flat plains were golden waves of grain in all directions. The bus jetted down the parted waters on its straight black track like a jet powered caterpillar on God's living room carpet. The brown and black bus was not like an ordinary school bus by any means. It had a bathroom and kitchen, fewer seats and room to move. It was two o'clock outside and hot as Hell. Inside the bus, time didn't exist and the climate of the space capsule was controlled by modern science.

Jim was all wired up with nowhere to go. They'd played every card game imaginable, told every joke umpteen times and heard every story worth telling... Jim decided he needed some exercise--or his heartbeat just plain wouldn't allow him to remain seated any longer. Running from the driver to the back of the buss afforded a seven yard sprint. Before long he and Barry had a series of races and bets going as they'd run the center of the bus and crash into the rear where they stacked up pillows and luggage to soften the splash-down. Bets were waged and friendly wrestling at the finish line got everybody huffing.

"Hey," Jim panted, "let's run a real relay. Let's get Sam to pull over and we'll run a relay along the highway."

"You bet!" Barry puffed with his white dry tongue. "Then at least we can get up to full speed."

"Yeah."

"Great!" Tom agreed.

"Sam!" Jim shouted to the front, "Pull over."

"Pull over," chorused Gordon and Tom.

Sam panicked, "Why? What's wrong? Somebody sick?"

"Okay boys. With our roadies, Frank and Tom, we've got two three-man teams."

"Sam, our beloved tour manager," Jim paused for a deliberate scowl, "is gonna be the checkered flag. Each runner must go around the drumsticks we stuck in the ground, then back to his team. The next runner must wait until he's been passed the stick before he runs." Jim looked around and emphasized, "Got that? You have to wait until you've got the stick before you run."

"What if you drop the stick?" Gordon took a big swig from his beer can.

"Well," Jim laughed. "Considering they're your sticks and how often you drop them onstage... I'm glad you're on their team."

Gordon didn't laugh with his teammates as they patted him encouragingly on the back.

"Remember," Jim finalized, "losers load and unload all the equipment for the rest of the week."

Unfortunately for Tom and Jim they had Russie the junkie on their team. He wasn't athletic at all. His fingers did the walking. They had him go first. Barry started the other team off to a long lead. Jim went next and closed the gap a bit. Tom and Frank were in the best shape, partly due to their physical duties of loading and unloading the equipment every night. They went last as their teammates cheered them on. Now that they were all done snorting lines, they shuffled out of the bus and lined up in the same order for the real relay race.

The prairie sun and passing cars gawked at this human spectacle. Jim's long blonde hair streaked behind him as he ran straight at Tom. They were losing so far.

Frank and Tom ran last against each other. Frank had a head start on Tom. The Razors roared their encouragement for both the relay runners. As Tom U-turned around the upright drumstick he slid sideways on the dirt and gravel roadside shoulder. But he kept upright like a surfer doing a cutback and began treading his feet like a race car burning rubber. Frank was quick though and still in the lead.

Tom's great turnabout closed the gap and had him only a few feet behind Frank. Tom could hear the cheers and shouts like indiscernible echoes. The sound of his breathing created an immediate awareness of only his body and the commands he imposed upon it. Tom strained to run faster but seemed to bog down into slow-motion with resistance from all of his muscles. When they were halfway to the finish line he remembered that Jane had always said relaxation is the key to speed and power. So Tom tried to relax instead of strain. It was immediately marvelous. Tom felt like he was on a smooth shiny train track and the air whistled loudly in his ears. Gliding with lightweight steps his stride seemed longer, easier, and faster. They crossed the finish line at full snort. Tom won by a half-foot margin.

Jim grabbed Tom in a bear hug. Tom was surprised and stunned. He'd run faster than ever. An unlocked secret. How much of his life, he wondered, had been inefficient because of straining instead of relaxing?

* * *

Tom was happy to be home at the Green Valley Commune. Only a couple of days until Christmas. In the communal recreation and dining lodge was a twelve foot Christmas tree. The fifty foot long A-frame ceiling could accommodate the evergreen only in the centerline of the room. At one end of the rec. room was a huge fireplace, at the other end the entrance and exit doors, separated by a very large service table. The tree had been decorated by everyone in the commune and stood proudly near, but not too close to the fire place. Between the tree and the doors were three long dinner tables.

During this time of the year everyone preferred to eat together for dinner. The dinner committee organized the contributions and delegated the cooking. It was a lot of fun eating together like a forty-one piece family. The tables were pretty long, seating over twenty each. The third table was occupied when visitors and relatives attended.

Becky was beautiful in a way Tom had never seen her before. Bearing a child had metamorphosed Becky into a new woman somehow. Her features were distinctly sculpted. Her sensuality was deeper and richer. Even her character was more controlled, and mature. Communication between them was relaxed and coherent. They sensed each other's needs and changes of mood before the detours were passed. As Tom ate lunch next to Becky in the lodge he wished he was sitting across from her so he could get a better view of her. He put his hand on her thigh as he ate. He remembered that first night he touched her.

He felt lucky. He didn't worry about the future. He didn't have to. He'd found his future.

A knock on Tom's cabin door interrupted the hot tea he was sharing with Becky as Erika ran around the room with Tom's fishing net.

Their neighbor, Bob, proudly announced his guest, "Tom, this reporter here is doing a story on our commune. He wants to take pictures of each cabin and--"

"Sorry but we don't--"

"Oh that sounds nice Tom," Becky spoke from beside the potbelly stove.

The journalist looked over Bob's shoulder for a better look at Tom.

"Sorry. Just take a picture from the outside." Tom scowled at Becky.

"Tom. Why not? Let's be in the picture too." Becky walked to the door.

"Cool it Becky. You know I don't like pictures taken."

The journalist stood on his tiptoes and raised his camera.

"Sorry guys." Tom shut the door as Becky tried to stop him.

Bob and the photographer could hear Tom and Becky arguing as they stepped off Tom's porch. The photographer took several pictures of Tom's cabin.

Tom packed up his fishing gear and backpack.   Good thing he'd planned to go fishing, this arguing made the house too uncomfortable. He kissed Becky goodbye, on the cheek, and headed out the door earlier than he'd planned.

That night Becky visited Bob's wife, Alice.   Jesse and Audrey were also over and they played a variety of card games.   Her mind was on Tom.   They rarely argued, and it felt especially strange to be away from each other, on bad terms.   She decided to make tomorrow's Christmas Eve dinner at home, instead of with the rest of the commune.

'Yeah, when he came home tomorrow, she'd surprise him with a great dinner and a special dessert.'

Becky's romantic imagination was pulled away as Alice repeated her question, "Becky?  Anyone in there?"

"Oh, I'm sorry, I was thinking of something else.   Uh, whose turn is it?"

"Jesse just won.  You all right?"

"Yeah, I'm fine.  Uh--"

The other card players giggled as Alice repeated her original question, "Becky, Jesse suggested we play poker, you have chips don't you?"

Becky laid down her cards.  "Sure, I'll go get them."

* * *

Tom and Bob lay in his truck camper on separate beds with a propane lamp between them.  Rolled up in their sleeping bags they wriggled like cutworms as they talked.

"What magazine was that photographer from Bob?"

"I don't know."

"Well, what magazine is the story going to be printed in?"

"He said that he was a freelancer and that a couple different publishers were, 'vying for the story.'"

"Did he say which two?"

"No, he said that he wasn't privileged to say until it was settled."

'Huh,' Tom thought.

"He asked questions about you too, Tom."

"Really?"

"Yeah. Maybe more than about anyone else."

"You teasin' me Bob?"

"No. Really. When you didn't let us come in he was very interested in where you were from and stuff."

Tom sat up in his sleeping bag. "What'd you tell him?"

"Well, I told him San Francisco, but I didn't know where you were born. And he asked about that band you went on tour with."

Tom felt nervous. Real nervous. Coincidence or danger? Tom was too deep in thought to even hear Bob, who was still talking.

"Hey Bob, I've got a funny feeling. I want to go back now."

Bob laughed. "Tom, don't be paranoid. Let's go back tomorrow afternoon, like we--"

"Bob," Tom said with cold authority, "I'm not gonna argue with you. We're going back now!"

\* \* \*

Becky opened the unlocked front door and walked into her house. A couple of lights were on so Becky walked straight to the hall closet and got the rack of poker chips off the top shelf. She was just about to leave when she noticed the bedroom curtains moving in the night breeze. Deciding to first close the window, she walked into the bedroom carrying the poker chips.

Becky pulled down the window and turned to leave. She'd left her daughter, Erika, back at Alice's' house where she was playing cards. Still, it felt strange to see her bed empty. It gave Becky a weird feeling in her stomach. Being pregnant was starting to make her more emotional. She missed Tom. She decided to get Erika's parka for when she had to carry her back home, later tonight in the cold Christmas air.

Becky opened the folding closet doors exposing Sid with a gun pointing at her.

He smiled.

* * *

"Tom, I'm going as fast as I can." Bob pleaded.

"Pull over, I'll drive," Tom snapped angrily.

"Damn it Tom. Cool it! It's my--"

"Fuckin' pull over Bob I can't take this piddling along!"

"Tom you're really freakin'. What's the--"

"All right Bob," Tom spoke with obvious restraint. "I'd feel a whole lot better if you'd let me drive." Tom gritted his teeth to suppress his anger and impatience.

"Please," he asked like a polite monster.

Bob was frightened by Tom's *'Jekyll and Hyde'* transformation. He pulled over and Tom took the wheel. Bob was even more frightened now by Tom's driving. Tom drove the truck and camper like a vampire racing the sunrise.

It was still dark when Tom skidded the camper into the commune's dirt parking lot. Tom left his fishing gear and ran straight to his cabin. The door was wide open and people were gathering outside.

"Tom!" Alice shouted.

He ran straight past her and into the house. He knew something was wrong. Oh God. Something. He ran to the bedroom.

Blood on the walls. Blood on the bed. Blood on the floor. No Becky. Oh God.

He turned to see Alice crying.

"WHERE'S BECKY? he yelled.'

Alice sobbed uncontrollably. Tom grabbed her.

Softer, he hissed through his teeth, "Where is--"

She pointed at the bathroom. Tom's heart stopped. 'No. No! NO!'

A sopping red bed sheet hung from the curtain rod. It still dripped blood on the edge of the tub. The rod bent under the weight of Becky's dismembered body. A handcuff dangled from the body bag.

"Where's Erika?" Tom asked in such a calm voice that he really scared Alice.

Bob entered the bedroom as Alice answered, "She's still . . . at . . . our place." She had trouble talking as she hiccuped from crying. "She's--"

Tom trotted out and over to Alice's and Bob's house. His steps were mechanical. Firm, quick, solid, like a robot.

A half dozen people were huddled with their children. Tom plucked Erika from them as they all watched him in silence. No one knew what to say and Tom's expression was cold and blank.

Bob caught up to Tom as he was getting into Becky's little import. "TOM! Tom, where you going? They called the police, they--"

"Bob," Tom started the engine, "I have nothing to say to the police and there is nothing left for me here. Don't tell them anything that might lead them to me." Tom finally looked at Bob, then at Erika who was playing with her seat belt. "Bob, he was after me. Don't give anyone any clues about me. Please."

Tom and Bob had been friends a couple years now. They fished together and understood each other pretty well. Although he didn't understand what was going on now, he reached out his hand through Erika's passenger window. They shook.

"Good luck Tom."

Tom drove off. Fast.

*Take me to a wishing well*
*Put a penny in my hand*
*Put the dreams that follow me*
*Back in -- my command*
*Quit at the junction of*
*The train's smoky gate*
*Blackness has captured you*
*You -- stayed too late*
*Half a dollar bill*
*Is all I've got*
*Half a dollar bill*
*Half a wish bought (20)*

# Chapter Seven
## *Underground Railroad*

Fuck. Fuck the news. Fuck the press. Fuck the President. Fuck the Governor. Fuck the system. Fuck education. Fuck politics. Fuck protest. Fuck freedom. Fuck sex. Fuck the laws. Fuck leadership. Fuck the establishment. Fuck trust. Fuck the Pigs. Fuck money. Fuck ownership. Fuck war. Fuck guns. Fuck violence. Fuck talking. Fuck demonstrations. Fuck prison. Fuck . . . A hate mantra. Free sex gone sour with freedom as a side dish, if you can afford it.

SDS, Hippies, Panthers, Yippies, Weathermen, countless undergrounds, countless movements, countless riots, countless arrests, countless deaths. The war is here. Amerika is a battleground. The CIA are here. The FBI are there. The police are everywhere. The courts are laundromats where invisible suit and tie lobbyists wash their laundry of the unkept youth. Justice is a word--like communism. Hope has matured into hate. Love is something you do where no one can see you. Survival is a way of life. Activists are over 30 and their audiences are tube viewers. Social consciousness is carnival game show reruns. Head bashing is a police sport.  Your name is on file.  You may be a contender. Revolution has been pushed off the street into the urban underground. Once again, guerrillas stalk the jungles of the cities.   Reagan has declared war.  Nixon has declared victory.  No one has declared peace— and lived.

"Wow Tom, you've really made the news!"

Tom shrugged back into the worn out mottled brown easy chair.  He wanted to sink into the puffiness of the cushions and be shielded from view.  Forget . . .

"Tom, listen to this."

Tom didn't want to listen.

She continued, "Tom Calder is also being sought in two other murders; one in Malibu, and one in San Diego.  And listen to this, there's a $50,000 reward just for information leading to your arrest."

Tom sat up in his chair.

"And, this Senator McLean says you represent, now get this, 'the bad apple of today's youth.'  He says you're a 'menace to society.'"  Corporal Kennedy chuckled in astonishment.  "Tom, this guy doesn't like you." She laughed.

"Did you say Senator McLean?"

"Yeah.  You know him?"

Tom rubbed his face as if splashing water to wake up.  "Met him." Tom thought but his logic was bouncing against a red brick wall.  The room they sat in, the living room of the safe house was strewn with newspapers, magazines, food wrappers and empty soft drink cans.  Tom shifted his weight, the soft easy chair was so soft it was more like a bean bag with arms, and just as hard to get out of.

"Hey, how 'bout this?!"  Corporal Kennedy asked with excitement. Her only excitement seemed to be in someone else's demise.  "Half the reward is being put up by him man.  Wow."

"By who?"

"This Senator McLean.  He's putting up half the reward to catch you." She chuckled a bit more.  "Man Tom, I don't think politics is your cup of tea."

'Shit. What did this dyke know about what's good for herself.' Tom looked with contempt at her. She had unevenly hacked multi-blonde hair. It looked like she was attacked by a helicopter and her hair was still being sucked upward into the rotors. And those geeky old granny glasses. Not even Granny would look good in those. The pink glass frame was the only hint of femininity she exhibited.

"Let me see that." Tom reached for the paper. His foot landed squarely in an open pizza box. Tom's butt was held to the chair cushion like a drain plunger in full suction. "Damn it, let me see that!"

Corporal Kennedy wasn't done reading, but Tom looked like a ferocious octopus wriggling out of the chair . . . Not to be argued with. She passed the paper to him.

Tom kicked the empty pizza box across the room as he sat back with the paper.

"Where does it say this Senator--"

"Back on page one."

Tom flipped angrily back to the cover of the newspaper. His own photo looked up at him. Fuck. His photo on the cover of the newspaper. Shit, they probably got that picture from his mom.

"Tom, you're gonna have to really lay low."

Captain Truman walked into the room. "And that's what I've got to talk to you about Tom," his Texas accent sounding both authoritarian and cartoonish.

Tom folded the paper in half, covering his cover picture.

"Tom," continued Captain Truman, "we're not only an underground railroad, we're also a revolutionary group. We live at high risk already. You're an incredible risk for us. Draft dodgers and bail runners are one thing, but you're front page now!"

"Man I'm sorry, " said Tom with head hung.

"Hey! Nothing to apologize to me for. But you're too recognizable and--"

"Hot!" added Corporal Kennedy.

Tom sneered at her gleeful expression and turned to Captain Truman,

"Fuck man, I told you that I'm not the murderer, I'm-"

"Hey! Calm down." Captain Truman approached and patted Tom on the shoulder.

"You've told us all that and we all trust you. So that speaks for itself."

"Well, I just want you to know--"

"Save it for court," Captain Truman mused.

"I ain't goin' to court!" Tom announced loudly. "They'd never give me a fair trial."

"Well, we'll get you to Canada, but you could be extradited. This is a heavier rap than AWOL or card burning."

"Anywhere is better than here."

Captain Truman took that comment a bit personal and replied coldly, "Well you'd better start liking it a whole lot more here. From now on you're not going outside."

Tom pivoted in the plush chair towards the Captain. "What do you mean?"

"Tom you're too hot to be outside. You're a security risk."

"Hey man. I'm a fugitive but I'm still a free man."

"No Tom, you're a wanted man. You're a marked target. It's open season on you."

"Wrong. Until I'm caught, I'm free!"

Captain Truman stood up from leaning against the window sill. "I want you to stay away from the windows at all times. The lace is to always be closed so no one has a clear look inside. Don't want no telephoto photos taken of us day or night."

Captain Truman walked across the room and into the kitchen where he pulled down the shade. "Tom, you are now completely underground. As a passenger on our underground railroad you will of course observe our regulations and restrictions."

Tom was amused by this almost airline hostess monologue in a Texas accent. Captain Truman had obviously delivered versions of this on many previous occasions.

Tom chuckled tensely. "Now c'mon guys. I came here to get out of the country. I appreciate your taking care of me but--"

Captain Truman cut him off. His tone more commanding. "Now you listen carefully Tom." Captain's index finger pointed threateningly at Tom like a pistol. He withdrew his arm and reverted back to his airline auctioneer hard sell Texan monologue, "Listen carefully Tom, this pertains especially to you." The Captain looked away as if reading from the walls or invisible cue cards, "And in the event that any fugitive should be our guest for a prolonged time . . ."

Tom wondered how much the rules were being written now just for him.

" . . . kept in custody for the duration . . ."

'What?' Tom thought. 'Custody?'

" . . . shall be considered a recruit and subject to the discipline and schedules of his commanding officers."

'Huh?' Tom felt like he was in a **Twilight Zone** episode. Not just watching it but in it. "Hold it!"

Captain Truman wasn't even looking at Tom. He stopped in mid-sentence. He was shocked at being rudely interrupted. He was the Captain.

"I've got a daughter who needs me. I have to see her."

Truman was less patient now. "Forget it Tom." The Captain straightened up into a formal posture as he faced Tom. "And we should probably find another name for you."

Every time we say, "Tom," we're cre-"

"Fuck it." Tom was pissed. Oops so was the Captain now. "I'm not some kinda prisoner of war. I'm not-"

The Captain stomped forward into Tom's face. "I don't care what you aren't! And I don't care what you are! But you're here, and that makes you MY responsibility. I'm making the rules here and you're going to learn to obey them. It's as simple as that. What I say is law here. Now Mr. Tom Whatever You Want To Call Yourself, you are the guest of The American Freedom Army. As such you are entitled to many of its benefits and subject to its many rules. Do you accept the challenge to fight for your freedom?"

"Fight? I've had quite enough thank you. Just tone down this-"

The Captain wasn't used to this rebellious disrespect. He slammed his open hands forward into Tom's chest knocking Tom straight back.

Tom felt a rush of fear, confusion and surprisingly--balance. Like a cat he landed poised and balanced, upright--instead of on the ground as was intended. This shocked the Captain as much as Tom.

"Yes, fight. This country is at war. Buffoons like you Tom make a mockery of democracy, abuse its privileges and like rotten apples you divert attentions from . . ."

'Oh man. Senator was burning him in the press. Captain Truman is roasting him in a safe house. Sid is a vampire in the attic--and the police are waiting outside. Just want to take a nap . . . lay down . . .'

"Tom listen to me! And fuck this Tom The Clown name, we're changing your name to--"

Tom raised his head smoothly, mechanically, relaxed and with a dreamy look in his eyes he stared into the Captain's robotic hatred. "The only name I answer to is Tom. It's always been my name and always will be. My name is Tom."

The Captain was ready to argue. The Captain was ready to fight. Hell. The Captain was ready to kill. Trained to kill. Trained to fight. Trained to obey. Trained to command. Trained to decide. Trained what to decide. He had decided to join up and be trained. Tom didn't.

* * *

Nancy's grey hung eyes might have appeared sad or pained on anyone else, but her internal anger burned a confidence through her tempered windows. She was tough, hardened by resentment and tightly wrapped by a colonial upbringing. Her parents fought, her parents drank, and her parents expected her to be a model citizen. So Nancy was a rebel to them. The staunch rules, hardline ethics, Sunday Bible readings in a fundamental orthodox sectarian denominational Christian reformist Bible worship church: Baptist. All those rules that were punishingly believed, inconveniently obeyed, were indoctrinated and proselytized upon her. Drilled from her parents own frustration she rebelled with enough anger to stretch the narrow boundaries into a contemporary lifestyle. Nancy was a Joan of Arc in a wasteland of crucified heroes; an angry girl, but a good girl.

"I've quit my job. I've moved. I've borrowed money. Given up my savings for you to go to Canada, and now you want me to come too? With Erika?" Nancy stomped and paced across her small apartment's living room floor. "Tom you're nuts! You've got enough problems without me, and now even Erika's been named in the papers as--"

"At least there weren't any pictures of her."

"Shit Tom, how do you expect to straighten all this out?"

Tom shrugged and stuck his hands in his pockets. Looking down he kicked at that invisible stone. "I guess we'll have to change her name. Erika isn't that common a name, like Tom."

They thought.

Tom got an idea. "Maybe Jane in Florida can take her."

"Just a minute. Hold on Buster! Becky was my friend. I'm Erika's Godmother-"

"Godmother, Godsmother--"

"Though that doesn't mean a lot to you . . . I am Erika's Godmother. I care about her and have a sense of duty and obligation."

"Nancy, go join the army. She's my dau-"

"Tom! Don't you talk to me about responsibility. Look at you. Look at what you've done. Look at-" Nancy choked up at the thought of Becky . . .

"Maybe I'm not going to Canada. Maybe I'll stay here, and be able to be with Erika."

"That guy follows you like stink on shit Tom. The best thing you could do would be to keep moving." She didn't even like looking at Tom.

"Well thanks a lot. I'm gonna play decoy for the wolf and lead him away from the nest?"

"Fine. That's about the only purpose you have left in life."

"Well maybe that's not fine. Maybe I'm tired of running from this fuckhead. Maybe I'll-"

"Yeah? Maybe you'll what? Everybody else does your fighting for you. Take care of your own problems. You're an overgrown liability."

"Fuck you," he said softly but sincerely. "Maybe I'll change. Maybe I'll stand up and fight right here. I'll just die in San Francisco. That make you happy?"

Nancy waved a hand at him to shut up.

"Well?"

"Shut up man. Keep it down, it's that old lady, the landlord out front. She's always pokin' around. Keep your voice down."

"I'm serious, you want me to fight?" he challenged.

"Calm down Tom. You're such a wimp. Now get serious!"

"Well, I am serious." Tom looked down. "And I don't know what to do."

"Fine. I'll tell you what to do," she started calmly. "Just proceed as planned. The A.F.A. will get you to Canada. Then you're on your own. We'll keep in touch."

"Yeah. A lot of touching. And just when am I gonna see Erika again?"

"That's up to you Tom. The sooner you get your act together, then the sooner we'll be able to see you."

"Well maybe I'm not going to Canada."

"Tom you're going. These are good people and they've-"

"Yeah, they're great people. John Wayne with a Texas accent leading a band of criminals and lesbians to revolutionary glory. Yee-haw!"

"You are so sarcastic-"

"Listen Nancy, I appreciate what you've done and how you've given up friends and conveniences for me, but I've gotta keep-"

"That's fine, and you're welcome. But I'm not doing this just for you. In fact this is hardly for you at all. I'm in this for Erika and I'm not running out on her like you're so inclined to do."

"I would never-"

"Well, what else have you to offer? Hitching across the country and sleeping on the side of the road?"

"No. I'd al-"

"I'll make a home for her," assured Nancy coldly.

"No." Tom ruffled his feathers. "No. I'll make a home for her."

"Fine. I'll believe it when I see it," she said flippantly.

"Nancy!"

"When you do, just give us a call," she now said matter-of-factly.

"She's my baby, Nancy. She's my little girl."

"She'll always be yours Tom. But for right now she's my responsibility. You're not capable of handling a family right now."

"And you are huh?"

"Yes I am. It'll be a lot easier for me to start over than for you, a headline killer. I can start over no problem. I can get a waitressing job anywhere I go. You? Huh!" Nancy forced a laugh. "Tom, I don't know what you're gonna do. You're all fucked up!"

Tom was deflated. Nancy was right. He felt like a loser. He thought to himself, 'I've lost everything. Lost. Everything. I . . . am, a loser.'

Because of the picture in the newspaper Tom couldn't look anyone in the face. The only aspect of a disguise was his short hair cut. Tom felt claustrophobic and alone on the sidewalk. The comfort of a crowd was evaporated whenever someone seemed to look at him too long. No taxis. The bus and cable cars were better camouflaged. More crowded.

\* \* \*

"How do you know we can trust him? This guy's a real clown."

"He could be an FBI plant," informed Field General Hoover.

"Or CIA" added Corporal Kennedy.

Corporal Harding sat silently soaking it all up.

"They've got as many of them everywhere as they possibly can," continued Field General Hoover. "You've all proven your loyalty. We've all done actions together. But this Tom, he's hardly good for even intelligence work. He doesn't seem aligned with our cause . . . He's too hot to be in public, and quite frankly his image as a murderer hardly garners public support. I say-"

"You don't say," cut in Captain Truman. A lower rank but responsible leader. "In this cell, I have final word despite rank. This is The Eagle Cell of the American Freedom Army. I am Captain here and run this cell by my authority. I may answer to you, but these soldiers answer to me." Captain Truman was constantly having to go over procedures with Field General Hoover. Hell, talk about buffoons. This guy was made Field General because there wasn't any room in the Committee of Four. The role of a Field General was designed as a Captain of Captains when doing urban missions. As of yet there was still only one cell of the American Freedom Army on the West coast, here in San Francisco. Actually, Oakland. Cheaper rent and the racial tension kept the cops at a distance.

"Why don't you just ship him off to Canada?" calmly asked Corporal Harding.

When she did say something it normally got extra attention and response, but they were avoiding this question.

"He should earn his keep and passage," said Master Sergeant Buchanan.

Tom had already paid $300.

Corporal Kennedy seemed to get excited. "Why don't we use him in the next armored car job?"

Master Sergeant Buchanan frowned, then sat even more rigid in his chair. "Out of the question. He's untrained. A foolish risk."

Field General Hoover seemed to like the idea. "Well, you've said we need more recruits."

Master Sergeant Buchanan stood his ground. "Sir! This Tom is a security risk. He's a civilian fugitive, not a soldier."

"Not all of our functions require soldiering," offered the Field General.

Captain Truman closed his eyes, shook his head and let it fall into his hands. 'Man, this Field General was an ass! This is an army. We're all soldiers. Just give me a day with this Field General in my command . . .'

"Sir, if Major Nixon were here I'm certain he would affirm my position. Tom is not fit for duty at this time."

"Well then, when could he be?"

"I . . . uh . . . couldn't say sir. He's very independent minded."

Field General Hoover was smiling and nodding to himself. "Then there. Now you have it." The F.G. ruffled his feathers in self-congratulation. "He's your newest recruit."

Corporal Harding sat up. Her question had never been answered. "What about his transport to Canada?"

They ignored the question. No one even looked at her.

When Tom arrived back at the safe house he was placed under arrest.

"You've got to be kidding!"

"Tom, I explained the rules to you," stated Captain Truman calmly. "You had two choices: one, as our guest you would be treated better than, but, by the same rules as a prisoner of war, as defined by the Geneva Convention; and two, you could be a recruit and would have the added advantages of serving your country as well as having more freedom and involvement."

"Okay then, I'll be a recruit. Now, would you kindly untie my hands and unarrest me."

"We'll see if you're accepted as a recruit first. But even as a recruit you're basically still a prisoner of war until you prove yourself. So if you don't get your butt in gear you could be a prisoner of war for a long time."

"Hey, what about my trip to Canada? Man, I already paid you."

Corporal Harding sat in the corner watching all this go down as if watching a TV show. Tom noticed that she was listening and watching . . . She was kind of cute . . .

"You'll go to Canada when the time is right."

"And when will the time be right?"

"That depends on you," Captain Truman said flatly. "Now shut up and work hard. Earn some respect."

The next morning Tom awoke with his hands still tied. 'Shit! These idiots are really crazy. How do you hijack someone who's being hidden by you? Under arrest? Fuck, what assholes. I only want to go to Canada and I'm under fucking arrest by the American Freedom Army! And just what are they going to do with me? Turn me in for a reward? Holy Shit!' Tom remembered he was worth $50,000 now. That's easier than robbing a bank. 'Shit-Fuck! I'm a captive of this cartoon Rat Patrol!'

> *I've been sleeping outside your bedroom door.*
> *I've been waiting permission to fight in your private war.*
> *I've lost track but still your mother's keeping score.*
> *So tell me who is winning and who I'm fighting for.*
> *But don't try to seat me in the loser's section,*
> *next to the guy who wanted to die when he failed to pass inspection.*
> *Just file my name under "A" for affection.*
> *The only promise I ever made in the House of Rejection. (21)*

"Load up on the sugar. Today we're picking up the exercises. We've got a new recruit and we are going to all set a good example."

Looks were passed over cereal bowls, but nothing was said.

Master Sergeant Buchanan continued as they ate. "This house is considered at Level Orange at all times now."

Tom looked at the Sergeant.

"Recruit Tom, Level Orange is just below Level Red. At Level Red we are at war and confronting the enemy. Do you understand?"

Tom nodded from across the table as he ate.

"Do you understand Recruit!?" he bellowed.

"Yes," Tom choked out. "Yes," he said more manly.

"This house is to be completely clean by oh-eight-hundred."

The safe house got cleaned up all right, and rearranged. Master Sergeant Buchanan even installed a chin-up bar and brought in some old tires for exercise purposes. Tom's recruitment brought a new sense of duty to this cell of the A.F.A.

Tom followed along and kept up with everybody reasonably well. He was in pretty good shape. He'd never been an athlete, but he did bodysurf, and his Tai Chi provided some physical discipline which he practiced whenever he thought no one was watching.

It was nearing lunchtime and the girls were exhausted. They were trying their damnedest to keep up, but . . .

"C'mon you sissified sweetheart. The army's got no room for housewives. Now you-"

"I'm," pant-pant, "doing," pant-pant, "my best," pant-panted Corporal Kennedy.

"Well, honey, your best and the Army's least have a lot in common. You don't want to be a casualty of war do you?"

The Master Sergeant was showing his real colors now. He loved to dish out discipline. Like an orchestral conductor he composed the bodies into chaotic movement. Corporal Kennedy was his current focus of abuse. Corporal Harding was lucky to be on post right now. Captain Truman was concerned that although they lived in a house without adjoining neighbors, they were still raising a lot of noise as they stomped and jumped and groaned and grunted... of course M.S. Buchanan was quite loud all by himself as he yelled out commands and threw objects that when successfully dodged created much noise as they bounced off the walls or broke an ornament. They were all at war in this safe house. It was them against him; of course he was supposed to win.

"Okay Corporal Kennedy. Go relieve Corporal Harding of her post. I'll deal with you later." Tom almost felt sorry for that dyke in men's clothing. Almost.

"What about dinner?" asked Corporal Kennedy as she walked into the kitchen.

"You just relieve Corporal Harding FAT ASS. This house is Level Orange. You'd best get used to it."

Tom watched Corporal Kennedy sulk off into the kitchen. Tom was running back and forth in the tires on the floor. This forced you to keep your knees high and step accurately. Tom had seen this done by football players on television. Somehow the image of them made it easier for Tom to learn it.

Corporal Harding appeared at the kitchen pocket door.

"Corporal Harding?!" bellowed the Master Sergeant.

She looked at him.

"Corporal Harding!" he snapped again.

She was as cool as a huge rock on a hot day. She blinked.

"Corporal Harding you are to address me as 'Sir' or by rank. DO YOU UNDERSTAND!?"

"Yes. Sir."

"Yes Sir," corrected the Master Sergeant in a resounding baritone.

"Sergeant Buchanan," the Captain addressed him calmly.

The Master Sergeant pivoted like a windup soldier to face his commanding officer at rigid attention.

"Sergeant Buchanan I feel that new sound control measures should be executed at once."

"Sir!"

The Captain almost wanted to smile at this well trained human bowzer. Tom and Corporal Harding were out of place like children on the front line. The Captain felt a little out of place here. In fact, the only one who was indigenous to this environment was Master Sergeant Buchanan. In only a few hours this safe house had transformed from a revolutionary pig sty to a bootcamp playground. Tom had stopped running and watched while straddling a couple of the black rubber doughnuts.

"I want an intensive report on our alternatives tonight."

"Yes Sir," chanted Master Sergeant Buchanan as he stared over the shoulder of Captain Truman. The Captain knew he didn't need eye contact with the Sergeant to confirm or acknowledge. If the Sergeant said, "Yes Sir," then his life was predestined to that cause. The lack of eye contact allowed his superiors to speak at him, not to him. The lack of eye contact meant this his emotions and feelings were unimportant, and not to be acknowledged or even dealt with. The lack of eye contact meant that his loyalty and obedience was to no face in particular. His was the devotion of blind faith of the highest order; he would kill without hesitation.

After a week of military exercise Tom's entire body throbbed in: not pain, not tiredness, not ache . . . kind of a soreness as if the bones in his body were waking up from a long sleep. The first few days had been Hell. Literally. Tom knew he would've been able to build up to all those exercises, but good thing for them The Captain made The Sergeant cut back a little. Mostly because of the girls. He was killing them by pushups.

No mercy from that guy. If jail creates criminals, and the military creates sadists, the colleges produce anarchists, the evil government creates wars, the police create laws... politicians are creating crime, the FBI are all pigs... What is America becoming?

Answer: a war zone like some Rod Serling black and white . . . doo-dee-doo-doo . . .

Pushups, sit-ups, running, wrestling, jump down, jump up, carrying a stick as if it were a gun . . . memorizing movement patterns with code names like football players. It got so fucking hot in the safe house that they began calling it, "the sweat house." Six hours a day they exercised. Six hours a day they sweat themselves into wet lather. The Captain and Master Sergeant participated in some of the exercises and some of the movement patterns. However, Tom was the recruit, the two female corporals were the pawns; these three were in bootcamp.

For drill and exercise everyone wore green army fatigues and the green and black army boots created specifically for Vietnam. Tom had gotten into a lot of trouble when he referred to them as, "nigger stompers." Corporal Kennedy, after chastising Tom herself, informed Master Sergeant Buchanan of Tom's racial statement. Tom had to stand watch all night and if found sleeping or making another racial statement was told he would be flogged like a black plantation slave until his back bled. The Sergeant said that after such an "all-American torture," Tom would have a new respect for the plight of the black man.

Tom decided he had an immediate respect for the plight of the black man and need not relive history's mistakes. He also knew that black Master Sergeant Buchanan was crazy enough and mean enough to really whip someone. The next day was a blur for Tom. No sleep, overworked, and now here we go again. Corporal Kennedy had a new life to her today. She reveled in Tom's weakness. He was tired, she was rested. Finally she could keep up with him, or better yet, even beat him. She pushed herself to the limit all day trying to outdo Tom, no matter what.

Corporal Harding tried harder so as not be left behind by Corporal Kennedy. The girls weren't really competing with one another, but they were trying to keep up with one another. Today, Corporal Kennedy was giving no consideration to Corporal Harding as she pushed herself to her physical limits, in effort after effort to outdo Tom.

"Beat you," chided Corporal Kennedy.

"Bully for you," panted Tom without looking at her.

"What's next?" excitedly asked Corporal Kennedy to the Master Sergeant.

"Move the tires out of the way. Next are combat drills."

Tom leaned a tire against the wall. His pants were soaked with sweat. The sweat that ran down his back had soaked the seat of his pants all the way down the crack of his ass. Tom took off his shirt.

"Captain Sir? You wish to join us for combat maneuvers?"

Captain Truman closed his book on weaponry and got up. "Yes, that would be fine." He continued to speak as he walked to the center of the room to join the three trainees. "We should be receiving a new soldier soon. He's being sent here as an arms expert."

"But I'm an arms expert," whined the Master Sergeant. "Sir."

"Yes I know. However, at last night's council meeting they decided that this soldier would be a positive addition to our force."

"What rank is he Sir?"

The Captain eyed Sergeant Buchanan's insecure interest. "He's a Sergeant. Not to worry. You'll remain Master Sergeant. As such he will be under your discipline. And both of you will be under my command."

Master Sergeant Buchanan stood as tall and cock-like as possible.

"Carry on with the drills Sergeant."

Master Sergeant Buchanan snapped out of attention trance and struggled to remember what he was doing before his ego had been confronted. "Yes, yes. Very good. Uh. Okay team. Team. Now we're going to drill. PICK UP RIFLES!" he yelled.

Everyone dashed for their wooden sticks.

Two weeks of playing combat and they finally got a day off. It was Sunday and it never felt so good to just sit down and do nothing. Tom was watching television, stoned. He'd stashed the last of his pot in the kitchen. They'd stated that under Condition Orange no one was to drink or take drugs. But Tom didn't take his recruitment very seriously. He was only here to help them pull off one job and then split to Canada, or somewhere. In the meantime he'd play along with them, blow smoke up the kitchen exhaust fan, while cooking, which also helped to cover up the smell of burning pot. Tom even had eyedrops to get the red out.

Someone knocked on the closed front door.

Electric jolt up everyone's spine. Although Tom was the only person on a wanted poster, the others had all performed missions ranging from robbery to conspiracy.

Everyone here was a fugitive.

Master Sergeant signaled Tom back into the bedrooms. As rehearsed, Corporal Kennedy took position behind the door with a sawed-off shotgun. Corporal Harding took position at the kitchen rear door with her Colt revolver. The Sergeant nodded approval to Captain Truman to open the door.

The man on the porch was tall, over six foot, and solidly built.

"My name is unimportant. I serve America."

This was the password phrase. "Which America?" asked the Captain.

"The America of the people. A free America for free people."

That wasn't part of the password phrase but it further satisfied Captain Truman. He opened the screen door outward. "Join us. Come on in."

Only after the door was shut did they salute. Then they embraced like old friends. "Front and center soldiers!" announced the Captain. "I would like to introduce all of you to Sergeant Roosevelt. This is Master Sergeant Buchanan."

Sergeant Roosevelt reached out to shake. Master Sergeant Buchanan gazed off between the Captain and the Sergeant and saluted robotically. Sergeant Roosevelt pulled back his outstretched arm and returned a relaxed salute.

"And these are our two Corporals, Corporal Harding-" they saluted, "and Corporal Kennedy." They saluted.

"And our newest recruit, Tom."

Sergeant Roosevelt looked over to the Captain who explained, "He has no rank, so he still goes by his civilian name."

"Glad to meet you all. I have been brought here to upgrade your weaponry skills. I don't know what your schedule is today. I'm prepared to start immediately."

"Well-" started the Captain.

"Fine idea," jumped in Master Sergeant Buchanan.

"Today's Sunday," continued the Captain. "We were taking a day off."

"Never a day off for the revolution," sang Buchanan.

"We'll begin tomorrow," the Captain sighed. "Take a day to settle in. Tomorrow."

This Sergeant Roosevelt seemed cool enough. He wasn't all gung-ho and amped-out like Master Sergeant Buchanan. He got a space of floor in the officer's bedroom.

The girls shared a room and Tom slept on the couch. It was somewhere around two in the morning when Tom was awakened by Corporal Kennedy as she rotated her night watch vigil between the kitchen and living room window.

Tom decided to get up and take a piss. He waited until she was in the kitchen and got up off the couch. The bedroom door opened as Tom entered the hallway.

"It's me," Tom softly sang to avoid surprising someone.

Then new Sergeant Roosevelt stepped out. "Oh. Hi Tom. I was just gonna use the bathroom."

"Me too. Officers first I guess."

The sergeant smiled. "Thanks."

Corporal Kennedy had heard the whispering and approached with her sawed-off shotgun.

"It's me, Tom," he said more nervously than before.

She continued to advance with her weapon pointed at him. There were no lights on in the house and Tom stood in the dark hallway.

"Hey," he whispered loudly. "It's me Tom. Tom"

Corporal Kennedy approached until her gun barrel almost touched Tom's chest.

"I know."

"Then stop pointing that thing at me."

"What's wrong? You're not nervous of a 'girl' soldier, are you?"

"C'mon," Tom impatiently scolded as he pushed the gun to the side. "Don't start with your feminist stuff again."

"It has nothing to do with fem-"

The bathroom door opened and Corporal Kennedy reflexed like an overanxious G.I.

"Relax, it's Sergeant Roosevelt," Tom informed her.

"Corporal Kennedy, you seem to be effectively patrolling this cell."

This compliment flattered the Corporal. Tom giggled to himself at her sudden shyness.

"Thank you sir."

"Keep up the good work Corporal."

"Thank you sir."

Tom entered the bathroom and shut the door.    It was getting dangerous to take a piss.   What he'd really like to do is smoke a joint, bu . . .

When he came back out the hallway was clear.    Good.    She was probably in the kitchen.   Tom went to his couch bed.   It was very dark in the front room but Tom could clearly see that Corporal Kennedy was sitting right in the middle of his couch, or bed as the case might be.

"Uh... hi Kenny.   Mind if I crawl back under my sheets?"

"I like that new Sergeant."

"Uh Corporal-"

"Here," she patted the couch next to her, "sit here."

Tom sat in the easy chair across from her.

"Tom you should try harder to fit in."

'Who's telling who about fitting in!' he thought to himself.

"You know Tom, we're like a family here.   You could be part of the fa--"

"Thanks but I'm not into settling down right now."

"I know your wife got killed and all, but you could start over here."

Tom closed his eyes and let his head fall back against the chair.   He didn't feel like arguing right now.   Especially not with her.   "Thanks, but--"

"Now just listen Tom."

Her voice was closer Tom thought.

"It's hard living underground.   None of us have many friends and life here can be very lonely.   Now that we're . . ."

Tom felt her hand on his ankles.   'No!'

" . . . and I was thinking . . ."

'Yes!'   She was massaging his calves.

" . . . you know.   It's a totally bourgeois setup, marriage."

Tom opened his eyes and sat up.   He moved his legs away from her.

"That felt real nice Corporal Kennedy but I have to go to sleep."

"You know you could be a little more generous--and friendly."

Tom got up as Corporal Kennedy sat where she knelt. He climbed under his two covers without saying anything else.

He felt the couch sag as she sat down next to him.

"Tom, we're soldiers together now. Comrades. Did you know that in the Weathermen Underground all soldiers have to have sex with each other to break down their bourgeois hangups?"

"Interesting," Tom moaned with his head covered.

"I think it would be a good thing, if we were to just have sex--and leave it at that."

"I'm tired."

"You're hung up. You're hung up on all your bourgeois ethics."

"I like ethics."

"They're ruining your life."

Tom thought for a second. His life was fucked up alright. But not from any ethical conflicts. In fact, Tom felt that whatever this dyke said, was the opposite of whatever is probably right--for him anyway.

"Good night Corporal."

Tom felt her hand rub over his hip and waist. She stroked atop the sheets. Tom ignored her. She kept rubbing. Tom wondered what to say. She rubbed harder. Tom rolled over, turning his back to her. She rubbed his side and waist. He felt her pulling down the sheets. Tom clung to the sheets near his neck preventing her from pulling them down. She kept rubbing with her other hand.

"C'mon Corporal Kennedy, I have to get some sleep."

"What about tomorrow night?"

"Oh--shit Kennedy. I don't feel right about it."

"See?! It's those bourgeois ethics I told you about. See how--"

"No, I don't think so."

"You don't what?"

"I don't think it has to do with my ethics."

"Then good. As a friend, as a comrade, as a fellow soldier I'm requesting we have sex together. There. Now you should have no problem honoring my request. Right?"

"Wrong."

"Tom," she stopped rubbing. "I can't figure you out. What--"

"Don't try. Just let me sleep."

"Tom I have a problem."

"I know," he replied hastily.

"Tom, I'm referring to my sexual needs."

"Oh," he replied hastily again.

She was silent. She didn't move. Tom kept the sheet pulled up to his chin and his face to the back of the couch. Silence. Maybe he really hurt her feelings. Maybe she was pissed off. Maybe she was undressing!

Tom sat up.

Corporal Kennedy was hunched over, sitting on the edge of the couch.

"Hey."

She didn't acknowledge. Great. Now she finally shuts up and Tom feels bad about it. "I'm sorry."

She still didn't acknowledge.

"You know I've really lost my appetite for sex, with anyone--since I lost my wife. So, nothing personal. I just ain't interested." He laid back down.

"I understand. But you don't understand. I don't want to replace your wife. I'm not interested in being your girlfriend or even a regular lover. It's like having a bug bite where you can't reach it, and you need someone to scratch it for you. I'd settle for just giving you head."

"You'd what?" Tom turned toward her.

"I'm serious. I really like to give head."

"Nice thought, but like I told you-"

"For me it's not really sucking cock . . . it's like milking a spiritual fruit or feeding on a flower."

"Are you being serious?" Tom knew she was but was hoping to embarrass her out of this fantasy.

"Yes I'm being serious. I'm--"

Tom rolled over away from her again. "Thanks sister, but I'm no honeysuckle flower and you're no ruby-throated hummingbird. Why don't you find a nice gay boyfriend. You'd be such a happy suckle--I mean couple."

Now she was pissed. "Fuck you Tom!" she said much too loudly for this time of night. "Fuck you Tom, you're no big macho prize!" She stuttered for an appropriate insult to his manhood. "You're a capitalistic hippie loser! Your dealing was just a pig enterprise with higher profits! The government controls the police; the police control the drugs; and you were just a small pawn in the government's own form of mass control. They control the public by drugs. And you were the government middle man. You're a stupid, duped cog in the wheel of the dying America, and you don't even realize it. You're so stupid Tom!"

"I'm smart enough to know what I like. And it isn't getting a blow job from a political lesbian."

She punched him in the ribs. Tom hurt and wondered if he could ignore her away. Another blow to the ribs convinced him of moving. The next hit he felt on his right thigh as he rolled over the back of the couch and onto the varnished wood floor.

"Fuck you! Fuck you pig! FUCK YOU!

"No thanks," Tom said from behind the couch, "you're not my ty--"

She lunged at the couch and it rolled over atop Tom as she leaned over its back.

Captain Truman and Sergeant Roosevelt dashed into the hall with weapons drawn. "What the Hell is going on here?!" yelled Captain Truman.

They untangled on the floor, both out of breath and Tom pinned under the fallen couch.

"Bad nightmare Sir," Tom said in mock sincerity.

"Corporal Kennedy, What is going on here?"

"Sorry Sir."

"Corporal I asked you a question."

"It won't happen again Sir."

The Master Sergeant entered the hallway. He realized his bedroom window post need not be covered any longer. Corporal Harding peeked out of her slightly opened door.

The Captain looked back and noticed Corporal Harding. "Corporal Harding, relieve Corporal Kennedy of her post."

"It's not-- Yes Yes Sir."

Even from the hallway Tom could feel Master Sergeant Buchanan scowling at him. 'Fuck. What a hassle.'


\* \* \*


'Tomorrow? Well, good. Do this job for the A.F.A. Get it over with, then Canada here I come,' thought Tom as his mind drifted from the safe house planning meeting.

Captain Truman laid out the maps and schedules and photographs of the bank exterior. Some showed the armored car and gunmen. Diagrams were hung on the wall. Drop points, car changes, backups and new code words and passwords . . . even contacts in jail were memorized.

Berkeley was different. Well, everything gets different--but not always better. And who's to say what's better. So everything is always changing. From mid-sixties liberation of race and gender to late-sixties liberation of the mind, it was always those in power who created conflict. Different wars against different enemies, the changing faces of good versus evil. It seemed that all the wrong people took LSD, or at least not enough of the politicians. Artists, musicians, and poets already break the boundaries and stretch reality as normal growing-up patterns. But the suit and tie crowd, the lawyers, the politicians, the rich and powerful; they're all too insecure of their reputations, and too indebted to the past, to change. They need the acid. They need the visions. They needed to be humbled with visual insobriety and powered with some respect of spiritual omnipotence.

Well all the best laid intentions were left behind. Burned up in the press, both sides were talked out and the public had heard it all. The Us versus Them was being fielded now by the more subversive government organizations: the F.B.I., the C.I.A., the D.E.A., the Defense Agency, the Secret Service, the I.R.S., the Department of Justice, and the countless temporary splinter groups they create for certain projects and activities. These groups were the antithesis of their enemies (Us), the Weathermen, S.D.S., the Yippies, the Black Panthers, and of course the A.F.A.

When citizens marched the streets, the police handled it. When the kids became spies and subversives, then the secret police grew accordingly. When Nixon declared his war on drugs, the drug dealers got guns. There is a balance in this world. Unfortunately.

* * *

The drive-up bank window did brisk business like a drive-through hamburger stand. Four cars were lined up hoping to make their calculated transaction before the window closed at 3:00. Tom liked the air suction tubes that transported the paperwork back and forth to the tellers. HWUMP.

The bank was on the street corner and catty-corner stood a small yellow grocery store. Apartments held their ground on the other two corners. It was a busy intersection with a traffic light. A blend of business and residence. The streets were more crowded than the sidewalks as cars hurried from work to the safety of their televisions.

A room on the second floor of the green apartments across the street from the bank overlooked the entrance to the bank. Captain Truman watched from the window as the Bank Manager locked the glass doors from the inside.

A white station wagon was parked directly below the Captain's window. Tom fidgeted with the steering wheel. He wasn't as nervous as he thought he'd be. It was like a sport, just higher stakes. But Tom didn't really like the whole idea, especially shooting the bagman. Tom was wanted for murder, but that still didn't make it any easier to be a party to it. They wouldn't allow Tom to even speak his disagreements, he held no rank and had no say… That's war.

The armored car turned across the intersection and parked across the street from Tom.

"I sure hope that traffic doesn't fuck us up," Tom said as he watched the bagman get out of the rear of the gray armored car.

"The smoke bombs should help. It's just a matter of getting through that intersection and we're home free," reassured Sergeant Roosevelt who sat shotgun next to Tom.

Tom watched the window clerk draw down her shade behind the bulletproof glass.

The unserviced drivers cussed and swore at the teller, at least so it appeared to Tom from across the street. The cars cleared out of the drive-up lanes and now Tom felt nervous. His heart beat louder.

The bagman did his normal routine inside and was carrying two money sacks.

The bank manager was waiting for him at the door and let him out, but not alone. The bank security guard was talking and laughing with the bagman. This wasn't supposed to happen. The bank security guard never walked outside before—when they were staking out this bank.

Captain Truman got uptight at this change in procedure. Nervously he turned back and viewed the array of weapons spread out on the bed near the window: two grenades and five smoke bombs.

Tom didn't want to see this old black security guard get hurt. Now Tom was really nervous. And worse, mad. Mad at being in this situation. Shit. Even if he was an outlaw. Even if he was a fugitive. Even if he was wanted for murder, he didn't want to kill anyone. This poor old black guy's probably got a family and--

The armored car bagman was walking slightly ahead of the security guard. Halfway to the sidewalk Master Sergeant Buchanan knocked him down with an M-16. A small gun but the Sergeant got three or four bullets in him before he hit the ground.

The bagman was dead before the security guard could get his gun out. Tom could tell he was scared shitless, yet the guard pivoted towards the van. Both Captain Truman and Master Sergeant Buchanan riddled him with rapid fire. Their opposing bullets kept him standing as he swayed back and forth, dead on his feet.

The armored car driver and other bagman in the rear tried to figure out where the bullets had come from. Master Sergeant Buchanan had fired through a hole drilled in the van door. Although they could figure someone was in the van with a gun, they had no target, no one to be seen.

Tom, Sergeant Roosevelt, and Corporal Harding watched from the white Ford station wagon.

"I think it's time to duck now," Corporal Harding reminded in an unusually high voice. The door panel had an extra layer of metal against it on the inside.

No one replied, they all just lowered their heads to between their knees and put their hands on the back of their necks, like a sit-up—going down.

The first grenade thrown landed in the middle of the street and bounced up and hit the side of the armored car. A car had just driven by and another was approaching when it detonated in the middle of the street. Its shrapnel and smoke puffed out in all directions. The side windows of the station wagon were blown out and a piece even stuck through the door near Tom's leg. No one moved. Sergeant Roosevelt tossed the next grenade like a basketball hook shot over their car with his arm out the passenger window. It landed under the armored car and rolled to the curb before exploding. The explosion physically jolted the guards inside as they still surveyed the street and the driver radioed for the police.

The smoke bombs landed around the armored car shielding it in bright red. The smoke blew into the intersection and down the street like a huge snakelike ghost. Traffic jammed up in the intersection. Some cars were trying to pass, others to get away.

The driver of the armored car probably thought he was on fire. Neither guard could see out except for glimpses between puffs of smoke.

Master Sergeant Buchanan opened the side door and ran to the two dead and bloody armed guards. Just as quickly he scooped up the two money bags and ran back to the van.

"Tom and Corporal Harding."

"Yes sir," they resounded simultaneously.

"Go round the corner and get into the other car with Corporal Kennedy. I'll be there in a moment," Sergeant Roosevelt calmly ordered.

Tom and Corporal Harding exited bent over and ran as such to the corner before straightening up.

Sergeant Roosevelt stayed head down, looking up every few seconds. He was responsible for covering the van's getaway. The intersection was packed full and no one was moving. The van couldn't pull out from the curb. Field General Hoover was driving the van and decided to drive across the front lawn of the bank where the dead guards were, over through the drive-up windows and exit there. The van almost ran over the dead bodies as it bounced through the planters and dug up the grass. The van drove right through the red smoke and past the armored car. The armored car driver suspected the van of being the enemy and attempted to pursue it. The hand grenades had flattened five of his six tires with shrapnel. The big gray metal elephant waddled and flopped a few feet.

Captain Truman dropped three pebbles onto the roof of the station wagon as Sergeant Roosevelt's signal to leave. The Captain watched the gray wounded truck waddle a few more feet to finally dock at the curb.

In the car parked around the corner, the Captain, Sergeant, Corporal Harding, Corporal Kennedy and Tom drove a few blocks to where they switched cars again and then headed home.

The others in the van would do the same with another switch car.

"There's no bond stronger than the fear of death, that unites men in battle."

Tom looked at the proud Master Sergeant Buchanan. A pockmarked black man who had just proven himself in battle, again. Tom didn't like talking with him, but he had found out a lot of stuff about him from the others. Seems this Master Sergeant Buchanan spent most of his life in jail, as an adult and as a kid. C.Y.A. at eleven, and then a choice of either jail for armed robbery or Vietnam. The idiot joined the Navy when he wanted combat. He was bored for the entire war. He hated the Navy . . . Got in brawls . . . But now he could play Marine in the A.F.A. Corporal Harding told Tom that M.S. Buchanan joined up through their prison system.

* * *

Master Sergeant Buchanan was getting drunk. "How many politicians were lost in Vietnam? Huh? How many?"

"Sergeant we are still at Level Orange." The Captain was good.

"Yes sir." Buchanan was embarrassed. "All right soldiers, let's straighten this place up. This ain't no rock concert. It's a war."

Tom walked over to the Captain in the kitchen. "Sir."

"Yes Tom."

"Since I did pull through so well today, you've got my fee, and you promised to reward me on this job: I'd like to just get my new ID and a passport, a few bucks and a way across the border." Tom shrugged and smiled mechanically at the Captain. "No big deal."

The Captain thought. Captain Truman did have a brain, unlike-

"Well, good work men." Field General Hoover strolled into the fluorescent kitchen light.

"Thank you sir," Tom piped.

"What's up guys?" The Field General looked at their faces. "Looks heavy."

"Tom and I were discussing his 'reward' and papers for transit."

"Well, that's fine and you should be rewarded," summed up the Field General.

The Captain seemed to be steering the conversation somewhere else though, "Wasn't it decided that if Tom pulled through we'd allow him to advance to Corporal."

"Thanks guys but just the paper and money."

"Now Tom," spoke the Field General, "we have a purpose here."

"That's fine. I have mine."

"Tom, we're all criminals here. We're on the outside, fighting to get back inside."

"I'm not fighting." Tom smiled, "I believe in love, not war."

"Tom that's what's wrong with you. You need to fight. You need to get mad and let it out. You need to stand up and fight for something."

"I will, my daughter Erika."

"That's fine, but you can do so much more."

"I've got my hands full, and it looks like you do too."

"Tom you'd best show some respect," Field General impatiently stated.

The Captain joined in. "I think you should also show some respect for this opportunity you've been given."

The Field General stepped back. "Tom stand at attention and be sworn in."

"But I-"

"'TEN-HUT!" the Captain shouted.

The Master Sergeant entered the kitchen like a dog being called for dinner. He wasn't about to miss a military drill.

The Captain saluted and held his hand to his forehead, palm out.

Reluctantly, Tom did the same.

The Captain began, "You Corporal Thomas Jefferson are hereby sworn into the American Freedom Army as a soldier. You are subject to all the laws of this body and to uphold the Constitution of the United States of America. We are at war with the current American military and police who are controlled by the corrupt government we seek to replace. As such we have declared martial law and thusly supersede the civil laws in order to regain the peace, equality, and freedom for all citizens. You will answer only to your military superiors and obey all commands with conviction and efficiency." The Captain paused and smiled at Tom. "We plan to win this war and have you back to civilian life in no time."

"Thanks," Tom replied half-heartedly. "But I just want a new identity now."

"You have one. You are now Corporal Jefferson," added Field General Hoover as he patted Tom on the back like a good doggey.

"That's not what I mean. A new civilian identity."

"Tom, all of us seek new identities, new lives. But we've had to sacrifice everything in the hope of attaining this. You too can earn your freedom." The Field General put his arm across Tom's back.

"I've already earned my freedom and given you my money and helped you out. Now if that's not-"

"Hey calm down Corporal Jefferson." His buddy-buddy routine wasn't working, and this "Thomas Jefferson" name was obviously preplanned. "As a freedom fighter Corporal Thomas-"

"It's Tom."

"Okay Corporal Tom Jefferson," he said sternly, losing his patience and removing his friendly arm.

Tom scowled. These guys weren't budging an inch. Talking wasn't working. "Maybe I should just collect my stuff, get back my money and find someone else to help me out."

"Hey now, just a minute Tom-boy." The Captain was getting serious. "You're like part of the family now. We have an interest in you-"

"Good then be interested enough to help me out. Like you originally agreed to."

"All right Tom," sighed the Field General. "Just stick with us for another action and we'll-"

"That's what you said last time. I've done an action."

"Well, this money is kind of important to us and we didn't get as much as we'd hoped to."

"How much did we get? The papers said seventy-five thousand dollars."

"Well Tom, you know the papers, they exaggerate everything."

Tom looked at this Field General Hoover and realized that he was just like any ordinary politician, dishonest. Selfish and unconcerned about the little guy. The pawns. He's just serving the ruling interests... Tom knew he could escape, but to where?

They had his money, he had no car, he had no ID  He was stranded, and it was safer here with these revolutionaries, lying cheating revolutionaries, than out on the street with his picture in the newspapers. How to play out this situation was confusing Tom.

Tom turned and walked out of the kitchen, leaving Field General Hoover and Captain Truman trying to read his mind. His angry mind.

Master Sergeant Buchanan stopped him. "You weren't dismissed Corporal."

Tom looked at the Sergeant's hand holding his shirt buttons crumpled up in his fist. Tom lazily panned his eyes upward to meet the hatred gaze of the Sergeant. "So."

"So?" The Master Sergeant exaggerated his voice, "SO?!?" he yelled louder.

"You mind letting go of my shirt, please," Tom spoke too calmly.

"Maybe I do mind. Maybe I mind a lot of things. Maybe I know how to mind. But you don't Tom. You're a rebel."

"Thank you."

"Without a cause."

"I'll decide what my causes are. My priorities are my-"

The Master Sergeant pushed Tom backwards into the kitchen. "You aren't capable of deciding your priorities Tom. You're just a lost kid."

"Yeah. And I think I'll just get lost again."

The Sergeant pushed him again. "You'll come and go as we see fit."

"Hey, I'm not a prisoner here."

"No, you're a soldier here," reinformed Field General Hoover.

"But-"

"Now if you'll excuse the Captain and me, we've got some business to discuss."

The F.G. turned his back to Tom.

"You heard the General. Corporal Tom report to the exercise room for drill practice."

The Field General winked at Master Sergeant Buchanan as he led, or pushed, Tom out into the living room.

The Captain was less settled about Tom's situation. "I don't know about Corporal Thomas Jefferson."

"Oh, don't worry about him, he'll come around. Anyway I have more important issues to discuss than him."

The Captain gave a quizzical glance to the Field General to continue talking.

"It seems that they've raised their price."

"Who?"

"You know, the Libyan training camp," replied the F.G.

"Oh yeah. Who are we sending to that anyway?"

"Originally, four; but now we can only afford to send three. They raised the price. I don't know why, but that's what I've been told," sighed the Field General.

"So we send three," the Captain sighed.

"Right, but which three? I don't want to go. After all I'm not really a soldier."

'You're right about that,' the Captain thought, trying not to grimace at the pussy Field General.

"And I know the rest of you all want to go, so I figure we just draw straws."

"Draw straws? Are you crazy? I mean, Field General Sir, this is the army, not a game show."

"Well it's the most fair way I can think of, anyway, didn't Burt Lancaster do that in the movie-"

"Sir, forget the movies. We are at war, lives are at stake--"

"Sure, sure Captain, now settle down. Unless you have a better idea."

"Yes Sir I do. We should decide based on merit, rank--"

"And who's to decide?"

"I will Sir," stated the chest puffed Captain.

"Very well, but do it soon, the candidates should leave for Libya next week."

The Captain and Field General walked into the living room where Tom was doing pushups as the Master Sergeant kept one foot on Tom's back for added difficulty.

"Master Sergeant, call the troops in.  We've got an announcement to make."

"Yes Sir," Master Sergeant Buchanan sounded as he removed a foot from suppressing Tom.

All the members of Eagle Cell, Western Division of the American Freedom Army sat in the living room.  Major Nixon and Lieutenant General Lincoln were back East right now.  They were married and Major Nixon's mother was dying.  So they both went back.

"Since all of you are here, it is time to make an announcement.  As some of you already know, one of the reasons for our last mission was to secure enough money to send some of our soldiers and officers to a guerrilla training camp in Libya."

Tom didn't know this.

"Unfortunately we are still short on funds to send all of you so a decision must be made as to who will go."

"I definitely want to go sir," shouted Corporal Kennedy with her arm waving in the air.

"The Captain will decide who goes," informed Field General Hoover with an appreciative smile.

Captain Truman resented this 'passing of the buck.'  He didn't smile back.  "Yes, I have decided who will go."

Master Sergeant Buchanan looked to the Captain with his biggest, beggingest, puppy eyes possible.

"Yes, Master Sergeant Buchanan you shall attend."

Buchanan smiled and stepped back happily.

"And of course I will go," stated Captain Truman, "So that leaves room for one more-"

"Me, me, me. Captain it has to be me. I want to go." Corporal Kennedy was desperate.

"Well-"

"Sir," spoke Corporal Harding. "I would like to go. I would be greatly benefitted by the additional knowledge, and could put it to good use for the revolution." Corporal Harding was the best educated of them all, at least civilian-wise.

Tom felt a certain despise towards this whole situation being as how he felt cheated and trapped… he decided to make things difficult. "I'd like to go also Sir," spoke Tom calmly, trying not to smile.

Kennedy snapped, "You can't let him go, he's not even a soldier, he's just a dope dealer hippie. He—"

The Captain interrupted Corporal Kennedy. "He's the same rank as you, we just initiated him in as Corporal Thomas Jefferson."

"Corporal Tom will suffice," Tom said belligerently to Corporal Kennedy.

She was so shocked, she couldn't say anything. She looked like she was having trouble breathing.

The Field General looked to Captain Truman with a smirk on his face. He seemed to be enjoying the added pressure on the Captain. "He is entitled."

Corporal Harding spoke again. "Sirs, I would very much like to attend this training camp. I have been looking forward to it."

The Captain frowned at the Field General who shrugged his shoulders with a restrained smile.

"Whatever I decide is final," said the Captain taking a large breath.

"Then please sir, choose me," pleaded Corporal Kennedy.

Tom looked at her. 'What a pathetic bitch.'

She looked at Tom. "And you can't consider him seriously. He's an unreliable asshole whose bourgeois-"

"Hey fuck you dyke. And don't be dreaming about my asshole anymore."

"Why you son of a-"

"At ease you two," commanded the Captain.

Master Sergeant Buchanan stood up to put his two cents in, "At ease Tom or I'll-"

"Excuse me," pardoned Sergeant Roosevelt who had been silent so far. "Perhaps there's an easier way to make this decision. Perhaps draw straws."

Field General Hoover could not contain the gleeful smile he beamed at Captain Truman. Captain Truman was cornered, very uncomfortably, by his soldiers, and fellow officers.

"Fine. We'll draw straws. We'll draw straws for all three trainees."

"Now, now," comforted Field General Hoover, slightly sarcastic. "You Captain should definitely attend. We'll just draw straws for the other two positions."

"But Sir," interrupted Master Sergeant Buchanan, "I should attend also so I can carry on the training here with-"

"You do a fine job now," comforted Field General Hoover. "But you've already had military training, I'm sure it would be good to make real soldiers of your young-"

"Begging your pardon Sir, that was the Navy, this is the-"

"All right, enough of this," disciplined the Captain. "We'll draw straws. The two shortest will go to Libya with me."

"Not Tom though," sounded off Corporal Kennedy.

"Corporal Thomas is now entitled," reminded Field General Hoover.

Tom smiled viciously at Corporal Kennedy.

"Sergeant Buchanan would you go get the straws."

Sergeant Buchanan got half way to the kitchen before he remembered they didn't have any straws. "Uh, Sir, we don't have any straws."

"Whatever, just-"

"Use pieces of spaghetti," suggested Field General Hoover.

Captain Truman looked over to the Field General scornfully.

"They should work as good as anything else," the Field General smirked.

The Captain sighed and shook his head slightly. This was becoming a carnival army, drawing straws of spaghetti, enlisting unwilling fugitives, girl soldiers . . .

Master Sergeant Buchanan returned while he still cracked and broke the pieces of uncooked spaghetti. "Here you go Sir," he said handing them to the Field General with a sullen face.

"That's fine Sergeant. You're doing fine by yourself, continue."

The Sergeant's face drooped further. He wanted to draw straws too.

Captain Truman realized his disappointment. "Here, I'll handle them, that way you can draw too." The Captain viewed and counted them. "Okay. There are five straws here. One for each of you. The shortest two will accompany me to Libya." He spun around 180 degrees so that no one could see how he arranged the 'straws' in his hand.

He turned back. "All right, Sergeant Buchanan, you draw first. Sergeant Roosevelt, now you."

Corporal Kennedy jumped out of her chair and cut off Corporal Harding for the next straw selection.

Captain sighed, "All right Corporal Harding, your turn."

She only had two sticks of spaghetti to choose from. She picked the one to the left.

Tom took the remaining piece. He didn't really even want to go. He was just trying to throw his weight around. Now he was... holding the smallest piece of spaghetti? No shit. Sure 'nough.'

"That's not fair," whined Corporal Kennedy, who held the longest piece of spaghetti. "It's not fair, that Tom-"

"That's enough," interrupted Captain Truman. He looked to his right and noticed that Master Sergeant Buchanan had his head hung. "Sergeant?"

Sergeant Buchanan held up his long pasta stick.

Sergeant Roosevelt shook his head side to side.

Tom was enjoying Corporal Kennedy's hysteria but realizing that he had just won a honeymoon in Libya: 'if this was good luck--then bad luck might be a good change of pace.'

Master Sergeant Buchanan wasn't taking this very well either. If Tom ever had a chance of befriending the drill instructor--he dismissed the thought. Like a big fat brown with black spots angry floppy lipped bull dog, he glared at Tom with hatred drooling hungrily. Libya looked like a good idea now.

Tom smiled at Corporal Kennedy with new conviction. Oh. She wasn't looking.

She and the bull dog went into the kitchen to commiserate. But Corporal Harding was looking at him. "So we're going to the desert."

Corporal Harding just looked at Tom. Brown eyes, big ones. She wore loose fitting apparel but Tom knew she was hiding something. She spoke softly, "Why are you going?"

"Change of scenery."

She tightened her lip. "Seriously."

"Actually I am being serious. I came here to get out of here and now I'm being kept here. Does that make sense?"

Corporal Harding shook her head 'no.'

"So off to Libya we go. Why are you going?" She was cute . . .

"It would be good training for me."

"So join the real army."

"This is the real army!"

"Ah, c'mon. You don't really think-" he looked around and continued quietly so the others couldn't hear, "you've got a chance of winning this war do you?"

Corporal Harding stood up aghast that Tom could talk such blasphemy.

"Hey, I'm sorry," he nervously tried to comfort her and hoped no one else heard him say that. Tom reached up and gently tugged her arm down. She sat.

"Hey," said Tom, "I like you and all. You're nice, and you're smart. I'll bet your parents have money. Right? That's what I thought. Now there must be some psychological reason that brings-"

"Don't talk to me about psychological things!" She was mad now. "I've heard it all. I've heard it all!" Corporal Harding pouted.

Erotic spots on the human anatomy and weak spots in the mind are both easy to recognize. Tom found the weak one.

"Sorry, I didn't realize you hated head shrinkers."

"They're not headshrinkers, they're doctors."

"Oh? Then I guess you've probably known some?" Tom said sarcastically.

"Tom, I know what you're getting at. Yes I've known some. But not the way you're thinking."

"'scuse me for thinking, but how do you know what I'm thinking?"

She laughed. "Tom, you're kind of funny, but you're an asshole."

"Oh, so you've been dreaming of my asshole too."

"Fuck off Tom. You ARE an asshole. Fact is my father is a psychiatrist."

"Ah, that explains being rich."

Corporal Harding scowled. Tom was goading her like a prosecutor in court.

"And," she continued, "his friends, who were also psychiatrists, and psychologists, would come over to visit or eat."

"Birds of a feather flock together."

"Tom, don't try so hard. It's been hard enough for me to deal with my parents without everybody else trying to make my life more painful because they think I've got it so good." She was trying not to be emotional. "If we're going to go to Africa together, we'd might as well get along."

'Hey! This chick is cool.' Tom respected diplomatic people, even when he was at fault. It's easier to apologize to someone you respect than to someone you don't respect. "Yeah, you're right," Tom began, "I'll behave myself. Like a soldier." He saluted her from his sitting position.

She smiled and saluted back.

* * *

Libya is a beige gritty desert, all of it. Fine if you want to build an ant farm. And hot. Not just hot, but double hot; sun from above, coals from below. Seriously, Libya is God's barbecue. Why do you think these Arabs are all so grouchy and unhappy--it's because they know they got a bum deal when their spirit got assigned to this Hell hole. Bad politics to get here, bad politics to survive here, and there's these fucking flies everywhere . . .

The twin engine plane landed on a straight gravel excuse for an airstrip. Middle of nowhere. Sun almost straight above, no clouds, of course, and no one there to meet them. The plane took off the moment they had their gear off. He blew a few seconds of sandblasting at them like a hillbilly farting, and flew off without saying or waving goodbye.

The two Spaniards that accompanied Tom (Corporal Thomas Jefferson), Corporal Harding, and Captain Truman, cussed at the barren sky. "Donde esta transportacion?" they chanted. The Spaniards cussed at the sand as they kicked it. And of course, to be impartial, they cussed with clenched fists at the plane... This amused Tom. 'Not gonna loan them any of my plastic army men.'

"What now?" Corporal Harding asked the Captain who was scanning all directions.

"Beats me. I'm sure they knew we were coming."

Nothing in sight. Nothing but sand, so... nothing.

"Maybe," continued the Captain as he scanned the lunar surface, "maybe he dropped us in the wrong spot."

Now Corporal Harding responded. She was emotionally cool, but the thought of being here on the planet mars, in the wrong place, finally broke down her cool. "No way," she said confidently, trying to convince herself.

They picked a place in the open to make camp. As long as there wasn't a wind, out in the open would be better. Tom warned them that snakes and spiders probably hung out in the rocks . . .

Tom tried to just look at the whole experience as just another campout. Somehow the thought of being in Libya, in the middle of the desert to take a two month course in terrorism, was a far fetched concept. This whole underground revolution was a far fetched concept. Being wanted by the law for murder, not having his van, and being without Barbara was--now that was strange. Tom bypassed his memories of Becky and went straight back to Barbara. Then Tom remembered Carey. 'Well, life on the run hadn't been all so bad . . .' Then he really remembered his daughter Becky and his body felt like the gravity of the hot sand had increased.

But what was a realistic concept? Tom tried to figure out where the Hell he was going. Not just here, to the guerrilla training camp, but somewhere down the line, a goal, a direction. Maybe even a family?

The thought of a family was both comforting and unsettling. He wanted it. He'd had it. He'd been emotionally numbed by it. But he needed to do it again, for Erika at least. How? Where? With who? When?!

'When' didn't exist for Tom. He was helpless against Time and Destiny. Like a leaf in the wind, Tom had been tossed about, here and there. Where was this wind blowing? 'No win,' Tom thought. 'My life's a no win situation.' Already he was wanted by the law, and now to complicate things, or simplify them for the police, he was hanging out with subversives. Not your ordinary, everyday liberal democratic whiners; these guys were big time. They even killed people. Tom looked around, this was not Canada.

But it was freedom. Kind of. At least he wasn't in jail, he was still free, well, that is if you consider being in the American Freedom Army freedom--Shit. Tom felt that he'd never been free. Even his memories from before the car accident were fading on him.

"Corporal Harding, we aren't carrying anything we can cook." The black desert night gave a sharp edge to the Captain's voice.

"I'll eat anything. I'm starved," she pleaded.

"Yeah Captain. What's for dinner?" Tom asked aristocratically.

"Well, we really didn't prepare for this. We're not carrying any foodstuffs or even water."

"We're gonna die out here," Corporal Harding said in wavering pitches.

The Captain continued. "We used up more than half our canteen of water today."

"I'm starved," she repeated.

"Calm down Corporal. Let's break down our back packs and see what we've got."

They all dug anxiously.

"Okay," announced Captain Truman. "I've got some chocolates and a bottle of wine."

"I've got some caviar," proudly announced Tom.

Both Captain Truman and Corporal Harding gave Tom a stern, questioning stare.

Tom realized they were looking at him like Corporal Kennedy always does. "I thought it might be fun to try."

They continued to gloat at his bourgeois taste.

"I've never tried it." Tom felt on trial. "Well, be that way. You don't want any, you don't have to have any."

The Captain smiled, they all laughed and went back to tearing up their packs.

Noon the next day was the hottest yet. Almost no water and only melted chocolates to eat. The hot-head Spaniards had not been seen since they took off yesterday.

Tom and Captain Truman played cards, mostly "Crazy Eights" and "Gin Rummy."

Corporal Harding said she didn't like to play cards. She sat in the shade next to Tom against a huge boulder.

Tom looked up from his cards and searched the sky. The barren hot horizon made Tom feel like Will Robinson of the movie, **Lost In Space**, or maybe Robinson Crusoe, or- "You hear that?"

"Hear what?" asked Corporal Harding.

"Yeah." Captain Truman stood up and scanned the horizon. "Maybe over there," he pointed.

From about 45 degrees to his right the first helicopter cleared the hill to the South. Two more helicopters came from the North. Then three helicopters cleared a hill to the West.

Tom, the Captain, and Corporal Harding ran out into the open, away from the rocks. They waved as the helicopters converged from all sides.

The copters had sited them but didn't appear all so friendly. They were moving fast and they all dropped down to about twenty feet off the ground. Now, their approach seemed like a head-on collision.

"What do we do?" Tom yelled. "We can't run away, and we can't fight. We don't even have any guns."

"So stand tall, and remain calm." Captain Truman was calm as stone.

"It's probably our escort," said Tom hopefully.

The copters were almost on them. The lone helicopter from the South was the closest and opened up with machine gun fire that was spreading dust in two parallel rows directly toward them like an invisible car.

Tom and Corporal Harding couldn't just stand there and be Swiss-cheesed. They both bolted off in different directions. Tom ran west, Harding ran east.

Captain Truman remained in position, standing tall, looking like a statue--or ready to die with honor. The approaching helicopter from the South released the trigger in time to not riddle the Captain as it flew directly overhead.

Captain Truman turned about face to watch the first copter fly right between the two copters approaching from the North. These two continued their course at the Captain and now they opened fire. Four lanes of bullets riddled the dirt towards Captain Truman but once again ceased fire in time to not blast him into noble hamburger.

The two side by sides from the West separated and pursued Tom and Corporal Harding. The center copter kept a bearing on Captain Truman. Tom couldn't believe this situation and how they were being played with like a cat plays with a half-dead mouse. The center copter fired a rocket which flew right over the Captain's head and exploded about a hundred yards away raising a cloud of dust and the hair on Tom's neck. Bullets sprayed around Tom. They were intentionally missing, but not by very much. All three copters kept their pace and flew by.

All six copters swung around and reversed directions reapproaching now at a slower speed. One from the South, two from the North, and the three from the East. They synchronized their approach so that they all arrived at the same time. Corporal Harding rejoined Captain Truman. Tom stayed by the rocks covering his face with his shirt to shield him from the dust and sand the copters were blowing up as they all hovered.

The copters landed in a semicircle around the conquered revolutionaries. Three men appeared from the dust. The two on the outsides had machine guns at ready. The Arab in the center wore a green cap and wore a pistol, as did his companions. He carried no gun. In one hand was a small notebook. They strode confidently forward and stopped fifteen feet away.

They were all dressed in army light brown with tan spots fatigues. The Arab in the center spoke first.

"Welcome to Camp Ansini. I hope that you appreciated our demonstration." He then smiled mechanically.

Captain Truman was pissed, hot, and hungry. Still, he was in their land and under their rules. "Captain Truman and fellow soldiers of the A.F.A. reporting for training. We were instructed to report to a General Fahizi."

"Good," the middleman replied. "Your group is unharmed?"

"We are fine."

"Good. Have your soldiers gather up their gear. My men will assist them. Captain, come with me."

As they walked to the choppers the Captain inquired why they had not been met yesterday.

"Policy."

"What do you mean, 'policy?'"

"This is a training camp and your training started yesterday."

"But we had no provisions or weapons."

"That was your mistake."

"How can you say that. We just flew halfway 'round the world to be here. Were this a mission we would have provided for it accordingly."

"Dear Captain, a soldier is always on a mission."

The Captain looked into the Arab's eyes as they climbed aboard one of the choppers.

The Arab repeated himself, "Always."

* * *

Six weeks of guerrilla training was the equivalent of four years of college in both a physical and intellectual manner. Exercise and hand-to-hand combat was from six in the morning to ten o'clock. Then two hours of shooting practice, bomb school, and gun smithing.

Lunch was good, usually being a spicy stew or fruits and vegetables. They socialized with soldiers from the entire world. From one o'clock to three o'clock was lectures and readings on different governments. Special speakers whose knowledge was of particular governments spoke. Propaganda was carefully avoided and both cheering and booing were discouraged.

From three o'clock to five was strategy, surveillance, and warfare. Psychology was a large part of the program.

Five to six o'clock was regimental formation and mock attacks. Sometimes these went on into the late evening. Supper was usually served at seven o'clock after everyone showered.

Tom was surprised how many women were here. Of the forty-five students there were eleven girls, including Corporal Harding. Corporal Harding had no interest in any of the other girls. She was however enamored with a French speaking mustached soldier of the F.L.Q. He spoke English well enough but preferred to speak French even though

Corporal Harding knew zero French. Their passion wasn't consummated but Corporal Harding talked incessantly about him.

Tom enjoyed the war games like high school sports. He paid attention during the lectures and was an overall good student. Tom had played with gunpowder as a kid and now he got an entire education on explosives. Guns were fun too, but this desert wasn't meant for human life. Maybe that's why these Arabs are all trying to wipe each other out. The environment is inhospitable. They're just in harmony with their surroundings.

Tom's hard work was recognized. He made the best of this death education in God's Libyan ashtray.

* * *

'Yeah, this place is safe. A real safe house. Three weeks back in the States and nothing. All that training and experience for what? They're planning something. Something big. Being cooped up here is as safe as smoking a cigarette in a room full of dynamite. Shit.'

They actually were sitting on dynamite. Although they hadn't even let Tom see any of the bomb materials, he was now their number two demolitions expert. Tom enjoyed the demolition training. Sergeant Roosevelt was also a demo man from the Seabees. First thing Roosevelt did was pick Tom's brain for new techniques when he returned. They were tired of being with each other for so long in such small quarters. No one had anything to say. This safe house was a time bomb of human explosives.

"What's with you?"

"Nothing," Tom replied.

"Bullshit," Corporal Harding taunted.

Tom didn't look at her as he continued to read the Sunday cartoons.

"Tom, I can tell you're upset about something."

"How very observant." She had gotten to know Tom pretty well during their vacation in the Devil's sandbox.

"You miss your kid, don't you?"

"Of course I miss my kid. I'm tired of waiting forever."

"We'll get a mission soon. They've been planning--"

"I'll tell you what they're planning. They're planning on keeping me here as long as they possibly can. I've had it. I want my money back and I want out of here."

"They did say just one more mission didn't they?" Harding encouraged.

"That's a laugh. They said that before the last mission."

"Of course, now with your guerrilla training, you're more of an investment to them. Maybe they think you might want to stay."

"I'll tell you what they think. They think that soldiers are just little pawns to be kept in a box until they're ready to play with them."

"How can you say that? Our purpose is to free the little pawns of society's manipulations. We--"

Tom started laughing.

"What's so funny?"

"You."

"What do you mean?" she asked as if there were food on her face.

"You. You really buy all that rhetoric about peace and equality."

"Tom you are a fool. Of course I do. Our country--"

"Our country depends on the little guy like the little guy depends on the little cows who depend on the blades of little grass who depend on the little drops of water. It's all just one big fucking pecking order." Tom started laughing to himself. "Actually, 'pecker order' would be a more apt description of our reality."

"You are so cynical. Joking about everything. You know Tom, one of these days you won't get the last laugh."

"Fuck you, I'll laugh whenever I feel like it."

"Fuck you Tom," Corporal Harding said flatly.

"Oh, get off it Har-dee-har-har. You're probably into lesbo politics too."

"Lesbo?"

"What the Hell are you doing here anyway? Why didn't you join the regular army if you wanted to be a soldier?"

"I wanted to do something good for the country."

"Then go get pregnant and raise some happy well-adjusted children. This country seems to be experiencing a shortage of them."

She was mad. Hot mad. An internal anger as Tom pressed her little red white and blue buttons.

Tom continued, "What's with you anyway? You don't date or even have any lovers. You don't even have any girlfriends. How happy are you anyway?"

Ouch. Tom stopped. He didn't even like listening to himself. He knew he'd hurt her feelings even if he did mean what he said. She was nice enough though. She was even kind of attractive, like a Siamese cat. She wasn't cross-eyed, she just had an exotic look to her. When her hair was wet it changed from brown to black, then she looked Asian. Small but overly plump lips provided her a genetic pout. She always appeared a little unhappy. Corporal Harding didn't pluck her eyebrows like most girls seemed to be doing, so they were long and black with a mean seductiveness, that wasn't threatening. Even if she was good looking, she was so sensually reserved that Tom hadn't even considered her. 'course, since losing Becky, he hadn't considered anybody.

Finally Harding spoke, "And you've got the perfect excuse for being here. Your wife is murdered and you can rationalize it as vengeance. A real death wish. A hero--"

"What are you talking about?"

"So you burn the bank, turn your back on the country . . . You're not even into politics. You take no interest in rallies or meetings. You're just an operative. Sucking off the revolution. You could probably work just as easily for the pigs or--"

"Oh, cram it with your party politics."

"See!"

"Politics, smallitics. Just a bunch of ass-kissing, brown-nosing, pencil pushers who fuck their secretaries and get to write off anything they do as part of their expense account."

"Well why don't you want to change that Tom?"

"Because they'd shoot me before they'd let me change their system."

"It's our system," she tried to say convincingly.

"Wrong. It's their system. They are in control. They are in power. They have control of the vertical, the horizontal... Don't try to adjust your TV set. They are in con--"

"Damn it Tom! Life is just a joke to you."

"And a funny one," Toms darker memories surged within him, "sometimes."

Tom made pancakes for the group. Master Sergeant Buchanan was still not talking to Tom. He really made life rough for him now that he was back from Libya. Captain Truman read the paper, and Corporal Harding looked at the movie section. Corporal Kennedy had shaved her head when Tom, Harding, and the Captain were in Libya. She really looked butch--or butchered, now.

Field General Hoover had been away for a week to the East Coast. That seemed to be their real headquarters. Tom didn't ask many questions about the A.F.A. He didn't care.

"I'd sure like to go to the movies," sighed Corporal Harding.

"Give up your bourgeois habits Corporal," scolded Kennedy.

"I'll go with you," agreed Tom.

"That's not a bad idea," nodded Captain Truman.

"It's a stupid idea," blurped Corporal Kennedy.

"We've got our disguises," added Corporal Harding.

Master Sergeant Buchanan summed it up, "We have been given instructions to stay inside with no one venturing out until told. Our food is delivered, and we have a TV and a couple radios. As an army we have more entertain--"

"Thank you Sergeant. Now listen troops," started the Captain. "I don't even know what they're working on. We may be aligning with another radical group, so we're waiting to see how that turns out before we continue."

Tom ate his pancakes now that he'd served everyone else. He chewed and quietly listened. 'Politics,' Tom thought to himself, 'politics is like talking about having a baby: it doesn't get the job done and it wastes your time.'

"But it's been months since we hit that armored car and some time before that when we torched the administration building. Why--we're hardly even a nuisance," complained Corporal Kennedy.

Tom wanted to say that she was a nuisance but . . .

"Now listen here," started the Captain again, "I told you something big is coming up. Everyone here has done a fine job. I don't want to hear any ragging. We will do as we're told, and we'll do it when we're told." Captain Truman eyed all the seated soldiers sternly. "Any problems with that?"

Everyone ate. No one talked.

* * *

The night fog was rolling in a little earlier each day. Berkeley was in the clouds, literally. Back at the safe house, probably still sunshine. Tom and Corporal Harding sat on their hilltop perch overlooking a canyon of nicer homes. One of them was inhabited by a Judge Willow. They were staking him out to keep track of his moves and habits.

From where they sat in the dirt lot between two large homes, the whole world seemed deserted.

They talked and eventually the topic came around to Jean Marchant, the F.L.Q. soldier they met in Libya.

"Do you think he remembers me?"

"I'm sure he always will," Tom patronized.

"I wish that I could write him," Hardy sighed.

"Why can't you?"

"I didn't get his address."

"Did you give him yours?"

"He didn't ask."

"Did you kiss him?"

"No."

"Then how do you know you even like him?"

"You don't have to fuck someone to know that you like them."

"It helps," Tom quipped.

Corporal Harding became angry again. "I don't have to prove my sexuality like you and Sergeant Roosevelt."

"We don't prove it, we just exercise it."

"Fuck you."

"See, there you go again with that Freudian slip."

"Damn you," she said softer but with more intent.

"Mellow out. You're bored, you're lonely, and you need to get laid."

"You are so crass!"

"But it's true, and it's perfectly normal."

"Tom. Maybe I don't know what's normal."

Harding's voice was cracking and Tom knew she was about to cry.

"Hey, hey," he said as he reached to pat her on the back.

Corporal Harding surprised him when she instinctively leaned into his shoulder and began to sob. She was more like a guy than a girl, and a buddy than a girlfriend. This felt very awkward to Tom as his fellow soldier compatriot weeped into his Levi jacket.

"I'm sorry Tom. I don't know what's wrong with me," she said wiping her eyes and trying to regain control.

"Is it your time of the month?" Tom asked gently.

She looked him in the eye with a shocked expression that meant, 'how could you ask me that?' then replied, "Almost."

* * *

Life at the safe house lightened up a couple days later when the orders came down.  Captain Truman was delighted also to get the ball rolling.  For the next few days they cased out three locales; the Judge's house, an officer's mistress, and several police stations.

"It seems that we're working in synchronization with at least two other units.  They're planning a major offensive.  Between the hijackings of the F.P.A. and the kidnapping by the Freedom Fighters, we'll force the government into surrendering some key political prisoners, forking out some big bucks for ransom, and supporting a couple of charitable organizations for public good will.  So let's pull our weight and look good in comparison to the other units."

"What are our projects?" Corporal Kennedy asked.

"They didn't say.  We'll be given our schedule and they'll be given theirs.  I've got a time frame of four weeks but no definite hits, yet."

"When do we start?" asked Corporal Harding.

"Now."

After only a couple more days the news began to explode like popcorn.  The other units had begun to act.  First there was a daytime bank robbery.  Then a school was bombed at night.  Next a post office bombing, several bomb scares, a hijacking to Cuba, then a sheriff was assassinated.  The underground movement was stretching its ugly arms and flexing its muscles.  The Feds were panicked and the public was screaming from the safety of their TV sets.  All the while, demands were being made for the release of political prisoners, freedom for the blacks and Indians, socialized medicine, remove the R.O.T.C., abolish nuclear arms and on and on . . .

The Freedom Fighters and the F.P.A. were the ones performing the actions, but they gave credit to the A.F.A. as an alliance in their communiques.  It gave the feeling of importance and prestige to everyone in the Eagle Cell safe house.  Although people didn't recognize them in public, it was like being a king disguised as a pauper. A rock star in sunglasses. They were constantly celebrating and toasting their press accomplishments. Then finally it came time for them to participate more actively.

They were told to abandon the judge surveillance and to keep surveillance on the Navy General. Tom was given a job as a driver for the company that serviced the police bathroom facilities. Tom delivered supplies and paper towels. He was brave in his makeup and disguises. Sometimes Tom wondered if he should have plastic surgery.

"Tom, it's tomorrow," Captain Truman informed. "You'll set a six stick clock bomb in a towel dispenser. It'll be set for five hours later."

"Which dispenser?"

"Which ever one is convenient."

"Where's the load?"

"I've got it in my room."

"Good, I'll set it up," Tom said eagerly.

"No. I and Sergeant Roosevelt will set it up. You just deliver it."

"I did good with explosives. I'd enjoy setting it up. I'm supposed to--"

"No. This is for me to do. Now get some sleep and don't speak of this to the others until after the job is done."

Tom felt strange about this. "Okay."

Tom made several deliveries carrying around his firecracker payload. Finally he arrived at the police station in Oakland. He was nervous of course and tried to act natural. Every move felt awkward. Every step seemed different. Every "Hello" was unnatural. The bathroom on the first floor was crowded. The second floor men's room was vacant. He opened the paper towel dispenser with his key and put some towels in leaving enough room on top for the blaster. He pulled the towels off the bomb in the basket and gingerly placed it in the cabinet atop the stacked paper towels. The timer was set for five hours already but the glass cover of the clock was a little loose. Tom could see the scratches in the ring that held the glass. Why would that be removed?

Too late to stand there and analyze this. Tom's heart was pounding and any moment someone could walk in.  He quickly connected the battery wires, pulled the alarm knob on the back of the clock and closed the dispenser.

Only as Tom locked the cabinet with the key did he realize his hands were sweating.

Tom still had two more bathrooms to go and went about stocking them very quickly.  Carrying his plastic basket down the ground floor hallway towards the side door service entrance, he noticed how many people were here.  Some were civilians, some were police, some were prisoners.  Men and women.  He looked at them and thought of what danger they were in.  He wanted to warn them.  He didn't want to kill any of them.  The police, didn't seem as much like pigs here.  This was their home, their job.  They seemed at home here, talking and joking with one another.  Human.  Out on the streets they were pigs.  Here they were just men in uniforms.  Yuck.  Uniforms: domination wardrobe of the government.  Well, pigs or not, most of these guys would be safely gone when the bomb went off in five hours.  It was almost twelve o'clock noon and a lot of cops were milling in for lunch.

As Tom headed for the exit at the end of the hallway, he tried to resolve in his mind how this terrorism was for the greater benefit of everyone.  Even these people would unknowingly benefit from the improvements they would make in society.  The police state was a disease that needed surgery.  'Perhaps this bomb would--'

The walls shook, floor jumped, and the ceiling collapsed behind Tom. The air wailed with screams, alarms, and dust.  Tom's bomb had gone off in five minutes, not five hours.  He was almost killed.  Tom walked as quickly as he possibly could.  He didn't know if he should run.  His basket was knocked from his hand as he squeezed through the crowd. An ocean of officers and civilians poured into the corridor.

Tom got to the truck and drove off.  Tom was afraid to return the truck but he wanted to get his bicycle he'd ridden to work.  Tom parked the truck around the corner from the office, snuck into the parking lot, unchained his bike and took off.

Tom took a different route home to the safe house.  The wind in his face was more like water.  He felt dirty yet clean, heavy but light, happy but sad, he was scared and confused.

An Oscar Meyer Wiener Mobile was parked in a grocery store parking lot. Kids were gathered around to meet Oscar. Tom remembered the Wiener Mobile visiting his San Diego neighborhood as a kid. He wondered what happened to the Wieney Whistle that the guy dressed like Oscar had given him. Tom sang to himself. It cheered him up. "Oh I wish I was . . ."

* * *

"I was nearly fucking killed!"

"I'm very sorry Tom, I was under orders not to tell you so that you wouldn't panic and blow your cover."

"Blow my cover? You almost blew the cover off my skull. I could have done it in five minutes as easily as five hours had I known. But why five minutes? Why lunch time? You must've killed--"

"Less chance of the bomb being found."

"FOUND my ass. That was calculated to kill more cops. They wanted prime time traffic."

"It's not ours to evaluate. You did well."

"Did well. I was lucky to survive that at all. I was in the hall when it fucking blew!" Tom wondered if it was meant for him too.

"I'm sorry Tom. I wanted to tell you," apologized the Captain again.

"Yeah. Thanks a lot. I'm never handling any bomb that I don't set myself. And I'd do a cleaner job of rigging the hands than you. I saw the scratches but never dreamed you'd cross me like that."

"Don't get cocky Tom. I apologized and that's that. Now shut up about it, here comes Corporal Kennedy and M.S. Buchanan. Don't stir up any trouble."

Tom gave Captain Truman a look of defiance. Mean defiance. He remembered all the people in that hallway and wondered how many were injured or even killed.

"Tom, I mean Corporal Thomas--we heard it on the car radio.  The F.P.A. took credit for the blasting of the police station.  They wouldn't say for sure but estimated nine killed and sixteen injured.  Wow.  What a score!"

Tom felt even more hate for Corporal Kennedy.  How could she be so excited about killing people.  'You pathetic bitch . . .'

Then Field General Hoover walked into the safe house through the back door.

"I wish I'd been there" she continued.

"Me too," Tom mused.

Captain Truman gave Tom a dark look.

Field General Hoover tapped the Captain on the shoulder.  "May I speak to you in private?"

Tom walked into the front room to be alone.

That night was a big celebration.  Corporal Harding and Sergeant Roosevelt returned from their stakeout with a jug of cheap rose wine and a couple six-packs of imported beer.  Tom drank methodically.  Corporal Kennedy was really whooping it up.

The Captain kept telling her to keep it down, but even the Master Sergeant was bellowing his war stories loud enough for the neighbors to hear.

"All right troops, let's go to the drive-in theatre.  We deserve some entertainment and--"

"Let's go shoot some pigs!" yelled Corporal Kennedy.

"Shhh."  Captain Truman was getting nervous and tipsy.

"Captain's right," said M.S. Buchanan as he stood up from the kitchen table.

"Let's go see a war movie."

"I don't really want to go out," spoke Corporal Harding.  "I'm really tired.  We did a fourteen hour shift today."

"Well, Corporal," spoke the Captain, "this is not an order, but we'd like to have you along."

"No thanks."

"Okay. Now everyone else pile in and let's go, it's almost dark."

"I'm not going either," spoke Tom.

The Captain looked at Tom's sour face. "Fine. But stay inside."

"Yes Sir."

The Captain was too busy rounding up his jacket and car keys to notice that Tom had called him "Sir."

"How come you're not going Tom?" asked Corporal Harding after the others had gone.

"I think I've killed God."

"What the Hell are you talking about?"

"Something hurts inside me." Tom took a long red drink.

"Tom, you're a hero. You've just accomplished something big."

"Yeah. Some hero. I'm just a messenger with a bomb."

"Tom, this whole scene isn't right for you. You're not happy."

Tom laughed, sort of, "And what the fuck is right for me? Huh? What is my scene? What is right for me? Shit. You know what makes me happy?"

Harding shook her head 'no.'

"I'll tell you what makes me happy." He took another long drink then slammed the empty glass on the kitchen table. "Fucking, eating, sleeping, body surfing and getting high. Oh, and I like music a lot. That's what makes me happy. And now I've lost it all. My life. I've fucking wasted it, killed my friends, lost my wife, lost my daughter," he paused, "and now I've lost my identity."

"No Tom, you're still Tom."

"No I'm not. I'm Corporal Thomas Jefferson, Eagle Cell, Western Division of the A.F.A., American Freedom Assholes."

"Tom!"

"It's fucking true . I just want to be Tom again. I want to be me. I

241

want to be free. I want to get high, go bodysurfing, camp in my van, sleep with beautiful babes and maybe someday settle down and have a radioactive family." He began pouring another glass from the green jug.

"Tom, you can still do whatever you want. Especially now. You're paving a path to freedom for yourself. You're helping other people. You are a benefit to society. I'm sure something good will come of--"

"You don't understand. I'm dead. I'm fucking dead. I've killed myself. I can see it now. I wish I'd turned myself in. I wish I'd never come to San Francisco. I--"

Corporal Harding grabbed Tom's glass and held it to the table so that he couldn't take another drink. "You've had some bad luck Tom."

"You call this bad luck?"

"You're still alive. You've survived-"

"Survived! Survival has been my religion. I don't know if I even believe in God, but somehow, I feel he doesn't believe in me. I don't."

"Quit feeling sorry for yourself."

"It seems the more you worship, the weaker you become, but how strong am I now? I've got nothing to worship, no one to turn to--"

"Tom, you've got us. We're your family now. You are such a rebel that you turn on whoever is in charge. Be it God or Master Sergeant Buchanan."

"Now there's a joke. That overgrown Boy Scout-"

"There, see? You rebel against everything."

"Not everything."

"Just about. It's a crazy world out there, full of crazy people. Murder is everywhere-"

"Yeah, like right here in my own clothes."

"Listen to me Tom."

"Ah. What's the use?" Tom pulled the glass from Corporal Harding and took a drink. Tom's gut clenched. Rotgut wine. Yummm. He thought of dying. He felt like dying. Crawl under a rock and sleep forever. What the Hell could he do now anyway? Anything he touched turned to dust. Perhaps this was the right place to be, to die. A parasite on Amerika's back, sucking its blood, killing its host. Tom felt morally numb.

Right and wrong sounded like a kid's game. The police were just pigs anyway. No, Tom remembered them in the hallway. They were people. But they were hunting him. Sid was hunting him. Who knows who was hunting him. At least here he had a fighting chance. Die fighting anyway. Better than jail.

Corporal Harding had been talking, he'd been thinking. He interrupted her, "Want a drink?"

"Uh, yeah, okay."

Tom relaxed a little and began talking of his wife and daughter. They continued drinking and talking of their pasts and memories.

"C'mon back to my room and I'll show you some pictures of my family," Harding offered in a slurred voice.

They peered through a couple of her scrapbooks. Tom teased her about being a tomboy but he also complimented her several times about how pretty she looked in some of the pictures.

They continued drinking and spilling wine. They laughed and giggled at the pictures until Harding pointed out that she had wet her pants while laughing too hard.

She was very embarrassed.

Tom looked and sure enough her Levi's were wet. She was so embarrassed and drunk that she started to cry. Tom reassured her and helped her into the bathroom where she fell on the cold ceramic tiles. Tom helped her take off her pants and sit on the toilet as she repeated over and over again, "I'm so embarrassed."

Tom wrapped a towel around her and helped her into bed. He pulled the covers back and she handed him the towel as she climbed in heavily.

"Tom, do you really think I'm pretty?"

"Yes, yes. You are very pretty," he mumbled manfully.

"Tom, do you think I'm a tomboy?"

"Well, yes. But there's nothing wrong with that. You're still a very attractive girl."

Tom pulled the covers up over her T-shirt. "Now Corporal you've had a lot to drink, just relax and close your--"

Harding pulled the sheet down and insisted, "I want you to kiss me. I want to know how."

"Now Corporal, I'm sure you kiss fine, now just calm down--"

"You don't think I'm pretty, you were just saying that to be nice."

"No that's not true, I meant it. You're an attractive girl."

"Then what do you care. You said you do it for exercise. I want to know how."

"Corporal, Corporal, Corporal." Tom chuckled nervously. He was a little dizzy still from the vino and this arguing was making him dizzier. He bent over the bed and kissed her gently on the lips. He sat on the edge of the bed as Corporal Harding reopened her eyes.

"Now show me how to French kiss."

"Corporal!?"

"Please Tom, I want to know how," she begged openly.

Tom smiled as he looked down on her. She looked more girlish than he'd ever noticed before. She seemed like a junior high student, inquisitive and still shy.

Tom leaned forward and kissed her again. They kissed longer and Tom used his tongue. She held her mouth open like a cavern. Tom kissed her top lip and sucked on it to get her to close her mouth. When he tried to French with her again she opened her mouth wide again.

"Relax your mouth and do what I do," he whispered.

They kissed again. This time she sucked his lips. He changed angles and they kissed and kissed.

"Use your tongue," he suggested.

Tom gently sucked on her tongue and flicked it with his own. He circled it and kissed it. With his eyes closed the sensations were magnified and the kissing became more than a lesson.

They intertwined and danced within his mouth. Harding shifted and squirmed.

She withdrew her tongue and Tom followed it with his. She now sucked on Tom's tongue and flicked it. Tom stroked her tongue and circled it.

Harding moaned some more and now hugged Tom tightly. Her hands gripped his back and rubbed towards his butt.

Tom was about to sit up when one of her hands reached over for Tom's hand.

She placed Tom's hand on her left breast.

* * *

When Tom awoke naked with Corporal Harding he was shocked. Yes, he remembered making love to her. They were intimate, nervous, serious, and passionate. He remembered her giggle and how they had rolled out of the bed when she tried to get on top for the first time. On the floor they'd laughed entwined in each other's arms and entangled in the bed sheets. But that was supposed to be a dream.

He had never meant to become sexually involved with Harding. He wouldn't have planned it and now he felt a strange unrest at his actions.

Harding lay in the bed asleep. She looked more feminine and girl-like than he'd ever noticed.

But he wasn't in love and felt a guilt accordingly. How would she react to him now? Would she be mad? Feel used? Guilty? Would she be in love?

She moaned. Tom instinctively reached over and gently brushed her hair out of her face. Tom quietly got out of bed and dressed. He noticed the red star around his pubics and commented to himself, "Well her period's started all right."

He opened her door quietly and snuck out. Quietly he closed the door behind him. He tiptoed down the hall to his couch in the living room. The rest of the house still slept. No one was on duty, they weren't on

Level Orange surprisingly.

The next few days passed quietly and very slowly. The house seemed to be a place of mourning. The press was backlashing on them. The P.F.A. and Freedom Fighters had even denounced the act, even though they were instrumental in its planning. Killing so many civilians was what they emphasized in the press. Sure there were a lot more cops killed than civilians, but the slain civilians got the press. Their families on the news . . . Politicians jumped on the bandwagon. Federal forces rallied. Promises of peace and vengeance were made on TV. Angry faces filled the screen. Nine citizens killed.

Field General Hoover disappeared back to the East Coast.

*Standing in the rain*
*There's no room to cry*
*Nothing to trust, nowhere to go*
*But where we will die*
*So what do we have now my love?*
*What is there to fight the decay?*
*But our love with which we feed each other*
*Beneath the bridge over which the soldiers parade (22)*

Tom and Corporal Harding didn't hardly talk. On Thursday they went shopping together. Friday they had to go on a pick-up to San Francisco. They drove over the Bay Bridge with the radio blasting until Corporal Harding reached over and turned it down.

"Tom, I'm sorry 'bout the other night."

"Hey," he tried to laugh. "It was no fault of anybody. We were drunk, it was an accident."

"No, it was my fault."

"Hardy, it wasn't your fault. It takes two to tango. It happened. No big deal."

She thought for a minute. "Well, I'm sorry."

"Corporal please." Tom looked over with an exhausted expression. She was looking at her nervously winding fingers. He tried to cheer her and himself up. "Heck. I never was much of a one night stand."

"Oh, you were wonder--" Corporal Harding began to say then stopped herself, embarrassed.

"Well, I really think that sex is best in a relationship, of some sort."

"You don't think less of me?" she asked demurely.

"Of course not. In fact I must confess that I've felt closer to you somehow. I mean we're best friends and all--but now I kinda see that you're a pretty girl too."

"You're just saying that."

"No. Really I'm not. I must admit that you've always been more like a buddy to me. But now you're more like a sister. I'll be watching and helping you."

"You think I need help?"

Oops. Wrong word. "Now Hardy, there you go again. Knock off this self-pity."

"I'm probably not very good in bed."

"For your information Miss Insecurity, you were great in bed. And you've got a great figure too. I enjoyed myself and I remember how you did too."

"Yes," she said softly with her head still hung. "I did."

"So stop the fuss and let bygones be bygones. There's no sense making a murder out of this."

"What about Captain Truman and M.S. Buchanan?"

"What about them? It's none of their business and they don't seem to care anyway."

Tom thought hard of a way to break the morbidness of this situation. "And I'm glad it happened anyway. I mean, what the heck. We're friends and compatriots, and you said you needed the practice."

Tom looked over with a sly smile, hoping that she'd return one.

"Yeah, I needed the practice," she said with a sad forced laugh.

"Okay then. So we're friends, right?"

Corporal Harding looked at Tom's profile as he drove. She smiled. "Yeah. Friends."

*Snow coldly blows upon our Summer*
*Burying greens in tides that know no aim*
*Thoughts struggling, frozen, moved only by the wind*
*I fear that the Spring will never be the same*
*Although the sun shines down upon my shoulders*
*It's not enough to cancel out the chill*
*As you open the door to leave me alone*
*I look to see the snow once again lighting on my windowsill (23)*

Captain Truman's phone conversation from the payphone was terse.
"Yes, I realize that the publicity- . . . But what do you expect? . . . Of
course, we all know that the press is manipulated by the-- . . . Yes, I
know that even in New Yor-- . . . Yes, well, it's bad for us out here-- . . .
No, our demands are not in print . . . Well The Barb is one thing but the
Hearst chain-- . . . No not even the-- . . . well perhaps our planning
wasn't right . . . No, I wasn't. But perhaps our original plan of making
certain demands against the five hour time limit would've worked better
to our benefit . . . No, of course I'm not-- . . . No sir, I'm sorry. I was
only saying-- . . . Yes . . . Okay . . . I understand . . . Sir, that's not
necessary is it? . . . Yes Sir, I'm listening . . . Uh-huh . . . Well Tom has
been very useful and-- . . . Yes Sir, of course, we're all willing martyrs . .
. No, I'm not arguing . . . Yes . . . I understand, but-- . . . Yes Sir, we
must do of course what we must do . . . Yes, yes . . . Tom is interested in
serving the best interests of the A.F.A . . . Really Sir? But why merge
now? . . . Well . . . The fact is Sir that Tom's involvement was more
accidental and he's-- . . . No Sir, but-- . . . Yes Sir, of course. I
understand. But those larger intentions and greater good-- . . . I know,
but Tom is-- . . . No Sir . . . I won't speak a word of this."

Captain Truman hung his head with the payphone receiver still
mashed against his left ear. He shook his head in unseen agreement
reluctantly. "Yes Sir, I'll carry out-- . . . Yes Sir . . . Yes Sir . . . If you
think that is the only way to take the pressure off us . . . Really? . . .
Thank you Sir . . . Yes Sir, of course . . . He's on stakeout . . . Yes,
that's right he'll be back tonight . . . Okay. I mean, Yes Sir. I'll keep
him home tomorrow . . . But Sir, it would take less-- . . . Yes Sir, we'll
leave everything just as it is . . . The Sergeants and Corporals will be out

by oh-nine-hundred . . . Uh-huh. We'll meet you there . . . Oh, I mean-- . . . Okay. We'll receive a message there . . . Yes Sir, we'll be there . . . --and Tom will be alone . . . Yes Sir. I will... Tomorrow."

\* \* \*

Corporal Tom and Corporal Harding sat on the backed-up freeway with a view of the San Francisco Bay from the Golden Gate Bridge. They would pick up Master Sergeant Buchanan and Corporal Kennedy down in Daly City, then return back to their safe house in Oakland.

"Tom let's get a bottle of wine tonight? I'm totally bored with this stakeout stuff and political backwash lately. Let's get drunk."

Tom looked over to Corporal Harding with a wicked smile. "Yeah, I agree. And Captain Truman's pretty uptight too. Maybe we should get him wasted too."

"Yeah. He needs to lighten up. Since the police bombing it's been dead city at the safe house."

"Yeah, a real mortuary."

"You've been uptight too, Tom," Harding smiled.

"Yeah," he chuckled lightly.

"But you were great. I mean I can just picture those pigs flying. What a ham house. You must've--"

"Harding, I didn't want to waste those pigs."

"What do you mean? They're our enemies. They're your enemies."

"That bomb was supposed to go off after quitting time, you know, five o'clock."

"Five o'clock? It went off at noon."

"Yes, I know."

"You were great at demolition. What happened?"

"I didn't set it."

"I thought you delivered it."

"I did, but I didn't set it."

"How could that be?  Rule one is never deliver an unchecked timer. You should've-"

"Oh, I checked it all right.  And it was set for five o'clock.  Yeah, but Captain Truman had tampered with it the night before so that no matter what I did it would be five minutes."

"Five minutes!?  Was he crazy?"

"I was nearly killed."

"Five minutes?  And you didn't know?"

"Are you kidding?  Of course I didn't.  I was in the hallway remember when it went off.  I was as surprised as they were.  I barely got out of there."

"But why?"

"I don't know.  El Capitan said he was under orders."

"Under orders?  What kind of orders are those?"

"I don't know.  He wouldn't talk about it.  I was under orders not to tell anyone before the bombing and then he told me not to discuss it with anyone afterward."

"He's been very secretive lately."

"I feel set up," Tom said quietly.

"The Captain wouldn't set you up," she countered in a surprised tone.

"Says who?  He plays the game like a good soldier.  He follows orders.  I'm expendable.  He almost killed me."

"Don't say that!  Captain Truman's like a father to us.  He cares--"

"He's a soldier, not a father," Tom reminded.

"He's been uptight to everyone.  He's under pressure.  The press is all screwed up right now.  They're crucifying us and he's taking it very hard."

"Well I don't trust him."

"DON'T SAY THAT!" Corporal Harding shouted.  "Captain Truman's the best.  He's the finest friend we could have."

"I'm glad you think so. But I don't trust him anymore."

"Tom this is ridiculous. Let's drop it."

Tom turned the car radio up.

Over the loud AM radio rock, "Tom, I'm worried about you."

"How romantic," Tom said sarcastically.

Corporal Harding slumped back and stared forward at the rows of inching cars.

"Fuck you Tom."

"Oh don't get pissed."

"Why shouldn't I?" She looked over to Tom. "You're my closest friend."

"And you're my closest friend."

"Oh, you don't understand," she said as if exhausted.

They listened to the radio, coldly. The traffic was stop'n'go... stop'n'go . . .

"Tom? I want you to kiss me again."

"Now Corporal, let's not go through this again."

"No Tom. I'm not talking about sex. I just want a kiss. Please?" She turned down the radio.

Tom turned to her to begin an excuse but saw her frightened eyes. He stopped the car behind another stopped car, pressed his foot a little harder than usual against the brake pedal to hold the car still, turned to her and kissed her cheek. He kissed her gently. She let him. She kissed him back. Then they kissed each other.

The car behind them honked.

Tom pulled forward. He would've kissed her longer.

Corporal Harding reached her arms around Tom in a tight hug as he drove with both hands on the wheel.

\* \* \*

Breakfast was weird.  Sergeant Roosevelt was being a comic, Harding was quiet, and Tom wasn't hungry.

Tom cooked pancakes but they weren't really 'his' pancakes.  When Tom made pancakes they were always different.    Experimental, expressive.    Tom seasoned or altered the recipe to suit the situation, desire, appetite, or adventurousness.  Today the pancakes were uniform, thick, flat and lifeless--pancakes without spirit.

The Captain began to explain the day as Tom sat down with his flapjack stack.

"We'll be leaving by eight-thirty.    We're gonna run an errand.  Corporal Tom, you'll stay behind and keep an eye on things here."

"What's to keep an eye on?"

Truman snapped, "I said you'll stay here!"

Corporal Harding was alarmed by this emotional outburst.    She looked at the Captain and then at Tom.

"Hey," piped Sergeant Roosevelt, "we don't want anybody running off with our tires."

"I'll stay too," announced Corporal Harding.

"No, we're all going except Tom."

"I'd like to stay," emphasized Corporal Harding.  I had too much to drink last night.  I don't--"

Captain Truman burned a stern look that silenced Corporal Harding.  "Now hurry up.  We've gotta run."

Corporal Harding didn't eat anymore.    Tom finished his breakfast without looking at anyone else at the table.

The Captain warmed the car engine.    Tom could hear the Fairlane humming in the driveway.

"C'mon Corporal," said Sergeant Roosevelt as he held open the screen door.

Harding stopped at the front door and looked at Tom in the kitchen, cleaning up the dishes.

"C'mon Corporal!"

She turned and left without saying goodbye.

They had driven about a half-hour in Thursday morning rush traffic when Corporal Harding finally burst out, "Why the Hell couldn't Tom come?"

"Corporal pipe down. I told you, he's staying behind."

"But why?"

"Corporal I have some important things on my mind. I'd appreciate your silence."

"I've had enough silence. Things have been very silent lately."

"Corporal shut up!" shouted Master Sergeant Buchanan from the front seat.

Corporal Kennedy took it all in. She kept quiet.

"Why?" continued Corporal Harding.

"Why?" mimicked Master Sergeant Buchanan. "What the Hell's got into you Corporal Harding? I'll jump back there and--"

"That's fine Sergeant. I'll handle this," said the Captain as he continued to commandeer the car slowly forward onto the freeway onramp.

"What's going on around here? Everything's mysterious and--"

"What's going on here Corporal is that you've lost your military discipline." The Captain continued coolly. "Just follow orders and mind your own business."

"Maybe I am minding my own business, and that means finding out the truth. What are you afraid to say?"

Corporal Kennedy leaned forward to look at Corporal Harding on the other side of Sergeant Roosevelt. More fury than she'd ever witnessed before.

"Corporal don't get yourself in trouble," Truman scolded.

"How much more trouble can I get in?" she countered, sounding more like Tom than herself.

"You're really pushing it," Buchanan boiled.

"Who's pushing who?"

"Corporal!" M.S. shouted turning to face her from the front seat.

She continued undaunted.  "And who pushed Tom into all this?"

"Corporal Harding I'm gonna--"

"What's wrong?" taunted Corporal Harding like a bullfighter teasing the bull.

"Something I'm not supposed to know?"

"There's nothing to not know," countered Master Sergeant Buchanan.

"Oh yeah?  Then why didn't Tom know about the five minute bomb timer?"

Captain Truman was silent as he tightened his grip on the steering wheel and sat up straighter. Master Sergeant Buchanan even looked at the Captain for a response to this accusation.

Corporal Harding wouldn't accept the silence.  "And where are we going?"

"I told you; an errand."

"An errand?  Where?"

"To Lake Ridge cabin."

"Lake Ridge cabin?  That's three hours from here.  What are we going there for?"

"An errand."

"Whose errand?"

"Corporal that's all.  What's got into you?  You've got a lot of nerve talking to me like this.  Now I'm ordering you to put a lid on it.  Act like a soldier--not a raving woman."

She was aghast.  "Oh yeah!?  Well I am a woman.  A raving woman and I want to know the truth.  Why couldn't Tom come?"

"Corporal I told-"

"No you didn't!"

Master Sergeant let the conversation continue now.  Everyone in the car had questions to be answered. Corporal Harding had stirred up more than just sand.

"Corporal, I'm under orders just like you. If I questioned authority like you're doing I'd be demoted."

"So demote me. Then tell me--"

"Corporal we're under orders to run an errand to Lake Ridge. Now if you'll kindly shut your face and quit being hysterical--"

"Hysterical? Why . . . I . . . I . . ."

Harding opened her door and stepped out of the car into the slow freeway traffic.

Despite the car only moving at about ten miles per hour, she fell and almost rolled under an adjacent car.

She got up and ran between cars, positioning herself on the white dotted lines as cars drove past her on both sides.

"Corporal!" yelled Buchanan.

They stopped the car. Master Sergeant Buchanan began to open the door to chase her.

"Let her go," the Captain stated angrily. He put the car back into gear and continued driving on.

Everyone else in the car watched Corporal Harding zig-zag to the shoulder and disappear off the side of the road.

It was almost noon before Harding got back to the safe house.

"Corporal? Where's everybody else?"

"They're going to Lake Ridge." She was a little out of breath.

"Why didn't you go?"

"I jumped out of the car."

"You what?"

"I jumped out. I got in a big argument with the Captain."

"Hardy, are you all right?"

"I'm scared. Something is wrong Tom."

"That's for sure."

"No, I mean, they said they were under orders."

"So," Tom shrugged, "we're all under orders."

"And Captain Truman was under orders to rig the clock, remember?"

"Now Hardy, don't you think you're a little paranoid?"

"Yes Tom.  I'm paranoid and I'm scared.  Something is wrong." Corporal Harding was pacing the living room. "Tom listen to me.  I can feel it.  Let's get out of here!"

Tom began to laugh. "Hardy, I've never see you so dramatic."

Harding walked up close to Tom.  They stood face to face. "Tom, I don't want anything to happen to you."

Tom chuckled and made a funny face.

"Tom I--"

A rustle in the leaves beside the house silenced their conversation. They listened as footsteps ran alongside the house.

Harding ran to the front window.  She saw a cluster of cars at the end of the block.

"Tom!  Something is going on."

Tom joined her at the window and saw two plainclothesmen enter the neighbor's house.

"Shit.  Something is going on.  Grab a couple pistols."

Corporal Harding ran back into the kitchen and pulled up a floor board.

The house was a one-story and Tom got a strange feeling from the roof.

"Harding let's get out the officer's window."

Corporal Harding parted the bedroom blinds to see a crouched suited man watching the back door. His revolver was drawn.

"Tom," she panted, "there are agents out there.  What're we gonna do?"

"I don't know."

Then the bullhorn blasted from behind a parked car in front of the house. "This is the FBI.  Please leave your house immediately.  Step outside immediately. This is an arrest! Vacate the house!"

"Tom." She looked up into his frozen expression. He stared out.

"I'm not going to jail," Tom said flatly.

"Tom we can't get out. There're too many of them."

"No, you leave now Corporal. They're probably just after me. You can plead innocent and say you knew nothing of my activities."

"No Tom, I won't leave you. We'll both surrender and--"

"No, I'm not going to be arrested."

"Then I'm staying too."

"No God damnit. Hardy give up now and you'll be all right." He grabbed her arm with his left hand, holding his pistol in his right.

"No I won't. I won't be all right if something happens to you."

"Hardy split God damnit!" He gripped her arm tighter and shook it.

"No. I'm staying with you!"

Tom pointed his gun towards the ceiling but held it in front of her face. "God damnit Corporal. I'm tired of running. I'm not going to jail, and I'm not gonna--"

With the crash of broken glass the rear door was smashed open. Tom turned and ran to the living room where he confronted the agent with a pair of blasts. The agent spun to the ground.

A window of the living room was smashed open and a rifle stuck through the hole. Tom fired but caught a bullet in the shoulder knocking him to the ground.

Corporal Harding ran in firing a barrage of shots. She knelt next to Tom firing a couple more blasts.

"Tom, Tom!" she sobbed slamming another clip into her Combat Commander.

"I'm all right. Give yourself up. You can still go. Just--"

"No. I'll get you out of here. Can you run?"

"Yes."

"Then we're going out the back. C'mon, before they dump tear gas in here. Let's go!" she proclaimed helping him to his feet.

The bullhorn was shouting, helicopters beating the air, more shots and the front windows shattered.

"NOW!" Corporal Harding commanded.

They burst out the back door and began firing in all directions as they ran.  They made it to the alley before Tom caught another bullet in the arm and they both dove through the hedge into the neighbor's backyard. They laid low on the grass as bullets whizzed overhead.

"Tom, look!  Over there."  She pointed to two bicycles next to the garage.  "We'll grab those bikes. You can still peddle can't you?"

"Yeah, yeah.  But Hardy, you've got to--"

"Hold on to me.  I'll cover you."

They got up to run but Tom was bleeding bad and in too much pain. Tom fell as bullets began to fan from over a brick wall.   Corporal Harding tried to drag him with one arm.  She stopped and began to fire at the hidden guns.   She walked backwards to the bikes.   "TOM!" she yelled.  "RUN TOM!"  She fired at a policeman in the alley and knocked him into a somersault.  She knelt down next to the bikes. "TOM!"

Tom couldn't raise his torso up, his arms and shoulder bled.  He lay like a hunchback pushing forward with his legs.

"TOM!" she screamed.  "RUN TOM, RUN--"

A bullet hit her in the hip.  She fell back against the bikes and another bullet tore through her back. As they laid down a swarm of bullets she flinched atop the bicycles with ricocheting sparks as she twitched like a puppet being jerked by its strings.

Tom saw it.  Like a snake he wriggled quickly to her.  Tears flowed. He knew but he shook her anyway as he laid beside her.  She didn't respond.   Tom last remembered a voice behind him and a gun barrel pressed to the back of his head.  The world went black.

# Chapter 8
## *Soledad Prison*

Jail was a grey blurr of weeks and weeks. From San Diego County Jail to the California Adult Authority to Soledad Prison, Tom had been shuffled and caged within paperwork walls and political bars. This mattress, two sheets, two blankets, a toothbrush and a Bible were the furnishings of Tom's new home. Soledad, for five to life.

Bullet wounds were the smallest scars left from the past four months of hospitals and guards, cells and steel, cuffs and chains . . . Tom sat in silence, an emotionless, dark brooding body.

The trial was a sensation. Tom's family never showed. He thought he saw Barbara once in the courtroom audience. Tom's defense was weak and plea bargaining had been denied. Tom spoke of no one. No names, no information, and no defense. He went through the motions knowing that "Guilty" was a guarantee.

Sitting in his private solitary cell Tom could still feel the chains and cuffs he wore to and from trial, day in and day out, for more days than he wanted to remember.

He could hear the rattle and clicks . . . Even sitting alone he still hung his head as if someone might be staring at him or taking a flash photograph. It was a relief to be out of that circus, even if that meant being here.

"Copkiller," is what they called him here. The stigma gave him a little more distance from the others and of course the guards. Tom could care less. He wished he'd died with Corporal Harding in that safe house battle. Tom's punishment was to be kept alive. His life was over but like a catatonic body, they would feed him in this box.

Dead among the living. Scraping together sunsets with Earth's talking rat population.

Most of these guys, including the guards, reminded him of characters in a Raid cockroach commercial. Twentieth century leper colony.

Tom didn't want any excitement or entertainment. Just breathe through another day, sleep another night, eat another meal, breathe . . . Lately however, the Mexicans were hassling him. One guy named, Ghost, was always trying to trip him and always had some derogatory comment to get a rise out of Tom. Tom ignored him but knew that there would soon be a confrontation. This unsettling possibility was the only thing to keep Tom from totally shutting off his brain.

The mess hall was the closest contact Tom had with other prisoners. Here he'd have to sit next to someone. Today a tall blonde kid sat next to him, intentionally.

"I've noticed you being bugged lately."

Tom didn't respond as he continued to chow down his corn flakes in milk.

"That Mex is just waiting for a chance to get on your case."

"Let him."

"I'd rather not. We don't like to see them get the best of one of our boys."

"Your boys?" Tom asked without looking up.

"Hey, you're not the only whitey in this prison. We stick together, they stick together, and racial problems are minimized."

"Oh." Tom munched on.

"Fact is you've been a loner since you came here. That's why Ghost would enjoy working on you. We don't want that kind of uncontrolled problem."

"So, what am I to do?"

"Just be seen with some of us. Make your alliance known. As soon as they see you're represented, they'll respect you and back off."

"I'm not interested in joining any gang."

"You know, you could play this a lot smarter. We all know about your underground life. You're a real rebel. That's fine. Around here violence isn't so noteworthy. Fact is that's your past. We've all got a past. But now is your present, and your present determines your future. So perhaps you'd better value some friendship."

"Yeah sure." Tom continued eating.

The blonde shook his head scoldingly. "Think about it."

"Yeah."

The tall blonde got up and went elsewhere to eat his breakfast. Tom didn't look up or say goodbye.

Later that morning when everyone was outside exercising, Tom was in the lounge reading magazines.

"Hey Copkiller."

It was Ghost, but Tom kept his eyes to the pages.

"Hey Copkiller, you run out of bombs?"

Tom ignored him. The old man next to him on the naugahyde couch got up and walked out. Ghost stood in front of Tom and pulled the magazine out of Tom's hands. Tom glanced around at the vacant area. He could see a couple other Mexicans at the outside exit keeping watch and figured there'd be one at the hallway entrance also.

Tom was still looking down into his open hands when he felt a stinging slap to his left cheek that snapped his head sideways.

"So Copkiller, I need some favors."

"What kind of favors?" Tom held his burning cheek.

"Oh, a little of this, and a little of that," he said in a sing song voice with a Chicano accent.

Tom was silent and still looking down. Another open handed slap rolled him onto the couch.

"Hey Killer. When I talk to you; you answer me."

Tom was still silent.

The Mexican's shoe dug deep into Tom's thigh muscle with a drop kick. Tom was hurting but lay motionless with his hands still on his face and his eyes closed.

Ghost looked down at Tom pathetically. "I'll come back later. Maybe you'll remember how to talk." He started walking away proudly. "If not, I'll teach you how to talk." He laughed, "Killer."

Tom's body throbbed in his self-contained darkness. Tom managed to avoid Ghost for several days. Tom got out of work details and exercise. He didn't need any money and wasn't interested in earning bonus points. He knew they'd never parole him. Tom stayed in his cell as much as possible.

Tom was walking by the gardens when Ghost finally intercepted him with a few of his brown buddies. Tom turned and walked into the kitchen side entrance. Ghost and company followed him. Tom was almost out of the kitchen and into the mess hall when he was hit in the back with a large metal mix bowl. Tom turned around to see another one aimed at his head which he barely ducked.

"Hey, you've been avoiding me, Copkiller."

Tom stood silent. Scared to run. Scared to fight . . .

"And you haven't learned to speak yet. I'm gonna teach you respect."

Tom ran for the door but was tackled by Enrique. Ghost pulled Tom up by his hair. One slap, two slaps, three slaps.

"Found your tongue yet?"

Ghost shook Tom like a limp rag doll.

"Game's over Taco," said a snide voice from behind the Mexicans.

Ghost and his buddies turned around to see two thin white boys holding a butcher knife and a meat cleaver.

"Now if you T-benders don't want to end up as enchilada stuffing, I suggest that you leave the cooking to the cooks and get out of our kitchen."

Ghost didn't say anything as he dropped Tom to his knees. They casually sauntered out mumbling in Spanish.

Tom got up and started to leave.

"You're welcome," said the skinny blonde holding the meat cleaver.

"Thanks," Tom mumbled as he walked away.

"Hey Tom, not so fast. What's the beef?" spoke the other one.

"How'd you know my name?"

"We know everyone.  What's the beef with those brownies?"

"They don't like cop killers."

The two blondes laughed.  "They've probably killed more cops than you.  So why were they pounding on you?"

"I guess cuz I'm a loner."

"Yeah.  Maybe so.  At any rate we can change that.  Can't we Bobby?"

"Heck yeah," replied Bobby.

"My name's F," he announced with outstretched hand.

Tom stepped back to them and shook his hand.

"And this is Bobby."

They shook.

"We're kitchen and the best friends a guy in this joint can have."

"How's that?"

"You know us--you eat well," F smiled.

\* \* \*

Tom was eating breakfast a week later when the tall blonde sat next to him again.  "I see you took my advice."

"Accidentally."

"Well, I wouldn't have guessed you for that crowd."

"What crowd?  They're your white boys."

"No not those.  That's F's gang.  We don't have much to do with them."

"Why not?" asked Tom with a mouthful of scrambled eggs.

"People's sex lives aren't my business but that gang take it religiously."

"Religious sex. New fad huh?"

"You really don't know, do you?"

"I can tell some of 'em are gay, but that's a popular religion around here."

"May be popular, but not a religion. F is a fanatic and he's got a lot of power around here. If that's your cup of tea then fine."

"I didn't say it was."    Tom stopped eating.    "Why are you so concerned?"

"I told you, we avoid trouble."

"So what's the trouble?"

"That's not a club or even a gang, it's a family."

"Like you and your boys."

"No, not like my boys. We don't have orgies."

"Oh c'mon.  You must be hard up for members to be using this slander."

"It's not slander.  It's true.  I don't suppose you've heard of the initiation?"

"They mentioned it."

"Did they tell you what it is?"

"No."

"Well ask them."

"I will."

The blonde got up with his tray of food.

"Hey," Tom asked. "Where you going?"

"Back to sit with my boys."

"What's your name?"

"Ken."

"Finish your meal Ken. I'm sorry I was so rude last time."

"Thanks, but I don't want to stir up trouble with F. See ya."

Ken left with his tray. Tom chewed in deep thought.

Bobby sat down where Ken had been. "Hey, what was that about?"

"He was checking up on me. He warned me about being a loner."

"Well you're not a loner anymore. You've got us."

Tom resumed eating. 'Yeah,' he also resumed thinking.

That night Bobby visited Tom in his cell escorted by a guard who unlocked Tom's cell and let Bobby in, then relocked it.

"Hey Tom, how's it going?"

Tom put down his book, "Fine. How'd you get the guard to bring you here? It's almost ten o'clock.

"Oh we get a lot of extra privileges. A lot of the guards are personal friends."

"What's up?"

"Well Tom, we're planning a party."

"What's the occasion?"

"You."

"What do you mean?"

"To celebrate your membership."

"An initiation," Tom said coldly.

"Yeah, but more like a party."

"And how do you expect to have a prison party?"

"Easy. We control the kitchen. So we get to have it for our personal uses."

"When's the party?"

"Probably Thursday."

"Day after tomorrow?"

"Yeah." Bobby smiled excitedly.

"So what is an initiation?"

"Just a big party. You know. We all have food, and even booze! It's a lot of fun and you'll get to meet more of the gang."

"I'm really not much for parties anymore."

"Oh you'll like this one, it's special."

"Thanks, but I'd like to think about it some more."

"What's to think about?  You're with friends and we want you to feel important."

"You know me.  I'm a loner.  I just want to ride this out here.  No excitement, no family, no--"

"HEY!" Bobby exclaimed, raising his voice.  "We rescued you from a bad situation.  You need protection here and we give it to you.  You could be more grateful."

"Yeah I'm grateful, but I'm not interested in social matters."

"Well get interested Bubba.  We're all here for a long time and we aim to make it as pleasant as possible.  So climb aboard Tom.  We can all help each other out."

With his last line Bobby put a hand on Tom's leg.

Tom left Bobby's hand there but said coldly, "I don't need that kind of help."

Bobby pulled back insulted.  "I don't need that kind of help," he imitated in a little kid voice as he stood up.  Shaking his hips with hands on his own waist he continued his high scolding voice, "Maybe I need that kinda help Tommy.  I helped you so why don't you help me?"

Tom looked down, sighed, and shook his head side to side as he contemplated his dilemma.

Bobby sat down next to him again.  "You've never been with a man before, have you Tom?"

"No."

"That's all right.  I can be your girl if you want."

"I don't want anyone."

"Shit.  You selfish mother fucker.  We hand you the world on a silver platter and you play righteous. And I suppose that you don't need us anymore?

"I didn't say that."

"Well I know when I'm not wanted."  Bobby got up and called the guard by name from the end of the hall. Bobby didn't say goodbye as he was let out of the cell.

Next morning F sat down next to Tom at breakfast. He was taller than Tom even when they sat. He had a hard look to him. His face, his hair, his bones were all angular and squarish. He reminded Tom of a punk surfer movie star.

"You really hurt Bobby's feelings."

"I didn't mean to."

"Maybe you could apologize to him."

"There's nothing to say."

F studied Tom as he ate. "We're planning a party for you tomorrow."

"I told Bobby, I don't like parties."

"This is a special party."

"I appreciate your help and support but I'm not really interested in socializing. I want to be alone." Tom thought 'disappear' a more appropriate word.

"When we found you in the kitchen, you were alone. Is that what you want? You want to be a slave to those Latin lovers?"

"Of course not."

"Then we're offering you the chance to be a part of our fraternity. It's invitation only. Your attitude is very unappreciative."

"Then maybe I'm not cut out to be a member of your gang."

"Now Tom. Let's get something straight. This is your future you're throwing away. Life insurance, security, and old age benefits. Rather than force you to make a decision now, think about it a little longer. Tonight Bobby will drop by and collect your answer. I hope you make the right decision."

F got up and left Tom who was now too perplexed to be hungry.

That night Bobby dropped in as expected. Only tonight he was accompanied by two other members whom Tom had not met. The guard unlocked Tom's cell and let them all in.

"Hey Tommy. How's it going?"

267

Tom was less than thrilled. "Fine Bobby."

"These are a couple of brothers I thought you'd enjoy meeting. This is Steven."

A hulk with a square headed crew cut grinned down at him like a retarded ogre, "How's it goin'?"

"And this is Teddy."

Teddy just smiled, crookedly.

"So what's your decision Tom? Is the party on tomorrow?"

"Well--no. I really don't want to go through with it. Not that I don't appreciate what you've done for me and all."

"We understand," Bobby smiled. "In fact F was so understanding of your indecision that he wanted to--as he said, 'unbias you.'"

"Huh?"

"Well we understand how new and different life is for you here in jail. So we decided to act as kinda of a welcome wagon. You know, to help you adjust to life here."

"I appreciate it but-"

"Please," interrupted Bobby impatiently, "let me continue. You see, life here has new rules and regulations that you aren't used to. It's important that you run with the pack. A lone wolf can't survive here. And we feel that your inexperience in certain 'personal' matters is making it difficult for you to make a proper decision."

"But I--"

"So--," cut off Bobby and leaning his face closer to Tom's face, "we've decided to help you adjust to life here."

Tom stood up realizing that these two guerrillas were here to control him.

"You just relax and all will go smoothly there Tommy boy."

"I'll call the guards," Tom said in a panic, stepping back with nowhere to go. "Back off Bobby, just get out of my cell!"

"Now, now Tommy. Just look at it as paying back a favor you owe me."

The bigger guerrilla took off his belt.

"GUARD! GUARD!" Tom yelled.

"Now Tommy, Tommy. The guard will return when '_we_' call him. So don't waste your '_precious_' breath."

The two goons crowded Tom all the way into the corner of the concrete cage.

Bobby had removed his shirt. "Just relax Tommy. You'll enjoy it if you relax."

Tom kicked one thug in the stomach and swung a roundhouse into the other.

Something snapped in Tom. He was a wildman. Like a Tasmanian Devil cartoon he spun, twisted, kicked and punched in a wild barrage. Bobby backed up against the door bars and let his monkeys handle business.

They were taken by surprise and hadn't expected such a fight from Tom.

"LEAVE!" Tom shouted at them swinging his fists. "LEAVE NOW! Get out and I'll forget all this."

The big chimp, Teddy, rubbed his jaw. He spoke for the first time, "But we don't want to forget this."

From his kneeling position Teddy lunged head first like a locomotive plowing into Tom's stomach driving him backwards into the concrete wall and over the white porcelain sink. The air was knocked out of Tom.

Steven got into the grapple and before long they had Tom pinned face down on the concrete floor. Tom tasted concrete as his teeth ground . . .

"Put him up on the bed," Bobby instructed.

"I'll kill you, you fuc--"

"Shut up!" commanded Steve as he shoved Tom's face into the mattress.

"I'll kill--"

Steven sat on Tom's torso atop the mattress and pushed his head down savagely muffling Tom's screams. He held a handful of Tom's hair like the reigns of a horse.

Teddy twisted one of Tom's arms to force him into even more pain.

Feverishly, Bobby yanked Tom's pants down and pulled the Vaseline out of his pocket.

\* \* \*

Tom laid on his back staring at the black concrete ceiling. He felt hollow inside his chest. His stomach twisted and his legs felt like dead logs. He was in Hell. Definitely in Hell. He'd made mistakes, mortal sins, capital crimes, fucked up his life and now was in Hell. Here he'd reap the rewards of his life as they butt-fucked him and fisted him. No escape from Hell. This was the end of the line and Tom knew what he had to look forward to. Hell tomorrow. Hell next week. Hell next month. Hell next year. Death was farther away than Tom could imagine because he'd only been alive twenty-four years. Tom wanted to cry but there was no sorrow left in him. He figured he deserved it. But he didn't want it. He didn't believe in it. Something wasn't right about it. He couldn't fully accept it. But he couldn't fight it. Yes he could! Why not fight? 'How much more can anyone hurt me?' he thought. He pictured pounding Bobby's face. Blood flying. He pictured kicking those goons in the balls. He felt better. He pictured himself taking on all those guys… at once. He saw it. He smiled.

Best feeling he'd had in a long time . . .

Prisons aren't known for having trees and Soledad didn't have but two in the entire yard. Security risk. At the South end near the kitchen was a tall Shamal Ash tree. Tom spent the day leaned against the tree trunk, scouting. He knew Bobby worked the morning and dinner shift. So somehow he hoped to catch him during his off hours. Somehow Bobby eluded him though. Tom couldn't find him anywhere. Tom decided to skip dinner to keep his post longer and locate Bobby.

Bobby was of the first to finish his kitchen shift and when he walked out the side entrance Tom followed him. It was almost sunset and Bobby was headed towards the tree that Tom had leaned on all day. Tom's only weapon was a thin belt which he would use to strangle Bobby. Tom wished he had a knife or gun. But maybe this was better. More personal. Feel him . . .

As Bobby approached the tree Tom quickened his pace. Tom caught up with Bobby as they were adjacent to the tree.

Tom's arms were upraised and crossed forming a circular loop with the belt. In a quick succession of movements Tom caught up with Bobby, whipped the circle of cow skin over his head, looped the belt over, uncrossed his arms separating them sideways . . . choking . . . pulling . . . tugging . . . choking Bobby. Choking evil . . . choking freedom . . . choking..

Choking Hell.. choking Sid . . . choking back . . .

As Tom had learned, there was an expected struggle from the victim. Tom raised his right knee into Bobby's back and pulled his neck backwards. Bobby's arms swung wildly, Tom pulled him down to the ground as he kneeled on top him keeping constant tension on the belt ends that knotted Bobby's neck.

Beneath the large ash tree Bobby gurgled and squeaked out his last moments of life. Tom held tight for another minute beyond Bobby's limpness to ensure his efforts.

Unconscious . . . forever.

Tom stood up. The tree seemed to be looking down. A certain vindication and the residual adrenaline gave Tom a feeling of exhilaration. He turned to reenter the premises on the North end but saw two others of the kitchen staff exiting in his path.

Tom disappeared around the South end of the commissary in the direction Bobby had been traveling.

When he rounded the corner he saw who Bobby was to meet. It was F and one of the cronies from last night's jail cell tango.

"Hey Tom," said F loudly from the distance. "You decided to make the party after all?"

F and Steven laughed.

Tom was still pumping inside with adrenaline like a panther after fighting a boa constrictor.  Tom tried to play it cool.  The anger was lightening to fear.

"Steven says you're a real natural," they both laughed some more.

Tom kept walking in an effort to pass them in a large arc.

"Sure you don't want to join us?"

"In Hell," Tom muttered softly as he walked away from them.  Then he remembered his resolve.  He felt that kamikaze euphoria of power and omnipotence.  Not afraid to die.  Today is all right.  Wager everything. There was no escape.  Who was he possibly kidding.  Nowhere to hide in prison.  Nowhere to run.  Not even an alibi.  And what about life in jail. His sentence.  Tom chuckled to himself sardonically, 'Sentence me to three life sentences.'

"Hey Tom, you're not gonna join the party?"

Tom slowed to a stop, pivoted his head to look F straight in the eye and with a cold smile replied, "Sure."

Tom walked straight at F.  So what if the other goon was there.  Tom could twist F's head off and tear out his throat before the goon could get his wang out.  Tom was like a robot programmed to kill. Methodically his feet lifted and stepped, lifted and stepped towards unsuspecting F.

From around the corner a couple of F's gang ran panting towards them.

"Bobby's dead!  Bobby's dead!" they yelled as they ran up.

Tom still had ten feet between him and F, whose head was turned the other direction now.  Tom ran and leaped on him.

F tried to sidestep him but Tom grabbed him by the hair and grappled him down on the asphalt with the loud smack of bones hitting stone. Everyone dogpiled.  Punches flew in all directions and Tom inflicted damage blindly but to no avail.

"So, Copkiller's now a fag killer huh?" F panted getting up holding the side of his head where Tom had pulled out a huge hunk of hair.  F looked at his hand covered with blood from his own head.

"Gag him and keep him in the kitchen until I get back.  NOW!" F said harshly to one of the death announcers.  "Show me Bobby," he said to the other one.

F fell to his knees next to Bobby's body in the dirt beneath the tree. He began sobbing. He shook his fists in the air as he looked up at the tree.

"I'd love to chop you down! I'd cut you up into little pieces and burn you. Not all at once either, you fucking tree. You fucking--" F sobbed and squeezed Bobby. The crony stood and watched. His name was John Tent. He was young for a place like this, only twenty-four, like Tom. He'd killed a couple in another car while driving drunk. He only had six months to go, three months off with good behavior. He'd known Bobby. He of course knew F, and he knew what kind of vengeance F was going to do to Tom. John just wanted to ride out his time. He couldn't get involved killing Tom.

"What're you going to do F?"

F kept crying with his head on Bobby's chest.

"We've got to report this."

F lifted his head but didn't face John.

"No," he said calmly. "Nobody tells nobody nothing. Okay?"

Okay, sure F. But I can't get involved in any of this. I've only got a few months to go. I can't get involved. I don't want trouble."

"I understand," F said in a moronic calm as he stared at the tree trunk. "Go back to your cell. We'll take it from here."

"Thanks F," John said walking away. "I mean, sorry F. I'm really--"

F still stared at the tree as if it was somehow responsible.

John ran back to the honeycomb.

F stretched out and laid down next to Bobby. He held him. Then the crying started again. F got on his knees. His tears fell on Bobby's shirt. He wanted to scream. He couldn't. He raised his arms out and upward with fists extended. F opened his mouth painfully wide in a screaming gesture that tensed every muscle of his body. A deaf person would have heard that tortured silent scream.

\* \* \*

Tom was strapped down naked, beaten until unconscious, with his legs tied to the legs of a butcher block table in the kitchen. F continued to pummel Tom's body with his fists.

"Here F, use this," Dennis suggest holding out a wooden roller.

"Nope. I want to feel my fists breaking his bones. I want to feel him die. I want to see him ugly and shredded. Yeah shredded." F grabbed a fork and pulled Tom's limp head up by his ear. In slow strokes F raked the fork down Tom's face in bloody furrows.

"Well, before he goes I'm gonna get in a last chance quickie." F put the bloody fork down.

"Line up boys," F proclaimed like a circus ringleader. "Line up for the one and only Copkiller. We'll all get a last chance with dear boy Tommy. Give me that cigarette."

F snatched a cigarette from one of the boys. He puffed on it a couple time, tapped off the ash and began to sizzle Tom's backside skin with its fiery red tip.

"Hey now," cooed F. "We won't have you pooping out on us now. Will we?"

They laughed as Tom's unconscious body twitched and flinched to the fiery pain.

"C'mon boys, make it quick. This chump isn't gonna make it much longer."

The kitchen double doors exploded open as armed guards ran into the room with riot sticks waving. John Tent peeked through the window in one of the kitchen doors.

\* \* \*

The hospital was white and rubbery like any other Lysol zone. Normally he'd be in the Alameda Hospital, but with so many internal injuries still hemorrhaging, they'd scheduled Tom for exploratory surgery here in the Highland Hospital. They figured that Tom's spleen was ruptured as well as one of his kidneys and liver. Several broken ribs and over a dozen crater-like welts with black blot clots on his back made lying in bed on his back the most sadistic of all his pains. Tom survived from one morphine shot to the next. As soon as Tom could begin to feel the pain he rang for the nurse. Heaven knows how long it might take her to arrive.

An armed guard was always stationed in or outside the room reading magazines. The waiting room of Hell. Can't go up to Heaven. Can't go down to Hell. Cops prevent an escape from Limbo.

Tom felt dreamy and somehow removed from the past. A strange Limbo where someone had misplaced his ticket. Tom was waiting for the final judgement, Heaven or Hell. Tom knew it was Hell, but as long as he could hang out here in Limbo . . . he wouldn't complain about the wait. Except when the nurse took forever to bring him his shot . . .

Tom rang again, pressing the buzzer on the end of the chord. To Tom's disappointment an unfamiliar priest walked in. The priest sat down next to the bed studying Tom with a cold stare.

The Marshal on the other side of the bed examined the priest.

"Here's the letter of permission from Sergeant Falwell," he stated passing the paper over Tom's sheeted body.

The cop took it, read it, and handed it back.

Tom had trouble moving his head, but his half-closed eyes followed the paper like a slow motion tennis ball.

"So what you got permission for?" mumbled Tom with a drugged out drawl.

"Permission to consult you."

"Great?" spittled Tom. "My travel agent's out of town and I--" Tom gasped and began coughing uncontrollably. He arched his back. "DAMN! DAMN FUCKING DAMN!" he screamed.

"Tom hold still." The prison chaplain stood up to calm him.

"My skin is burning. MY BACK IS ON FIRE!"

"Tom, calm down. You--"

"I'll get a doctor," the cop said as he walked out.

Tom continued coughing. The priest wiped some blood from the corner of his mouth.

"Relax Tom. You're scheduled for surgery tomorrow."

"Fuck it Father," Tom blurted between coughs. "Just let me die." He arched his back up and pulled on his arm restraint straps—rocking side to side. "I'm not going back. I wish they'd-" cough, "killed me!"

The priest put his hands on Tom's shoulders to steady him. "If someone hadn't informed the guards, they would have."

Tom relaxed out of breath gasping for air. "Father, I killed Bobby."

"I know," said the priest hovering over Tom.

"So, if F doesn't get me, I'll die in prison anyway."

The priest released Tom. "No one knows his time to die."

Tom sobbed and gasped. "I want to die. I want to die!"

"Don't talk like that, its' a--"

A nurse stepped in with the Marshal following. She felt his pulse.

"Nurse I hurt everywhere." He coughed. "Just give me--"

"Just hold on young man. I'll have--"

"Hey Priest!" Tom laughed. "Say my *Last Rites*." Tom coughed a bit of blood up again.

"Find the strength to live Tom."

The nurse walked out.

"HEY!" Tom yelled at her with his weakened lungs. "Give me my shot!"

She ignored him. The Marshal followed her out.

"Damn it Father. I can't even die peacefully. I hurt everywhere. My--"

"Tom, try saying a prayer with me."

"I can't sing and I don't pray," Tom grimaced.

"Our Father," the chaplain began.

"Our Father who's not in Heaven," Tom echoed.

"Hallowed be thy name."

Tom gritted his teeth. "Make it a short one Father, I don't have much time."

"Thy kingdom come, thy will be done."

"AAAAAAGGGGH! No prayers are gonna save me!"

"Pray Tom."

"I pray for all the people whose lives I fucked up. I hope THEY will forgive me. And Father-" cough . . . cough..cough . . . "Father I pray-- I pray with all my heart that Sid burns in Hell one day longer than I do."

"Tom you can't blame other people for your mistakes."

Tom's expression changed from grimacing pain to a clenching hate. His eyes narrowed to a snake's coldness. "Wrong Father! I accept my guilt. I accept my blame. Especially the sin I carry for not killing Sid when I had the chance."

The priest stood up looking impatiently down. "You've killed plenty Tom."

"Hah!" Tom coughed and choked. "I would live again to kill one more time."

"TOM! That's crazy talk. Don't talk like--"

"I'd kill him, kill him--" Tom spasmed from his internal bleeding.

"Calm down Tom. You're making this worse."

"GOOD!" Tom yelled. "I had my shot and missed it. MY LIFE'S OVER!"

The priest grabbed Tom's bicep and squeezed it roughly. "Find something to live for. A reason--"

Tom laughed and coughed . . . coughed and laughed . . .

The nurse finally reentered and Tom got his ticket to Nirvana.

McCales's Navy was on TV and Tom enjoyed being on that island . . . until he was interrupted by a guest. It was the tall blonde from the prison who had originally told him to join a gang.

Tom dreamily rolled his head. "How'd you get over here?"

"I'm a trustee, and it took a lot of doing."

"So why'd you come visit me?"

"See how you are."

"Oh, I'm dandy. My guts are jello. I'm pissing blood. My face is the Phantom of the opera, but I'm getting free drugs."

"Good deal." The blonde sat down next to Tom. "Actually I'm here to do more than wish you well. I've got some information for you."

"They electrocuted F Queen?"

"No, nothing like that, although I hope they do. It's about Sid."

"Sid? How'd you know about Sid?" Tom rattled his poppied head.

"Everybody knows about your life. Your story's been in **Newsweek**."

"So I'm famous--what about Sid?"

"A couple of guys back in Soledad have worked for him."

"You sure?"

"Yep. In fact they say he works for the government."

"Fuck off! That guy's a murderer."

"Right. It seems they pass off dirty work to him."

"And these friends of yours?"

"He passed a couple contracts to them."

"How do you know it's the same guy?"

"**Newsweek** did a pretty long story on you and published your description of him complete with that artist rendering you submitted in court."

Tom thought a minute. "Do they know how to find him?"

"I don't know. You can ask 'em when you get back."

"Get back? I'd just as soon die here," Tom laughed but that started a pain shock wave.   He grimaced.   "Hell, I'll probably just die here. They're cutting me open tomorrow."

Tom looked up as the next theme song played.   "Yeah I'll stay here with 'the skipper too, a millionaire and his . . .'"

"You don't learn do you?" Ken stood up and began to walk out.

"Hey!"

Ken stopped and looked back to Tom.

"Thanks," Tom offered.

"Yeah.  See ya 'round."

"Hey Ken, do me a favor.  Find out more about Sid."

"I'll see what's available."

Tom felt suddenly lonely.  Some warmth had come, and gone.  "See ya."

"See ya."

# Chapter 9
## *Sid's Place*

*Forests, mountains, green trees, rocks*
*Nature carved*
*Where car walks*
*Flat black oil*
*White paint lines*
*Sliding engine roars*
*To the next sign*
*A wild cat steps out*
*A reason all its own*
*The lights and noise confuse*
*Wheels roll over bone*
*Bloody eyed coughing*
*Calm, in infinite pain*
*Only one eye*
*The leg tucked in*
*Concrete street is stained*
*Houses made of trees*
*Forests are backyards*
*Wild cat of the city (24)*

"They're going to be transferring you back to Soledad in a few days Tom," the white collared Father spoke half-heartedly.

"So much for your **Last Rites.**"

"You came close to dying Tom. Even the doctors were betting against you," he smiled to one side.

"I found a reason to live."

"That's marvelous, then you considered what I said."

"Partly." Tom looked over at the tube in his arm.

"What do you mean, partly?" The priest shifted in his chair.

"The part about undoing evil."

"Then you're repenting."

"I will," Tom stated looking at the turned off TV screen.

"Tomorrow is today Tom."

"If the Lord is as forgiving as you say he is, then I suppose he's forgiving the bastard that murdered my wife."

"If he has repented."

"If he's repented?" Tom barked back. "Father you live in a vacuum! There is evil out there you can't wish away with a prayer. Murderers and rapists you can't chase away with a crucifix!"

"If they received Christ, there would be no murderers and rapists."

"If, if, if, if. And in the meantime you can hide behind your white collar, drive your Cadillac, and so matter-of-factly explain to everyone suffering that God is forgiving and we are forgiving, and expect us to pretend like nothing ever happened. Well that's bullshit Father. You're just tucking in the sheep while the wolves wait until dark. You're setting up the world for slaughter."

"And what are you suggesting Tom?"

"Preach justice. Not an eye for an eye, but justice. People shouldn't forgive so easily. Not forgive others, not forgive themselves."

"So you'd like to see everyone take the law into their own hands. You'd advocate vengeance?"

"People should demand it."

"And where would you be? If people discovered your identity while you were living on the commune they could, by your policy, have sentenced you to death, made your wife liable and removed your daughter."

"Don't be ridiculous," Tom scoffed.

"You're being ridiculous Tom. I'm not saying crimes should go unpunished. I'm just saying that people should rest their hearts and souls from the evil and hatred so easily manifested there. We have to find peace in the world by finding it in ourselves."

"And the world would be a better place . . ." Tom sang from a song.

"Yes, it would. The courts and police can handle crime. People should live their lives--"

"The police and courts are rigged."

"Tom, you've got to believe in something."

"I believe the world is fucked up and that the Devil lays waste to the best made plans."

"You'll never accomplish anything with that attitude."

"What's for me to accomplish? I'm a loser Father. A big time loser. I've lost my family, my wife, my daughter, my friends--" Tom thought of Corporal Harding. "I've lost my future. Except for--" Tom stopped.

"Except for what?"

"Except for a chance to redeem myself," Tom said defiantly.

"There. Now that's true. You can still redeem yourself."

"Yes Father. But I can't do it in jail."

"You must find a way. You will be in for a long time. In the meantime you mustn't lose sight of your spirituality. Even in jail, God's deeds can be done."

"Yeah," Tom said, but didn't mean it. He was thinking of a way to find Sid. F Queen could live. Fuck him. Forget him. Or F Queen could die if Tom got a clean chance. But Tom had to save himself for Sid. Tom wanted Sid. Sid dead. And now he had a lead. Tom daydreamed of tracking down Sid as Sid had done to him . . . Somehow the grosser it was, the more realistic and satisfying the dream. If only Tom could find Sid. First kill Sid, then Tom would repent. The killing to end killing. If he was going to Hell, then Sid was going with him.

"Father."

"Yes, Tom?"

"I need to speak to a guy who visited me from Block C. A trustee named Ken."

"Ken who?"

"I don't know. But he got permission to visit me once. I need to talk to him again.

"Why?" the patient priest asked with suspicion.

"Because he gives me hope," Tom said nonchalantly.

"Let the Lord guide you and you'll overflow with hope."

"Yeah, well, any hope I can get right now suits me fine," Tom placated. "I'm tired of being an empty cup. And Father, leave me a Bible."

"Good start son. I'll find this Ken, and you can read mine for now."

"Please Father. Get him."

* * *

"Hey Ken, I see the preacher found you."

"Yes, he found me all right. How you doing?" Ken sat down beside him.

"I need some more information on Sid."

"What's the hurry?"

"I need to know now." Tom couldn't contain his anxiousness.

"Well I did find out something?"

"What?" Tom blurted out.

"Sid is a Vietnam vet," Ken spoke calmly.

"So," Tom retorted with disappointment.

"So somebody just happened to know his last name."

"What?" Tom sat up anxiously. He grimaced in pain accordingly.

"Hodges."

"Sid Hodges?" Tom groaned, still hurting.

Ken nodded his head.

"You sure?" Tom double-checked.

"One of our boys came back with him. They were in the blackmarket business for a while."

"Then what?"

"Sid went solo."

"Where does he live?"

"My boy thought it was Tennessee."

"Tennessee?"

"He wasn't sure."

"What else?"

"That's it."

"That's all?" Tom's expression collapsed.

"Sorry, that's all I know yet," Ken confirmed with upraised shoulders.

Tom blew a gust out of his nostrils. "Thanks Ken. It's a start."

"Sorry that's it."

"I know. Just keep me posted."

"When you coming back to the big house?" Ken asked, getting up.

"Couple days they say."

"Good. Take it easy," Ken offered with a friendly wave.

"Yeah. Real good. Back to the cage," Tom spoke in another direction.

Ken laughed. They shook an old-fashioned handshake.

\* \* \*

The two armed marshals entered the hospital room to escort Tom back to Soledad. Tom offered no resistance, but no assistance either.

The doctor watched as a couple of nurses slid Tom off his bed onto the new one.

Tom grimaced and made the exchange look very uncomfortable. The nurses wheeled him to the door.

"Okay. He's yours now," the doctor said to one of the marshals as he passed the clipboard for a signature.

One of the nurses wheeled Tom down the corridor flanked by the two marshals.

Into the elevator. No one talked. The sounds of the hospital seemed deafening. Tom hadn't noticed the buzzers and voices so much as now. Now he was leaving. Now he missed the mechanical sounds, and intercom voices. Now he wanted to stay. Recuperating in pain had been his holiday from jail. But now the vacation was over.

The marshals picked the bed Tom lay upon from its wheeled frame like a serving tray. They slid him into the paddy wagon ambulance like a pizza into an oven. The rolling gurney frame folded up and was placed in the back beside Tom.

One cop got in back with Tom. The door slammed shut.

The drive back to jail was only a few miles. A thick metal grill separated the driver from the rear. The cops occasionally exchanged a brief comment.

The stop lights seemed the only saving grace. They were the last extensions of Tom's temporary freedom.

"Hey Bob isn't that Corvette the same color as yours?"

The marshal next to Tom hobbled up to peer through the grille and verify his partner's question. As Bob clung to the grille and looked for the car his gun hung above Tom's head.

With hardly a hesitation Tom cleared the leather snap with his left hand and pulled out the pistol with his right hand.

The cop reached down as quickly as possible to grab his gun but--

"FREEZE!" Tom yelled so loud that he rattled the driver and made him swerve.

Time stood still as Tom lay on his back with the gun pressed firmly into the cop's gut.

"Turn right!" Tom yelled at the driver.

"There's no street to turn on."

"As soon as there is, turn right!"

The cop above Tom was so angry he seemed to drip with hate. He started to move back--

"Just keep your hands in the grille. I don't want to hurt anyone. But I've got nothing to lose. Driver, throw your gun out the window."

Tom smiled wickedly. "So where's your 'vette? Huh Bob?" Tom poked him with the pistol.

"At home mother fucker," the marshal hissed.

Tom clicked his tongue at the officer. "Such language. You shouldn't talk that way to someone with a gun in your gut."

"How far do you think you're gonna go?" the marshal asked as he still leaned on the white metal grate.

"As far as possible. In fact, where do you live from here?"

"None of your business punk."

Tom cocked the trigger and shoved the gun into the cop's stomach. "Answer me."

"Twenty-second street."

Tom shouted to the driver, "Let's go to Bob's house!"

"That's clear across town," the driver whined.

"Good, that'll give us more time to talk. And unlock these cuffs."

"You've gotta be nuts. Give it up Tom," the driver pleaded

"Just drive. No one gets hurt if you do what I say."

It only took about ten minutes, but it seemed like hours to everyone in the police van.

"Okay driver. No hero stuff. Just open the rear doors and stay back with your hands in the air."

The van doors opened to a quiet middle class street. Trimmed lawns, bright stucco houses.

"Now your turn Bob. Back out slowly and keep your hands up. And move slowly. Any fast moves and this hammer's gonna fall."

Tom sat up. He was still in pain. Weak from no exercise and hospital food he scooted out the rear doors.

Bob's 'vette was poised at the sidewalk. Bright metallic blue.

Oversized tires. It was gorgeous and looked fast.

"Stick the keys in the door . . . Bob!"

The marshal grimaced.

"C'mon copper. Just do what I say and you'll live to drive your 'vette again."

Tom felt like a thug in a fifties gangster movie. "Toss your wallet inside the car. Good. Now lay down on the street, both of you."

Tom hobbled to the Corvette and opened the door. Before getting in he tried to lower the window. It was an electric. 'Shit!' He plunked down into the low bucket seat keeping the door partially open and one leg outside. It was an automatic. Tom fired it up. It sounded fast.

"Keep your head down and kiss the street Officer Bob."

Tom kept the gun pointed at them with his left plaster casted arm stuck out the door. He lowered the window down, pulled his left arm in, shifted into 'drive,' then released the brake.

"Take it easy boys."

Tom pulled away, then stopped abruptly and reversed the car. He pulled back to beside the van pointed the gun out the passenger window and shot a tire flat.

The 'vette screeched off and skidded around the corner in a squeal.

Tom chose the most accessible border crossings, Nevada, Colorado, as he headed East. He parked off the road and slept in the car mostly. With the officer's cash, and driver's license he had a chance. He wanted to use the officer's license as an I.D., get a motel... but that would be leaving too many clues. Tom didn't have any clothes except his hospital pajamas. He was only interested in getting to Tennessee. When he got there he'd figure out a plan.

After three days of gas station snacks and little sleep, Tom arrived in the rectangular state. He found a V.A. number in Nashville and called. He explained himself as an old war buddy and was looking for Sid Hodges. He got an address. Tom bought a map and discovered the town was a speck on the map called Draketon. Now he needed a plan. Tom only had twenty dollars left.

He drove to a drug store. A lot of people looked at him oddly dressed in his lime green hospital pajamas. There were still purple bruises on his face and railroad fork streak wounds on the left side of his face. He bought sulfur and potassium nitrate. At the grocery store he picked up a small bag of charcoal briquettes, some wooden matches, string, small finish nails and some plaster.

The mountains were beautiful as Tom wound up and down the narrow roads to his destination. What if this wasn't the right Sid? Tom figured that either way this was the end of the line. He planned his bomb strategy and relished the thoughts. He pictured Sid being blown to bits in a gust of fire as the nails ripped his skin and pin-cushioned him into a government sponge.

'Garlic. In the old days gangsters put garlic on their bullets. I should have got garlic for the nails,' Tom thought.

Tom drove through the tree lined mountain roads merrily daydreaming of destruction, but sometimes gripped with fear. He was weak and tired. Probably still hemorrhaging inside. 'What if I have to fight Sid? No chance!' Tom knew he had to surprise him. 'Somehow . . .'

With the help of a couple kids on bicycles Tom finally found the small cabin. A real wooden log cabin. 'This was Sid's place? A CIA blackmarket hitman, Vietnam vet lives here? This place looks like Daniel Boone's house... or Davey Crockett's cabin . . .'

There was no car in the driveway but Tom drove away just the same. He pulled off the road and hid the car behind a thicket of trees.

Tonight he'd investigate. For now he'd make bombs.

Tom made six bombs the size of coke cans. For fuses he wrapped wooden matches in black powder and paper so that just the heads of the matches stuck up out of the plaster casting. Pieces of the large flint from the side of the match box were tied to the middle of a half dozen lengths of string. If secured properly, pulling the string would rub the flint on the match heads and boom . . .

Tom could only carry three bombs at a time and had to be very careful not to rub them against each other. These match fuses were instantaneous. No time to run or throw them.

No lights were on in the house as Tom crept around to the rear window. No one home. The doors were all locked. Tom broke in through the bathroom window. Even after he turned on the lights he felt spooky. Tom wondered if Abraham Lincoln's log cabin was decorated with the same colonial knickknacks. 'Fucking spooky!' There was a feeling of extreme danger to this quaintness. A sensation of hidden death. Tom felt as though he were in a black jungle with eyes upon him from the darkness.

The book case had photo albums. Tom pulled them out and skimmed through.

Family pictures, family pictures, baby pictures . . . pictures of a teenager in military uniform. Must be Sid Hodges. But didn't quite look like the Sid that Tom was after. Tom kept looking. No, if this was Sid, it was the wrong one. Tom opened some books that were stamped in the inside cover, "Property of Sid Hodges."

Right place, wrong guy. Tom's heart sunk.

"He was an officer it seemed. Army. Lieutenant Sid Hodges. It looked like Sid. But he knew it wasn't. Tom went to the bureau and rummaged through some drawers.

He found a loaded Smith & Wesson .357. That's normal. Especially for a vet. Tom stuck the gun in his pajama waistband. When he started to walk it fell down inside Tom's pant leg and scared the shit out of him as it bounced on the wood floor. 'Could've blown my foot off!'

Tom set the gun down on the bureau next to a large green dragon carved out of jade, and went into the bedroom.

The bed looked fifty years old. Bouncy springs and a patchwork quilt. The closet was a wooden, free standing pine armoire. No mirrors on it. The clothes were nice.

Tom decided to get dressed. He found a nicely fitting suit. So this Sid Hodges was about the same size as Tom. Tom decided to look for some food and money before splitting.

The refrigerator was fully stocked. Lots of meat in the freezer. It appeared that Sid was a hunter. The white butcher wrapped parcels were labeled: deer, duck, trout . . .

Some opened milk was still fresh. Sid was in town. Tom realized he'd better hurry up. Sid could come home at any moment.

Tom tried to think where a vet would keep his money. 'With the guns! Of course!'

Other than the pistol, Tom hadn't yet seen any rifles or weapons. It was a small house. There wasn't an attic in this little A-frame . . . so, where? Under the floorboards?

Tom glanced around the house and stomped the floor for clues. Then he noticed the scrape marks in the floorboards near the bureau.

Tom was weak and it took the last of his strength to push the bureau away from the wall into the center of the room. Sure enough. A couple floorboards had been cut.

Tom had to get a butcher knife from the kitchen to pry up the three short boards.

This guy was a veteran all right. Rifles, ammo, surveillance equipment and several attaches. The first attache was full of more pistols in a foam lined case. The second one was full of money. Literally full. Tom couldn't believe it. Thousands of dollars. Maybe hundreds of thousands. Maybe even a million as Tom thumbed through the neatly packed bundles of various denominations.

Tom put the pistols back down in the hole, closed up the money attache and set it down beside himself. Tom pulled up the third attache. This one was full of files and papers. Probably explain what kind of illegal business this guy was into.

Tom was hungry. He closed up the third attache and carried it and the money into the kitchen after putting the cover on the hole. He tried to push the bureau back but was too weak. He felt so weak that he might faint. Tom went back to the kitchen for his glass of milk.

As Tom sat and drank the milk he peered through the files. They were locations, blueprints, and files on different people. Tom kept glancing through until he gagged and choked on his milk. A file was labeled, Tom Calder. It was a file on him . . . Tom.

Newspaper clippings of the original accident, pictures of him and the police info . . . actual police files and records. 'How did Sid get these?' Was this the same Sid who'd been trying to kill him? The Sid Hodges from the pictures in the scrapbooks wasn't. But the owner of this attache surely was. 'But how?' Tom pondered quickly turning the pages of his life.

Tom's heart pounded. He was drinking the milk of the man who killed his wife, raped Jane, killed the guy in Malibu, and chased him for three years. Tom had his money. Enough to start a new life. But how could he? Sid would always be there. Somewhere. A threat to any comfort he may enjoy. No future in fear. Tom knew that he still had to finish what he'd started.

Tom put one bomb in the armoire so that when it opened it would blow out someone's midsection. Tom put the other two he had in the bathroom medicine cabinet on two different shelves. He used scotch tape to hold them down, he fastened the strings to the inside of the cabinet door with tape.

Grabbing the attaches in the kitchen he headed for the front door as a car pulled noisily into the gravel driveway.

Tom ran for the bathroom window and dropped the two attaches outside. He forgot to get the gun. He'd left it in the living room next to the jade dragon. Too late.

Tom slid out the window and ran into the woods.

Tom had left the lights on and the bureau out in the center of the room. Hardly a clean burglary. Tom could only see the rear side of the cabin from the woods. Impatiently he waited for something to happen. Holding a fortune in cash, no gun, outside an assassin's house, who . . . he'd just burglarized.

Tom felt stupid. Tom was scared.

Then he heard it. A low toned explosive whoosh. It must have been the one in the bedroom. Tom listened and waited. No sign of movement in the house, no sign of life. Did he kill him? 'Or just injure him again?'

He couldn't leave until he knew for sure that Sid was dead. If he even got the right Sid . . . or someone else . . . Tom had to know for sure.

Leaving the attaches in a bush, Tom snuck around the house, peering in the windows. The bedroom was packed full of smoke and the armoire door was shredded.

No sign of anyone on the floor through the smoke.

If only he had a gun. Walking into an injured tiger's cave unarmed seemed stupid, stupid, STUPID!

The gun he'd left next to the jade dragon was visible from the kitchen window.

Tom could dash for it, then check out the bedroom.

Tom snuck to the front door. He gently turned the knob. It was unlocked. It would be a straight run to the gun. The bedroom door was open and Tom would have to run right past it.

Tom stood on the porch holding the front door knob. He wanted to run away.

He wanted to be somewhere else . . . not running into this den of death . . . he had to . . . this was it.

No sense thinking about it. He was ready. He burst the door open and ran inside.

Tom's feet seemed to be in slow motion as they pounded the wood floor towards the gun.

The front door slammed shut behind him. Tom kept running . . . he reached the gun-

"You want to die?" a voice asked from behind. Tom froze reaching the pistol. He could feel the aim of a gun from behind him. Tom looked over his left shoulder to see Sid pointing a small 9 mm at him. It was the right Sid--or wrong Sid from where Tom stood.

"Well, look who's here. I just heard about your escape. You've saved me the trouble of finding you."

"You're welcome," Tom said in a surprising calm.

"Glad to see you made yourself at home here," Sid almost smiled.

"Whose home is this?"

"Mine," Sid replied with eyes that felt like the aim of a rifle.

"But you're not Sid Hodges."

"I am now."

"What happened to the real Sid?"

Sid laughed. "You're pretty smart for a punk kid. How'd you find out about Sid Hodges?"

"I looked through the photo albums and stuff."

"We were in Nam together." Sid glanced at the bookshelf.

"Where's he now?"

"Dead." Sid straightened up from leaning back in the corner behind the door, injured but seemingly under control.

"Then who are you?"

Sid walked closer. "I told you, I'm Sid Hodges."

"But he's dead you said."

"That's poetic," Sid laughed slightly.

"You took his name."

"And house." Sid's hair was black. Dark shadows under his eyes.

"Why?"

I decided to change identities. I had a lot to gain by it."

"How'd he die?"

"You ask too many questions." Sid's face was a rough skin.

Tom backed up. "You killed him."

"Not exactly."

"But--"

"That'll do. I've waited a long time to finish this job. Don't bore me with your stalling. How'd you find me anyway?"

Tom wanted to keep the conversation going. Stay alive longer. "In jail." He backed up without the gun.

"How, in jail?"

"There's a guy who knows you."

"Who?" asked Sid with heightened interest.

"Maybe he knew the old Sid Hodges. Who do you work--"

"Who knows me?" Sid questioned impatiently.

"How'd Sid die?"

"Answer my question. Who is this guy?" he commanded pointing the gun out more.

"If you tell me how Sid died."

"A grenade. Now who told you about me?"

"He's a friend of a friend. He told him you were a black marketeer. Was it a Viet Cong grenade?"

"No, mine fuckface. What's this guy's name?" Sid closed the distance.

Tom decided to stay honest, keep the questions going, though he wanted to protect Ken . . . "I don't know his name. A friend passed the info along."

"What friend?"

"Ken. But why'd you kill the real Sid?"

"He was already dying. He got hit by a Charlie bamboo trap. He was standing there with a dozen shafts of bamboo through him--screaming and crying. I kept his ID and put him out of his misery. Later that same day I got hit in the shoulder. When I woke up in the chopper I decided to make the change." Sid kept the pistol pointed in his right hand and round-housed Tom with his left. "Now that's everything to know."

Sid jammed the gun up Tom's nose as he pulled Tom's head back by the hair. "Now tell me: Who's your friend?"

"Ken. I don't know his last name," Tom groaned with his neck arched back.

"Describe him."

"Tall blonde. Handsome. Head of the Arians or something."

"I wish I'd killed you in Malibu," Sid whispered.

"Like my wife?"

Sid smiled. "You're a fool. You shouldn't have ever married her or laid hands on Barbara."

"Barbara?"

"You'll never catch on, will you?"

Sid threw Tom to the floor and aimed the gun at Tom's temple.

"Fuck. I don't want to clean up your mess in here. Get outside."

Tom stood slowly, stalling for even just seconds of time. He brushed himself off as if his appearance mattered.

Sid reached to push him towards the door but Tom ducked and rolled towards the kitchen. Sid turned to fire as Tom ducked into the bathroom.

Tom didn't have a chance to get to the window. Sid stood in the bathroom doorway with his gun leveled at Tom's messed up face.

"Fuck it. I'll clean up your mess."

Tom grabbed the medicine cabinet door and yanked it open. The blast knocked Tom back through the shower curtain and into the tub.

*   *   *

When Tom tried to open his eyes--they were caked shut. He reached to touch them and cut his fingers. His face was a jagged pincushion of broken glass from the mirror. Tom could only barely open one eye.

The room wasn't full of smoke any more. He sat up in the tub. The suit he wore of Sid's had absorbed most of the glass fragments. With every movement he was pricked and cut by thousands of glass shards, and splinters.

Sid lay on his back in the doorway. Tom could see only his feet.

Painfully, very painfully, Tom stood up, stepped out of the bathtub and walked agonizingly in robotic steps over to Sid's body. Sid's face was completely sheared off.

His throat was torn wide open in a pool of black blood.

The smoke had cleared--so it'd been some hours since the explosion. Tom stumbled half blind to the bedroom. The mirror on the wall had been shattered by the bomb in the armoire that had missed Sid. In the few remaining fragments Tom could see his face was packed full of glass. It hurt even more to look at it as Tom held up a larger piece of broken mirror he picked up from the floor. Blood still dripped from his chin.

Tom sat heavily on the bed pondering what to do now. Throbbing, wet with blood, in pain, salty tears burning his sheared sockets . . . A shiver, then hot pain, then more cold shivers. He felt numb, scared, weak, but triumphant, in a way that made him cry. Ouch! Tears burned. He was bleeding badly, injured . . . but he knew now that he didn't want to die. He felt alive as he chuckle-cried, ouch... ouch . . . he pulled another piece of glass out of his cheek.

*  *  *

Jane's clothing store in Miami was doing well. She enjoyed the buying trips to Europe and was beginning to carry African jewelry she'd been picking up in Jamaica.

Jane didn't notice the man following her from the grocery store. She didn't notice him follow her home. When she went to work the next morning he was still parked outside. He followed her to the clothing store, then drove away. At about eleven-thirty he walked into the clothing store and approached Jane directly.

"Yes, sir, may I help you?" Jane inquired professionally.

"I hope so. I'm interested in something sheer, fancy," he paused, "and sexy."

"For your wife I suppose."

"We're not married, but she's a very close friend."

"In what size?" Jane asked over the counter.

"Well, I'm really not familiar with women's sizes. But she's the same height as you are."

"Then she's probably a size seven. Can you be more specific? Are you interested in something formal? Perhaps an evening gown?"

"Yes," he pondered. "That would be fine."

"Follow me."

Jane led the gentleman to a wall two rows high. The blouses were on the upper row. Skirts on the bottom row of hangars. A circular chrome stand near this wall was stuffed around with beautiful long dresses.

"This section here is size seven. Do you see anything you like?"

"Yes, this is attractive. But please, I'm not used to buying for other people, a girl especially. Show me what you like the best."

Jane felt odd about this man. She'd never seen him before, but his voice was familiar. He looked at her strangely, it seemed odd that he'd be here buying a dress . . .

"So what's the occasion?" she asked looking at him more attentively.

"It's for a friend I haven't seen in almost four years."

"Must be a good friend," she quickly replied. Jane shuffled through some gowns.

"She was very helpful to me before. I hope to repay her kindness."

"Here. I like this one a lot. I brought this back from Paris," she announced, holding it chin level against herself.

"That is very beautiful. But I don't quite know how it will fit her-- without seeing it modeled." He smiled strangely, "Would you please try it on for me?"

Jane was slightly perturbed by this request. She'd never had to model her clothes in the store before. Still, she didn't feel threatened. "All right," she said awkwardly. "Just have a seat over there."

When she exited the dressing room she was stunning. The dress fit her very exquisitely and dramatized her slim waist and healthy figure.

"That is very nice," the man complimented with another strange smile.

Jane admired herself in the mirror. "Would you wear it to lunch with me?" he asked so softly she could barely hear him.

Jane flustered, "Are you kidding?"

"I'm buying it for you," he said shyly.

Jane was shocked. "You said it was for an old friend."

"It is," he smiled sheepishly now.

"But I don't know you." Jane kept her distance.

"Yes you do."

Jane looked at him closely and shook her head sideways.

He looked over to make sure no one was close by, "My name used to be Tom Calder, then Tom Brady when I met you."

Jane's mouth fell open.

"Now my name is Sid Hodges."

"Sid?" she gasped.

"Are we alone?" Tom looked around again.

"Yes, my other girl isn't due in 'til noon."

"Sid is dead."

"But your face is . . . different! And I read in the papers that they found your body in some car wreckage in Tennessee!"

"They found Sid's body."

"Oh my God!" she said with goosebumps and adrenaline stirring up her heartbeat.

She leaned back as if to fall, against the circular dress rack.

"It's a long story. I've a new life and a lot of money. May I take you to lunch?" Sid asked calmly.

"I have to wait until Susan get here."

"Susan, your cousin?"

"Yes."

"Okay, but remember, from now on my name is Sid."

Jane had already begun walking back to the counter. She stepped over to the cooler and got a paper cup and took a small drink of water.

"How much do I owe you for the dress?"

"Oh that's all right Tom, I mean Sid. GOSH!" she looked around, "Gosh I'm sorry."

"It's all right. I'm still getting used to it too."

"It's a very expensive dress-"

"Turn around," Sid politely commanded. He leaned over the counter and reached for the price tag dangling from the neckline. "Okay." He pulled out a thick money clip.

"Here's three hundred dollars. Keep the change. I'll be back-"

"Oh, here's Susan now."

Jane's older cousin walked in.

"Uh Susan. This is a friend of mine--Sid," she forced out.

Sid shook her hand like an old fashioned gentleman keeping her palm down and holding it gently. "Glad to meet you."

"We're going out to lunch. He's an old friend. I'll be back soon. Well, maybe an hour," she stammered, "I'll be back later. Oh heck--see ya later."

Susan smiled as her flustered cousin exited with Sid. "Hey, isn't that one of our dresses you're wearing?"

"It's her dress now," Sid informed Susan as they walked out the door.

"Oh yeah. Ring it up, the tag's on the counter. The cash is in the till," Jane said loudly walking away.


* * *


Sid and Jane walked happily arm in arm from the nightclub restaurant. The out-of-uniform policeman accompanying them was happy also.

"Nice place," the cop complimented.

"Thank you," replied Sid.

"I don't suppose I'll always get treated so well and have it in on the house?"

"You'll always be treated so well. But I wouldn't want it to look as though we have an arrangement of any sort. I'm just glad to introduce one of my neighbors to my restaurant. Tell your friends at the station. I would appreciate their business. We welcome our men in blue and think we have one of the finest restaurants in Miami."

"Yes, you're right on both counts Sid. It doesn't look good for officers to be on the tab and this is one of Miami's finest." The officer leaned over to Jane and whispered to her, "Your husband is a very honest man."

"Yes," Jane smiled. "He believes in the letter of the law."

The following day the policeman is on the phone with his Captain. "I've been to the best new restaurant."

"Oh yeah? What's it called?" the Captain asked indifferently.

"Sid's Place."

"Who owns it? . . . What?!" the Captain asked looking at the jade dragon atop his desk and sitting up behind his desk. "Sid Hodges? Are you sure? . . . Yes, I mean, No. I don't know him. Where is this place?" The Captain leaned forward in his chair.

"You remember that place, it used to be called 'The Wagon Wheel?' It's totally remodeled. None of the western atmosphere. Real modern."

"Any good?" the Captain asked, but he wasn't concerned about the food . . .

"Oh yeah. I told you. Real good food. Live entertainment. The owner and his wife treated me last night. They're neighbors of mine."

The Captain relaxed a little. The Sid he used to know would never have gotten married. "What kind of food? . . . Huh . . . Really? . . . Sounds good. Well, maybe I'll check it out sometime. Sid's Place huh? . . . Thanks for the tip." He hung up the phone gently.

The Captain looked at his Vietnam war souvenirs hanging from the wall to his right. He pressed an intercom button on his phone and spoke curtly, "I'll be out for an hour. I'm going to lunch." He pulled the center drawer out and removed his Colt .45 Combat Commander.

"Where to?" the phone asked via its desk speaker.

He stuck the gun in his shoulder holster and repressed the comm-line button,

"Sid's Place."

Richard Del Connor
1978 San Diego

Richard Del Connor
2017 North Hollywood

# Song Credits (Lyrics)
# used in Sid's Place NOVEL

### 1. *"Heaven In Smoke"*
Lyrics by Richard Del Connor, "The Hippy Coyote"
Written for the book, **Sid's Place**
Used by permission of *Shaolin Records*
Copyright 2008 *www.shaolinMUSIC.com*
All rights reserved.  ASCAP

### 2. *"Nectar Of Love"*
Lyrics by Richard Del Connor, "The Hippy Coyote"
From the poetry book, **Autumn Flavours** of **Seasons Of Fours**
Used by permission of *Shaolin Records*
Copyright 1972 *www.shaolinMUSIC.com*
All rights reserved.  ASCAP

### 3. *"Our Time Is Through"*
Lyrics by Richard Del Connor, "The Hippy Coyote"
Written for the book, **Sid's Place**
Used by permission of *Shaolin Records*
Copyright 2008 *www.shaolinMUSIC.com*
All rights reserved.  ASCAP

### 4. *"Illusion"*
Lyrics by Richard Del Connor, "The Hippy Coyote"
Written for the book, **Sid's Place**
Used by permission of *Shaolin Records*
Copyright 2008 *www.shaolinMUSIC.com*
All rights reserved.  ASCAP

### 5. *"Headin' To Heaven"*
Lyrics by Richard Del Connor, "The Hippy Coyote"
Written for the album, **Bonita**, by the group Lotus
Used by permission of *Shaolin Records*
Copyright 1974 *www.shaolinMUSIC.com*
All rights reserved.  ASCAP

**6. *"Fade Away To Stay"***
Lyrics by Richard Del Connor, "The Hippy Coyote"
Written for the book, **Sid's Place**
Used by permission of *Shaolin Records*
Copyright 2008

### 7. *"Acid Time"*
Lyrics by Richard Del Connor, "The Hippy Coyote"
Written for the book, **Sid's Place**
Used by permission of *Shaolin Records*
Copyright 2008 *www.shaolinMUSIC.com*

### 8. *"Moonlit Drive"*
Lyrics by Richard Del Connor, "The Hippy Coyote"
Written for the book, **Sid's Place**
Used by permission of *Shaolin Records*
Copyright 2008 *www.shaolinMUSIC.com*

### 9. *"Run, Run, Run"*
Lyrics by Richard Del Connor, "The Hippy Coyote"
Written for the book, **Sid's Place**
Used by permission of *Shaolin Records*
Copyright 2008 *www.shaolinMUSIC.com*

### 10. *"I've Got My Life To Live"*
Lyrics by Richard Del Connor, "The Hippy Coyote"
From the rock opera, **In Violence**
Used by permission of *Shaolin Records*
Copyright 1976 *www.shaolinMUSIC.com*

### 11. "Loving You"

Lyrics by Richard Del Connor, "The Hippy Coyote"
Written for the book, **Sid's Place**
Used by permission of *Shaolin Records*
Copyright 2008 *www.shaolinMUSIC.com*
All rights reserved. ASCAP

### 12. "Marina"

Lyrics by Richard Del Connor, "The Hippy Coyote"
Written for the book, **Sid's Place**
Used by permission of *Shaolin Records*
Copyright 2008 *www.shaolinMUSIC.com*
All rights reserved. ASCAP

### 13. "Backseat Love"

Lyrics by Richard Del Connor, "The Hippy Coyote"
From **The Village Recorder Sessions 1979** by The Rich
Used by permission of *Shaolin Records*
Copyright 1979 *www.shaolinMUSIC.com*
All rights reserved. ASCAP

### 14. "Sand Castles"

Lyrics by Richard Del Connor, "The Hippy Coyote"
From the rock opera, **Underground** (based upon the book, **Sid's Place**)
Used by permission of *Shaolin Records*
Copyright 1975 *www.shaolinMUSIC.com*
All rights reserved. ASCAP

### 15. "Luxury"

Lyrics by Richard Del Connor, "The Hippy Coyote"
Written for the book, **Sid's Place**
Used by permission of *Shaolin Records*
Copyright 2008 *www.shaolinMUSIC.com*
All rights reserved. ASCAP

### 16. *"Gypsy Knights"*
Lyrics by Richard Del Connor, "The Hippy Coyote"
Written for the book, **Sid's Place**
Used by permission of *Shaolin Records*
Copyright 2008 *www.shaolinMUSIC.com*
All rights reserved. ASCAP

### 17. *"Together And Free"*
Lyrics by Richard Del Connor, "The Hippy Coyote"
From the rock opera, **The Pauper**, by Richard Del Connor
Used by permission of *Shaolin Records*
Copyright 1977 *www.shaolinMUSIC.com*
All rights reserved. ASCAP

### 18. *"Dear Mom"*
Lyrics by Richard Del Connor, "The Hippy Coyote"
From the rock opera, **Underground** (based upon the book, **Sid's Place**)
Used by permission of *Shaolin Records*
Copyright 1975 *www.shaolinMUSIC.com*
All rights reserved. ASCAP

### 19. *"I Am"*
Lyrics by Richard Del Connor, "The Hippy Coyote"
From the rock opera, **Underground** (based upon the book, **Sid's Place**)
Used by permission of *Shaolin Records*
Copyright 1975 *www.shaolinMUSIC.com*
All rights reserved. ASCAP

### 20. *"Half A Dollar Bill"*
Lyrics by Richard Del Connor, "The Hippy Coyote"
From the rock opera, **Coyote In A Graveyard**
Used by permission of *Shaolin Records*
Copyright 1984 *www.shaolinMUSIC.com*
All rights reserved. ASCAP

### 21. "House Of Rejection"
Lyrics by Richard Del Connor, "The Hippy Coyote"
From the album, *Level 3 = I Want You To Love Me, by American Zen*
Used by permission of *Shaolin Records*
Copyright 2008 *www.shaolinMUSIC.com*
All rights reserved.  ASCAP

### 22. "What Do We Have Now?"
Lyrics by Richard Del Connor, "The Hippy Coyote"
From the album, **Bonita**, by Lotus
Used by permission of *Shaolin Records*
Copyright 1974 *www.shaolinMUSIC.com*
All rights reserved.  ASCAP

### 23. "Precious"
Lyrics by Richard Del Connor, "The Hippy Coyote"
From the album, **Bonita**, by Lotus
Used by permission of *Shaolin Records*
Copyright 1974 *www.shaolinMUSIC.com*
All rights reserved.  ASCAP

### 24. "Wild Cat" 217
Lyrics by Richard Del Connor, "The Hippy Coyote"
From the album, *Level 2 = Christ Killer by American Zen*
Used by permission of *Shaolin Records*
Copyright 2007 *www.shaolinMUSIC.com*
All rights reserved.  ASCAP

*Spotify ARTIST:  Kung Fu Cowboy*

*TikTok ARTIST: @KungFuCowboyClassicRock*

*YouTube ARTIST:  Kung Fu Cowboy*

*www.KungFuCowboy.com*

*www.ScorpionResurrection.com*

*www.AmericanZen.org*

*www.CoyoteRadio.TV*

*www.ShaolinRecords.com*

*www.CoyoteRadioTujunga.com*

# DISCOGRAPHY

**Richard Del Connor** 1954 to 1979
**Richard O'Connor** 1980 to 2005
**Richard Del Connor** 2006 to current year
**The Coyote** 1984 to 2006
**The Hippy Coyote** 2007 to current year
**Master Zhen Shen-Lang** "Spirit Wolf of Truth" 1992 to 1999
**Buddha Zhen Shen-Lang** "Spirit Wolf of Truth" 2000 to current year
All the above pseudonyms are me, Richard Del Connor. Each year I write more than one dozen songs and copyright them as an album with a dozen songs listed as "Alternative Titles" to reduce my copyright expense. I wanted to list many of these "Annual Songwriter Albums" below, but I decided to only list the actual projects that were recorded in studios as albums, performed onstage as rock operas, licensed to movies, or released as vinyl records, cassettes, cassingles, or CDs.

Visit *shaolinRECORDS.com* to purchase many of the following albums and songs.

All songs listed below were written/composed/authored by me under one of the names above. My birth certificate reads, Richard Del Connor.

I founded Shaolin Records in 1984. I had interns until 1991 when I moved to Utah to be a Mr. Mom. Big mistake. Since then I've referred to Shaolin Records as, *"My record company in a shoe box."*

I'm hoping to hire my first Shaolin Records employees in the next year or two. First, I need to sell some records to pay their salaries.

# 1974 Bonita

(album originally titled **The Thrush**: 16 songs)
Band: **Lotus** (featuring Richard Del Connor on lead guitar, lead vocals).
Only released at the Shaolin Records online record store.
Produced and engineered by Richard Del Connor at Bonita Studio.
I need to purchase a 1/2" 4-track Tascam recorder to mix these songs and
create the album these songs were destined for. Buy my albums and
songs so I can be a record company.

### Shaolin Records RECORD STORE:

*www.shaolinrecords.com/RecordStore-R/AmZen_Lotus-R.html*

*songs:*
*Headin' To Heaven*
*Stay Away*
*Precious*
*Insanity Back Or Your Money Guaranteed*
*What Do We Have Now?*
*Divinity*
*Dance Of The Lepers*
*What Do We Have Now*
*Laundromat (by Rory*
*Gallagher)*
*We Found The Love*
*Centerpoint*
*Meet Me Soon*
*Nothing To Do*
*Outlaw*
*Wishwood Bridge*
*You Are My Song*

# 1975 Underground
(rock opera based upon first chapters of **Sid's Place**)
Band: **Lotus** (featuring Richard Del Connor on lead guitar, lead vocals).
Sheet music only with no studio or live recordings (performed live).
All Shaolin Records albums are composed and produced by Richard Del
Connor.

## Shaolin Records RECORD STORE:
*www.ShaolinRecords.com/RecordStore-R/underground-R.html*

*songs:*
***Underground Suite / Dance Of The Lepers***
***I Am***
***Dear Mom***
***My Family***
***Headin' To Heaven***
***How Many More Times***
***I've Got My Life To Live***
***Paper And Film***
***Sand Castles***
***Cold Day In Hell***

# 1976 In Violence

(rock opera based upon last chapters of **Sid's Place**)
Band: **Lotus** (featuring Richard Del Connor on bass, lead vocals).
Sheet music only with no studio or live recordings (performed live).

## Shaolin Records RECORD STORE:

*www.ShaolinRecords.com/RecordStore-R/in_violence-R.html*

*songs:*
*In Violence*
*Outlaw*
*Five Before Noon*
*F Queen*
*Stalker*
*Bring Me In (From The Cold)*
*For You*
*My Life And Me*
*My Name Is Tom*
*We Are The Hunted*
*What Do We Have Now?*

# 1977 The Pauper

(rock opera performed at keg parties: 12 songs)
Band: **The Rich** (featuring Richard Del Connor on flute, lead vocals).
Sheet music only with some live rehearsal recordings and 4-song demo.

## Shaolin Records RECORD STORE:

*www.ShaolinRecords.com/RecordStore-R/the_pauper-R.html*

*songs:*
***Without You Day By Day***
***Don't Forget***
***Beggar's Call***
***Together And Free***
***The Pauper***
***Hello Again***
***Heather***
***Lady Fate***
***Queen Of Mercy***
***Stallion***
***Show Girls***
***The Forest***
***The Revolt***
***Time After Time***
***Turn Key***
***The King's Song***
***To Return***

# 1978 The Rich KPRI Radio Show

(Radio Show for winning San Diego "KPRI Battle of the Bands")
Band: **The Rich** (featuring Richard Del Connor on bass, lead vocals).
Live recording of 3-piece band with flute and vocal overdubs.
Original masters owned by Shaolin Records.
Aired as 1978 Best San Diego Band (although we'd just moved to LA).

## Shaolin Records RECORD STORE:

*www.shaolinrecords.com/RecordStore-R/TheRich/KPRIradio1978/TRich-ColdDayInHell.html*

*www.shaolinrecords.com/RecordStore-R/TheRich/KPRIradio1978/TRich-HelloAgain.html*

*songs:*
**Hello Again**
**The Pauper**
**Cold Day In Hell**
**Show Girls**

# 1979 The Rich In Venice

(12 songs recorded live in Venice, California)
Band: **The Rich** (featuring Richard Del Connor on bass, lead vocals).
Live recording of 3-piece band in Venice Beach, California.

## Shaolin Records RECORD STORE:

www.shaolinrecords.com/RecordStore-R/the_rich-VENICE-R.html

*songs:*
*Play To Win*
*Feel This Way*
*Jealous Guy*
*Without You Day By Day*
*Show Girls*
*Carol*
*You And Me*
*I Love You So*
*Leaves To The Wind*
*Other Girls*
*The Reason Why*
*On The Streets*
*Runaway*

# 1980 The Rich - The Village Recorder

(4 song masters recorded at Village Recorder, Santa Monica)
Band: **The Rich** (featuring Richard Connor on bass, lead vocals).
Studio recording engineered by Gary Starr remixed by Marc Paladino.
Masters owned by Shaolin Records.

### Shaolin Records RECORD STORE:

*www.shaolinrecords.com/RecordStore-R/TheRich/VillageRecorder79-81/
TheRich-VillageRecorderALBUM.html*

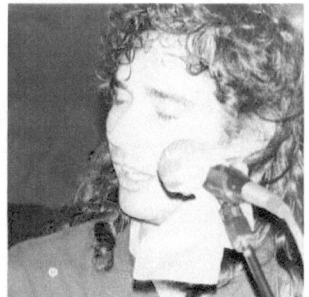

*songs:*
**Play To Win**
**Jealous Guy**
**Without You Day By Day**
**Show Girls**

# 1984 Temptation

(EP vinyl record release of Shaolin Records: 4 songs)
Band: **The Rich** (featuring Richard O'Connor on bass, lead vocals).
Recorded at Cherokee Studios and Capitol Records.
Released by Shaolin Records, September 1984.  1,000 vinyl records.

## Shaolin Records RECORD STORE:

www.shaolinrecords.com/RecordStore-R/Temptation-R.html

*songs:*
***Temptation***
***We're Not Working Out***
***My Child***
***Carol***

# 1985 Coyote In A Graveyard

(rock opera recorded at Cherokee Studios)
Band: **Coyote Graveyard** (featuring The Coyote on guitars, vocals).
Unreleased 24-track album mixes by Darin Prindle at Sound Castle
Studios. Some overdubs at Studio 54, Hollywood, California.
Album ONLY available from Shaolin Records online record store.

## Shaolin Records RECORD STORE:

*www.shaolinrecords.com/RecordStore-R/CoyoteGrave-R.html*

*songs:*
**Bang Bang Boom Boom**
**It's Your Shadow**
**Out Of Touch**
**Mother Mary**
**Out Of My Mind**
**All Around The**
**World**
**Jealous Guy**
**Other Girls**
**Elaine**
**Coyote In A**
**Graveyard**
**I Can See You**

# 1987 It's Your Shadow

(cassingle: cassette single)

Band: **The Rich** (The Coyote on lead guitar, lead vocals).

Released with college radio play in 1988 by Shaolin Records.

1,000 cassettes with "Instrumental Versions" on SIDE-B.

## Shaolin Records RECORD STORE:

*www.shaolinrecords.com/RecordStore-R/CoyoteGraveSINGLE-R.html*

*songs:*

*It's Your Shadow* (A-side vocals / B-side instrumental version)

*Coyote In A Graveyard* (A-side vocals / B-side instrumental)

# 1989 Love, Always & Forever

(journal of songs and poetry from 1988 to Angie)
Band: **Coyote Graveyard** (featuring The Coyote on lead guitar, vocals +
solo shows of Coyote performing acoustic or electric guitar).
Unreleased album of songs with accompanying book: 25 copies printed.

## Shaolin Records RECORD STORE:

*www.shaolinRECORDS.com/RecordStore-R/LoveAlwaysForever-R.html*

*songs:*
*No, It Wasn't A Dream*
*I'm On My Way*
*Musical Woman*
*What You Fear*
*Sacrifice Your Heart*
*Married Man's Mistress*
*You'll Find Me*
*Songs Last Forever*
*You're Lazy*
*Angry Blues*
*Hurts To Know*
*Winter Flowers*
*A Long Time Now*

# 1989 "Backseat Love"

(song mixdown by Richard O'Connor at The Village Recorder 1979)
Band: **The Rich** (featuring The Coyote on bass, lead vocals).
Used in soundtrack for movie: **A Hard Sell** 1989.
Performed from 1979 to 1991.

### Shaolin Records RECORD STORE:

*www.shaolinrecords.com/RecordStore-R/TheRich/VillageRecorder79-81/*

*TheRich-BackseatLove81.html*

# 1989 "Show Girls"

(song mixdown by Richard O'Connor at The Village Recorder 1979)
Band: **The Rich** (featuring The Coyote on bass/lead vocals).
Used in soundtrack for movie: **A Hard Sell.**
Performed from 1978 to 1979.

### Shaolin Records RECORD STORE:

*www.shaolinrecords.com/RecordStore-R/TheRich/VillageRecorder79-81/*
*TheRich-ShowGirls79.html*

# 2005 Level 1 = Peace Of Mind

(11 songs = 11 poems orated)

Band: **American Zen** (The Coyote on flute, acoustic/lead vocals).
Recorded 4-track in Utah and mastered by Richard O'Connor,
Released on CD, and at *shaolinRECORDS.com*

## Shaolin Records RECORD STORE:

*www.shaolinrecords.com/RecordStore-R/americanZenLevel1-R.html*

*songs:*
*Peace Of Mind #2*
*Black Of Night*
*Whose Heaven Is This?*
*In The Darkness*
*You've Been Sold*
*Free The Change*
*Trust Me*
*Simple Lady*
*All Screwed Up*
*A Long Way Home*
*Thank You*
*Introduction*
*Get Out Of My Dream*
*In The Darkness (poem)*
*Last Year*
*When Children Are Unwanted*
*Nurturing Your Life*
*The Power*
*The Teacher Was He*
*Spring Rain*
*It's tough…*
*My Woman is My Wife*

# American Zen LEVEL 1 = Peace of Mind

This is **Rock Opera 11** of the
**Kung Fu Cowboy 36-LEVEL Spiritual Rock Opera Metaverse**.

In 2022 I created this collection of MUSIC NFTs. There are 22 NFTs. Each contains one of the 11 POEMS or 11 SONGS from the **LEVEL 1 = Peace of Mind** album by American Zen. The pictures on the NFTs are mostly from when the album was written and recorded on my 4-track tape recorder in Salt Lake City, Utah.

## Music NFTs at OpenSea

*https://opensea.io/collection/american-zen-level-1*

The **LEVEL 1** of **American Zen** is *Rock Opera 11* of the *Kung Fu Cowboy Spiritual Rock Opera Metaverse*. This is when I moved to Utah with my 1-year old daughter Caitlin. I was a Mr. Mom. My wife worked for Xerox. We had a medical plan for the family and I made money teaching Tai Chi Chuan in my Kung Fu school I founded in 1992: Shaolin Chi Mantis. This was a romantic year. A year of hope. A year of family dreams. I wrote and recorded these songs that tell that story.

# 2006 Tai Chi Magic 1

(11 songs for Tai Chi and Kung Fu performances)
Band: **Buddha Zhen**: flutes, pipa, Buddha drum, shakuhachi.
Recorded 4-track in Utah. Finished and mastered in Tujunga, California.

## Shaolin Records RECORD STORE:

*www.shaolinrecords.com/RecordStore-R/taichiMagic1R.html*

*songs:*
*Tai Chi Magic*
*Sparrows In Daoist Courtyard*
*Inner Mountain View*
*In The Pool Of Enlightenment*
*Inner Will*
*Path To The Mountaintop*
*Dao Mountain Monastery*
*Silk Mushroom*
*Boundless Space*
*Pushing Hands*
*Night Blue Sky*

## Also available at Special Website:

*www.taichiMAGIC.com*

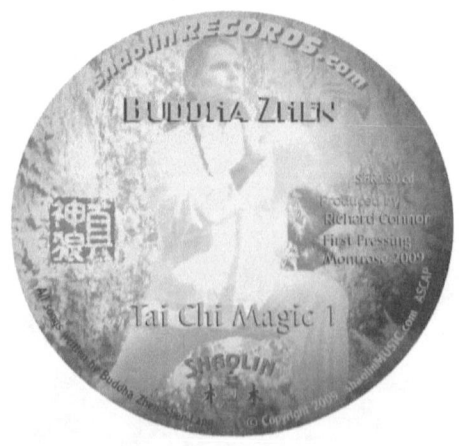

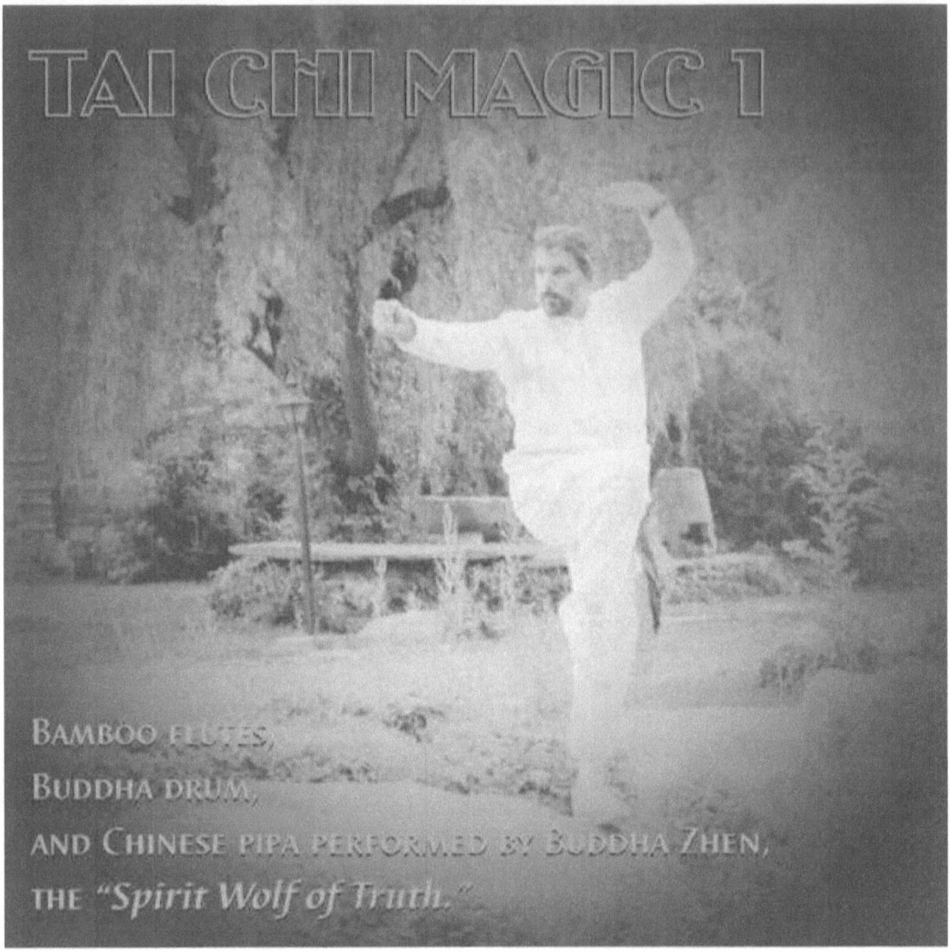
TAI CHI MAGIC 1
BAMBOO FLUTES,
BUDDHA DRUM,
AND CHINESE PIPA PERFORMED BY BUDDHA ZHEN,
THE "Spirit Wolf of Truth."

Some people have called this, *"Chinese Folk Rock."*

ShaolinRECORDS.com
BUDDHA ZHEN
Produced by
Richard Connor
First Pressing
Montrose 2009
Tai Chi Magic 1
SHAOLIN
ASCAP

# 2007 Level 2 = Christ Killer
### (15 songs + 7 poems orated)
Band: **American Zen** (The Hippy Coyote flute, acoustic guitar, vocals).
Recorded 4-track in Utah. Completed with ProTools Tujunga, California.
Released on CD, and at *shaolinRECORDS.com*

## Shaolin Records RECORD STORE:
### www.shaolinrecords.com/RecordStore-R/americanZenLevel2-R.html

*songs:*
**Great Salt Lake**
**Wild Cat poem**
**Peace Of Mind #1**
**American Zen LEVEL 2 poem**
**God Will Protect**
**Can't Hold Me Down**
**5th South**
**Best Is Blessed poem**
**I Know**
**Even Or Odd poem**
**Land Of Mediocrity**
**If I Can't Die poem**
**Christ Killer**
**I Want To Laugh #2**
**33 Bass Players**
**Loyalty poem**
**I Am Not From Here**
**Daryoon**
**Just For You**
**Quiet Army**
**Quiet City poem**
**The End The Horizon**

# ALBUM: LEVEL 2 = Christ Killer

The Mormons are fighting the Catholics. The Catholics are fighting the Protestants. But they all agree that killing Christ is a GOOD IDEA. This album is about me disagreeing with all of them by saying, *"Don't kill Christ for me." (No animal sacrifices either—please.)*
Even if you do believe in human sacrifice—buy this album!

### Shaolin Records RECORD STORE:

*www.shaolinrecords.com/RecordStore-R/americanZenLevel2-R.html*

LEVEL 2 of American Zen is *Rock Opera 13* of the *Kung Fu Cowboy Spiritual Rock Opera Metaverse*. Entrance NFTs are at:

## Music NFTs at OpenSea

*https://OpenSea.io/collection/christ-killer*

Each song on the album is an NFT. Each music NFT song has a photo taken from the year this album was made except for the pictures of my son which were a few years later.

When I was a kid I bought lots of 45rpm black vinyl singles. NFTs are the NEW SONG SINGLES of the 21st Century. I'm in the lead. I'm a pioneer. I started making my music NFTs in 2021. What makes them really cool and better than 45s is the DESCRIPTION TEXT in each NFT. I pack these with information and links to my websites. Check out the "DESCRIPTIONS" in my NFTs. I put a lot of work into some of them with "Markdown Text" editing to make them look cool...

# 2008 Level 3 = I Want You To Love Me

(11 songs + 12 bass poems orated)

Band: **American Zen** (featuring The Hippy Coyote on acoustic guitar, flute, drums, vocals)

Recorded 32-Track digital at Shaolin Records in Tujunga, California.

I invented "BASS POETRY" on this album. Poems + Ricky bass tracks.

Released on CD and downloads from *shaolinRECORDS.com*

## Shaolin Records RECORD STORE:

*www.shaolinrecords.com/RecordStore-R/americanZenLevel3-R.html*

*songs:*

*I Want You To Love Me*
*All Around The World*
*I Just Want To Be With You*
*In Line*
*House Of Rejection*
*Change Your Mind*
*All Alone*
*Hurts To Know*
*Musical Woman*
*Carol*
*In Dreams*
*My Lesbian Neighbors*
*Whatever*
*Everything*
*Magic Lady*
*1000 Sorrows*
*Let's Go To Church*
*God Is Smaller Than You Think*
*Civilized World*
*Omnipresence*
*Intuition*
*My World*
*Patience*

SFR056cd
Produced by
Richard Connor ASCAP

# ALBUM: LEVEL 3

**LEVEL 3 = I Want You To Love Me.**  Although some people may graduate the battles of Christianity and other religions, this is the first LEVEL of Buddhism.   When the Original Buddha in 250 BC was creating disciples and Buddhas, this is where they began their Buddhist compassion for helping people.

*www.shaolinrecords.com/RecordStore-R/americanZenLevel3-R.html*

## Music NFTs at OpenSea

*https://opensea.io/collection/level-3*

Right now, as I'm doing my FINAL EDIT on this book, I've created this MUSIC NFT COLLECTION.   But I haven't made the NFTs yet. Hopefully, when you click that link up there—there will be 23 MUSIC NFTs of this **LEVEL 3** album by American Zen.

This album features songs written from 2001 about a love affair I had with one of my Utah Kung Fu students.   She knew I had a crappy marriage and wanted me to come back to Utah and replace her husband who she had recently divorced. My wife/ex-wife was already engaged to Federico from where she worked.   Lara sent me a plane ticket and we spent seven days in a nice hotel having sex all day, all night, all day… then we went to see the movie **Crouching Tiger Hidden Dragon**.

# 2010 Level 4 = Kung Fu Cowboy
# PART 1: King Solomon's Temple

(14 songs + 14 bass poems orated)

Band: **American Zen** (featuring The Hippy Coyote flute/drums/vocals). Drums Recorded in Gymnasium of Crescenta Valley Park Gymnasium. Recorded 32-Track digital at Shaolin Records in Montrose, California. Released on CD, and at *shaolinRECORDS.com*

## Shaolin Records RECORD STORE:

www.shaolinrecords.com/RecordStore-R/americanZenLevel4-P1-R.html

*songs:*
*Kung Fu Cowboy*
*Boy And King POEM*
*Spirit Gun*
*A Lucky Man*
*33 Bass Players POEM*
*My Life Belongs To Me*
*Elaine*
*Christmas Is*
*Dear Lara POEM*
*You're Lazy*
*You'll Find Me*
*Flintridge Fire*
*From Within*
*Horses And Harleys POEM*
*King Solomon's Temple*
*Hiram Abif*
*Kill The Spider*
*I've Been Thinkin'*

# ALBUM: LEVEL 4 = Kung Fu Cowboy PART 1: King Solomon's Temple

I was a Freemason when I recorded this album. I transformed my tragic marriage romance story into the story of Hiram Abif, a hallmark of all Freemasons who was the architect of King Solomon's Temple in Jerusalem. I thought I could make Masonry more interesting for young people and modern by telling this Masonic tale in a rock opera.

I recorded 36 songs and poems for this album and realized that was too many songs to fit on one CD in 2010. So I divided the album into **LEVEL 4 Part 1 = King Solomon's Temple** and **LEVEL 4 Part 2 = 3rd Degree Master Mason**.

This **Part 1** album begins with the birth of King Solomon and the death of his Architect Hiram Abif when the Jerusalem Temple was almost completed. Hiram is murdered by three 2nd Degree Masons who want Hiram to tell them the secret passwords of a 3rd Degree Master Mason so they can escape the slavery of building the Temple and go home to their families. This is the foundation story and "3rd Degree" of Freemasonry.

*shaolinrecords.com/RecordStore-R/americanZenLevel4-P1-R.html*

**Music NFTs at OpenSea**

*https://opensea.io/collection/level-4*

# 2010 Level 4 = Kung Fu Cowboy
# PART 2: 3rd Degree Master Mason

(15 songs + 2 poems + 1 bass poem orated)

*NOTE 2022: Album = unfinished and unreleased.*

Band: **American Zen** (featuring The Hippy Coyote flute/drums/vocals).
Drums Recorded in Gymnasium of Crescenta Valley Park Gymnasium.
Recorded 32-Track digital at Shaolin Records in Tujunga, California.
Released on CD, and at. *shaolinRECORDS.com*

## Shaolin Records RECORD STORE:

www.shaolinrecords.com/RecordStore-R/americanZenLevel4-P2-R.html

*songs:*
**3rd Degree Master Mason**
**Masonic Kung Fu**
**But I Got**
**I'm Certain I'm Not Sure**
**Run To Me**
**Dizzy, My Toxic Daughter**
**Mother's Pearl**
**My Mockingbird**
**Montrose Cuckold**
**Tell The Truth**
**What Do You See?**
**I Want To Improve Everyone**
**Patriot**
**Eye To Eye POEM**
**Blue Skies**
**Time To Go Home**
**Proud To Be A Hippie**
**Bottom Line**

Kung Fu Cowboy
3rd Degree Master Mason
AMERICAN ZEN
LEVEL 4 - Part 2

# ALBUM: LEVEL 4 Part 2

**Kung Fu Cowboy PART 2: 3rd Degree Master Mason** is the rock opera album completing the story of the three 2nd Degree Fellowcraft Masons being caught by King Solomon and executed by him for the murder of his Jerusalem Temple Architect, Hiram Abif. This is an important legend that lays the foundation for the morality and virtues of being a modern day Freemason. Hiram Abif died without revealing the secret passwords of Hebrew Masonry, making him a role model hero.

I made this album believing that I could bring a new and interesting view of Freemasons that would attract a young audience and new generation of Americans enrolling in Freemasonry as their membership dwindles significantly.

Unfortunately for me, and unfortunately for Modern Masonry, I was urged to quit my Freemason membership because I became homeless and was a *"burden on the lodge,"* as I requested free meals at weekly meetings. The new Masonry is only a shadow of the old Masonry.

### Music NFTs at OpenSea
*https://OpenSea.io/collection/kfc-17*

### Dizzy, My Toxic Daughter SONG SINGLE
*www.ShaolinRecords.com/RecordStore-R/DizzyMyToxicDaughter-R.html*

_Table_of_Contents_

# AUDIOBOOKs by Richard Del Connor

This walk-in closet is my audiobook recording studio. It's very quiet until Bear scratches on the door for something to eat. I can record professional quality. My first audiobook has been released. It's available from Audible.

**Masonic Kung Fu**
**Entered Apprentice**
Audiobook written and read by Richard Del Connor.

**Shaolin Records RECORD STORE:**
*www.shaolinrecords.com/RecordStore-R/MasonicKungFu1-R.html*

335

I wrote this novel when I was a Freemason back in 2010.

First, I discovered the actual *"MASONIC KUNG FU"* that had been passed down in China since 1937. This "Ling Po" Kung Fu form was created by a Chinese Kung Fu Master to teach European Freemasonry to Chinese martial artists, even in public, without anyone being aware of it. The Chinese were banned from being Masons, so this was the only way.

Only because I became a 3rd Degree Master Mason was I able to decode this secretive form. Evidently, all the Chinese Masters who were aware of this form were killed in WWII by the Japanese. So I am the first person since 1937 to decode it and realize the hidden secrets, signs and stories encoded within this Kung Fu form.

I wrote this book based on stories I discovered from Chinese research.

This is MY FIRST AUDIOBOOK. Write me a good review!

# 2014 Level 7 = End Of The Line

(11 songs + additional mix of *"End of The Line"* by Scott Karahadian.)

Band: **American Zen**

| | |
|---|---|
| The Hippy Coyote | vocals, flute, electric guitar |
| Rory G | lead guitar, slide guitar |
| Tom Calder | bass |
| Steve Hixon | drums |

Drums Recorded in North Hollywood apartment.

Recorded 4-Track digital in Tacoma Studios (my truck) in North Hollywood, California.

Released July 4, 2014, by *shaolinRECORDS.com*

## Shaolin Records RECORD STORE:

www.shaolinrecords.com/RecordStore-R/AmZen_EndOfTheLine.html

*songs:*

*Use Me*

*High School Graduation*

*Scorpion Resurrection*

*Secret Asian Girl*

*Rock Me Hard*

*Kung Fu Cowboy*

*Take Me Apart*

*End of the Line*

*Honor and Obey, Cherish and Protect*

*Black Hills Ride*

*Starting Over Again*

*End of the Line - Scott Mix*

# American Zen 8-LEVEL
# Spiritual Journey to Nirvana

I released my **LEVEL 7 = END OF THE LINE album** in 2014 on the 4th of July.  If enough persons bought my album my homelessness could be ended.  Help me.  End my homelessness by buying this album and buying one for someone else.  I recorded this album in my Tacoma Truck in North Hollywood.   I'd like to create a rock band to perform this album.  Any rockers out there?  I think I'm one of the last ones still alive.

## Music NFTs at OpenSea
*https://opensea.io/collection/level7*

The **Supersoul 13** BOOK tells the story of making this album and getting $18 million dollars that Homeland Security took away because it came from a Panamanian Bank, through a German Bank, through...

Anyone want to make the **Kung Fu Cowboy** movie with me?    All the

directors and producers I worked with in the 1980s are dead. This is a ROCK 'N' ROLL MOVIE. So this movie title is:

### *Kung Fu Cowboy: Rock & Roll Movie 1*

# 2014 Level 8 = Memorial Day Album

(9 songs + 1 poem orated)

*NOTE 2022: Album = unfinished and unreleased*

Band: **American Zen**

| | |
|---|---|
| The Hippy Coyote | vocals, flute, electric guitar |
| Rory G | lead guitar, slide guitar |
| Tom Calder | bass |
| Steve Hixon | drums |

Drums recorded in Gymnasium of Crescenta Valley Park Gymnasium.
Recorded 32-Track digital at Shaolin Records in Tujunga, California.
Released on CD and at *shaolinRECORDS.com*

## Shaolin Records RECORD STORE:

www.shaolinrecords.com/RecordStore-R/AmZen_MemorialDay-R.html

*songs:*
***War Sucks! INSTRUMENTAL***
***Friendly Fire***
***Camp Tehr Ohr***
***Every Breath I Breathe***
***Pictures Of Home***
***Memorial Day***
***Bags On Their Heads***
***Bombs From God***
***Father To Son (Poem)***
***War Sucks!***

# ALBUM: LEVEL 8 = Memorial Day 2014

A half-dozen ghosts woke me up on Memorial Day and told me their war stories and how they died. I wrote a song for each of them and sang the vocal as each of them seemed to use my body to express themselves. I saw their battles and cried their tears as I recorded the album and sung their songs. When I finished the recordings they vanished and have never reappeared. You don't have to believe me. It's still a great album whether I get all the credit or not.

I recorded the bass, vocals, guitar and SLIDE GUITAR in my Tacoma truck. I call it, *"Tacoma Studios."* It is a very emotional album.

Best of all, this song is antiwar album with most of the songs actually be true-life war stories. One of the songs was written (or inspired) by a Lakota Sioux Air Force Military Officer. He is VERY PRO-WAR.

I hope that this album is enlightening and inspirational. I'm just telling their stories. The only song actually written by me is, ***"War Sucks!"*** That song I will take full credit for. I made two versions of the song.

### Music NFTs at OpenSea
*https://opensea.io/collection/level8*

I had clear visions of what those ghosts had seen before they died. I even saw images of the home of the soldier in ***"Pictures of Home."*** I could have identified his home easily back in 2014.

# 2017 Zombie Holidays

(7 songs + ? poems orated)

*NOTE 2022: Album = unfinished and unreleased*

Band: **Kung Fu Cowboy & Zombie Three** (featuring **Kung Fu Cowboy** on lead guitar/vocals).

| | |
|---|---|
| Kung Fu Cowboy | lead guitar, vocals |
| Clean Zombie | surf guitar |
| Fuzz Zombie | metal guitar |
| Bone Banger Zombie | drums, percussion |

Recorded 4-Track digital in Tacoma Studios (my truck) North Hollywood Park, California.

## Shaolin Records RECORD STORE:

www.shaolinrecords.com/RecordStore-R/KungFuCowboy/ZombieThree/
KFCzombieBAND.html

*songs:*
***Zombie Thanksgiving***
***Zombie Christmas***
***Zombie New Year***
***Zombie Elf***
***Zombie Reindeer***
***Zombie Santa***
***Chasing Mrs. Clause***
***You Called It Sex ("Empty Beds")***

# Kung Fu Cowboy & Zombie Three

This is me at the **Action On Film International Film Festival** in 2015.
I entered the screenplay, **Kung Fu Cowboy: Rock & Roll Movie 1**.
I co-wrote the screenplay with Scott Karahadian. We won the FIRST
PLACE AWARD for *"Best Action Scenes" in a screenplay*.

### Official Zombie Three Website of Shaolin Records

*www.ZombieThree.com*

### Kung Fu Cowboy & Zombie Three of Shaolin Records

*www.shaolinrecords.com/RecordStore-R/KungFuCowboy/ZombieThree/*
*KFCzombieBAND.html*

### Kung Fu Cowboy & Zombie Three album: Meet The Zombies

*www.shaolinrecords.com/RecordStore-R/KungFuCowboy/ZombieThree/*
*MeetTheZombiesALBUM.html*

### Zombie Three single song: "Zombie Christmas (No Bones)"

*www.ShaolinRecords.com/RecordStore-R/KungFuCowboy/ZombieThree/*
*ZombieChristmasNoBones.html*

# 2023 Scorpion Resurrection

(10 songs + ? poems orated)

Band: **Kung Fu Cowboy**

| | |
|---|---|
| Kung Fu Cowboy | vocals, flute, electric guitar |
| Tom Calder | Rickenbacker bass |
| Rory G | lead guitar |
| Steve Hixon | drums |

Scorpion Orchestra arranged by Richard Del Connor

Drums recorded in Lancaster, California.

Recorded 32-track digital in Lancaster, California.

## Shaolin Records RECORD STORE:

www.shaolinrecords.com/RecordStore-R/KungFuCowboy/KFC1-ScorpionRes.html

*songs:*

**Scorpion Resurrection**
**High School Graduation**
**Rock Me Hard**
**Take Me Apart**
**Honor and Obey, Cherish and Protect**
**Use Me**
**Secret Asian Girl**
**End of the Line**
**I'm Certain I'm Not Sure**
**In Dreams**

## Music NFTs at OpenSea

*https://opensea.io/collection/kungfucowboy1*

I will finish this album next year, 2023, then I can make the MUSIC NFTs. Actually, I'm considering NOT PUBLISHING this **Sid's Place** book until 2023 so I can do some advance marketing. Hmmm… What date would I choose to release this book, **Sid's Place**? Hmmm… The last album I released was on July 4, 2014, by American Zen. Hmmm…

I had cancer last year. I had a surgery, chemotherapy and 100 days of Cobalt Radiation Therapy. They cooked all the hair off my butt and groin. I looked like a chihuahua and bled every day for the entire year.

If it weren't for 2021 being a miserable year I would've released more than a few songs from my **Scorpion Resurrection** debut album as the **"KUNG FU COWBOY."** I spent the year laying on my back watching YouTube videos about crypto, WEB3, and creating a DAO. I thought I might die, but I couldn't stop writing songs. I released a few of my songs called, *"Dogecoin," "Kung Fu Cowboy 2,"* and *"Rock Me Hard."* I'm also *www.tiktok.com/@kungfucowboyclassicrock*

I decided to create the **AMERICAN ZEN PEACE FOUNDATION** to be my legacy and keep my websites and albums and books on the digital shelves of the internet. Maybe you can help?

*www.AmericanZenPeaceFoundation.org*

# AUDIOBOOK of Novel, Sid's Place

**As of the FIRST Release in 2012:**
The **Sid's Place** audiobook will be released June 2, 2023?  I hope so.
Check *ShaolinRecords.com* for updates and book reading podcasts.

### *Produced by Richard Connor for Shaolin Records*
*www.ShaolinRecords.com/RecordStore-R/sidsplace-R.html*

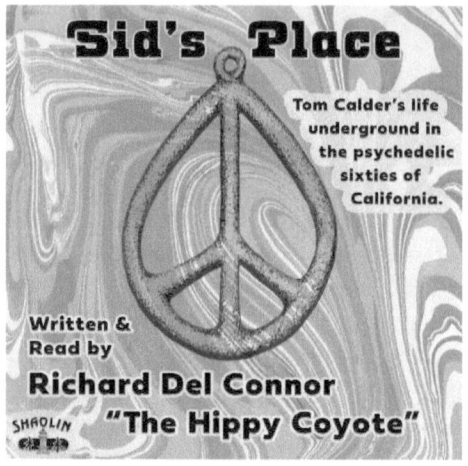

# Sid's Place BOOK NFTs

*https://opensea.io/collection/sids-place*

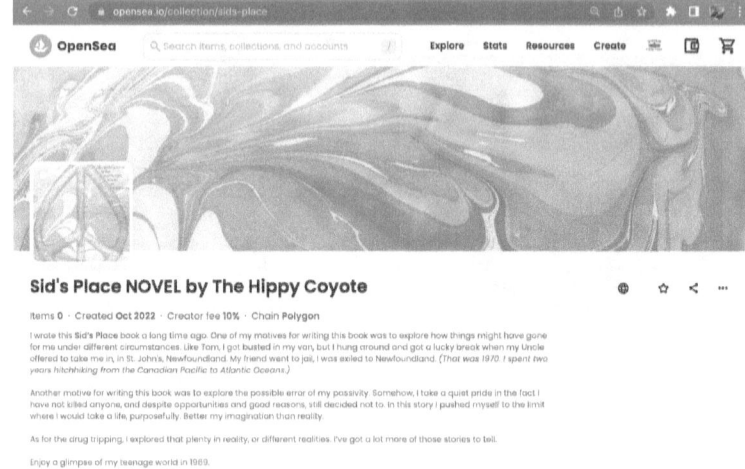

## Sid's Place NOVEL by The Hippy Coyote

Items **0** · Created **Oct 2022** · Creator fee **10%** · Chain **Polygon**

I wrote this **Sid's Place** book a long time ago. One of my motives for writing this book was to explore how things might have gone for me under different circumstances. Like Tom, I got busted in my van, but I hung around and got a lucky break when my Uncle offered to take me in, in St. Johns, Newfoundland. My friend went to jail, I was exiled to Newfoundland. *(That was 1970. I spent two years hitchhiking from the Canadian Pacific to Atlantic Oceans.)*

Another motive for writing this book was to explore the possible error of my passivity. Somehow, I take a quiet pride in the fact I have not killed anyone, and despite opportunities and good reasons, still decided not to. In this story I pushed myself to the limit where I would take a life, purposefully. Better my imagination than reality.

As for the drug tripping, I explored that plenty in reality, or different realities. I've got a lot more of those stories to tell.

Enjoy a glimpse of my teenage world in 1969.

# Sid's Place

**Tom Calder's Life Underground in the Psychedelic Sixties of California**
by Richard Del Connor, *"The Hippy Coyote"*

1969, Tom Calder's van is involved in a car crash, it's loaded with kilos of marijuana. He runs from the law, he runs from a hitman, joins a rock band, lives on a hippie commune, learns real Tai Chi, joins the underground railroad, trains in a Libya terrorist camp, bombs a police station, goes to jail, escapes imprisonment and finds revenge with a new identity.

This story is based upon what might have happened to Richard Del Connor if he had not been exiled to Newfoundland in 1970 for LSD and marijuana trafficking. Richard hitchhiked across Canada several times before hitchhiking home years later being hunted by the FBI.

Here are three years of romantic psychedelic turbulence described in detail by someone who lived amongst the fugitives, exiles, criminals, and AWOL Green Berets of the flower power years. A rare inside look at the underground lifestyles of the President Nixon *"War On Drugs."*

All song lyrics by Richard Del Connor, "The Hippy Coyote."

Cover design and art by Richard Del Connor, "The Hippy Coyote."

*produced by*
**SHAOLIN RECORDS**

*A Shaolin Communications company*